William Gill was born and brought up in Argentina. He trained as an architect and came to practise in Great Britain in 1972. He now lives and works in London. *Sugar and Spice* is his first novel.

D0231842

WILLIAM GILL

Sugar and Spice

Grafton
An Imprint of HarperCollins*Publishers*

Grafton
An Imprint of HarperCollins*Publishers*
77–85 Fulham Palace Road,
Hammersmith, London W6 8JB

Special overseas edition 1991
This edition published by Grafton 1992
9 8 7 6 5 4 3 2 1

First published in Great Britain by
GraftonBooks 1991

ISBN 0 586 21087 3

Set in Sabon

Printed in Great Britain by
HarperCollinsManufacturing Glasgow

To Clare, for a million reasons

ACKNOWLEDGEMENTS

Research is inevitable in any novel, particularly when, as in this case, the characters lead infinitely more eventful lives than their author. It involves travelling, and the compilation of information from many sources. But none of these can be as helpful to the author as the patience and kindness of those knowledgeable on a particular subject. I am grateful to John Alexander, Kin Coombe, Robert Hancock, Debbie Hutton, Nora Jaureguiberry, Julio Nuñez, Mandy O'Flynn, Rolando Paiva, Neil Shaw, Juan Suaya, Saxon Tate and Mary Wiggins for their most valuable advice and help.

I am also grateful to Lynn Nesbit and to Imogen Taylor. In many ways *Sugar and Spice* is as much their book as mine.

Prologue

'Go faster!' Pandora urged the driver. The moon was covered by clouds. Only the road ahead was visible in the car's headlights as they took the sharp turn leading up into the hills. The evening breeze had become an ocean wind, bending the plumes of pampas grass at both sides of the narrow country lane. The trees yielded to it, and the sound of summer foliage, beaten and blown, muffled the roar of the engine at full throttle.

The wind suddenly broke the cloud, and at last she saw 'La Encantada' ahead of them, the fairy-tale palace that had been brought from Spain stone by stone, a monument to the money and the madness of Simon de la Force. The walls shone a watery silver in the moonlight, but behind the trees that concealed the tower from sight Pandora could see an orange glow in the sky.

The car drew up outside, and Pandora stared at the tower, its top completely wrapped in flames. 'Call the firemen!' she screamed to the driver. Then she ran to the house and opened the huge front door. Inside was complete darkness. The wind blew in, making the Flemish tapestries flap against the stone walls of the hall.

Pandora pressed the light switch, but the lights did not come on. Only the moonlight filtering through the landing windows faintly outlined the stairs ahead of her through the haze that was rapidly filling the vaulted passage. She could hear Arianne's cries of terror from her room at the top.

Pandora rushed upstairs. Her eyes streaming, she could feel the grittiness of the smoke in her throat as she approached the final flight. It seemed forever until she reached the top. Blinded by smoke, she crawled towards the door somewhere in front of her. She *had* to save Arianne. A line of orange light at the bottom of the door guided her through the last few yards of smoke-filled blackness. The Moorish tiles on the wall around the door were cracking from the heat. The only other sound was the sinister hiss of the fire beyond the closed door, nothing else. The screams had stopped.

Pandora fumbled in the darkness until her fingers gripped the door handle, her skin blistering at the touch of the incandescent metal. She had to open the door. A banal, everyday action, a reflex almost, had become the most important thing in her life. She pushed desperately at the heavy door. It gave a fraction, and a slap of heat rushed through the opening, singeing her eyelashes. Her lungs ached for air, sweet, cool air. Will and instinct clashed for a second. Her friend was almost within reach, but Pandora found herself turning back towards the ocean wind. She staggered a few steps, and then collapsed at the top of the stairs.

All she could see now was the glint of the heart-shaped diamond on her finger. Ted Carson's ring, the ring that had caused her so much doubt, just as Charles' behaviour over the last ten days had fuelled Arianne's suspicions. Yet both women had both disregarded their instincts. They were separated only by a burning door, a sheet of Spanish oak that had been lovingly carved four hundred years ago, now slowly crumbling to ashes.

As Pandora's consciousness faded away, she remembered her own home as it had been long ago, the horizon immense and new to a child's eyes. But it was all irrelevant in the end; she realized that she had misunderstood so many things . . . perhaps millions. Yes, maybe millions . . .

Part I

1

NEW YORK
April 1987

'Fifty-two million,' the auctioneer said, as the woman's hand rose in the air. The spotlights caught first the gloss of her nail polish, then the matt finish of the gold pencil she was holding, and finally the square-cut emerald of her ring. The gesture was precise, just enough to be noticeable from the dais, no more.

Murmurs filled the room while the electronic board above the rostrum converted the figure from dollars into yen, deutschmarks, sterling, French and Swiss francs. As expected, Manet's long-lost *Portrait de Madame Claire* had become the world's most expensive painting.

Displayed next to the auctioneer on a velvet-lined stand, as if on a shrine, its calm beauty contrasted with the commotion around it. The painting depicted an unknown sitter, supposedly one of the models for the *Déjeuner sur l'herbe*, standing in front of a gilt-framed mirror. She was seen from the back but her head was turned over her right shoulder, as if her attention had just been caught by someone behind her. The face was partly in profile and partly reflected in the mirror, two incomplete images adding to a whole in the viewer's eye.

It was this counterpoint between reality and reflection, representing a mature development of the painter's earlier *Bar aux Folies-Bergère*, that had caused such a sensation in the art world when the painting had been discovered a few months before in the attic of a house in upstate New York. The old woman's great-uncle had been the painter's assistant, and she had inherited the house from him. The rolled canvas had lain forgotten in a dusty cupboard for decades, and it had only been found after her death. The woman had died in poverty.

Such poverty was unimaginable in Christie's main auction room tonight. Famous paintings were being fought over by the fantastically rich in an atmosphere of almost

13

erotic tension. Money had ceased to matter and possession became all-important. The excitement was now at a new peak after the woman's offer.

Pandora Doyle's professional interest was stirred as soon as she heard the bid and caught sight of the emerald on the woman's raised hand. She had no idea who this woman was.

At first, a number of people had taken part in the bidding, but once the price had reached thirty-seven million, it had become a two-man contest between Jacob Kugler, the New York dealer, and someone who was bidding by telephone. Pandora heard the man next to her whisper to his companion that the call was surely from Tokyo, and that Kugler was acting on behalf of Ted Carson, the Anglo-Australian business tycoon whose eagerness to collect paintings had earned him the nickname of 'King Kong' within the art world. From forty-eight million on, the Tokyo bids had been more cautious, and they had finally stopped when Kugler offered fifty-one million. At that point, the tension in the room had slackened: the hand had been played. Pandora was about to leave to beat the rush to the door, when the woman's bid stopped her.

Pandora stretched her neck, trying to catch a glimpse of the bidder, but the rituals of money are ruled by strict codes, as polished as Court ceremonial, and the woman was close to the auctioneer's dais, while Pandora stood near the very back of the room, the difference between someone who could bid fifty-two million and a budding young journalist. Pandora had phoned Christie's that afternoon to reserve a place in the magazine's name, otherwise she would have been outside, among the crowd of celebrity-watchers. She could not see much of the woman from where she was: very shiny black hair pulled tightly into a chignon, a long neck, the collar of a sable coat and, almost tangible, the aura of opulent wealth.

There was a story here, and that was exactly what Pandora needed. She had been at *Chic* for almost five weeks and had by now realized that the 'Shopping List' section was the magazine's Siberia. Her predecessors had been either Upper East Side girls killing time until they found a husband, or rich divorcees waiting for their settlement. As soon as one or the other materialized they moved on, leaving behind them a brief memory of Chanel suits and spelling errors, both displayed in awesome quantities. Pandora badly needed a scoop.

Now she watched as Jacob Kugler hesitated for a moment, then raised his catalogue. The auctioneer was about to say 'Fifty-three million,' but the woman raised her gold pencil before he could even acknowledge the bid.

'Fifty-five million,' she said firmly, and a frisson of excitement ran through the room. Bidders do not normally announce their bids, let alone double their last increase unless prompted by the auctioneer. Both the impatience and the foreign accent were just noticeable in her voice, but the message was clear: 'Get out of my way'.

All eyes were on Kugler, waiting for his next move. Pandora decided to break the rules of polite behaviour: she left her place and, after treading on the feet of the man next to her and ignoring his icy look, she walked slowly down the side aisle until she reached the woman's row. Pandora stood against the wall, looking at her.

The face combined handsome Latin features with British aloofness, something that Pandora had previously noticed in rich Italians or South Americans. The nose was slightly aquiline, the golden-brown eyes slanted upward, and the smooth olive skin was tight against perfect cheekbones. The woman was neither young nor old. She had the early-thirties look of women just past forty who have a magnificent bone structure, and perhaps a great plastic surgeon as well.

The man next to her was about the same age. Framed by his prematurely silver grey hair and deeply tanned skin, his sky-blue eyes were almost luminous. He was dressed in the standard uniform of the international rich, a navy-blue double-breasted suit, crisp white shirt, and red silk tie. He was superbly attractive and, from his constant attention to the woman's smallest gesture, clearly not her husband.

'I have fifty-five million dollars on my left, fifty-five million.' The Hon. Henry Lyndhurst-Smythe had come from London to conduct the auction, a polished performance in eagle-eyed nonchalance that managed to make the actual bids seem slightly insignificant – an infallible formula for achieving a record price. He paused now, apparently scanning the room but never losing sight of Kugler, who remained silent.

'Fifty-five million, any more bids?' This time he looked directly at Kugler. His eyes moved on after a few seconds, enough time for him to know that the dealer was beaten.

'All done? Last time,' he announced. 'Fifty-five million dollars once, fifty-five million twice,' he raised the old ebony gavel a few inches, paused, and then brought it down.

'Sold for fifty-five million, thank you. For you, Madam.'

Pandora noticed the woman's eyes light up for a moment, but the impassive expression soon returned. She left her seat followed by the man, and moved swiftly to the nearest exit, where she was surrounded by well-wishers and dealers, complimenting her on her wise choice, her courage, her vision. A nod from her well-coiffed head was all they got in return. She paused for a moment to shake hands with Christie's Impressionist expert, while a uniformed porter held the door open for her. Once outside, the woman took no notice of the waiting television crews; even under the hard glare of the lights, both her beauty and her stance were flawless. The small crowd of onlookers cleared a path in front of her, partly in recognition of her grandeur, but mostly because of the effective push-and-shove work by her chauffeur and a bodyguard. She ducked into a light-grey Rolls, seemingly unaware of the flashbulbs exploding around her. The man waved at the crowd and then walked around the car to climb into it from the street side.

Pandora, no chauffeurs or bodyguards to clear her path, had some difficulty in following them. She managed to reach the front line, and caught a glimpse of the man getting into the car. Their eyes met, his automatically sending out an instant flash of sexual charm.

The car pulled out and the crowd moved forward, pushing her into the road. She had often dreamed about a

16

moment like this: a taxi would instantly appear, she would climb in, push a large note into the driver's hand and say 'Follow that car!' Then they would fly off in pursuit, tyres screeching. But there was no taxi. She just stood there, breathing the cool April air and the warm traffic fumes, and watched her would-be story slowly vanishing into the New York night.

Fighting disappointment, Pandora turned into 59th Street towards Madison Avenue and began to walk the few blocks home. It did not feel quite like home to her, though: it would always be her father's apartment. His sudden death from a heart attack last year had rattled her, but the simultaneous troubles in her marriage had prevented her from fully grasping the implications at the time. She had come to New York then to attend his funeral and deal with the lawyers, but had kept her visit as short as possible. It was suggested to her that the apartment should be sold, but she could not bring herself to do it. She simply cleared out her father's clothes, burned his personal papers, and locked the door behind her. She was strengthened by the thought that she could now have a second home, the chance of a new life somewhere else, but that had been only part of the reason behind her decision. The apartment was still evidence of her father's presence, and she could not part with it while, after all those years apart, she was still reassessing what he had meant to her.

It was difficult for her to accept that so much had changed since Christmas. She had always looked for certainties, for life to be safe, organized. Like the little pig's house, they had all been blown away. After eight years as Mrs John Lyons, she was once again Pandora Doyle.

She stopped by the Laura Ashley window, and stared at its nostalgic reconstruction of English life. The window dummies were set up as mother and daughters in a scene of Edwardian domestic bliss. When she was little, Viyella nighties and dresses with sailor collars from Liberty's had failed to make up for a father who had decided to leave England and return home to New York when she was only five. Her mother had never been able to disregard the polite scorn of her friends when her marriage failed, scorn

17

which could have been anticipated from their equally polite surprise when they had first heard she was going to marry a handsome American serviceman from the nearby base, rather than one of the local gentry. Pandora had grown up in the loneliness of a rectory in Norfolk, within her uncle's estate. She had longed to go to boarding school, because for her it was the chance to be with other girls who would not know that her father had left.

But school had underlined her isolation. She was too posh for the girls sent to Benenden by *nouveau-riche* parents in order to improve their prospects, too diffident for those whose mothers had gone there, and generally too odd for either group, this half-American girl with little money and no father to take her out to lunch on exeats. Only with her friend Geraldine, also considered odd by the other girls at school because of her looks, did she feel at ease during those difficult years.

As she entered adolescence, Pandora had become more and more torn between her father's hopes for her, constantly preached in his letters from the other side of the Atlantic, and the aspirations of her mother. Her father wanted her to embrace a career as a marriage; her mother saw marriage as a career.

Partly because of her unadmitted resentment towards her father, and partly because of her own need to belong, her mother's values had prevailed. A worshipper taking up a faith for reasons other than true belief, she had embraced it without allowing herself any doubts. At school she could not wait to grow up, leave, and fall in love, as people did in books. She won her dream, but it had ended in disaster. Johnny was gone.

Not only was he gone, he had shattered her life. During the last years of their marriage she had been cook, valet, and once-a-week lay during the commercial break just before *News at Ten*, not allowed to have children, 'not yet', because they would interfere with Johnny's progress. His career at the bank required her full-time support, he said. Only later she found out that he was having an affair with a power-dressed trader who dealt in Japanese securities and was 'like one of the boys' which probably meant she didn't mind anybody's hand up her skirt while getting plastered after work in a City wine bar. It was the final episode in a long line of disappointments. At least she knew it had been hurt pride, not love, behind her explosion when she threw him out. Love had died long before.

After leaving school, she had wanted to develop a career in interior decoration, and a friend of her mother's had introduced her to Mrs Ogilvy, London's Queen of Chintz. Pandora took her job very seriously, but she wished Mrs Ogilvy had been equally serious about her, instead of putting her in charge of a string of atrocious jobs for rich Arabs to keep the cash-flow rolling; in the meantime Mrs Ogilvy took the kudos for her much-publicized country-house work for the National Trust.

She had found it easy to give up work for Johnny, but soon after their marriage she opened a small shop of her own. It had ended in failure, to Johnny's not-so-silent satisfaction.

Pandora turned into 64th Street, almost bumping into a jogger, oblivious to the world around him thanks to his bright yellow Sony Walkman. The distraction broke the bitter, brooding mood into which the subject of Johnny inevitably cast her. 'Don't brood, darling' had been Geraldine's advice when she had told her the story two months ago in London.

Geraldine had been asked by the Sainsburys to the Royal Gala at Covent Garden and was staying with Pandora for the night, her first house guest in the new flat in Campden Grove. She had sold the house in Fulham as soon as Johnny left: the rooms had become unbearable, stage sets for a play suddenly without the male lead. Thanks to the housing boom and her father's inheritance, Pandora had ended up a modestly rich woman. 'If you must cry, it's better to cry in a Rolls than in the Underground,' Geraldine had told her a long time ago. She would prefer not to have to cry at all.

Ever since they had met, sixteen years ago, Geraldine had either done all the things that Pandora would have liked to do but didn't, or done them better, or simply first. When they left school, Pandora had drifted into

19

her Season while Geraldine had had a well-publicized affair with a famous columnist, at least twenty-five years older than she was. Her own column soon followed, a stepping stone towards the editorship of *The Diary*, a moribund magazine that even Pandora's mother found rather old-fashioned. Geraldine turned it into the Bible of London glitz in just six months. Her success had been the springboard to her appointment as editor of *Chic* in New York, with a salary and perks to match. She had been even more successful in America, and three years ago she had married Solly Goldschmidt, a very rich real-estate man.

'Don't brood, just think about what you'll do from now on. You're bright, you're young, you're beautiful in spite of what you do, or rather don't do, to yourself, and there are no children to tie you down. The world is yours,' Geraldine had said. 'What you need is a break, something completely different. Come back with me to New York and help me at the magazine for a while. You were very good at writing at school. We'll fly back tomorrow, early morning Concorde, my treat, don't say a word. You have dual nationality, no immigration problems: use what you've got, that's the secret.'

Was it? Pandora wasn't sure, but it had been better than sitting in London doing nothing. At least it gave her a chance to try a different road. As she let herself into her apartment, her thoughts returned to the auction; if she could only find out who the woman was, and if there really was a story there . . . Geraldine would know. She would ask her tomorrow.

2

NEW YORK
April 1987

The elevator stopped at the 37th Floor. Pandora glanced quickly in the mirror, although she already knew that her clothes were all wrong. Everything she owned had seemed charming in London, variations on the early Princess Diana theme. Here they made her feel ready for the Salvation Army. She had to go shopping for clothes, but she didn't feel in the mood.

That morning, the *New York Times* had reported the auction on the front page, but it had said that the buyer was an anonymous woman. No one that rich could be totally unknown unless she wanted it that way.

The receptionist showed her into Geraldine's office. Pandora was no longer startled by the walls covered in newsprint, the 1950s furniture, or the tiger-skin print velvet curtains framing the New York skyline. The room had been one of Terry Cappello's landmark interiors, a brief moment of glory just before the onset of AIDS and his premature death.

Geraldine greeted her by the door, and Pandora, as usual, felt dwarfed by her height. Geraldine had been six foot tall since the age of fourteen, a laughing matter at school, but now a key ingredient of her stellar presence. Geraldine believed in making the most of what she had: her very high heels and the short skirt of her tight dress emphasized her superb legs and the starved leanness of her figure. Her straight flame-red hair reached her elbows, her heavy fringe covering the top of her glasses.

Smiling warmly at Pandora, Geraldine kissed her on both cheeks. In a city where capped teeth are as common as dyed hair, only her outsize self-confidence could explain why she had not felt it necessary to do anything about hers, once described as the dental example of an earthquake.

'Dearest, I forgot to ask you to come to my party tonight. It's for Paloma and Rafael, they arrived yesterday.

Come around 8.30.' Geraldine scanned Pandora's clothes. 'Maybe you could treat yourself to something nice for tonight, and get out of those things you wear. You're not ready for the pyre just yet. Come and sit down.' She pointed towards a kidney-shaped sofa, the gesture accompanied by the clanking of her huge crystal bangles.

Pandora glanced at Geraldine's portrait by Andy Warhol hanging over the sofa. The strong face had been glamorized but, even behind the huge glasses, it was impossible to conceal the shrewdness of her narrow eyes.

'What can I do for you, darling?' she asked.

'Last night I went to the Christie's sale . . .' Pandora began, but Geraldine interrupted her.

'Arianne de la Force,' she said, glancing at the claret-coloured polish on her nails.

Pandora was astonished. 'How did you know what I was going to ask you?'

'I know lots of things, my darling, and one of them is that you are desperate for a story. There's a good one there.'

Pandora at least had a name, a lead to follow.

'Do you know her?' she asked hopefully.

'I've come across her a few times, but we are not friends. If you are going to write about her, be careful. She does not give interviews, and she sues if the copy isn't factual. It is difficult to be completely accurate when writing about someone who can conceal her past behind a mountain of money, and Jaws might vacillate before biting the kind of lawyers she employs. What do you want to know about her?'

'She looks South American. Do you know where she comes from?'

'The CIA might, just, find the answer to that one.' Geraldine chuckled. 'She told me once that she had been born in France and brought up in Brazil, but then she said the opposite to someone else. She is one of those people who has an accent in every language she speaks. I've also heard her say that she is Argentine, which could be true because of her husband.'

Pandora remembered the handsome man at the auction.

22

He did not look South American and he did not act like a husband, but she was eager to keep the conversation going before Geraldine became distracted, and she did not want to appear totally clueless.

'He was with her last night, he is very handsome,' she said.

Geraldine raised one elegant eyebrow. 'Darling, if you really saw them together last night, I am going to make a lot of money out of you,' she laughed. 'She married Simon de la Force, an incredibly rich Argentine, and much older than her. Mind you, that's the right way to go about getting a husband if you want to keep him long term. But she didn't need to think long term because he died very soon afterwards.'

Pandora blushed at her misfired attempt to appear knowledgeable, Geraldine's amusement adding to her embarrassment. But she was finding the story more and more interesting.

'How did he die?'

'I think he had a good old-fashioned heart attack. Not surprising if you think about a man in his fifties, before aerobics and non-smoking, trying to impress the divine Arianne. She was one of the three top models in Paris when she married him. I wonder what she does to look so damn good still. Must be that wizard surgeon in Rio, but maybe it's just all that screwing under the palm trees with that wonderful music! Chica-boom, chica-boom, nothing better for the skin.'

The secretary came in to say that a Mrs O'Connor had arrived, but Geraldine was obviously having a good time, and waved her hand in a dismissive gesture.

'Tell her to wait.' She continued talking. 'All I've told you is gossip, and anyway you and I were playing lacrosse at the time it happened. She must have married him at least fifteen years ago.'

It was difficult for Pandora to understand a woman like that, and she couldn't help feeling a twinge of disapproval. It was the old, old story of a wonderful-looking woman marrying a very rich man.

'What does she do?' A stupid question, she thought.

23

What do rich women do? Have couture fittings and get bored.

'When he died she took over his company and ran it extremely well. She has apparently doubled its size. It is the largest everything-to-do-with-sugar business in South America, or something like that, plus a lot else all over the world and no shareholders anywhere. Some say she is worth nearly a billion, others insist that two billion would not shake her. She lives most of the time here or in Europe now; something to do with guerrillas in Argentina in the 70s.'

The woman was not quite as predictable as Pandora had thought, but if she was so able, so powerful, why wasn't she in the public eye?

'Why is she so secretive?'

Geraldine smiled. 'You *are* sweet. Privacy is the ultimate luxury. Any greaseball can go to the South of France, but only the really rich or the penniless can live without being seen unless they want to be. Besides, there were all kinds of stories when Simon de la Force died, then the guerrilla episode. She has good reason to dislike journalists.'

'What kind of stories?'

The clock on the side table struck the hour. 'I can't keep that O'Connor woman waiting the whole afternoon. My time is too expensive to use it for research, anyway. If you want to write about Arianne you'd better do some work yourself, but remember those lawyers.'

Pandora stood up. She had heard enough to confirm her interest, and she made her plan instantly. She would go to the library and look up any available information on Arianne de la Force. As she followed Geraldine towards the door, she felt excited by the prospect. She had found her story at last.

Geraldine stared at her, obviously amused.

'I can see you're looking forward to the chance of playing Sherlock Holmes, but perhaps you should wait until my party this evening before spending hours breathing dust in libraries. I thought that a bit of South American glamour was necessary for the occasion, so I asked Arianne. I'll introduce you, and we might be able to arrange an interview with her. It's always better to hear it from the horse's mouth, even if it's a lie. And be nice to Charles Murdoch. In the magazine I would call him her constant companion, but to you I would describe him as her regular, and very expensive, lay. He's gorgeous to look at, and he might provide you with some interesting angles. Don't be too nice, though: she doesn't take competition kindly, and I'm using the best silver tonight. I hate bent knives. Mind you, Arianne is too polished for that. She'll probably send you poisonous orchids from one of her plantations. And try to buy a new dress, darling. Your mother is a lovely lady, but you've dressed like her for long enough.'

On her way out, Pandora felt full of anticipation. She would go and buy the new dress right now. She had always been careful about money in the past but to hell with it . . .

The apartment had cost six million dollars to buy, and three million to decorate not counting the antique furniture and pictures. It meant a price of half-a-million dollars per window for the pleasure of looking at Central Park from high above Fifth Avenue, but the last thing on Arianne de la Force's mind as she stood in front of one of her expensive windows was the cost of anything other than Charles Murdoch's silence.

They were in the library. The fire in the Louis XVI fireplace threw a red glow on the green and gold tooled Cordoba leather on the walls, and brought out the gilded outline of the picture frames.

The night before, on the way back from the auction, Charles had told Arianne that he wanted to talk to her. Alone, he had added, pointing at the chauffeur and the bodyguard in the front seat.

When they arrived home she felt tired and had gone straight to bed after checking her diary for the following day's engagements. Her personal trainer was arriving at 8.00 a.m., Michelle would arrive at 9.30 to do her hair, then a fitting at Oscar de la Renta which would take some time. Lunch with Pat Buckley, and she was seeing Ted Bosco at Shearson Lehman in the afternoon to review

25

her bond holdings. They agreed to talk early in the evening, before changing for Geraldine's party.

Charles was already there when she walked into the room, standing by the drinks tray and pouring himself a whisky.

'Would you like anything?' he asked.

'The usual,' she said, sitting down on the Thomas Hope chair by the fireplace, her back to the fire. He poured her a glass of Salus, the Uruguayan mineral water she had shipped over wherever she was, brought it to her, then sat facing her.

'Are we alone?' he asked.

'Yes.'

'Where is Gloria?'

'She is long past the age of telling me where she is going. I don't know. She went out. I probably ask less about what Gloria does than I could, but *you* have been asking about her a good deal more than you should lately. I don't like it.'

She looked at her watch. 'Before you tell me anything, phone Rick and remind him to have the car downstairs in an hour. We still have to change, and Michelle is waiting to dress my hair for tonight.'

Charles walked to the desk, picked up the phone, dialled and waited for a while. 'He is not there,' he said, replacing the receiver. 'I told him earlier anyway, but I'll try again later.' He went back to his chair and took a sip of his whisky, his eyes on her.

'You are lovely,' he said admiringly.

She noticed his eyes on her body, and pulled the hem of her skirt down over the top of her knees.

'I thought we were long past all that.'

'Don't you miss it?' Charles asked.

'If what you wanted to tell me is that we should screw again, once in twelve years is enough for me. Why are you suddenly getting so romantic, and what is this all about?'

'My future,' Charles snapped. 'I've reached the age by which most people have arranged some pension scheme. I have none.'

26

Arianne smiled.

'You know that for as long as you keep your mouth shut, I will look after you. There can't be a better pension scheme than that.'

'Probably not,' Charles responded, 'but what will become of me if, perish the thought, something ghastly were to happen to you in ten years' time? It's not easy to rearrange your life when you are over fifty.'

Arianne smiled. 'No, particularly not in your profession.' Her contempt was clear.

He glared at her.

'Since keeping my mouth shut is what this is all about, I will not remind you of the details, but don't get holier than thou, Mrs de la Force. Or is it Madame? Señora? You are so international . . .' He smiled. 'But there's no point in getting angry. Old couples do that, and we are not old yet.'

'And we are not a couple,' said Arianne. A long silence followed, his eyes on hers.

'But we can be one,' he said at last.

'What are you talking about?' She tried to conceal her fear.

He walked towards her and leaned down, his hands on the carved arms of her chair, until their faces were inches apart.

'I am talking about Mrs Arianne Murdoch, the former Mrs de la Force. I think it sounds very good.'

She stood up, pushing him aside, and walked towards the window.

'Why?' she asked, her back to him.

'I told you why,' Charles said coolly. 'Fear of old age, a perfectly reasonable motive. I am sure you will outlive me, but imagine my position if you don't.'

'I can provide for you in my will.'

He helped himself to another whisky.

'Don't think that this is a rash proposition, because it isn't. I know that you could provide for me, but the problem is that you are not just a rich woman, you are enormously rich, and I'm used to your lifestyle now. If you were to provide for me, but made me merely rich, I

27

would have to drop my standards; not easy at any age and cruel when you are getting old. If you were to leave me enough money to continue to live like this, any lawyer worth his fee will advise Gloria to contest your will. I know the calibre of the lawyers you employ: they will be Gloria's lawyers, spurred on by endless money. My lawyers will be interested in the *possibility* of money, but only if their client wins, a far weaker motivation when things get tough. With their fees on top, I would probably end up worse off than with the small legacy option.'

He took a long sip from his glass, then went on.

'No, there is no acceptable alternative but to get married. Then the law would be on my side, and I will keep to the deal. I promise you I will never leave you.'

Arianne laughed. 'I am sure you won't. The gossip columns always say that the only two women richer than me are the Queen of Holland and the Queen of England. Neither is likely to leave her husband for you.'

Her face hardened. 'But I'm impressed by your understanding of lawyers. You've obviously thought carefully about your situation. We have been together for twelve years, and neither of us is the hurrying type. Not about things that matter, at least. I'll think about what you've said, and let you know in due course.'

She stood up, and walked towards the door.

'I don't want to be late. Please phone Rick again,' she said over her shoulder as she left the room.

Pandora was applying Chanel's *Ombre couture Jersey ambre* to her right eyelid while struggling to keep the magazine open with her left hand, when the phone rang. After many attempts, she had at last achieved a passable imitation of the model's make-up in the photograph. It had taken quite a while to acquire a 'perfect porcelain finish with *Teint naturel fluide* and *La Poudre de Chanel* in *Lumière midi*', and then she had tackled her cheeks, 'gently contoured with *Rose turbulent joues contrastes*'. She had already applied the *Ombre couture Jersey pêche* to both eyelids, and then it would only be a matter of brushing on the *Cils lumière brune*.

While looking for her new dress at lunchtime, she had walked through Bloomingdale's cosmetics department and realized that her make-up was hopelessly basic. Not knowing what to do about it, she had bought a copy of *Vogue*: the colouring of the dark-blonde, blue-eyed model on the cover was similar to her own. She had then gone to the Chanel counter at Bloomingdale's, and bought all the cosmetics listed in the caption, plus a few other suggestions from the salesgirl as well. Her heart stopped when the bill came to $384, but she was too embarrassed to ask the girl to take anything back. The experience prepared her for the next step, a short, wonderful black faille Valentino dress. She was full of excitement after her conversation with Geraldine, and was spurred on by the store's atmosphere into a sort of hypnotic shopping abandon, made easier by her credit card.

A few hours later, she was cruelly aware that she had spent nearly three thousand dollars for the sake of one evening, and she had been standing in front of the mirror for the last hour to achieve an apparently effortless look. It had been worth it, though; the carefully applied make-up brought out her blue eyes and her cheekbones, while the lipstick underscored the softness of her mouth and the golden streaks in her dark-blonde hair. But she was horribly late, and now the damned phone was ringing. As she put the eye-shadow box on the bathroom shelf, her hand brushed the foundation bottle, which crashed to the floor, splashing liquid make-up all over the tiles. Shit shit shit. She ran to the telephone, only to find out it was a wrong number.

Pandora rushed back to the bathroom, applied a last coat of mascara, and decided to leave the mess until later. She walked to her bedroom, took her dress off the hanger and put it on, her high spirits cheered on by the rustle of new silk, and stood in front of the mirror; for the first time in months, she was pleased by what she saw.

She picked up her black wrap from the armchair and walked to the door, eager to leave. She was going to a wonderful party, where she might find the first break in her new job. Maybe her life was beginning to fall into place at last; she even found a cab outside her building.

The man was lying on his back, his ruggedly handsome head propped up by pillows, watching the girl sitting on top of him, astride his thighs. The phone rang and he tried to pick it up, but the girl leaned down, her small breasts just touching the hairs of his belly, and grabbed his wrists to stop him. Her tongue encircled one of his nipples first, then the other, faster and faster, until they were taut, smeared by her lip gloss, the hard edge of her teeth against the soft flesh moistened by her saliva. Her fingers encircled his swelling cock, her thumbnail gently following the thick vein along the shaft. He gasped with pleasure.

'Let me fuck you, please, baby, please.'

She raised her head, smiling. 'Not yet. You always want it too soon, and I am not ready yet.'

He watched her hands cup her breasts, her thumbs rubbing her nipples, her eyes closed and her teeth biting her lower lip. She then lifted herself up, just enough for the head of his cock to slip between her thighs. She moved up and down very gently; he arched his spine in a desperate effort to enter her, but she raised herself slightly to prevent him. A drop of semen appeared on the tip of his penis: she quickly wiped it with her finger, and licked it greedily.

'Oh, I like it, I want it,' she sighed, 'but not yet, naughty boy, not yet.' She eyed him slowly, taking in the strong body, the broad shoulders, the arms almost as thick as her thighs. 'Baby needs to calm down, he is so impatient. Baby needs something sweet.'

She looked at the bedside table. Next to his keys and his wallet, there was a Mars bar. She picked it up, tore the wrapping off, rubbed it against his lips until it was soft, and then slipped it inside her, pushing the Mars bar in and out, her fingers smeared by the slowly melting chocolate.

'Baby is going to like this,' she whispered. She pulled the moist chocolate bar out and slowly moved her body forward, until she could feel the grittiness of the five o'clock shadow on his cheeks rubbing against her inner thighs, his breath on her skin.

'Now have some nice warm chocolate. Lick me, baby, I'm all sweet for you.'

The tip of his tongue touched her, first gently, then faster and more firmly until she felt herself begin to melt. Suddenly he caught the soft ridge between his teeth, and she screamed.

'Oh, yes, baby can have me now.' She leaned down and kissed him deeply, her tongue rubbing against his, her nails digging into his chest. He suddenly rose, one arm around her waist, and pushed her on to the bed, face down, the weight of his body crushing her. Slipping his arm under her belly, he entered her from the back, his fingers digging into her rear. She felt the rush swelling inside her, bit her lips, and buried her face in the pillow as his animal roar filled the room, the waves of her pleasure in unison with his hot outpouring.

As he lay on her back, panting, his body pinning her to the bed, the phone rang again. He picked it up.

'Yes, sir, immediately.' He jumped out of bed. 'That was Mr Murdoch. Sorry, Gloria, I have to drive your mother to a party now,' he said, pulling on his chauffeur's uniform as fast as he could.

3

NEW YORK
April 1987

The taxi swerved across two lanes of Park Avenue traffic in a crescendo of enraged hooting before turning into 70th Street. Pandora slid along the back seat, clinging to the metal grille behind the driver to regain her balance as the cab slowed to a halt outside Geraldine's house.

Pandora got out, took a deep, steadying breath, and walked up to the double doors, their gloss black paint reflecting the streetlights. The brass bell-push was the size of a side-plate, and polished to a mirror finish. As she waited, her eyes wandered along the beautiful street, its mansions and brownstones softened by the tracery of the large trees, taking in the lovely house nearby, a Parisian toy in New York. 'We live just a few steps from the Mellon house,' Geraldine had told her proudly when she had given her the address. Pandora, at that time completely ignorant of the finer points of New York society, thought she meant a very expensive East Side grocer. By now she knew better.

The door opened and Compton, the English butler, let her in and took her wrap.

'Good evening, Compton. Am I terribly late?'

'Good evening, Miss Doyle. No, you're not. I believe that Mrs Goldschmidt has asked forty guests, and only about half are here so far. If you'll excuse me saying so, Miss Doyle, I think there's nothing prettier than a good-looking English girl.'

Compton's voice was pitched at the right tone of polite and cheerful deference. Pandora felt both flattered and uncomfortable, her usual reaction to compliments.

'Thank you, Compton, but I think that you're just being patriotic,' she laughed. 'I'd better join the others before you start singing God Save the Queen.'

Her guess was that Compton was not the name he had been given at some small church in Derby but Geraldine's

32

choice, another facet of her clever strategy to conquer New York by combining outrageous idiosyncrasies with upper-class British mannerisms.

The house was typical of her approach. It was the perfect New York Upper East Side residence from the outside, but as soon as the door was opened another of Terry Cappello's interiors engulfed the visitor. The circular foyer had industrial flooring in steel plate, its walls pock-marked with dents and scratches, covered in graffiti and painted to imitate the rotting walls of a slum in the Bronx. Two plasterers had been brought in from Italy, at the rate of $100 per hour plus expenses, to achieve the distressed surface effect. It had taken three attempts, and four weeks, to please Terry and only then had the painters moved in. The ceiling, a nineteenth-century French canvas, combined nymphs, cherubs and clouds. Opposite the entrance door, two huge Ron Arad panels in gashed steel sheets slid silently to the sides as Pandora approached them, revealing the crowded hall.

Here, the décor was in faultless Regency style, down to the staircase copied from Sheringford Hall, and the elaborately swagged drapes, which, according to Geraldine, had been inspired by the Brighton Pavilion. The room was carefully lit by spotlights behind huge arrangements of quince branches and leaves in terracotta urns in the corners.

Pandora noticed at first glance that most of the women were blonde and ageless, their hair and their diamonds glowing brighter than the dimmed lights. Geraldine was close to the door. Not close enough to give the impression that she was standing there to greet the guests as they arrived, but sufficiently close for her not to miss anyone coming in. Like most of the women in the room, she was wearing Lacroix, hers in yellow and black and very short.

She was talking to a small group of guests, and quickly introduced Pandora to them. Paloma Picasso looked ravishing in red and black, with enormous jewels. The others in the group were equally famous: Marco Bellini, the film director laden with Oscars and Palmes d'Or, Nick Abrams, the anchor man, Roz Rittner, whose photograph seemed to be a permanent feature of American glossies, and a man whose name she did not catch. After the brief interruption of her arrival, they continued their conversation. They were discussing *The End of Dreams*, a new novel about life in New York which had become the success of the decade.

'I found it too exaggerated,' Roz Rittner said, wrinkling her nose.

'Exaggeration, like beauty, is in the beholder's eye,' replied Bellini.

In spite of her social smoothness, it was clear from her face that Mrs Rittner did not like being contradicted, and Geraldine intervened.

'I wouldn't know, Marco, I'm always beautiful but never exaggerated,' she said with a smile. They all laughed politely, relieved that the moment had been saved, then launched into further praise of the book. Pandora cut in.

'I thought it was marvellously well-observed, and . . .' She realized that no one was paying any attention to her, and stopped. Their simultaneous monologues finally ran their course, and a brief silence followed.

'Pandora has just arrived from London. I've been begging her to do some special writing for me. She's fantastic, everyone wants her. She has agreed to do Mrs Thatcher for us; the Prime Minister is *very* particular about who she'll give interviews to,' Geraldine explained. Her tone underlined the importance of the secret she had just revealed, and Pandora could sense the group's attention suddenly turning to her for the first time.

'Do you know Mrs Thatcher? I admire her enormously,' said the man whose name she had missed. He was in his fifties, with a face as shrewd as his watch was expensive. Although amused by Geraldine's fabrication, Pandora felt annoyed at being turned into the centre of attention on the back of a lie, but she could not deny it without embarrassing Geraldine.

'I don't know her at all, but I once did a profile of Mrs Gandhi for a journal which may have caught the Prime Minister's attention.' Geraldine's almost imperceptible wink confirmed to her that she also remembered Pandora's contribution to the school magazine many years ago.

'English girls err on the side of excessive modesty,' Geraldine said to the group at large.

'You always have one of everything at your parties, Geraldine, but I had never come across a modest guest before,' Nick Abrams teased.

'Perhaps you did, but you just weren't listening,' Pandora replied sweetly.

Geraldine cast her eye around her, and turned towards another group nearby.

'Solly darling, please be an angel and show Pandora your new Schnabel before everybody arrives. Ever since I told her about it she's been dying to see it.'

A terror to the world, chewing up deals and people for twelve hours a day, Solly Goldschmidt yearned for domestic peace, and had learned soon enough that the easiest way to have it was not to contradict Geraldine. He excused himself from his guests, and led Pandora towards the library.

Relieved to be taken away, she smiled at Solly. Everything about Solly was solid: his head, his body, and his views. He was short and compact, his bright brown eyes and black curly hair his most noticeable features.

'I would never have guessed that you are such a fan of Julian Schnabel,' he said.

'I've no idea who he is.'

He stopped and stared at her, obviously nonplussed.

'What the hell is going on?'

'I don't know. Geraldine launched into a fantastic story about me, and then asked you to take me away. Maybe she was trying to make me look more important than I am, and then sent me away before the others could find out.'

He smiled, picked up a glass of champagne from the tray presented by a waiter, and handed it to Pandora.

'She was probably right. No one listens to details at parties; after five minutes the only thing they will remember is that you are somebody worth knowing. Have a drink, and I'll show you my Schnabel anyway.'

They walked into the empty library and Solly pointed at the huge painting above the sofa: dozens of broken white plates embedded into a thick crust of paint in vibrant colours.

They stood silently in front of it. Uncertain what to say, Pandora hesitated before asking:

'Do you like it?'

Solly gave her a sharp look.

'What's that got to do with anything? Geraldine told me that I must have it, and I beat the dealer shitless on the asking price. He was selling on behalf of a guy in real trouble and wanted the money quick. I don't look at paintings, I only go to museums for the parties. But do *you* like it?'

Pandora inspected the painting for a moment.

'I don't think so, no, I'm afraid I don't,' she finally said, almost apologetically. She knew that it would have been wiser to flatter Solly, but she also knew that she would not have been able to sound sincere about what, to her, looked like a mess of broken crockery.

'You Brits are funny. Why are you "afraid"? I ain't gonna kill you for it. Just say "No, I don't." Life is easier if we know where we stand. Come on, let's go back; I'm supposed to be the host here.'

They left the library and walked up the wide staircase to the first-floor landing leading to the drawing room. The big double doors were open, and they heard the sound of party laughter. As they walked into the room, a woman rushed towards them.

'Solly! Solly daaarling!'

Pandora was pushed aside by a swirl of rustling silk, bare shoulders, tempestuous black hair and dramatic eyes made up in Maria Callas style. Solly disentangled himself from her embrace, and introduced them:

'Pandora, this is Maria Dimitrescu, Pandora Doyle.'

The woman's eyes scanned Pandora from top to bottom, and then she focused on Solly with extraordinary intensity, as if he were the one and only person in the room.

'You are *méchant*, so naughty. When are you going to come to my encounters? It's just a weekend, and you'll discover a new dimension to yourself, a deeper meaning to our life in communion with our brothers and sisters.'

36

Solly's black tie was perfectly straight, but she tugged it while she talked, her eyes on his. 'Promise me that you will come. And Geraldine, of course. I *adore* Geraldine, she is my best friend.' A minute ago they had been three people chatting at a party, now Maria had turned the scene into a couple in intimate dialogue, and Pandora had become an intruder.

'I don't know,' said Solly. 'You'd better ask her.'

'Ah, how you love each other. You are both a-dorable! Geraldine told me that I should ask *you*. Why don't you come the first weekend in May? La Duchesse de Brie-Montval will be there, and Barry Leen is coming specially from London. Do come, Solly.' She smoothed his lapels. '*Please* do.' There was a sly expression in her eyes now. 'David Blomfield will also be there.'

David Blomfield, or Lord Blomfield as he had been for a few years, was a financial titan who had recently surprised everybody by unloading all his stocks in spite of the buoyant markets. He was now sitting on a mountain of cash, and was supposed to be interested in property deals.

Solly's voice softened a fraction. 'We may have something to do then, but I think we can make ourselves free.'

The change in Solly's tone obviously pleased Maria, and she flashed a huge smile, her capped teeth shining in the half-light. 'I'll drop you a little note, not a *billet-doux*, just to remind you.'

The corners of her mouth turned up into a coquettish smile. '*Au revoir*, darling.' She then turned her face just a fraction towards Pandora, murmuring 'Nice to meet you' as her eyes checked out the other guests.

'Who is she?' asked Pandora as soon as Maria left. She had realized long ago that parties are hunting grounds for business or sex as much as a social occasion. Even she was here tonight with an ulterior motive. But in London the cards were played close to the chest; here they were laid on the table.

'Oh, one of those people who crops up everywhere. Her parents fled from Romania to Paris when she was little. They struggled to educate her, and eventually she got a degree in something or other. When she was at University she fucked some very old professor who knew everybody, and got herself launched in Paris society. Hasn't stopped since. She moved to New York when she realized it's where the real bucks are.' Solly grinned. 'But she's probably learning Japanese by now.'

'She doesn't seem to waste much time. What was she inviting you to?'

'There isn't any point in wasting time if you know what you want. She has some method of talking to God, direct line, or some crap like that. She's done very well with it.'

Stung by his reference to wasted time, Pandora looked sharply at Solly, but realized from his face that there had been no personal edge to his remark, and was as annoyed by her own insecurity as by Maria's brazenness.

'At least she knows what she wants,' she told Solly.

'Don't you?' There was genuine surprise in his voice. Pandora smiled.

'I thought I did, but I was wrong.' She sensed that Solly might think she was asking for sympathy. 'But I'm finding my way now,' she added quickly.

They were half-way down the stairs when the doors to the hall opened, and Arianne de la Force came in.

At the auction, Pandora had been struck by her beauty, but there Arianne had been surrounded by a quietly elegant audience. Now Pandora saw her among the most glamorous women in New York, and realized that this woman was truly unique. She stood as straight as a plumbline, shoulders thrown back, her long neck and exquisite head slightly tilted. Yet there was nothing contrived or rehearsed about the way she moved, just instinctive grace.

Her beauty was underlined by her dress, the simplest long sleeved, body-skimming sheath in thick satin the colour of ice. In a room full of frills and bows, her refined elegance pushed every other woman into the background. Her shiny black hair was drawn back in the same style as the night before, and even at a distance Pandora noticed the size of the pearl studs in her ears. Charles Murdoch was one step behind her. As Geraldine greeted them, she glared over Arianne's shoulder at the nearest waiter, who rushed to offer drinks to the newly-arrived guests.

38

Solly led Pandora back to Geraldine's group.

'Ah, there you are, my darlings. Arianne, this is Pandora Doyle, my oldest friend in the world. Pandora Doyle, Arianne de la Force and Charles Murdoch. Pandora is going to write a series of profiles of the world's leading women for the magazine, or at least I hope so. She's so hard to get.'

Charles Murdoch's eyes latched onto Pandora.

'Are you?' he asked pointedly. The flirtation was so blatant that it was obviously for the benefit of the company as much as for her. Perhaps it was his retaliation for being cast into Arianne's shadow.

'Pandora should tell us about Mrs Thatcher,' the man with the shrewd face said to the group at large, then he turned towards Arianne. 'She is one of her favourite journalists.' Pandora guessed that, at this rate, she would become Mrs Thatcher's *éminence grise* before the evening was over.

Arianne gazed at him, an amused expression in her eyes.

'You are always very well informed, Bob. Miss Doyle reminds me of that lovely looking secretary you used to have a long time ago.' Her voice was soft and very low, a mixture of a Brazilian lilt and a French cadence in her accent.

Geraldine cut in. 'I've been desperately trying to talk Pandora into writing your profile, Arianne. I would be delighted if you would consider helping her.'

Arianne turned away.

'I love those foliage arrangements, Geraldine. Who does them for you?' Arianne asked, as if she had not heard the question.

Geraldine smiled.

'A marvellous girl I found in London; she used to be at school with Princess Diana. I fly her in when we have a party. Much more sensible than paying New York florists' prices.' Pandora wondered if either woman really knew the price of flowers, in New York or anywhere else.

'I know. I fly orchids from Brazil for my parties· if I can, but here it's so difficult to bring plants in,' Arianne

39

said, and then took a sip from her glass of mineral water. Pandora saw that she was wearing identical square emeralds on both hands.

'What wonderful rings,' she exclaimed.

Arianne smiled. 'You are very observant, but that's not surprising. You are a journalist, after all. How unusual for an English person to comment on one's possessions.' The silky rebuke was delivered in an equally silky voice.

'England is no longer what it used to be, darling,' Geraldine cut in, 'but your jewels get better and better.' She showed Arianne her massive gilt and faux-pearl cuff bracelets. 'I don't wear real jewellery any more, I can't be bothered with the insurance. These are by Mercedes Robirosa, she is absolutely the best designer around now.'

'I gave up costume jewellery a long time ago,' Arianne replied shortly.

'It's understandable, with emeralds like yours,' Geraldine said acidly.

'Simon gave them to me sometime before our marriage. He said that he could see no reason why he should favour one of my hands over the other.' Arianne's eyes wandered over the room, a constant smile of recognition on her lips as she came across one familiar face after another.

'I wish Solly had heard that,' said Geraldine. 'I might ask you to repeat the story when he's around. Where is Solly, anyway? We should sit down to dinner now. Please come with me, Arianne. I've put you and Paloma at Solly's table.' She led Arianne away.

The guests began to drift towards the just-opened gilt and mahogany doors at the back of the room.

'Have you checked where your seat is?' Charles Murdoch asked Pandora, offering her his arm. She did not like the man, but his charm was evident, even in trivial conversation.

'No, I haven't.' It had not crossed her mind to do it. She was not used to going to dinner parties at friends' homes with forty guests or more and seating plans.

Charles stopped by a gilded console between the doors leading to the dining room. New York hostesses went to great efforts of imagination and money to display seating plans for their guests, but Geraldine considered it common. A sheet of white paper, typed by her secretary and pinned to a cork board, rested on the marble top.

'We are sitting next to each other. Well done, Geraldine,' said Charles.

Looking at the plan, Pandora noticed the name on the left side of her seat.

'Who is Sheridan Crabtree?' she asked.

'I don't know, but don't waste your time,' Charles retorted, escorting her into the dining room.

Pandora had seen it before, but the transformation for just one night amazed her. The huge French doors to the garden had been removed, and a conservatory-like structure had been added on, doubling the size of the room. The whole space was tented in pale silver gauze shimmering in the candlelight. On the tables, candles burned in *Empire* silver-gilt candlesticks in the shape of Egyptian goddesses, forming a circle around the mass of wild flowers in the centre; more candles burned in the huge Waterford chandelier hanging from a tasselled silk rope, their light refracted into miniature spectrums by the faceted drops. The floor was strewn with kilims, adding to the opulent atmosphere. A row of veiled girls, dressed up as harem slaves, was lined up against the rear wall of the room.

There were two tables for twenty. Pandora was at Geraldine's, within the room, while Solly presided over the second table in the conservatory. As they sat down, she was at first disappointed not to be at the same table as Arianne, but then she realized that she would not have been able to talk to her anyway: there would have been at least one man between them. Geraldine had done the best possible thing for her, placing her next to Arianne's lover.

Pandora glanced briefly at Sheridan Crabtree as she picked up her napkin. The most remarkable things about him were his extremely old dinner jacket, and a pungent smell of rancid sweat, drowning the combined strength of the world's most expensive perfumes. Pandora turned away from him.

41

The conversation around the table was at that fragile stage when people are still sitting down and finding out about their neighbours. As the line of waitresses started to move around the tables pouring Puligny-Montrachet 1971 in the first of four St Louis crystal glasses, Charles Murdoch asked Pandora if she had been in New York for long.

'I've been here for a few . . .' She was going to say weeks, but it would have been at odds with Geraldine's version of her career. Star journalists don't stay anywhere without a definite purpose.

Another slave presented a huge silver dish. Grateful for the distraction, Pandora helped herself to lobster and Burma lettuce salad.

'I've been here for a few days. Presumably you came here with Mrs de la Force. She seems such a fascinating woman. How did you meet her?' she asked abruptly.

Charles glanced at her, amused.

'I thought this was dinner party conversation, but you seem to be writing your profile already.'

Pandora smiled, regretting her impatience.

'I'm sorry if you thought I was interviewing you. It was not at all my intention. I use a tape recorder when I'm on duty, and it would be very difficult to hide it under my dress.'

'I wouldn't mind checking up on that later,' Charles grinned.

'I thought this was dinner party conversation, not a seduction,' she laughed.

'You seem old enough to know that that's what most dinner party conversations are.' He picked up his knife and fork.

'Odd that Geraldine, who is such a perfectionist, would not know that one needs fish cutlery to eat lobster,' he added.

Already annoyed with his smugness, the pretentious remark brought out the worst in Pandora.

'Fish cutlery is a Victorian invention. Only *nouveau-riche* people inherit *that* kind of silver,' she said, sounding exactly like her mother.

He gave her a sharp look.

'I can't imagine Solly's family bought much silver in the eighteenth century,' he replied, and then carried on as if the exchange had not taken place. 'Have you been to the Liechtenstein exhibition? It's fascinating. We went to the Benefactors viewing.' He launched into a long description of the exhibits. Pandora was certain that he was not the type to care about art collections: he was steering the conversation away from the one subject she was interested in. She had to regain control.

'. . . and apparently his Titians are fabulous.' Charles paused to take a sip of his wine.

'You seem amazingly knowledgeable about paintings, but I can't imagine that you are an art dealer. What do you do?' she asked, then went on eating her salad, which was delicious. Once again, Charles seemed amused by her question.

'I run a very lengthy educational course. The subject is "how to have a good time", and the only student is me. By and large, it's running very well.' He stopped talking and watched Pandora as she took another bite of lobster. He smiled.

'You must be the only woman in New York who actually eats at dinner parties. Stop eating and tell me more about yourself. Are you married?'

'Separated,' she said tersely. She hated to discuss her personal life.

'You ought to be more expansive, otherwise I won't have time for even one mouthful myself.'

'My husband and I . . .' It did not sound right, and she started again. 'We separated five months ago. We were married for eight years. We married very young.' She knew that perhaps she ought to say more. Making this man feel she was confiding in him might encourage him to talk about himself, but she drew the line at using her private life to entice confidences.

'Where are you from?' she asked. 'Your accent is almost American, but not quite.'

'I lived in Europe for a very long time. Your accent changes if you live abroad.'

'You sound like a character in a Henry James novel.

43

Where did you live in Europe?' She had to get the subject back to Arianne, but at least the conversation was now on personal ground.

'South of France, mostly. Very good place for educational purposes.' He was not going to volunteer much information either, she thought.

'I haven't been to the South of France for years, it must have changed so much,' she carried on glibly, to put him at ease. 'Did you meet Arianne there?'

He smiled.

'No, I met her at Formentor, a long time ago.'

The main course, very pink *noisettes d'agneau* garnished with courgettes, minute carrots and infinitesimal potatoes cooked to perfection, was presented to Pandora. She helped herself, and Charles Murdoch turned towards the woman on his right. As Pandora turned her head to her left, she caught a snippet of conversation across the table.

'You shouldn't be so cruel about poor Nathan,' a woman wearing rubies said to the man next to her. 'I know him well. He's one of my best friends in fact, and he's really a sweetie when he's sober.' Pandora decided to concentrate on the man next to her.

The *'Bombe glacée à la délice des Indes'* was served, and Pandora thanked God for his Mercy. For the last half hour she had been listening to Sheridan Crabtree's adenoidal voice. He had informed Pandora that he was an architect, but that he really did not practise because buildings today were not worthy of his talent. Instead, he was the editor and founder of *The Palladian Gazette*, an exquisite architectural journal of limited circulation, which he ran from his home in Wiltshire. He was in New York because of work: he explained that he was 'chief design consultant for a large historical reconstruction project', adding that his wife was Geraldine's cousin.

Pandora remembered Geraldine mentioning his arrival and describing him as a pompous bore, and the wife as rich and ugly in equal measure. She had also said that his visit was to advise on the decoration of a new health club called 'Boodles', where the aim was to re-create an English country house atmosphere.

During the conversation, Pandora had noticed that suddenly Charles Murdoch's leg was beside hers, not touching, but close enough for her to feel the texture of his trouser leg through her stocking, the warmth of his body reaching her skin. She looked at him, but he seemed to be completely immersed in conversation with the woman on his right. She moved her leg away, and kept on listening to Crabtree.

As the Roederer Cristal 1976 was poured, Charles turned towards her and said:

'Where were we?'

'Mrs de la Force.'

'You can call her Arianne. I'm sure she won't mind, not here at least.'

The edge of sarcasm in his voice was evident. An embittered lounge lizard, she thought.

'I've heard that she had a problem with the guerrillas in Argentina.'

'That was a long time ago. I met her after she and Gloria went to live in Europe.'

'Who is Gloria?'

'Her daughter.'

Pandora was nonplussed.

'I thought her husband died very soon after their wedding.'

'Simon de la Force was not Gloria's father,' Charles explained. 'Gloria was two or three years old when Arianne married Simon.'

'Who was she married to before?' At last she was making some progress.

'You'd better ask her.' He smoothed over his terse reply, adding, 'I don't know, I think he was a Frenchman. I am sure Arianne told me all about him, but I've forgotten. I'm sorry that I make such a poor gossip, but I never remember other people's personal stories. And now that you know that I am reliable, or at least that my discretion is, perhaps you will tell me more about yourself?'

'What could you possibly want to know?' Her guardedness was more genuine than she would have liked it to be. There was little in her life at the moment she felt at ease about.

'What are you doing tomorrow, for instance. The afternoon is better, but mornings can be fun.'

His boldness was irksome but, after months of solitary dinners in front of the TV set in London, a very handsome man making a pass at her was like *Grande Champagne* cognac. But Pandora was not attracted to him, so it was easy to exaggerate her annoyance. She gave him a frosty look.

'I do something rather unusual: I work. My mornings and afternoons are busy, and I'm very tired in the evenings.'

Her right hand was on the table: he moved his left hand until they almost touched. She lifted her napkin to her lips, and then rested her hand on her lap.

'You are exceptionally unfriendly,' Charles said. 'Is it because you are having an affair with Solly, or something?'

Pandora felt her cheeks burning with rage.

'How dare you say something like that, here of all places. Geraldine is my oldest and best friend, and I will not tolerate you making that kind of suggestion about her husband and me.'

She was furious now, but Charles seemed genuinely puzzled by her outburst.

'Please excuse me if I have offended you, but I don't think that you should take it like this. Going to bed with the wives of my best friends is what I have done all my life. Let's not get upset about trivial things.' She was about to reply when the slaves reappeared with minute gilded cups and antique Turkish coffee pots. Perhaps it was better to drop the subject.

Pandora noticed that Geraldine was talking to the man Arianne had seemed to know, the man with the shrewd face whose name she had missed earlier.

'Who is the man on Geraldine's left?' she asked.

'Bob Chalmers. He's a financial genius: got most of the Third World into debt, then was paid huge fees for suggesting ways to get them out of it. He now advises

46

just a few private clients: Arianne is one of them. Since Geraldine seems transfixed by everything he says, I would guess that he has something to do with Solly as well.'

At that moment Geraldine left the table and led the way to the drawing room upstairs. Her red hair glowed in the candlelight as she walked across the room, quickly surveying the scene, the success of her dinner party confirming to her, once again, that the richest, the brightest, and just a very few of the most boring had been awed by her style. But this verification was unnoticeable; the guests could only see her walking past, her hostess smile in place, a perfect New York star.

As soon as Charles and Pandora left their table, they were joined by Bob Chalmers.

'We haven't played tennis since Lyford Cay, Charles. How about Piping Rock next Saturday? I hope your serve has suffered during the winter, otherwise it will be very boring for you.' He smiled at Pandora and, as they approached the marble staircase, he offered her his arm. Charles stayed behind to talk to some people at the bottom of the stairs.

'I am very impressed by someone as young as you being so successful,' he said. 'You must be very good. Have you published anything recently?' After dinner with Charles Murdoch, Pandora was wary of men's flattery and Bob Chalmers' interest seemed excessive. On the other hand, she had been introduced to him as a successful journalist.

'I have a few things in the pipeline,' she said, 'but only one of them will be in *Chic*, the rest will be published in England. Right now I am doing research on some new material.'

'I'll ask my secretary to keep an eye on *Chic*.' Bob pulled out a gold-trimmed wallet from his pocket and gave her his card. 'I would be delighted if you would send me a copy of your English features as soon as they're published.'

'Of course,' Pandora said with a smile, slipping his card into her evening purse. They walked into the drawing room, which was buzzing with conversation. Geraldine was sitting at the end of one of the two black and gold Regency *chaises-longues* by the fireplace, with Rafael Lopez Sanchez in the middle, and Arianne at the other end.

As Pandora and Bob walked in, Geraldine saw their reflection in the huge gilded mirror above the fireplace. She waved at them.

'Come here. Rafael is telling us about his theatre days in Buenos Aires in the Sixties.' She pointed towards the huge tapestry stool by the fireplace, and asked them to sit down.

'. . . and they were half-way through the play when the General's wife in the audience couldn't restrain herself any more: she climbed on stage, pulled a rosary out of her bag and whipped the actors with it, shouting "Blasphemy! Blasphemy!" It was so awful . . . The play was banned the following day. I left for Paris soon after.'

Rafael turned towards Arianne. 'Were you in Buenos Aires then? I can't remember, it's such a long time ago.'

'No. Simon and I got married in 1969,' Arianne replied. 'I missed the Sixties there.'

'Where were you in the Sixties, Arianne?' Geraldine asked. 'Mind you, now that Pandora will be doing your profile, I should save the answer for my readers.'

'There's no point in boring your readers.' Pandora noticed that Arianne had clenched her left hand, the thumb folded under her fingers, and she was turning the emerald ring round and round.

Geraldine raised her hands in mock horror. 'Goodness me, I've never come across anyone so un-cooperative. You are worse than Garbo, darling, but at least she wants to be alone. You must be used to talking about yourself at parties. Conversation would be so boring otherwise.'

'Where is Charles? We have to go soon,' Arianne said, picking up her purse from the coffee table.

'Pandora dear, I think that I will have to fly you to Rio on a research trip, your interviewee is *very* unhelpful. It's beginning to look as if she may have something to hide.'

Geraldine's tone made the phrase sound like a joke, but she stared at Arianne with a deadpan face.

Arianne stood up. She smiled at her hostess.

'I'm not as interesting as all that.' She turned towards Pandora. 'Please phone my secretary to make an appointment. I'd rather talk to you for half an hour than be cross-examined by Geraldine every time we meet. Goodnight everybody.'

'I'll walk with you to the stairs. You are my favourite guests, but I've been sitting here for far too long. I must mingle,' Geraldine said, leaving her seat.

The two women walked towards the door, chatting and laughing like old friends, as if their contretemps just a moment ago had never happened.

4

NEW YORK
April 1987

The grey sky was getting darker, and Pandora hurried along 57th Street. She began to cross the road as the first drops hit the ground. By the time she reached the other side the rain was crashing down on the sidewalks, and the gutters had turned into streams. Damn it, she had the best of her Fulham-princess wear on, and her favourite shoes. Neither would survive this monsoon-like storm. She took shelter in the doorway of Hammacher Schlemmer just in time to avoid the sheet of water sprayed over the pavement by a bright-red delivery van.

She scanned the street for a taxi. It was ten past three, and she was supposed to be at Arianne de la Force's apartment in twenty minutes. Unless she found a taxi soon, she would have to walk in the rain.

Her mood and the weather had run parallel that morning. She woke up full of anticipation at the thought of her meeting with Arianne, arranged last Friday. She had asked Geraldine's secretary for Arianne's number as soon as she arrived at the office the morning after the party. She had expected Arianne's secretary to have a sharp voice and the polite kindness of a cheetah. She was right. But the cheetah had not put up any further struggle than to say: 'Madame de la Force is going abroad on Friday. She's terribly, terribly busy. Let me see if she has any gaps in her diary,' and then abruptly added, 'She can see you next Thursday at 3.30 p.m.'

She had walked to the office under a blue sky and in high spirits. She loved early morning in New York: the buzz of the street life, the traffic, the street salesmen creating a miniature bazaar-like atmosphere at most corners. The short walk was a pleasure, although she knew her morning meeting with the Advertising Manager was not going to be one of the day's joys. As she entered into the chrome, black marble and mirror 1930s' foyer of the *Chic* building, she suspected that this second meeting with the advertising ogre was likely to be as unpleasant as the first, which had occurred two weeks after she had started work at the magazine.

Pandora had arrived in New York with a very vague notion of what her job entailed. She had thought that her relationship with Geraldine at work would be an extension of their friendship, but she soon realized that while Geraldine was genuinely trying to be helpful, she now lived in a world of Concorde flights and lunches with Nancy Reagan. Only crucial matters concerned her, and then only those critical to either the success of the magazine or her personal career.

It was true that on her first day Geraldine had received her warmly, asked her to come up for a cup of tea in her extraordinary office and given her a lurid account of who was screwing whom, but she soon cut the meeting short because she had an urgent engagement. When Pandora asked for a briefing on what she was supposed to do, she was told to wait for 'someone to contact you, and explain the ropes. It's really quite simple, you can do it in your sleep. I'll call you, darling. Maybe you can come for dinner tomorrow, Sam and Jessica are in town, you will adore them.' She had gone to dinner at Geraldine's home the following night, with fifteen other people, but she still had no idea of her job.

The next week boredom began to overwhelm her, and she started a list of possible subjects for feature articles to discuss with Geraldine. It was during one of those afternoons, as more and more pages of her note pad became slowly covered in doodled daisies, that her phone rang for the first time. It was Connie van Naalt's secretary, asking Pandora to come up to see Miss van Naalt in her office in an hour's time.

The reputation of Connie van Naalt, *Chic*'s fashion editor, was formidable. She had discovered struggling designers in the Bronx and made them Seventh Avenue superstars, turned girls glimpsed in the street into international models, and started more fashion trends than she had swallowed ginseng tablets. Obsessed with perfection, she was known to rip dresses off the back of her terrified assistants if she found them 'common', an expression picked up during a brief stay in London during the Sixties. After years of cleverly hopping from one job to the other on an ever-upward route, she had joined *Chic*, eventually achieving the prize of American fashion journalism, second only to the editorship itself.

Some of this Pandora knew from her sessions at her Fulham hairdresser. What she did not know was that when the previous editor-in-chief had retired, Connie had made no secret of her bid for the succession. She was sure that her legendary sense for the most subtle fashion vibrations ensured her right to it.

However, Mrs Greene, the owner of *Chic* and a dozen other titles, had an equally legendary nose for profits and she had not failed to notice the magazine's disappointing balance sheet and static circulation. She needed someone who understood how to make money through style, not a fashion legend. She had heard of Geraldine Freeman, and flew to London for an overnight visit, where she asked Geraldine to dinner in her suite at Claridges. Geraldine's appointment was announced in New York the following week.

Connie's silence was as elegant as everything else about her because there was nowhere to go but down from *Chic*, and she was too skilful to antagonize Geraldine in any way or show the slightest sign of dissatisfaction. But when she heard that a new girl had been appointed for the Shopping section, a protégée of Geraldine's without any previous journalistic experience, she felt the joyous expectation of a vulture who has circled the sky for hours and suddenly notices a limping rabbit on the ground.

'Another new girl for the Shopping page?' Connie had asked Geraldine casually.

'Yes, that idiot Bibi Sohnnental had a skiing accident in Gstaad two weeks ago. She has to stay in a clinic there for God knows how long. I asked Pandora Doyle, a girl I know from London, to stand in. She is very competent. I've sent a memo to Tony to brief her,' Geraldine replied crisply.

'I'm sure she will be fabulous, Geraldine,' said Connie enthusiastically. Geraldine was momentarily nonplussed by the sudden change in Connie's usually haughty demeanour, but put it down to a sporadic impulse to show her willingness to be friendly. Perhaps the back-stabbing phase was over.

'You know Tony. He is always so worried about figures that he will take as little time as possible over the briefing. If you agree, Geraldine, I could have a chat with Pandora to brief her, and explain our total concept, our philosophy.' Nothing but constructive concern showed in Connie's voice, and Geraldine agreed to her kind offer.

Back in her office, Connie spoke briefly to Tony Andreotti, the Advertising Manager. She then called up the draft Shopping section for the forthcoming issue on her PC, and the facing-editorial advertisers for the following issue already approached by Bibi Sohnnental before her multiple fractures. The subject of the feature was to be Italy on the East Side. She asked her secretary to make a copy of the advertisers' list, and then call Pandora to her office.

An hour later, her secretary announced Miss Doyle. She went to her light box and switched it on, pretending to look at the shots of the American summer collections taken in the Maldives by Anahi Paivakis, the sensational Greek photographer she had discovered while in Paris for the last collections.

'Please sit down,' she said to Pandora without turning around, pointing at the chair facing her desk. Connie inspected the transparencies for a few minutes, and then turned towards her visitor.

At the sight of Connie's blue-black hair cut into a severe bob, shaved eyebrows, black and white Kabuki make-up, black skin-tight dress and steel jewellery, Pandora's first impression was that she was facing Cruella de Ville. However, Connie's mortuary look was belied by the warm smile that flashed briefly on her lips; a month later, Pandora would have been able to appreciate the very special honour of a smile from a higher-ranking colleague in an American fashion magazine, but she was still unaware of such fine points.

'My dear, I've heard so much about you from Geraldine that I was dying to meet you,' Connie gushed, fixing an admiring glance on Pandora. She leant forward, her elbows on the desk, her chin resting on her hands, a look of warm complicity in her eyes. 'I'm supposed to brief you about your job, but I feel it's almost embarrassing. It reminds me of that charming saying in your country, teaching mother to suck eggs or something like that; so expressive. Please tell me if you want me to explain the basics, but I really don't dare. One look at you is enough to make me realize that I would be insulting you.'

Overwhelmed by the compliments, Pandora could not bring herself to contradict Connie. Geraldine had vaguely explained to her that her job was very simple, and would entail writing about interesting shops. Pandora just hoped that it would all become clearer in the course of the conversation.

'Here is the list of the F-E ...' As she uttered the abbreviation of 'facing editorial', the code word for those advertisers who have to be specifically mentioned in the text and their ads placed on the opposite page, Connie coughed violently and the initials were lost in the noisy spasm. '... Oh, I'm sorry, excuse me, advertisers for the next issue. As you can see, the subject is Italy on the East Side.' She handed a sheet of paper to Pandora.

'I so regret that people have just not been willing to be more imaginative or creative with your section,' Connie went on. 'The scope could be immense. Just imagine, Italy for instance ...' She stopped for a moment. 'I must restrain myself, and not put impossible ideas in your head, but I know that Mark Brody, our Advertising Director, is always keen on new angles.' Fond memories of their affair a few years ago flashed through Connie's mind. 'But it may not be easy with that section. Maybe a real journalist could do something much more exciting with it, but I will not bother you with my boring views. You must report to Tony Andreotti, the Advertising Manager, as soon as your material is ready. He is a *very* dynamic man.' She did not consider it necessary to inform Pandora that his flashes of temper could justify the evacuation of the building.

Connie then launched into an enraptured vision of what fashion meant in people's lives, putting much emphasis on the fact that fashion, far from being frivolous, was perhaps as important an aspect of culture as music or literature. Her passionate delivery was accompanied by much fluttering of hands and rolling of eyes. After ten minutes, she let Pandora go, and sent a memo to Geraldine confirming that the briefing had taken place.

Pandora could hardly wait to get back to her office and start planning the new section. Over the weekend, she checked old issues of the magazine, and understood what Connie had meant. The section was predictable, month after month going on about restaurants, clothes and other everyday necessities, expensive but trivial. Pandora considered a number of options, and finally decided that her subject would be Italian music.

She spent the next three days in a fever of excitement, combing antique dealers and rare book traders, from cosy little shops on Second Avenue to grand galleries in stone town houses in the Upper Seventies. It took her a day in the office to draft the two pages of copy, further polished at home in the evening and then redrafted the following morning. At last she decided that she had done her best, and phoned Andreotti's secretary. She was told to bring the copy upstairs immediately, because they were very close to the deadline.

She walked into Andreotti's office, terror clamping her stomach. He did not stand up when she came in, just waved his hand towards the chair facing his desk, cigarette ash dropping on the papers in front of him. Pandora guessed that he was not very tall, but his one continuous eyebrow, the scowl and the deep lines on his face made him fearsome. As soon as she sat down, he held out his hand. Pandora gave him her draft, and waited.

He began to read it, then stopped and looked at her, his continuous eyebrow knotting into a frown. Pandora saw his face go red as he raised his closed fist and then brought it down, rattling the desk with terrifying force.

'Who the fuck cares about Puccini's desk or Aida's gold bra from the 1879 Milan performance, and who would want to buy them? How do you imagine I'm gonna get ads out of the jerks who sell them, you smart ass?' Pandora began to mumble some explanation, but his ranting was unstoppable. He stood up and leaned across the desk, his hands flat on the desktop. His face almost dusky now.

'I'm fed up with all you cocktail party queens who can't even write a fucking shopping list. Where do they find you? None of you has ever been good for anything other than acting snooty, but you're the tops, Miss Puccini. You've even put on a Brit accent!' He flung the papers onto Pandora's lap. 'You'd better appear tomorrow at the same time with something the advertisers will appreciate. Now get out.'

She collected her copy, stood up and coolly walked out of the office, her head high as she swept past the giggling secretary. As soon as she was outside the department she felt the hot flush on her face and the tears pricking behind her eyelids. While waiting for the elevator she lost her control at last, and began to sob quietly.

Back in her office, she reread the section as published over the previous six issues, and suddenly realized that virtually all the shops mentioned had ads immediately adjacent to the text, or within the next few pages, and she at last understood the implications of the advertisers' list Connie had handed to her. She rushed out of the building and managed to visit all the shops on the list before closing time. The following morning she typed the copy in two hours flat and rushed it upstairs, where she left it with Andreotti's secretary.

A week went by. Finally Pandora phoned his secretary, who told her that if there had been any problems she would have heard from Tony. Pandora then checked past columns, wrote a list of possible subjects and city areas to cover and sent it to the advertising ogre for his approval. His secretary phoned to say that Tony had approved the list, and he liked the open-air party theme for her next article. Now the advertisers were lined up, the deadline was close, and this morning she had to face Andreotti for the second time. Their meeting was scheduled for 11.30.

She walked into her office, a larger than average station-ery cupboard with a superannuated desk in it. Its vicinity to the copy-editors' room gave it some credibility as office space. After checking her mail, an assortment of invitations to a few of the shops she had been to as well as many she had never heard of, she began to write a letter to her mother to take her mind off the imminent meeting. She had long lost the habit of making her mother party to anything that really mattered to her, and New York's small talk of the kind Geraldine excelled in would be incomprehensible to someone whose weekly highlight was her bridge evening at a friend's.

Pandora looked at the photographs of her father and of Walsham Hall in the *faux* tortoise-shell frames on her desk, one of her many wedding presents, and the only two objects she had brought over from London. She preferred to keep them in her office; this was alien territory, and she needed family support.

To anyone else, the photographs would have seem incon-gruous, lost in the impersonal room. They were meant for a little round table draped in Colefax & Fowler chintz, to be surrounded by a bowl of *potpourri*, miniature boxes, and Herend china. But to Pandora they were a link with people, things and times she loved.

She dropped her notepad on her desk, and stared at the photograph of Walsham. The picture of the Queen Anne brick house had been taken in the afternoon, the sun shin-ing on its graceful white turret with the weathervane on top, and the wistaria climbing up over the east corner. This was the magical house of her childhood, when her Uncle Harold had been a kind eccentric, fond of his niece within the limitations of his stunted affections. His expressions of love were a sweet after Sunday lunch, permission to look at the pheasant chicks with him in the spring, and a doll for her birthday, bought in Norwich by Hayward, the driver.

Occasionally, Uncle Harold would take her for a walk with Whisky, his West Highland white terrier. They would always take the same route, up the path to the stables, then alongside the kitchen garden, its crumbling brick wall covered in honeysuckle, and into the wood until they came to the small Greek temple folly by the lake, a ruin buried in the rhododendron bushes. He would hardly say a word, other than to perhaps comment on the shrubs, trees or birds they came across, and then they would walk back to the house. She had never been at ease with Uncle Harold when he was silent, and she was always slightly afraid of his gruff voice when he spoke, but she had loved those walks.

They had been the only semblance of a father/daughter relationship in the long gaps between holidays and Christmas, when her real father would appear with a mountain of toys from New York. She would not admit then that she looked forward to his visits, because it would have been a betrayal of her mother's martyrdom. Once he was there, the long silences and stilted conversation between them confirmed to her that Daddy was not easy, a point stressed by her mother often enough.

Uncle Harold was now a recluse living in shuttered rooms, dust settling on his models of great ships of the 1914 war. The only thing that brought any shine to his Parkinson-dulled eyes were cricket matches on television, and Mrs Thomas' bubble-and-squeak. Mrs Thomas had been the cook at Walsham for nearly forty years, and Uncle Harold had never tired of her over-cooked nursery food.

Pandora glanced at her watch and realized that she had to be upstairs in five minutes. Relieved, she abandoned her letter and rushed out of her office.

The scene began as a rerun of their first meeting. She handed over her copy, Tony Andreotti waved his hand in the direction of the chair, she sat down and he began to read. He read through the whole piece, then smiled.

'This is great, Pandy, really great.' He was genuinely pleased by her witty style, and by now he was also aware that he was dealing with a close friend of the Great Bitch Upstairs. He stood up, came around to her, and patted her on the shoulder.

'It's really good, honey. You and I are gonna do good things together in the future.'

Pandora thought that perhaps he was more bearable when he was unfriendly.

She was about to ask if there was anything else to discuss when the door opened, and a Richard Gere look-alike walked in. He was tall, in his mid-thirties, broad-shouldered and he had obviously been in the sun recently. Pandora found him very attractive and tried to keep her eyes fixed on the photograph of New York by Tony's desk.

'Hi, Tony,' the good-looker said, 'I'm back from the Comores. You ain't gonna get many ads from there, but it's a great place.' He patted Tony's stomach. 'You could do with some healthy living yourself. Maybe you should go there.'

'The only good thing for my health is getting more ads,' said Tony sourly. 'Paying for expenses during your fancy travels for nothing really kills me.'

'Don't worry, I've also been to Sri Lanka and Tahiti. Lots of flabby credit card holders on vacation there and a long list of multi-storey hotels to tap for you. Let me show you.' He put a folder on Tony's desk, and opened it.

Pandora stood up. 'Excuse me, but I have another appointment,' she said. If she hurried, she might be able to get a sandwich before there was a long line at the counter.

The man looked at her, then back at Tony. 'I also have to go. Have a look at the file, and I'll phone you later.' He held the door open for Pandora, and they left together. He began to talk as soon as they were out of the room.

'I'm Tom Cansino. I'm the travel editor, that's why you haven't seen me very often. Who are you? You are the first woman I've seen in this place for a very long time who looks real.'

Pandora hesitated for a second, wary of his instant charm: a particular reaction she had had since Johnny's departure, whenever she came across an attractive man. There had to be life after Johnny. She kept her reply as terse as possible, but she adorned it with a friendly smile.

'I'm Pandora Doyle. I am in charge of the Shopping section,' she answered. They reached the elevators and, conscious of his proximity, she averted her eyes from his.

'I'll take the stairs. It's getting late for me,' she said, and began to walk towards the door.

'Don't walk so fast, I only go to the gym three times a week,' Tom said, coming up behind her. As they reached the stairs, he bowed in an exaggerated way.

'I'll show you what a gentleman I am. First, have the handrail side, and second, please be my guest for lunch.'

She smiled, and began to descend on the handrail side.

'I'm sorry, but I have a lunch engagement already, and I'm late.' Her voice echoed up the huge stairwell, just as she noticed through the windows that the sky was getting dark. She began to run.

Tom dithered. He had already run behind her once; twice in a row was once too often. She was great looking, but she was not the next Calvin Klein girl.

Pandora realized that she had been too abrupt. He was nice, he was attractive and she did not have many friends. She stopped at the landing, two floors below, and turned around.

'I would love to have lunch any other time.' She beamed up at him, and rushed on.

Arianne de la Force answered the internal phone.

'The doorman just called to say that Miss Doyle is on her way up, Madame.'

'Thank you, François. Show her to the library. No, perhaps it's better if you take her to the drawing room instead.' It would be more difficult for this mousey journalist to ask probing questions while sitting in one of the grandest rooms in New York. Keeping your distance, putting people in their place, *de haut en bas*: these were useful tactics when dealing with bothersome small fry.

Arianne took off her emerald rings and put them on her dressing table, then opened a drawer of her jewel case. After a quick look at the velvet tray where gems sat edge to edge, she picked up a diamond ring. The flawless stone was an inch square: Simon had surpassed his high standards of ostentatiousness when he had chosen it. She never wore it, but this girl seemed to notice jewellery. The ring would help to divert the conversation, if necessary. She slipped it on while glancing at the clock on the mantelpiece, then sat down and picked up a magazine from the pile on the low table. She looked at it until she was exactly fifteen minutes late, then left the room.

Sitting in one of the gilt armchairs ordered by Catherine the Great for the Winter Palace, Pandora felt as if she were waiting in the Wallace Collection. She had seen a few rooms like this in England, also full of exquisite furniture and paintings, but those were put together by generations of aristocratic privilege; now she was staring at the raw power of money. Pandora was usually able to read many things about the owner by looking at a room, but not in this case, other than the fact that the mistress of the house was immensely rich and fond of eighteenth-century decor at its most magnificent. There were perfect flower arrangements where they should be, obviously placed by experts, but there were no photographs in silver frames of loved ones or mighty personages, no piles of artfully arranged picture books on the low tables hinting at private predilections, no slip of taste betraying an object favoured by the owner for personal reasons. There were none of the touches that even interior decorators allow to give the illusion of life to rooms used only for entertainment. Like Arianne at the party, the room was expensively elegant, impeccably mannered, and gave nothing away.

At last, one of the double doors flanking the fireplace opened, and Arianne walked in. As Pandora stood up and watched her walk across the vast room, an enchanting smile on her face, she thought that most people take second place to their possessions, but only a few outshine them.

'Sit down, please,' Arianne said as she approached, her left hand outstretched in a casual gesture towards Pandora's seat, the diamond sparkling in the light for a second. 'I'm so sorry to have kept you waiting, but I was on the phone and I couldn't get away.' They sat, and the butler walked in with a silver and ivory tea set. He placed it on the table between them.

'Would you like a cup of tea? Or anything else?'

'I'd love some tea,' Pandora replied. 'Thank you so much for seeing me. I've asked the photographer to be here at quarter to four.'

Arianne poured the tea, and the butler took a cup to Pandora.

'Would Madame require anything else?' he asked.

'No, François, that will be all, thank you. When the photographer arrives, please show him in.' Arianne stirred her tea, then raised her eyes. Her expression indicated that she expected the interview to begin.

Pandora opened her bag and pulled out a small tape recorder. 'Do you mind if I use it? It's easier than taking notes. I wouldn't want to use up more of your time than necessary. I understand that you are going away soon.'

'Of course I don't mind,' Arianne said. 'I'm leaving for Buenos Aires tomorrow. I am not involved in the day-to-day running of my business any more, but I like to keep in touch. The sugar industry is going through difficult times.'

Pandora was too polite to mention the curious contradiction between the purchase of a fifty-million dollar painting and an industry in trouble.

'This room is magnificent. How did you start your collection?'

'I inherited most of it from my husband,' Arianne explained. 'He had agents all over Europe buying for him. He was like a magpie, but I don't think he ever saw most of the pieces, they were just stored away in warehouses. I only buy paintings. In fact, I only buy portraits.'

'Why?' Pandora asked. She felt excited: this was an angle worth exploring. It gave her an opening into what this woman found interesting in people, or at least their painted images.

'I like them. I'm sorry that I cannot be more articulate about it. I just like them.'

'Perhaps it might be easier to concentrate on one picture,' Pandora said. 'Why did you buy the *Portrait de Madame Claire*?'

Arianne stared at her.

'Who said I bought it?' she asked.

Pandora was astonished. 'I saw you there!'

Arianne smiled. 'You may have seen me, but you must have read the papers the following morning, and I was not mentioned. As a journalist, you should trust your colleagues. Sometimes I bid for friends who want to remain anonymous, and they do the same for me. Things are not always what they seem.'

Arianne leaned forward, picked up her cup of tea and took a sip. She turned her head towards the windows.

'The storm has cleared up, thank God. Would you like some more tea?'

'No, thank you,' said Pandora, conscious that she was getting nowhere. She tried again.

'Were you born in Brazil?'

'I grew up there.' Arianne was going to leave it at that, but then remembered Geraldine's comment about sending Pandora on a research trip. This girl was beginning to look like a pushover, but Geraldine wasn't: better to feed her what she wanted rather than letting someone else scavenge over her past.

'My father had a *fazenda* not very far from Bahia. He grew spices. I can still remember the smell in the house, the cedar floors and the spices in the air.' She proceeded to give Pandora a long description of life on the estate, the black maids dressed in white flounced dresses, the horse-drawn carriages. For a second she wondered if further embellishments were necessary, but Pandora's attentive expression reassured her, and she carried on for a while with her evocation of her childhood in rural Brazil. '. . . and I did all my schooling at home, with private tutors. It would have been unthinkable for us to go to school, my sister and I were so sheltered from the outside world. When I was eighteen, I was sent to finishing school in France. My mother was a favourite client of Balenciaga, and he offered me the opportunity to model his last collection. Then I met Simon. Perhaps you know he died soon after our marriage. It was a terrible, terrible blow.' She paused, her voice trailing away, as if the memory overwhelmed her, then she smiled. 'Otherwise, I have had a very protected, privileged life.' She crossed her arms,

63

her left hand resting on her upper arm, the diamond in full view.

Pandora realized that this woman was more than adept at glossing over any subject while giving the impression of a personal conversation. Her sheltered childhood would make entertaining reading, but it was not enough for a profile. She decided to probe cautiously.

'I have been told that you had some serious trouble with guerrillas in Argentina . . .' Arianne seemed unruffled by the reference, and Pandora went on. 'It must have been a traumatic experience for you. Did it have any lasting consequences?'

Arianne picked up her cup of tea.

'That's a very old story. It was of no consequence, and there were many similar episodes in Argentina at the time. If you want more details, you'll find them in any newspaper library.' She gave Pandora an apologetic smile.

'I know I'm a difficult interviewee, but you journalists seem to think that I have some fascinating story to tell. My life is about running my business. It might be of interest to the *Wall Street Journal*, but I fear I'm rather dull for *Chic*.'

Difficult maybe, but dull unlikely, Pandora thought. There had to be some way of cracking her glass cage. She decided to try a roundabout approach.

'Is there a particular aspect of your work which interests you?' she asked, concealing her impatience. Arianne rolled her eyes.

'So, so many . . .' she sighed. She suddenly leaned forward in her seat. 'I'll tell you one particular aspect I'm sure you will find fascinating . . .' She paused, as if to allow Pandora to fully take the implications of what she was about to hear, then continued. 'I'm very interested in Eurosterling bonds, and the future relationship between UK government and non-government stocks. There are major questions there. Are we going to see long-dated corporate issues maintain their value, or will the spread widen to dangerous levels? There could well be a flight into liquid, quality stocks; it all depends on the relationship between swap rates and bond spreads against gilts.'

She went on and on, until Pandora tried to stop her in desperation.

'Mrs de la Force, perhaps our readers . . .' Arianne interrupted her with an imperious wave of her hand, balanced by a disarming smile.

'You must listen to this, it is very important. If we look at five-year swap rates . . .' The torrent of financial wisdom poured forth, and Pandora gave up. It would take time to crack Mrs de la Force's façade, and hers was running out. The door opened and François came in, followed by a street-worn photographer carrying an aluminium case, his camera and flash dangling at the end of a wide shoulder strap.

Arianne stood up. 'We'd better do the pictures now. I would be delighted to continue talking to you, but unfortunately I have so many things to do.'

While Pandora switched off her tape recorder, Arianne struggled to conceal a grin; life would be so easy if all journalists were like this one. She quickly posed for the photographer, standing next to the fireplace, her arm resting on the mantelpiece. Her elegance gave new life to the cliché pose of a society woman at home.

The photographer took several shots. He was in the process of explaining a different set-up to Arianne, when a magnificent *ormolu* clock struck the hour. Arianne looked up.

'Oh dear, I am very sorry, but I'll have to leave you now. I hope you've got everything you need.' She walked briskly towards the door and waited until the photographer packed his case, then held the door open.

Arianne led her visitors through the marble foyer. Pandora and the photographer stopped by the front door to say goodbye, and Arianne held out her hand.

'If there is anything else you need, just . . .'

She was interrupted by a crescendo of screams from the other end of the long gallery. A door opened and a naked girl burst through, followed by Charles Murdoch shouting at the top of his voice:

'You little whore! You slut! So that's what they taught you in Switzerland, to suck the chauffeur's cock!' He threw

65

a dog lead and collar on the black and white marble floor. 'And don't forget your props, you little pervert!'

The girl was sobbing violently, almost hysterical.

'Who are *you* to teach me anything? You are nothing, just a paid cunt-licker. Where would you be if you didn't fuck my mother? I hate you, you shit!'

Pandora glanced at Arianne: her face was white, but her eyes were burning with anger.

'Gloria!' screamed Arianne, walking towards her. 'Enough! Behave yourself! You disgust me!'

The girl was now completely out of control. She turned towards Arianne, shaking with fury.

'Oh, I disgust you, Mummy dearest. I'm so sorry! Sorry to upset your stud. You, hypocrite, *you* are disgusted . . . Tell me, my wonderful *mother*, what does Nana know about you and your precious secrets? I despise you, I . . . I loathe you!' Her voice became higher and higher until, in a frenzy, she picked up the huge Ming vase on the console table and smashed it onto the marble floor.

'François! François!' called Arianne. Charles tried to restrain Gloria, who bit his hand until it bled. He roared with pain, then punched her in the stomach. Gloria fell on her knees, gasping for air.

Pandora was repelled by the sight. 'Let's go,' she whispered to the photographer, who was leering at Gloria's nakedness. He did not budge. She tried to touch his arm to catch his attention but he moved suddenly, and her hand fell on his camera instead, pressing the shutter. The brutal white light from the flash filled the gallery for a blinding second, bathing the smashed vase, the naked girl, and Arianne's horrified expression in its glare. The butler put his jacket over Gloria's shoulders, and led her away. Pandora found the ensuing silence even more difficult to stand than the scene before.

'We'd better go now.' Her timid voice echoed down the gallery. Charles Murdoch looked at her, then turned around and walked out, slamming the door behind him. Arianne rushed to Pandora.

'My dear, I'm so embarrassed. I hope you will forgive me for this awful incident. Perhaps the best thing is if we all forget that it ever took place, don't you think? I'll call you as soon as I am back. We must get together. Would you like to come to Venice with us? Or maybe sail the Aegean with me on the yacht?' She seemed to be getting no response: what the hell was this girl going to write? She had heard about Nana, God damn it, she had heard about Nana . . . And that picture. It would probably be in every tabloid from coast to coast, by tomorrow morning.

Arianne felt fear growing in her. She thought of grabbing the camera to pull the film out, but the last thing she wanted was to be sued for assault: she was in America. She carried on in an ingratiating voice. 'I'm sure you don't want to take those pictures back to your office. Why don't we take some better ones tomorrow morning? I could wear my new Valentinos. Would you care to give me the film?' There was no reaction. Her fear became panic, shattering her control for a moment. 'I noticed you admiring my ring while we talked,' she went on. She took the ring off and held it out to Pandora. 'Would you like it? I hardly ever wear it, I've got so many . . .'

Pandora wondered why this icon of perfection was shaken to the point of making ridiculous offers. It could not just be the picture. It had to be something else, but she no longer cared to find out; she could not stand this place a second longer.

'No, thank you,' she said. She gently pushed the photographer, and they stepped into the waiting elevator.

Arianne heard the elevator's door shut behind them. She began to shiver violently. Shoulders hunched, she closed her eyes and wrapped her arms about herself tightly as if protecting herself from an imminent blow. Then suddenly she opened her eyes in a ferocious glare, ashamed of her performance, ashamed of herself. Enough self-pity. Head high, she walked to the nearest telephone.

Geraldine switched on the intercom to her secretary.

'Vanessa, get me the reception desk downstairs. Immediately. Find out who the photographer was who went to Mrs de la Force's apartment with Pandora Doyle.'

She leaned back in her chair. Her ear was still buzzing

from Solly's outburst over the telephone. Bob Chalmers had phoned him to say that Arianne was so upset by a *Chic* journalist and photographer, that she was reconsidering the 'Los Milagros' deal, and had asked Bob to approach Lord Blomfield. The incident had just taken place. Arianne would only review her decision if the undeveloped film shot at her apartment was returned to her at once, and nothing was published about the incident.

'Los Milagros' was to be Europe's largest shopping mall, outside Madrid, on land that belonged to a de la Force company. Solly had been looking for the right opportunity to branch into Europe, and Bob Chalmers had put him in touch with Arianne. After a year of careful negotiations, the deal was almost signed. The dinner extravaganza had been a covert attempt to strengthen the personal contact between them. Paloma Picasso was wonderful, but Solly would not have spent $30,000 in one evening to entertain the Twelve Disciples, let alone her, unless it would show a profit somewhere.

Geraldine had played a role in these manoeuvres, by underlining to Arianne the potential nuisance value of her magazine. Pandora had been perfect for the charade: a real journalist would have been dangerous, and difficult to control if the scent of blood was in the air. Geraldine had no intention of shattering her relationship with Arianne; a slight rattle was enough for her purpose. Two days after the party, Bob had phoned Solly to say that Arianne would sign the agreement before going away but now, obviously, she had to be appeased.

Her phone buzzed.

'I've got Luke at the reception desk for you, Miss Freeman. The photographer is Robert Lopinski.'

'Thank you, Vanessa.' There was a click in the line, then she heard the Southern drawl. 'Good afternoon, Miss Freeman.'

'Good afternoon, Luke. As soon as Miss Doyle and Mr Lopinski come through the door, you bring them straight here. Don't just *send* them here, you accompany them, and see that they don't stop anywhere on the way up.'

'They are coming through the door right now, Miss Freeman.'

A moment later Vanessa showed them in. Geraldine stood up behind her desk, her hand outstretched, palm upward. Pandora had never seen Geraldine looking so stern.

'Now, Bob, you don't say a word, and you give me the film you shot at Mrs de la Force's apartment. You then go back to your lab, and I'll do my best to forget this episode.'

While he rolled the film back and took it out of the camera, she addressed Pandora, ice in her voice.

'I cannot tell you how displeased I am by what has happened.' She took the film from Bob, dismissed him with a nod, and turned to Pandora. 'You must learn that there is no point in upsetting people unnecessarily. I am telling you I will not tolerate . . .' As soon as the door closed behind Bob, she left her desk and rushed to Pandora.

'Sweetheart, as they say in the best circles, you must have her by the snatch!' She roared with laughter. 'Let's sit down. I can't wait to hear all about it. What the hell did you find out?'

5

NEW YORK
April 1987

The photograph showed the most beautiful evening dress Pandora had ever seen, a sculpture in fabric as stunning as the woman modelling it. The caption pasted at the bottom read: '*No 30 – Robe du soir en satin bleu – Collection Printemps /Eté 1968*', and the back of the picture was stamped '*Balenciaga – Reproduction interdite*'.

The pictures in the photo-library file were spread on her desk. There were a few others from the last Balenciaga collection in 1968, and an agency picture of 'Arianne, Paris' latest star model, and Simon de la Force, South-American magnate, arriving at Maxim's – December 1968'. The other photographs, four or five in total, were all taken during the summer of 1976, on the South of France social circuit.

Pandora was trying to replace the photographs returned by Geraldine. Arianne's archive pictures were dated by her clothes and make-up but not by her looks, which had barely changed over twenty years. Pandora's eye was caught by a head-and-shoulders shot of Arianne looking entrancing in a fruits and flowers headdress: '*Bal de têtes*, Villa Alexander, Cannes, July 1976'. The costume gave a timeless quality to the photograph, and she set it aside.

However, it was the picture with Simon de la Force that really interested her. It was a standard *paparazzo* shot: the couple surprised as they were stepping out of a shiny black limousine. Simon de la Force's right hand was stretched towards the camera in an attempt to block the lens, an enormous cigar between his fingers, and an angry expression on his face.

The face would have been awesome even when smiling. There was an Indian cast to the features, and the hooded eyes blazed an iguana-like malevolence. The superb cut of the Savile Row suit was defeated by his barrel-chested body, a vicious fairground wrestler ill at ease in his Sunday finery.

Arianne was behind him, but this did not conceal the fact that he was noticeably shorter than his companion. She looked impossibly thin in the simplest of black dresses and a chinchilla jacket, a string of huge pearls around her neck. The festive air, suggested by the smiling doorman and the edge of the canopy with its Art-Nouveau lettering, was denied by the absent look in her eyes.

The library pictures had been Geraldine's idea. After she had heard the details of the incident, she had been as helpful as ever. She encouraged Pandora to draft the piece, but suggested that they wait for a couple of days.

'I may not hear anything else from dear Mrs de la Force, in which case we write a nice flattering profile, but if there is any more damning criticism of you from her, darling, then we do a hatchet job. We keep mum about her little darling's pastimes, but you could just hint at the starving peasants while Madame shops. Nothing heavy-duty, of course, gloves on all the time.' In the meantime, Pandora could check the library for pictures, or any additional information useful for the piece. She had felt grateful for Geraldine's support.

She was putting the pictures back in the folder when the phone rang.

'Are you free for lunch, or shall I join the line?' She recognized the voice, and smiled. 'It's Tom, Tom Cansino. Please say yes.'

She was flattered. She found him attractive, but that worried her. She could probably do with a little flirtation but she feared involvement, and she was too vulnerable still not to get involved. Loneliness could be reassuringly snug.

'I'd love to have lunch with you, but I have to finish something for Geraldine. Thank you very much for the thought though, it's *so* kind of you.' She masked the nagging edge of regret behind her polite refusal.

'My goodness, that *is* heavy-duty name-dropping. Maybe I should learn to keep my place. Don't work too hard,' he said cheerfully, and hung up.

As soon as she put the receiver down, she wished she

71

had been less cautious. She thought for a moment, then impulsively picked up the office directory, and dialled Tom's extension. Somebody else answered it. 'He has just left for lunch,' the voice said.

She grabbed her coat and bag, and ran downstairs as fast as she could. She rushed through the door, and saw him walking down Madison Avenue. He turned into 53rd Street.

She caught up with him, and he contrived to retain his moody countenance.

'I though you were working,' he said acidly.

'You would be amazed at how *incredibly* fast I work,' she replied with a smile. He looked at her, and then he smiled too.

'Sure,' he said, 'but I was going to take you to Le Cirque, and I cancelled my reservation when you turned me down. The best I can offer now is Between the Bread.'

'I've never been to either, so it makes no difference to me,' Pandora replied. It was a crisp New York day. As they walked past Paley Park, the waterfall was sparkling in the sunshine. She glanced at Tom for a second, and was glad to have changed her mind. They stopped at the traffic light, and she was suddenly full of excitement at the sight of the palisade of buildings lining into the horizon, and the sudden expanse of sky over the park. She had had this feeling the first time she saw Fifth Avenue just before Christmas, as a little girl holding her father's hand; by now it was difficult to say if she still reacted to one of the world's great city views, no matter how familiar, or to the memory of a simple, wondrous emotion, only possible when places are still seen through unjaded eyes.

The light turned green. Tom held her arm, and they crossed the avenue. She was conscious of his touch.

'I will now tell you my favourite story for tourists,' Tom said as they walked past St Thomas Church. 'This was the smartest church in New York at the turn of the century, and a lot of those American girls with trunkfuls of greenbacks married here. There was an Italian stonemason working at the church when it was rebuilt, and he carved a dollar . . .'

Two small boys ran up to them from behind, and hugged Tom's legs.

'Daddy! Daddy!' they shouted, jumping up and down.

Tom whirled round. 'What are you doing here?' he asked incredulously. 'I was going to phone you tonight. I thought we could go fishing on Sunday.' He picked them both up in his arms.

'Mommy brought us to see Grandma. She's taking us to the movies this afternoon.' A slim and, to Pandora's eye, very American-looking girl, caught up with them. She quickly scanned Pandora, then turned to Tom.

'Hi, this *is* a surprise,' he said.

'Yes, it is,' the girl replied tersely. 'Tommy, Ben, please get down, it's time for lunch now.'

The boys did not move. One of them hugged Tom. 'Daddy, please have lunch with us. Please, Daddy, *please*.'

The woman seemed amused by Tom's obvious discomfort. Noticing it, Pandora glanced at her watch. 'It's getting late. I think I'd better go.' One of the children had begun to mess up Tom's hair, while the other pulled at his tie.

'I'll talk to you later,' Tom said. 'Maybe we can go to the movies one evening.'

Pandora turned around and crossed the avenue again. And maybe not, she thought.

Their meeting at an end, Bob Chalmers collected his papers and locked his briefcase. Arianne led the way out of the room.

'. . . and that settles "Los Milagros". Please phone Solly, and arrange to sign the agreement today, Bob.'

'I will. I'm glad that the problem with the magazine was solved. I thought the girl seemed very nice at Geraldine's party.'

Arianne looked at him knowingly.

'It was pretty obvious that you did, and I think Betty noticed it also. It must be difficult to be your wife, Bob.'

'Not at all. Every time I'm found out after a one-night stand, Betty goes to Bill Blass and buys a couple of evening dresses. She's told me that if she had to really start worrying about it, then she'd go to Bulgari, for the heavy-duty stuff.

I can't afford to have a serious affair, but now you are putting ideas into my head. Maybe you can organize a small lunch when you are back and ask that charming girl. I must be entitled to some gratitude for the brilliant deal I organized for you at Los Milagros.'

Arianne raised her hands in mock horror.

'Are you suggesting that I become your procuress? You know how fond of Betty I am.' She smiled slyly. 'But maybe I ought to give a lunch for you when I come back. I haven't done much entertaining lately.'

'I'll look forward to it.' As they approached the door, Bob stopped in front of an elaborate flower arrangement on top of a marble console. 'Where is your beautiful vase?' he asked.

'With the restorers. One of my idiotic maids must have been thinking about her boyfriend while dusting it. She dropped it on the floor,' Arianne said casually.

'I'm sorry to hear that. Such a marvellous piece.'

Arianne patted him on the arm, and smiled.

'You'll have to make me an extra million, Bob, and then I will be able to buy another one.' Her tone indicated that the subject was closed. He opened the door, and leaned forward to kiss her cheek.

'Have a good trip. I'll call you tomorrow morning.' She closed the door behind him.

She returned to the library and sat at her desk, absent-mindedly toying with the ivory letter opener. She closed her eyes and sighed. For almost twenty years she had never looked back. Her money had become her shield. But it was just a greenhouse, an exquisite world protected by a layer of thin glass, and now Charles was throwing pebbles at it.

She picked up the phone, and dialled Charles' bedroom extension. He answered, with a somnolent voice.

'Come to the library immediately. I have to talk to you.'

'What's the time?' he asked.

'Late enough. I'm leaving in half an hour.'

Charles appeared a few moments later, dressed in his silk dressing gown. A handsome man wearing only his dressing gown can be a sexual turn-on or an endearing picture of everyday domesticity. To Arianne, he was simply repellent.

Charles picked up the phone, asked for coffee, and sat down on the sofa. Arianne fixed her eyes on him.

'I've been thinking about your proposal. What I'm going to say is not a gut reaction; there's too much at stake.' Someone knocked at the door, and she stopped. After a moment, François came in with a silver coffee service. He placed it in front of Charles and left the room.

Charles poured coffee into the Sèvres cup, and then concentrated on Arianne, waiting for her to go on.

'I have given a lot of thought to what you said. We know the facts, and I have to admit that you have a very strong hand.' Both her head and her voice had dropped as she spoke. When she raised her face, she noticed a gleam of triumph in his eyes. She might enjoy this conversation, after all.

'Your analysis was entirely correct with regard to your position, but you forced me to think about mine and, much more important, yours in relation to mine.' He sensed her likely answer, but had lost his grasp on her thoughts.

'There is one real threat you hold over me. Not publicity, because what you would get paid for the story is nothing when compared to what you gain by remaining silent. Your only option is to go to Simon's family. They can claim my money once they know what you have to tell them, but they cannot pay you the sort of figure you would want until they win the case. You'll have to drop your trump card before the bets are on the table.'

She glanced at the clock on the mantelpiece. She had to leave in fifteen minutes.

'You are worried about your chances of upholding your rights in court if I were to change my will now and provide for you. Maybe you are right, but they are certainly higher than your chances against Simon's family in court, if they decide not to honour whatever unsavoury agreement you might strike with them. If they have any sense, they will not sign anything outside Argentina, and I wouldn't rate your chances in court there against the de la Forces once they became the richest family in the country.'

She checked the time again; she ought to go now.

'Alternatively, we carry on as if these conversations had never taken place, except that I will alter my will. You mentioned your concern about the passage of time, and I can understand it. But you shouldn't worry about the future, my dear, and you've never struck me as the worrying type. I'll see you in a few days.' She turned around and walked out of the room.

'Give my regards to Nana. I'm sure you two will have a great time talking about the good old days,' Charles said venomously as she left, but Arianne did not hear him.

Charles stood up, walked to the drinks tray, and poured himself a large Scotch. Arianne was right: he was not particularly keen on a dubious deal with the de la Forces. Only Arianne's fear had made their bargain possible at the beginning, but apparently she had learned to live with it after twelve years, enabling her to call his bluff. But he had not been bluffing when he had told her about the vulnerability of his position, *his* fear of time running out.

It was worse than that, though. He still had sufficient years ahead of him to find another rich woman, more than likely far less glamorous than Arianne, certainly less rich, but equally capable of providing the lifestyle he coveted. But he could no longer stomach the chase, the perpetual pretence. With Arianne, he was able to make love to any woman he fancied as long as he kept it quiet. His relationship with another woman would have to be based on the fallacy of her attractiveness, his daily praise of her beauty and the nightly evidence of his admiration. His years with Arianne had made him lose the dedication required to make a woman feel wanted if he didn't mean it.

Only his own money, or somebody else's under his control, was the answer. He stopped in mid-thought. The solution was so simple, so pristinely simple. The realization warmed his blood as effectively as the Scotch.

Arianne was right. Charles needn't worry about the future. There was Gloria. Young, screwed-up, silly Gloria.

* * *

Nana walked slowly up the stairs. It took her quite a while to reach the top, and she was breathing hard. She was getting too old for this task, but Arianne did not allow anyone but Nana to come into her bedroom here at 'La Encantada', her favourite room in her favourite house. It was locked while Arianne was away, but she would be here any moment now, and Nana wanted to make sure that everything was tidy, although she had been here every day.

The bedroom occupied almost the whole of the top floor of the tower. It was very plainly decorated. The panelled walls matched the dark wood of the carved ceiling and the wide floorboards. The furniture was Brazilian, from Colonial days: a large bed, a wardrobe and a dressing table, all in solid mahogany almost black with age, waxed by Nana every week. A few chairs, a bookcase, a bedside table, that was all. No curtain at the windows, no pictures on the walls, just two photographs in silver frames on the dressing table.

Nana began to dust the room. It was unnecessary, because she had done it in the morning, but at her age routine had become almost obsessive, a day to day process to keep death away.

She had never asked why she was the only one allowed in the room. Nana already knew too much. Arianne needed her silence, she needed Arianne's protection. That was their bargain, and they had both kept it.

Nana polished the rock crystal toilette set on the dressing table. As usual her eye was caught by the carved monogram 'A'. She had accepted so much and yet the name, even the initial, still distressed her.

She picked up one of the silver frames, gently rubbing it with her cloth. She had seen the picture a million times but she looked at it again. Little Gloria, so happy. She did not want to think about Gloria, it was too painful.

She polished the other frame on the table. It held a cracked old photograph in fading greys, the work of a street photographer. The mountainous background had the unmistakable outline of Rio de Janeiro's *morros*. The scene had been shot in a large public square, its paths lined by tall, slim palm trees, an equestrian statue in the centre. On the monument's steps, a poorly dressed woman held two children by the hand. Her faintly mulatto face would have been beautiful, even stunning, if she had looked less worn. The children were very young. When she had first seen the photograph, Nana had guessed that the older girl was about five years old, the other one perhaps three. Both girls bore a striking resemblance to their mother. The woman wore a tattered dress outside fashion, but judging from the people in the background, the photograph must have been taken sometime around 1950.

She had never asked about this photograph, not even when she saw it for the first time in Paris, many years ago. Then, as now, she did not want to know any more. It was difficult enough to live with her own ghosts.

While she was being driven through the airport, Arianne studied the back of the new chauffeur's head. François had found him through the Christian Welfare Association; the man had both an impeccable record as a driver and a speech impediment. She took in the grey hair, the wrinkled neck and the narrow shoulders. This man was obviously much more suitable than the last one, and she made a mental note to raise François's pay on her return to New York.

Out of the window, she could now see the familiar shape of 'Sugar One'. Of all her possessions, the plane and 'La Encantada' were the ones she valued most. The key to her life had been to run away: from what she was, from where she was, from her husband. Then it had been necessary to stand her ground, and she had won. She did not need to run away any more, but she enjoyed the knowledge that she had the means for flight. 'La Encantada', a Moorish castle by the Uruguayan coast, was her refuge from reality, 'Sugar One' her magic carpet.

The driver managed to get out of the car slowly, and opened her door. Arianne waited impatiently. It had taken her years to get used to having small things done for her by servants. She had learned to adapt her own tempo to it, but any change in the usual pace reawakened her old instincts.

She rushed up the steps and walked into the plane. As usual, Maria and José were waiting for her. Once she was inside, Maria closed the aeroplane's door. By the time Arianne had reached her private quarters at the front of the cabin, the ground staff had removed the steps. As soon as he heard Arianne was on board, the pilot started the engines.

In the cockpit, the co-pilot confirmed to the control tower that they were about to taxi towards the runway holding point. Arianne was now in her leather armchair, her seat belt on. José informed the cockpit that they were ready.

As Arianne sprayed a thin mist of Evian mineral water on her skin to protect it from dehydration, the mixture of compressed kerosene and air flared in the combustion chambers, the searing exhaust rushing out of the huge engines. Inside the cabin, Arianne felt a slight chill, and asked Maria for her cashmere shawl. Then she flicked through Italian *Vogue*.

The Boeing 737 began to move very slowly. Ninety-eight feet long, the huge machine burned two pints of fuel per second just cruising along the tarmac while its solitary passenger admired Gianfranco Ferre's sashed shirts in her magazine. The plane reached the holding point and stopped. Engines running, the Fowler flaps and slats in take-off position, the captain waited for the control tower's clearance.

Arianne did not like the moment just before take-off: it made her feel vulnerable. Her whole life was about being in control, and now she was not. Anxious for distraction, she noticed that Charles' Walkman was in one of the pigeon holes by her seat. She picked it up and put the headphones on. Turning the volume knob up, she pressed 'Play', and closed her eyes. She did not bother to look at the tape; any music would do. She just needed to close her eyes, and let her mind drift away for a few minutes.

Beethoven's Ninth Symphony, the great choral setting of the 'Ode to Joy', burst within her head. She tore the headphones off as if they had burned her, trembling uncontrollably. At first, she thought that Charles had set the whole thing up to hurt her, a cruel plot to hit her with one of her worst memories at the moment when she would be most vulnerable. Then she realized that it was impossible. Only Nana could know what nightmares were unleashed by that particular music.

At last, the pilot received take-off clearance from the tower. Engines at full throttle, 'Sugar One' raced along the runway. The outside world began to shoot past Arianne's window like a speeded-up film, but she paid no attention. Her eyes tightly shut, she was sobbing quietly, as her memories ricocheted in her mind.

The plane began to climb towards the cloudless sky. Arianne's eyes were also fixed on the sky, but she did not see it, nor the ocean below, the same ocean that thousands of miles southwards washed the beaches of her childhood. The carefully built fortress in her mind, untouched for so long, had been demolished in seconds by the 'Ode to Joy'. A prisoner on her magic carpet, she remembered. She remembered Florinda, she remembered Silvia, she remembered Brazil.

Part II

6

'Mamãe! Mamãe!'

The terrified shriek broke the quiet of the night. Carlota Souza jumped up from the rags spread on the dirt floor, and fumbled in the dark until she found the torch.

Aiming the light at her sleeping children, she saw an enormous black rat run towards a dark corner. But it was Silvia's leg, bleeding where the rat had nibbled at it, that made her cry out in horror. She picked up the bottle of *cachaca* from the upturned crate, and rushed to the girl.

Silvia flung her skinny arms around her mother, sobbing hysterically while Carlota poured rum on the wound, then held the child tightly against her, kissing her head again and again.

Florinda had also been wakened by her sister's anguished scream. She leapt to her feet and lit a candle. Picking up two long sticks, she cornered the scurrying rat, pinning it to the dirt floor with one of the sticks while savagely hitting it with the other. She beat the repulsive creature until one of its eyes popped out of its socket, and blood dripped through its sharp, clenched teeth. The furry body twitched in its last convulsions, then its squeals ceased. Florinda picked up the limp remains by the long tail, pushed aside the corrugated sheet which served as a door, and flung the dead rat down the hill. She hoped it would land in the garden of one of the nice houses at the bottom of the cliff. Florinda was only ten years old, but she had already learned to hate.

She went back inside, into the damp heat of the shack, and lay down again on her pile of newspapers and rags. Her sister was still weeping. 'Shut up, I want to sleep!' Florinda shouted at her before closing her eyes.

In the dark, holding her moaning child, Carlota prayed for rain. Only the downpour would cool the overheated *favela*, wash away the turds on the dirt paths, make life a bit more bearable.

Life had never been kind to Carlota. She looked like a middle-aged woman, but she had been born only twenty-seven years ago, on an estate in Pernambuco, the daughter of one of the women who cooked for the workers in the estate's *cantina*. Her mother had not been able to tell her who her father was. In fact, she had been able to tell her very little about anything, and Carlota had not had much schooling either. The local priest attempted to run a school on Sundays, but she was rarely able to attend.

She grew up to be a stunningly beautiful girl, as her mother had once been. Carlota's looks and unusual height were the result of hundreds of years of racial mix. The Indian blood showed in her straight blue-black hair and her slanted eyes, her black ancestors in the high cheekbones and the slenderness of her body, and generations of white Portuguese masters in the pale honey colour of her eyes and her olive skin. But beauty was a handicap for women like Carlota; hard work would destroy it before it could be used as a tool of escape from her miserable life and, for a brief period, it would make her too noticeable to the men around her.

In Carlota's case, eleven years ago it had brought her to the attention of one of the gangs of migrant labourers hired to harvest the sugar cane. Their job finished, most of their pay went into a last night celebration at the dusty local bar, a few miles down the road to Natal. After many rounds of drinks and tales of sexual prowess, they walked out into the hot, damp air of the tropical night. Singing and shouting obscenities, they went to the hut where Carlota and her mother lived and kicked the door down.

Her mother tried to resist. It was a mistake. Her struggle did not save Carlota, and one of the many blows she received broke her neck. The men threw Carlota onto the bed, where she was a toy for the use of the drunken gang until the morning, when they finally left, after tying her up and gagging her.

It was while waiting for someone to come and release her, the bed damp with her own blood, the smell of men burning her nostrils, that Carlota made up her mind. After her mother was buried in the small cemetery by the white-washed chapel, she went home and removed the slim wad of *cruzeiro* notes hidden in a tin. Her mother's savings would pay for her trip to Rio, to a new life, to freedom.

The savings barely covered the cost of the third-class train fare and it took Carlota four days to make the journey. She finally arrived in the enormous city; she had no idea what to do or where to go, and her money had run out.

It was nearly dark when she left the terminal. Terrified, she crossed the wide avenue outside the station, and wandered into a park which reminded her of the scenery she knew, the fichu trees with their huge roots above the ground, the little *agoutis* playfully running on the grass. 'Campo de Santana' said the enamelled metal sign, but she could not read it.

She settled down on a bench, but was awakened in the middle of the night by a torch shining in her eyes. A policeman, his coarse face barely visible in the dark, asked for her papers, and began questioning her. When she had finished her story, he pulled out a notebook, gave her the address of a domestic employment agency, and let her go.

The following morning she went to the Vargas de Moreira Agency, and by the afternoon she was employed as a maid in a beautiful house in Rua Redentor, near Ipanema Beach. The family was very nice. The *senhor* was an executive in a big company with a difficult name; the *senhora* slept late in the morning, and took the children to the beach in the afternoon. Carlota did all the housework other than the shopping, cooking and kitchen work, which was done by Otilia, the cook.

For the first time in her life, she had a small room to herself and the use of a bathroom with running water. It was her job to clean the bathroom; Otilia, who shared it, purposely splashed water on the floor every time she used it but Carlota did not mind. She was happy. When she was paid at the end of the month, she spent a considerable sum on a bathing suit, and she was then able to go to the beach with Otilia on Sundays, their day off.

In the joyfully sensual atmosphere of a Rio beach, a girl like Carlota could not go unnoticed, but no matter how friendly the invitation, how funny the remark, she was not interested. The pervasive *samba* beat, the primeval shape of the mountains, the oiled bodies under the sun, everything was redolent of sex, though not for Carlota. When smiling men leaned down to talk to her, the sight of their hairy chests frightened her.

Her monthly bleeding stopped. Her mother had told her once that this bleeding was something that happened to women: she guessed that its disappearance must be due to the change of place, that women living in big cities were smart and did not have the same troubles as women in the countryside.

Her breasts swelled up, and she began to have difficulty in doing up the buttons of her uniform over her waist. One morning the *senhora* told her that she wanted to talk to her. Carlota was non-plussed at first, then embarrassed by the *senhora*'s questions.

That evening, one of the *senhor*'s many cousins, a doctor, was asked to dinner with his wife. Just before dinner, Carlota was told that the doctor was going to check her over. She found the examination unpleasant, but it did not take long. The doctor told her she was expecting a baby.

The following morning the *senhora* told Carlota that she was shocked by her irresponsibility, and that she could not employ someone so unreliable in her home, but she was kind and did not want to upset a girl in Carlota's condition. Carlota could stay until the *senhora* found a reliable replacement for her. Four days later, the new maid moved in.

Her few belongings in a cardboard box, her wages in her pocket, Carlota walked back to the agency. The woman at the desk took one look at her and told her that she was no longer suitable for their clients.

Carlota left the building, the midday crowd rushing around her, feeling desperately alone. She walked for a long time until she found the station. She had decided to go back home, but she was told that there was no train until the afternoon. Longing for a familiar place, she went into the park across the avenue, and found her bench. She sat down, stretching her aching legs. Suddenly the full extent of her predicament became clear.

There was nobody waiting for her back home. She did not even have a home; she had nothing. How would she be able to look after her baby? Lonely and very miserable, she burst into tears.

The sight of this unhappy young girl caught the eye of many passers-by; some were moved, some were intrigued, most were indifferent. But one of them took one look, and accurately assessed the situation. Chico Ribeiro had seen this scene many times before, and he knew exactly what to do.

He sat down next to Carlota and said, 'Come on, there's nothing to worry about,' again and again, wiping away her tears with his heavily scented handkerchief. Carlota had never seen a young man with so many gold chains, wearing such magnificent white crocodile shoes with beautiful Cuban heels.

Chico patted her hand, and her relief at another human being's concern was overwhelming. Carlota buried her face in his shoulder, crying out her despair. He put his arm around her, and helped her to sit up again. It was the easiest thing in the world to take her money from her pocket.

Chico muttered soothing words until she calmed down. Then he glanced at his gold watch, said, 'My God, I must rush,' and left, wishing Carlota good luck. He did not go far, just far enough to find a bush to hide behind while keeping watch on Carlota. After a while, she stood up and walked away, disappearing from his sight. It didn't matter; Chico knew she would come back.

He only had to wait for fifteen minutes. Her face was a mask of fear; she crawled on her knees around the bench, looking at the grass behind it, raking the gravel under it with her fingers. He could almost hear her sobs. At last, she sat down, her hands covering her face.

Chico walked towards her.

'You're still here! *Tudo bem?*' he asked cheerfully. The

traditional 'Everything all right?' Rio greeting felt like the stab of a knife to Carlota.

'Don't go, *senhor*, please don't go,' she begged him.

He did not go. Far from it; he took over her life. When he heard about Carlota's problems, he immediately suggested that she move in with his fiancée until she found a job and somewhere to live. Carlota could not believe her luck, and followed him to his car, clutching her cardboard box.

The fiancée lived in a small apartment near Maua Square, in the dock area. She greeted Carlota warmly, and told her that her name was Lula. She asked Carlota to come with her to the kitchen, where she was cooking supper. She emphatically refused Carlota's offer to help with the cooking, and listened sympathetically as Carlota told her her sad story.

When they sat down at table, Carlota was suddenly aware of her hunger, and tucked into the steaming plate of steak, rice, and fried bananas in front of her, an inconceivable feast a few hours ago. Lula said that since Carlota had had experience in domestic work, maybe she would be interested in a job at the exclusive institute that she managed. The institute's speciality was *massagem relaxante*, given by live-in girls. They were all like one happy family, but the girl who was in charge of domestic chores had just left. Carlota accepted immediately, full of gratitude for Lula's kindness.

The next morning, Chico drove them to a house in a run-down section of the district. Lula quickly scanned the street before opening the door, and pushed Carlota inside. The cheap scent in the air hardly concealed the miasma of cat piss, and they could hear the sound of *samba* from a radio somewhere in the house.

As they climbed the stairs, a mulatto girl walked across the first-floor landing. She was wearing very high-heeled sandals and nothing else, her large breasts partly concealed by the enamelled washing bowl she carried with both hands. She greeted Lula without stopping. Carlota heard her open a door, followed by the splashing of liquid in a sink.

A moment later, the girl returned, holding the empty

bowl. Lula introduced her to Carlota; her name was
Nerinha. A door at the end of a corridor opened and
a blond sailor appeared. He shyly said 'Goodbye' as he
walked past. Nerinha pursed her lips and held her breasts
up, blocking his way and thrusting her bosom against
his chest.

'*Ingrato*, make present, dollars, Nerinha all night, *sim?*'
The boy pulled the note carefully. She was about to tuck
it under her left breast, when Lula snatched it away with
a smile, and put it in her pocket.

Carlota settled in quickly. There were two other girls in
the house: Mimosa, who came from Ceara, and Magnolia,
who had been born in Pelotas and kept two cats, Café, a
brown mean-looking tom, and Leite, a fat, placid white.
Each girl had her own room off the first-floor corridor, the
glazed doors obscured by flowered curtains. Carlota's was
a small attic, accessible by steep stairs next to the kitchen.
It was stiflingly hot at night, even when the breeze blew
in from the harbour, but Carlota was proud to have her
own room again. Her job was to cook for the girls, wash
the floors, and make the beds.

Carlota's gratitude was the first step in Chico's plan.
At present, she was not very useful to him, but he could
afford to wait until she was able to offer the full range of
services to his customers. And the baby would be useful
for his other business, the beggars ring. Once the child
was born, and under Chico's control, Carlota would be
willing to do whatever he wanted her to do.

Life settled into a routine for Carlota. The mornings
were very quiet. The girls slept late and went to the beach
around midday, when Carlota would do their rooms. They
would come back around three or four in the afternoon and
have a siesta; then they would all get together in Nerinha's
room and listen to her new RCA Victor radio, speculating
endlessly about the plots of the soap operas while they
knitted or sewed clothes for Carlota's baby.

Some nights Lula would let the customers in. She would
sit in a bentwood rocking chair in the hallway, waiting for
them, while chain-smoking 'Dourado' cigarettes; on other
evenings they were greeted by Chico or Morena do Sul, a

friend of Lula's who worked at one of the bars near the docks. Carlota stayed in her room in the evenings. She was afraid to go out on her own, worried that something might happen to her baby.

One night Chico and Lula asked her if she wanted to come with them to their *terreiro*. Carlota had been deeply religious, but she had not been to a place of worship since she had left home. Lula allowed her to make a white dress from an old sheet. She sat in the car in silence as they drove through a very long tunnel, then uphill, until the road turned into a dirt track. They stopped by a wooden fence. The house behind it was barely visible through the banana trees.

There was no moonlight, only the stars, the fireflies, and the city lights in the distance. They walked into a large shed where a small crowd of worshippers sat around the room, their white clothes reflecting the yellow glow of the candles on the floor. A large crucifix on a table dominated the clear area in the middle of the room, flanked by the statues of the Jesus-like Oxala, the beautiful Iemanja, goddess of the sea, and other images. Also on the table were many glasses or small vases holding flowers.

The singing started and Carlota joined in, losing herself to a feeling of abandon and well-being. In the clear space by the altar the *cavalhos*, in their white robes, swayed to the music, humming loudly. Suddenly one of them grunted, and his face contorted into a mask. He fell to the ground and rolled backwards and forwards, hissing and muttering in an incomprehensible language. Soon the two other *cavalhos* followed, and the *macumba* rite began.

During the long night, in the constant dialogue between spirits and worshippers through the *cavalhos*, Carlota came to terms with her current circumstances. When her turn came to interrogate the spirit, her *cavalho* shook violently, until a beatific calm overcame him. His eyes suddenly opened and, looking at Chico who stood next to Carlota, he made an unmistakable sign. The spirit had chosen Chico as a force for good in Carlota's life. The *cavalho* reinforced the bond with special herbal mixtures, and the cleansing ritual sealed it. The spirit had clearly said that Chico was

90

to guide Carlota, and she accepted it. They returned to the house soon afterward, the peaks of the *morros* on the horizon outlined in gold by the rising sun. Carlota did not know that the *cavalho* was Chico's cousin.

Very soon Chico gave her a new job. She and Morena do Sul were to travel in Rio's crowded buses. Carlota was to stand next to the most prosperous-looking passenger, her huge belly thrust forward. The man would then give up his seat out of kindness. If he didn't, Morena would lecture him in a very loud voice about people's manners. In either case, the man would leave his seat. In the ensuing commotion, Morena would pick his pocket. She would then get off the bus immediately, and Carlota would meet her at the following stop, where the two would wait for the next bus.

One afternoon, they were working the bus route along Nossa Senhora de Copacabana Avenue. They had just completed their routine, and Morena was elbowing her way to the door through the standing passengers when the man she had robbed shouted that she was a thief. Morena jumped out of the bus, the man in pursuit. Carlota began to wonder what she ought to do when she felt a flash of pain and water poured out of her, flooding the seat and the floor. Deeply embarrassed, she left the bus, ignoring the offers of help from other passengers.

She started to walk aimlessly, when the pain came again. Gasping, she stumbled and managed to balance herself against the trunk of a huge palm tree. She could feel the sweat on her face.

A woman came up to her, a woman with a kind face. She began to question her, but Carlota felt her strength flowing away. The woman asked her a question she could not hear, and she passed out. An ambulance took her to the Rocha Maia Hospital. Seventeen hours later, she was holding her newly-born daughter to her bosom. She had never felt so much love in her life; her baby needed her, and she would protect it.

During her stay in the hospital, she became friendly with a cleaning woman who came from Recife. The old woman's interest made Carlota wish that her mother could be there to see her beautiful granddaughter, Florinda. Carlota had named her daughter after her favourite soap opera character. She hoped that her baby would one day be rich and famous, like her namesake.

Chico did not bother to look for Carlota; he knew that she would return. And he was right. A few days later, Carlota came back. The house was in commotion as Lula, Nerinha, Magnolia and Mimosa cooed over the little Florinda until the first customer arrived. Then they quickly cleared Mimosa's bed, and got back to work.

A month later, Carlota was cooking *feijoada* for supper, slowly stirring it with a fork, when Chico walked into the kitchen. He was smiling, and holding Florinda in his arms.

'The little one is ready for some fresh air,' he said. 'Tomorrow morning I'll take her out with some friends of mine.' Carlota did not understand at first. She walked Florinda in her arms every afternoon, and they went around the square at least twice before coming back. Her baby had plenty of fresh air.

'But I can't go tomorrow morning. I have to help Lula here.'

'You don't need to come. In fact, from now on you will see Florinda only when I say so. I am taking her away.'

Months of coexistence with Carlota had accustomed Chico to her meekness. But he had misjudged her. Carlota leapt at him, her eyes wide open. While grabbing Florinda with her left hand, she gashed his face open with the fork from eyebrow to chin. Blood covered Chico's eye, and his screams brought the girls rushing downstairs. The front door was open, and Carlota and Florinda were gone.

Mimosa and Nerinha ran after them, while Magnolia looked after Chico. They turned into Avenida Venezuela, but wolf-whistles and hooting cars made them realize that they had left the house dressed in their work clothes, high-heeled sandals and black underwear. They could not afford to be stopped by the police, so they had to rush home again.

Carlota kept running. Sweat trickled down her neck, and her heart beat wildly, but she did not stop. After a while,

Florinda began to cry. Carlota stopped in the doorway of a church, and fed her, the baby's soft mouth on her breast soothing her fears. Looking at Florinda, she remembered her first feeding in the hospital, and she thought of Maria, the old cleaning woman who had befriended her. Maria was her only hope.

Florinda went to sleep, milk dribbling down the sides of her mouth, a placid smile on her face. Carlota kept her watch for as long as she could, until she too fell asleep, just after hearing the church bells chime two o'clock.

When she woke up, it was still dark, and her body ached all over. Florinda's nappy was soaked and dirty. The baby stirred, and began to whimper. Carlota lifted her up gently and began to walk down the empty streets. She saw a small alley, by the side of a house. Looking in every direction to ensure that nobody was watching her, she walked into the alley and relieved herself on the pavement. She noticed an open window nearby, behind ornate bars. The edge of a curtain was just visible.

Carlota scanned the ground around her, and found a piece of broken glass. She laid Florinda carefully on the sill of the adjacent window, then swiftly pulled the curtain out through the bars and slashed a square piece from it with the sharp edge of the glass. Holding the piece of fabric, she picked up the baby and ran away. She ran for two blocks, until she found a sheltered doorway. Folding the piece of curtain into a triangle, she improvised a clean nappy for her baby.

People were beginning to appear on the street. She asked for directions several times, and at last she found the hospital. She waited outside until she saw Maria. Calling her name, Carlota felt safe for the first time since leaving Chico. She burst into tears and explained her predicament. Maria went into the hospital; after a while, she came out with coffee in a paper cup and a roll. She told Carlota to wait for her outside until the end of the shift.

Carlota sat on a green wooden bench under a palm tree, holding Florinda. At last, exhaustion took over, and both mother and daughter fell asleep in the warm morning air.

93

Inside the huge white hospital building, Maria thought about Carlota while mopping the tiled floor of an interminable corridor. She could do with help at home and Nelson, her son, needed a woman. Carlota seemed a nice girl. She also produced beautiful, healthy babies. Nelson would be pleased.

When she left work, Maria told Carlota that she could come and stay with her; she also mentioned her son, and said that she was sure Nelson would like her. She explained that they lived in a nice part of town, overlooking the Jockey Club and the lagoon. Carlota was impressed that Maria lived in such a smart part of the city.

After a long bus ride, it took them nearly an hour to climb the steep hillside. It was difficult for Carlota to walk up the rocky path holding Florinda in her arms, the ferns and lianas growing on the rocks brushing against her. Maria offered several times to carry the baby but Carlota refused.

At last they reached the *favela*, and began to walk among the hovels built at random on the mountain face. Carlota could hold Florinda with just one arm, because she needed the other to wave her way through the clouds of flies swarming over the piles of rubbish and excrement. She did not particularly notice the naked children playing here and there, their scrawny bodies caked in mud. They were a familiar sight from her childhood.

Maria pushed open the tin door of one of the shacks. Inside, Carlota saw a young man, wearing only his trousers. He was snoring on the floor, an empty bottle beside him.

'Nelson . . . Nelson,' called Maria. The man did not move. Maria shook him until he woke up. He struggled to stand, and Carlota noticed his lame leg.

'Nelson, this is Carlota,' Maria said. 'She is going to live with us. Her baby is called Florinda.'

'Fine,' said Nelson, eyeing Carlota's body under the cotton shift. He did not need further explanations. His mother kept him, and she had now produced a fine woman; Nelson was pleased.

Ten months later, Carlota gave birth to Silvia. She named

her second daughter after Silvia da Costa, the movie star who had rocked Brazil.

On Silvia's third birthday, Maria fell ill. They had planned to go to the square and have their picture taken as a memento of the girl's birthday, but at the last moment Maria developed a terrible headache, and preferred to stay at home. Nelson announced that he would look after his mother. Shortly after Carlota and the girls left, Maria went to sleep and Nelson rushed off to the race track.

The next day, Maria was checked into the hospital where she worked. A brain tumour, they said, and she died a short while afterward. It took an even shorter time for Nelson to leave Carlota and the children. With Maria's savings he took himself to São Paulo, where he had been told that living was easy.

Carlota never saw him again. She had to make a living, but she could not go to work and leave Florinda and Silvia alone. If she did, she knew that, sooner or later, she would not find them there on her return. Begging became the only way for her to earn a few *cruzeiros*, and sifting through garbage cans the usual way of feeding her children. Two years after Nelson's departure, she began to cough. One year later, she began to cough up blood.

No, life had not been kind to Carlota. Sometimes she wished that she had been luckier, but then she thanked God for her girls. She loved them, and had given them all she could.

She also worried about them. Not so much about Florinda; the girl was tough, and would survive anything. But she could not bear to think what would become of Silvia if she were not there to protect her.

At last, the child fell asleep in her arms, and Carlota gently moved her to her bed of rags. She kissed Silvia on the forehead, and then lay down on her own pile of rags. She felt feverish, but did not think much of it: it was to be expected after such a commotion.

She looked at her sleeping children. As usual, she was struck by their beauty, and proud of it, and yet she feared for them. Her own beauty had been no protection. She made a point of taking the girls to school every morning. At least they would learn to read and write. They would not be illiterate like her, but what would they become?

Closing her mind to disquieting thoughts, she tried to sleep.

7

RIO DE JANEIRO
31 December 1962

The sun had just gone down over Copacabana beach. The purple-blue darkness had almost rubbed out the pink light from the horizon when Florinda and Silvia joined the vast crowd of worshippers on the sand.

It had taken them the whole morning to prepare the beautiful flower wreaths for the sea goddess, Iemanja: white roses from Florinda, red bird-of-paradise flowers from Silvia. Florinda had stolen the flowers early in the morning from the stall near the Jockey Club while Silvia, following her sister's instructions, had distracted the owner's attention.

The crowd stood away from the water's edge, and the sand glowed in the light of thousands of candles. The singing muffled the sound of the waves but the noctilucas turned the breakers into a festoon of light in the darkness, a sign to the faithful that the goddess of the sea would visit them at midnight.

On one side of Avenida Atlantica, the world's most spectacular sweep of seaside apartments shone in the night. Servants could be seen on the terraces setting candle-lit tables for the New Year parties that would begin in a few hours. On the other side, past the wide pavement of black and white stones that formed a ribbon of undulating lines, one million people gathered by the sea to honour its goddess, a ritual brought over from Africa four hundred years before. At midnight, men in black tie and women in Dior and diamonds would toast the New Year from their penthouses while they watched, like benevolent gods from the clouds, the dancing crowd below them.

On the beach, Silvia and Florinda joined in the festivities, singing and dancing to the rhythmic beat of the drums. They were nearly the same size, both exquisitely proportioned, their long narrow bodies giving the impression of weightlessness, so supple were their movements. They both looked strikingly like their mother.

The music made them forget their worries. They had always come to the beach with Carlota, but now her health prevented it. For the last few days she had been running an extremely high temperature, but she refused to let the girls bring a doctor from the local dispensary. The herbal remedies from the *macumba* were all she needed, she said, and she insisted that the children should go to the beach that evening, otherwise the goddess might take offence.

Carlota had been unable to make a present for Iemanja. The effort had been too much for her. At the last moment she explained to Silvia what she wanted. At the bottom of a beer crate full of assorted pickings from garbage cans, Silvia found the square of material her mother had asked for. The edges were roughly cut as if a primitive tool had been used, and there was a large stain in the middle, which had caused the floral pattern to fade.

Carlota stared at the piece of material for a long time, before focusing her eyes on her children.

'Please bring me two of your flowers, both of you. And needle and thread as well.' She made an effort not to let her tiredness show in her voice.

She stitched the flowers to the corners of the fabric, then gave it to Silvia.

'When you bring your offerings to Iemanja, put this next to them. She knows what my wish is.' Her head sank onto the rags spread on the floor. In spite of the heat, she shivered constantly.

'Go now, children, go,' she managed to say before falling asleep.

Silvia did not want to leave her mother, but Carlota insisted they should go. Even now, dancing under the stars, she worried about her mother.

The sisters' dancing caught the attention of others, and soon there was a circle of people around them, clapping their hands to the obsessive beat of the drums. Suddenly, the ring of people surrounding them broke up and everybody joined in their dance. The girls found themselves dancing with ever-changing partners, until two men held

98

their stretched-out hands to them, shielding them from the crowd. The whole beach was now covered by a swaying ribbon of people dressed in white, folding and unfolding to the rhythm of the tribal sounds.

Just before midnight, the crowd rushed to the shore with their gifts. Lace cloths were spread along the tide line, and were instantly covered by the offerings of the faithful: flowers, fruits, ornaments, silk ribbons – a million gifts for the goddess of the sea. If Iemanja accepted their presents, she would send the tide to collect them at midnight and grant the donor's wish.

Silvia and Florinda ran towards the sea with their trinkets and laid them down just in time, Carlota's cloth flanked by her children's floral offerings. Holding hands, they faced the sea with the rest of the crowd, standing shoulder to shoulder along the water's edge.

As the surface of the water swelled in the distance, a murmur passed among them. The swelling became a huge wave, then it crashed into an explosion of phosphorescent foam, rapidly approaching the beach in a tidal surge. The water rolled towards the spectators, covering their feet. The goddess had come to them, and the crowd cheered in their joy.

The receding surf carried away the offerings, and the roar from the crowd silenced everything, including the explosion of fireworks which, at the stroke of midnight, covered the skies of Rio de Janeiro in a shower of gold. As the tide continued to wash the shore, the people began to disperse. Soon the endless stretch of wet sand was clear. Only Carlota's offering, entangled in some driftwood trapped by the sand, was a reminder of the gifts that had been collected by the sea.

An incessant incantation ran from one end of the beach to the other: 'Happy New Year!' 'Happy New Year!' 'Happy New Year!' 'Happy New Year!' said the older of the two men next to Silvia and Florinda. 'I'm Carlos, and he is Omar,' he explained, as he produced a hip flask full of Scotch. Omar, just a few years older than Florinda and very good-looking, smiled at her.

'Let's toast the year in,' Carlos said, taking a swig from

the flask. 'Welcome, 1963!' He passed the flask on to Silvia. Trying to conceal the fact that her only experience with drinking was an occasional beer, she gulped down a large mouthful of whisky. She choked, and tears came to her eyes. Carlos slapped her on the back.

'You have to be careful with this stuff.' Carlos slapped Silvia's back once again, then his hand slid carelessly down her spine.

'Why don't we try to find somewhere to sit and watch the fireworks in peace?' Carlos asked. 'We could go back to my apartment. I can drive you home later. You ought to see my car, it's very nice.' He began to walk towards the road, his hands resting lightly on the girls' shoulders. Omar took Florinda's hand in his. She recoiled slightly at his touch, but noticed the Rolex watch on his wrist.

They walked along the avenue, zig-zagging their way through the crowd. Carlos and Omar cracked jokes and constantly offered the flask to Silvia. Florinda had declined it after a second tasting, but Silvia had accepted every offer. She was impressed by the men's conversation, their constant references to cars, yachts and famous people, their obvious ease in a world she longed for. In the meantime, Florinda studied them. The fit of their clothes made it obvious to her that they were not carrying wallets.

Omar suggested they take one of the side streets to avoid the crowd, and Florinda readily agreed. As they turned the corner, Omar held her arm and began to walk faster, until they were a few yards ahead of Carlos and Silvia. Omar talked to her without a break, trying to take her attention away from his arm, now encircling her waist.

The lights hanging from wires across the road cast their pale yellow glow on the empty street ahead, and Florinda saw the square at the end. As they got further away from the main road, the noise from the crowd became fainter, and she could now hear Carlos chuckling and whispering to Silvia behind her.

They crossed the road and walked into the square, under the jacaranda trees. They were completely alone, the darkness all around them. Florinda gave Omar a coy look. 'I feel dizzy, I would like to sit down somewhere very quiet,' she said, placing her hands on his bare forearm, as if to keep her balance. 'I'm so tired,' she muttered, her head now resting on his shoulder.

Omar pointed at a gazebo, smothered by a bougainvillaea in full bloom. He almost had to carry her inside, her body limp against him. He could feel her breasts pressed against his chest, her hand carelessly rubbing against his groin. Florinda heard his breathing become quicker. Her eyes were half-closed, but she was able to see Carlos steering Silvia towards a nearby bush, his hand on her sister's buttock. The sight pleased her; she had work to do, and it would be easier if she and Omar were left on their own.

She collapsed on the bench inside the gazebo, Omar next to her. He took her in his arms. Florinda moaned softly, as if semi-conscious. Omar was familiar with girls and their ways: this was one of those who liked to pretend they weren't there. He began to caress her breasts through her thin blouse, and guided her hand to his bulging prick.

While moaning and sighing, Florinda was methodically running through the lessons she had learned from Mario, the boy next door in the *favela*. His price had been one blow job per lesson; she would soon find out if it had been worth it.

Omar stood up to undo his belt, and Florinda saw her chance.

'Oh, you drive me crazy,' she whispered, falling on her knees in front of him. She pulled down the zipper of his trousers, took hold of the top of his shorts and pulled his clothes down to his ankles. Gasping, she took his cock in her mouth. While her lips moved slowly up and down, she could sense him tremble with pleasure, oblivious to anything else. She slowly caressed his legs until she reached his feet. Then, as rapidly as she could, she tied his shoelaces together.

She took his wrists in her hands, as if to retain her balance, and began to gently caress the ridge between the head and the shaft of his penis with the edge of her teeth. Omar grunted with delight, and she felt a salty taste in her mouth. Time for action, she thought, otherwise this pig was going to shoot.

Suddenly she sank her teeth into his flesh. Overwhelmed by the horrendous pain, Omar did not feel her fingers unfastening the Rolex from his wrist. Florinda ran out of the gazebo. Screaming with rage, Omar tried to follow her but he fell flat on his face, his feet tied together.

'Silvia, let's go! Police! Please help me! Police!' Florinda screamed at the top of her voice, running towards the street. She saw Carlos appear from behind the bush, his clothes undone; Silvia was behind him, tears in her eyes. Florinda grabbed her sister's hand and pulled her away. She ran as fast as she could, and kept on shouting for the police until she noticed that Carlos was running in the opposite direction, Omar stumbling behind him.

Florinda did not stop until they reached the main road. After making sure that they were not being followed, she turned to Silvia.

'You are a revolting whore, a shitty little slut. Wait until we get home, and I tell mamá,' she said angrily.

'No, Florinda, don't tell mamá, please. You know she is ill,' Silvia pleaded. Florinda felt a surge of pleasure; her sister was in her power.

'I'll think about it, but I don't know if I can ever look at you without feeling sick,' she said. She dropped the watch inside her blouse, where she felt it come to rest against the tight waistband of her skirt.

Silvia walked in silence, her eyes on the pavement. Sex was as much a fact of everyday life in the *favela* as the grinding poverty, and she had long been aware that men found her attractive, as attractive as Florinda. But that night, for the first time, she had come across a man who not only was attracted to her but who could offer her the opportunity to escape from a life of squalor. Men could be a way out of poverty. But she did not have Florinda's ruthlessness, her complete disregard for anything other than her own objectives. She often wished she could be more like her sister.

It was nearly morning by the time they reached home. As they walked in, the pale light of dawn coming through the door caught Carlota's body on the floor. Her pained expression had been replaced by a look of serenity, restoring her features to their original beauty.

'Mamá, mamá . . .' Silvia choked, kneeling down and taking her mother's hand. Even in her ignorance, the cold skin confirmed her fear. She looked up at Florinda in despair.

'Mamá is dead.' Tears came to her eyes in sorrow for the person who had shown her so much love.

She stood up, sobbing uncontrollably, and embraced Florinda. Her sister remained motionless, looking at their dead mother. Things would be easier now: *she* was in control.

8

RIO DE JANEIRO
February 1966

'*La plume de votre tante est sur la table,*' the voice said.

'*Non, la plume de ma tante n'est pas sur la table, elle est sur le dre . . . dre . . .* Oh, shit!' Florinda slammed her fist down on the coffee table in front of her armchair. She switched off the record player and closed the book on her lap.

'How long are you going to go on with that?' Silvia shouted from the kitchen. 'I know it far better than you by now.' She stood in the doorway, languidly leaning against the doorframe, her hand on her hip.

'*Voulez-vous du café?* she asked in a mocking tone.

Florinda glared at her.

'I'll go on for as fucking long as it takes me to speak it. I may not be as clever as you, but I'm going to be a model in Paris while you're stuck here, still being screwed by your fat car dealer who will probably give you the pox if he doesn't get you pregnant first.' She looked into Silvia's eyes. 'I've told you a million times that I don't like you wearing my eye-shadow. You have your own, leave mine alone.'

Silvia pursed her lips and blew her a kiss.

'I'm sorry, don't get so upset. Some of the things you say *might* be true, but if it weren't for my fat car dealer, you would still be skidding on the shit in the *favela*. I would wait until that photographer of yours lives up to his promise to make you famous before making too many plans about Paris.'

She walked across the room and turned on the radio.

'. . . General Castelo Branco received a delegation of . . .' Silvia rolled her eyes and changed the station. The voice of Astrud Gilberto singing 'The Girl from Ipanema' filled the room.

'*Ah que coisa mais linda, mais cheia de graça, e ela*

menina . . .' Silvia sang, dancing around the coffee table, her hips swaying to the tune.

'You ought to tell your Ruben to try to sell more cars, or be less stingy,' Florinda said. 'You're not living in Ipanema yet.'

Silvia paused for a moment. 'Maybe, but at least Ruben pays the bills and you live here thanks to him. If you don't like it, you can climb up a *morro* any time and stay there.' She sat on the arm of Florinda's seat, and put her arm around her sister's shoulders.

'Let's not fight. I love you more than anyone else in the world. You know, Florinda, I've always envied you, wanted to be like you, and now we are bickering about stupid things. Don't be nasty about Ruben, and I won't say anything about your Marco. When am I going to meet him? You're very secretive about your photographer friend.'

Florinda didn't reply. Silvia leaned forward and picked up a packet of Kent cigarettes from the table. She lit one, blew several smoke rings in the air, and continued.

'And my Ruben sells a lot of cars, you know. He's just done a big cash deal with someone who's bought a Jaguar,' she said proudly. 'You should see it, Florinda, such a lovely car. White, with red leather seats. The man's coming to pick it up on Friday at six o'clock on his way to Cabo Frio. He must be one of those guys who think they're so important they can't stay for Carnival with people like us on the street. If you want, I can take you to the showroom tomorrow, and you could see the car before it goes.'

Florinda stood up, her eyes wide open, staring at Silvia.

'You know I can't stand the smell of cigarettes, put it out!' she screamed. Shaken by her sudden outburst, Silvia stubbed her cigarette out in the ashtray. Florinda walked towards the door.

'I'm going to have a shower and get ready,' she said. 'I can't waste any more time with you. Marco is taking me to the Copacabana Palace. He's picking me up at seven, because he wants me to have a drink with some film producer he knows.'

'I'm sure you will look beautiful, and you must have something new and lovely to wear, you always do. You know how I get my money, but I'm never quite sure how you get yours, Florinda. I'd better not ask, I suppose.' Silvia instantly regretted her words. She knew that only undiluted flattery kept Florinda under control during one of her moods.

'It's none of your business,' Florinda said curtly.

Silvia quickly changed the subject.

'Promise not to come into my room,' she said sweetly. 'I have to finish my costume for tomorrow night, and I don't want you to see it before then. I think you'll like it.'

Florinda shrugged her shoulders and walked across the hallway into her bedroom, closed the door and leaned against it. Eyes closed, she bit her lip. She could not go on like this, not for much longer.

During the first year after their mother's death, Florinda had been in charge of their survival. She thieved and prostituted herself when necessary, while Silvia stayed at home, listening to the transistor radio Florinda had stolen for her. Silvia refused to go out. She lay at home in a daze, day after day, numbed by her mother's death. Her vulnerability was soon obvious to the gangs of young louts in the *favela*, and her fear of them increased her reluctance to leave their shack.

One afternoon, Florinda went past a group of men on her way home. They cracked jokes about her little sister: she just kept on walking but one of the boys followed her. He began to describe in detail what he would like to do to both Silvia and to her. Suddenly she stopped and picked up a dog turd from the road. She turned around and smeared it over his face, kicking him in the balls for good measure. She had no further trouble. Then, soon after the first anniversary of Carlota's death, Silvia regained her spirit. She began to frequent the beaches, where her looks drew as much attention as Florinda's, even more so. Silvia craved admiration, and she got it. It was during one of those lazy afternoons that she came across Ruben. They began meeting every day, and eventually the middle-aged car dealer rented a furnished apartment in Rua Palmeira, not far from his office. Silvia insisted that she would only live there if Florinda could move in with her.

Sometimes Ruben stayed for the night, but not always. He was in the process of separating from his wife, and he had to keep up appearances until all the legal matters were settled. He lived with his mother in a house near São Conrado.

The apartment was small, but it had two bedrooms, one of them big enough for a double bed, a sitting room, kitchen and a bathroom. To Florinda and Silvia it was a world of inconceivable luxury, with hot and cold water coming out of the taps, and electricity in every room. They soon learned to use knives and forks, the difference between towels and sheets, between a tumbler and a wine glass. Their life appeared to have changed only for the better, but not from Florinda's point of view.

In the *favela*, she had been in charge of their lives. Ruben was the benefactor now and, for Silvia, the source of love and money. It was only a matter of time before Florinda became a secondary factor in Silvia's life, a possibility that the elder sister found intolerable. She wanted to be first in anything she did. Always.

There was also another, deeper layer to her dissatisfaction. Florinda had used sex for her own purposes since she was thirteen. Men meant nothing to her, and she felt nothing with them. But they were easy to pluck. She knew that her beauty made her irresistible to them, and she used it. Someday she would find a really big catch.

But in the meantime she had to carry on, a quick grope here and there to pick some sucker's pocket, occasionally a night in a hotel if the money made it worth her while. Most of the men were fairly repulsive, with soft bellies and varicose veins, but she did not look very closely at them.

Silvia's affair with Ruben had shaken her. Her sister had achieved all the material benefits she craved for, and had found someone who adored her. It was this last aspect which aggrieved Florinda most.

She had invented Marco out of hurt pride. She had picked up his name from the captions in fashion photographs in O *Cruzeiro* and other glossies, and then told Silvia that a photographer had stopped her at the beach in Leblon and asked her to pose for him. She described him as tall, broad-shouldered, with blue-grey eyes and blond hair, the proud owner of a red Ford Thunderbird. Silvia had actually seen the car when the photographer came to pick up Florinda. What Silvia could not see from the window was that the man inside the car was Epitacio Barbosa, a fifty-four-year-old scrap-dealer. The man was bald, overweight, and had difficulty in controlling his wind. He had picked up Florinda from his car one evening as she strolled up and down Avenida Atlantica, waiting for an impressive car to stop beside her. It was easy for Florinda to hook the podgy businessman into a weekly meeting, when they would spend an hour together in a hotel before he went back home to his family. She would then go off on her own to the late show at one of their local cinemas. The following morning she would tell Silvia about the fabulous places she had been to the night before.

While watching *Charade* at the Joia Cinema, the sight of the exquisitely dressed Audrey Hepburn walking along the river in Paris had given Florinda the idea for her next fabrication. Over breakfast she had announced that Marco had told her that she was too classy for modelling in Rio, and that he was going to get her a job in Paris. When Silvia had asked how she would manage when she couldn't speak the language, Florinda had replied that she would learn it in no time at all. Later in the day, after spending most of the afternoon applying for a passport, she had used part of the money her scrap-dealer had given her the previous night to acquire a 'Teach yourself French' record set.

She regretted the idea after the first lesson because she found the exercises intolerably boring, but she could not face Silvia's predictably smug look if she gave up, so she sat every evening listening to the records, exercise book in hand.

Now she was trapped in her own story, pretending to learn a language which was useless to her, fêted by a non-existent admirer, supposedly on her way to an incredible job. Epitacio had warned her, now that Carnival was upon them, that he had to be home early, so tonight he would pick her up at seven. She didn't even bother to dress up for the sake of her story. She decided to ask Epitacio to drive to a quiet spot in Tijuca, and they could have a quick screw in the back seat. He liked that, and she could then be back home in less than an hour, in time for dinner with Silvia. Maybe she could even cook; she had not done so in a long time.

She left her room and opened Silvia's door just a fraction.

'I'm going now. I think I'm getting the curse, so I'll be back home after drinks. Don't go out tonight, I'll cook for you,' she added.

Silvia smiled.

'For Ruben too. He was taking me out, but I'll tell him we'll eat here. Don't come in, my costume is all over the bed.'

She left the apartment without replying. The sound of samba bands playing and singing in the streets came through the open windows.

Florinda walked into the sitting room carrying the tray with the coffeepot and cups. She saw Ruben holding Silvia's hand, and felt a stab of jealousy.

'That was a delicious dinner, Florinda,' Ruben said, carefully picking his teeth. He slid his hand inside his shirt, almost undone to the waist, and patted his stomach to corroborate his compliment. 'I haven't had such good *vatapa* for a long time.'

'It's the only dish my mother taught me how to make,' Florinda said. 'She used to cook it once a year.' Memories of the open fire inside the tin shack, the food cooking in discarded oil cans found in garbage dumps, the stench of the slum temporarily masked by the smell of shrimp frying in *dende* oil, the rice simmering in coconut milk, all flashed through Florinda's mind. Her eyes involuntarily drifted for a moment to the solid gold identity bracelet on Ruben's wrist. She knew how easy it would be to slip back into the hell they had left behind, and she knew she should be grateful to Ruben. But she was not.

'I have a very worried man here,' Silvia said. She patted Ruben's cheek affectionately. 'I'm going to change and then we're going to go out and dance all night. You shouldn't worry so much about a broken safe,' she added, finishing her coffee.

'What's the problem?' Florinda asked after Silvia had left the room.

'It's nothing,' Ruben said. 'The lock in my office safe doesn't work. I want to have it fixed tomorrow but you can't get anyone to do work on Carnival Friday. It doesn't really matter.' He began to tap a rhythm with the tip of his fingers on the edge of the table, a smile on his lips. 'Carnaval-carnaval, carnaval-carnaval,' he sang, his fleshy shoulders moving in time with his beat. He suddenly stopped and glanced at her. 'You look fabulous tonight. Why don't you come out with us?'

'I may not have much fun on my own,' she said coyly. Her arms crossed under her breasts, she leaned forward across the table. Her silky tank top slid downwards as she moved, and her bosom was almost fully exposed. 'Maybe *you* could amuse me later,' she purred, pursing her lips.

She sensed his surprise, and acted upon his uncertainty. She swiftly left her chair and sat on his lap, putting her arms around his neck.

It suddenly became clear to her that, at the bottom of her disquiet, was the fact that she wanted Ruben for herself. She wanted him because he had money, because taking him away from Silvia would reinstate her sister's dependence on her. After all, if Silvia could love him, so could she.

'It's so nice of you to ask,' she said softly, stroking his cheek, just as Silvia walked into the room, wearing a gold lamé bikini and a feathered headdress. Florinda was pleased to notice the anger in her eyes. She stood up and walked towards the kitchen.

'I'm going to do the dishes,' she announced cheerfully, exaggerating the sway of her hips as she walked away.

Silvia glared at Ruben.

'You must be sorry that I interrupted you, you pig!' She tried to keep her voice low, so Florinda would not hear, but she could not hide her distress. 'Leave my sister alone!' she said as Ruben led her towards the front door, vainly trying to explain what had happened.

Florinda heard every word of their exchange. She felt more cheerful, and began to whistle as she tackled the pile of dishes by the sink. In her new mood, she briefly considered going out and joining the merry crowd on the streets, but she decided to stay at home. She had a lot of planning to do.

The Jaguar XKE stood in splendid isolation in the middle of the showroom, the high gloss of its perfect finish distorting the faces of Florinda and Silvia like a fun-fair mirror. Florinda slid her hand along its side, the cold metal giving her more pleasure than the touch of any man. Opening the wide door she looked inside the car; the heady smell of brand-new leather upholstery enveloped her as she slid onto the low red seat. She was wearing shorts, and the feel of the soft hide on her naked thighs sent a shiver up her spine. She caressed the knob at the top of the gearshift, then set her hands on the steering wheel, looking at the instruments on the polished walnut dashboard. She patted the smooth wood affectionately as Ruben leaned down to look at her inside the car.

'I can't take you for a ride. The owner is picking it up tonight, and I can't take any risks with a beauty like this one.'

Florinda got out of the car and closed the door. Even the solid 'clunk' sound made by the lock gave her pleasure.

'Some day I will own one of these in every colour,' she said.

Over breakfast, while listening to Silvia's stories about all the places she and Ruben had been to the night before, Florinda feared that her sister might have forgotten her offer to bring her to the showroom to look at the car. Eventually, Silvia asked her if she would still like to see it. Florinda pretended not to be very interested, and went to the kitchen to make some more coffee, knowing that Silvia would insist. She enjoyed showing off the evidence of Ruben's money.

'Come on, Florinda, we'll never get to the beach at this rate,' retorted Silvia, looking at the clock on the showroom's wall.

111

'I need the toilet,' Florinda said curtly. Ruben pointed towards a door. In the small hallway off the showroom, Florinda rapidly checked the ladies' toilet. No good. She then inspected the room marked 'Gentlemen', and found what she wanted. She locked herself in.

The vertical rock face of the Sugarloaf glowed in the sunset light. The thimble-shaped mountain stood out like a cardboard cut-out against the sky, but neither Florinda nor Silvia took any notice of the extraordinary sight. For them it was familiar, a backdrop for the Carnival frenzy that was just beginning, and would last for five days, until Ash Wednesday.

They had walked from the centre of town to Leme, at the start of the long arc of Copacabana beach. They had danced most of the way: as soon as they left Ruben's office they had come across one *banda* after another. Near the showroom the *bandas* were small, ten or twenty people, but as they approached the beach both the bands and the crowds following them became much bigger. Now, among thousands of other dancers, the girls followed the *Banda do Leme* as it progressed along Avenida Atlantica. The tops of the palm trees rivalled some of the extraordinary headdresses among the dancing crowd. The girls had not said a word to each other; they did not need to. They just danced, *samba* after *samba*, both carried away by the fantasy of Carnival where millionaires were dressed in loincloths, beggars from the *favela* were covered in silks and feathers, and reality faded away. They had been dancing for five hours now and Silvia suddenly felt very thirsty. She touched Florinda's shoulder as she twirled next to her.

'Let's sit over there,' she shouted, pointing towards the awnings of a bar on a side street. 'I'll buy you a beer.' She had to say it again, Florinda reading her lips in the roar of the music and singing around them.

They elbowed their way through the thick crowd and, suddenly aware of their tiredness, found the nearest empty table and collapsed on the green metal chairs. 'Two *chopps*,' Silvia gave their order to the waiter standing by the door as they sat down. The waiter went inside, and soon returned. In the fierce February heat, the coarse glass beer mugs on his battered round tin tray were already covered in a dew of condensation.

Silvia took a long drink, then licked the white foam from her upper lip.

'I needed this,' she said, and burped. 'Excuse me,' she muttered, covering her mouth with her hand.

'Oh, "Excuse me". You've become a real sissy! Ruben has turned you into a doll,' Florinda laughed.

'What's wrong with you?' Silvia asked. 'I know that tone; you're trying to pick a fight. But I'm not going to have a fight while the *banda* plays like this. Listen, Florinda,' she said, her fingers tapping on the table to the rhythm of the *samba* being chorused by thousands of voices nearby. 'Just listen, and don't think about anything else.'

'He has turned you into a whore,' Florinda continued, her voice full of venom.

Silvia glared at her. Angrily, she took Florinda's wrist, her grip as tight as her lips.

'Listen to me, you bitch, I'm fed up with you going on about Ruben. Yes, Ruben keeps me and you benefit from it, but he hasn't turned me into anything. I have always needed someone to protect me, to look after me, and you don't – or maybe you just think you don't. If a guy you loathe gives you a present after screwing you, then you are clever, but if I'm given things by a guy I love then I'm a whore. You ought to realize how lucky you are, and how much easier things are for you. You're tougher than me.'

Florinda pretended to be enraged.

'Do you think I'm lucky because a fat car dealer screws my sister, because you pay the rent with your ass? You are an idiot. Maybe we should split. I've had enough!'

She stood up and walked away. Silvia threw some money on the table, and ran after her.

'Florinda, please, you don't understand. I wasn't criticizing you. Please, Florinda, stop and listen to me.'

Florinda began to run. Silvia followed her, but in a second Florinda had disappeared into the crowd.

Florinda fought her way through the dancers until she

113

reached the Princesa Isabel Avenue, where she waited for a bus to take her home. She wasn't in a hurry any more. The first part of her plan had worked to perfection, but the knot of tension inside her tightened. It was always easy for her to quarrel with Silvia: the really difficult task was still ahead.

Naked but for a silver sequined G-string and bra and silver high-heeled shoes, Silvia looked in the mirror and put the final touches to her eye make-up. She heard Ruben hooting his car horn outside. She spent a few more seconds putting on her long black gloves, then picked up her headdress from the bed and left the room.

As she walked past Florinda's empty bedroom, she wondered where she could be. After their argument a few hours ago, she had gone to see Ruben at his office, arriving at the same time Ruben was saying goodbye to the happy owner of the beautiful Jaguar. Silvia waited until the man climbed into the car and drove away, and then she told Ruben about her argument with Florinda. At first she refused to tell him the reason for it, but Ruben pressed her until she eventually said that Florinda was very upset because she had borrowed her eye-shadow. Ruben raised his eyebrows, but said nothing, then suggested that they have dinner together at a nice new restaurant he had found at Barra de Tijuca, where it would be cooler than in the city.

During dinner, Ruben announced that he thought it was time they had a proper holiday together. They would go to Europe for a few weeks either in April or May, and he mentioned the name of the places they would visit. Most of them meant nothing to Silvia, but the excitement of planning and discussing their trip made her forget the earlier incident with her sister. She felt so happy and safe with Ruben that she almost told him of her suspicions, but she decided not to break the news to him yet. She did not know how he would react, and she did not want to upset him, not now. She was not even sure if she was pregnant; she was only three weeks late. Better to tell him once Carnival was over. She would be absolutely certain by then.

Now, as she left the building, she glanced towards the full-size mirror on the wall by the front door. She was sure that she would be noticed that evening.

She walked to Ruben's parked car, put her headdress on the back seat, and got in. As they drove away, the car lights just missed Florinda, who had been hiding in the doorway of one of the neighbouring buildings for the last hour, waiting for Silvia and Ruben to leave.

Once the car disappeared, Florinda rushed upstairs. She stood by the window for ten minutes to make sure that the couple would not return. Then she walked into her bedroom and changed her clothes. She picked up her passport and the aeroplane ticket she had bought that afternoon, and slipped them into a bag she had stolen the day before. She added the old photograph from the shelf and a plain cotton dress from her closet. Nothing else. A new life was waiting for her in Paris. She would not lack for anything there, and her success tonight depended on moving fast.

She scribbled a mis-spelled note on a piece of paper: 'Silvia, *we cant liv together. I am going.*' She stared at it for a moment, decided it could not be improved, and then left it on the sitting room table.

She walked around the rooms for a last time. Perhaps she had been happy here, but she was not sure. She picked up her bag and left the apartment without looking back.

The noise in Avenida Rio Branco could be heard from half a mile away. The parade of the *Escolas do Samba* was now in full progress, and a million people cheered on their favourites.

For months, the poor people of Rio had gathered at their local *Escola do Samba*, impromptu social clubs where the miseries of everyday life would fade with the elaborate preparations for the Carnival parade. Routines for hundreds of dancers had to be rehearsed, songs written, costumes made. Now it was parade day, and tens of thousands of people descended on Avenida Rio Branco dressed as Versailles courtiers, mandarins, Thousand-and-one night princes, birds of paradise. Miles of satin and velvet had been turned into crinoline skirts and coronation robes, tons of sequins and rhinestones stitched into intricate patterns, mountains of feathers shaped into towering headdresses, all paid for from their miserable earnings. Only by scrimping and saving from the day Carnival is over would it be possible to pay for next year's costume and next year's dream.

The parade had been going on for hours. Several *escolas* had already appeared, filling the wide road with thousands of people. Each *escola* developed a theme set by the huge float at the front, a fantastic construction as dazzling as the costumes of the dancers and the beautiful girls on it. Then came standard bearers, waves of dancing children and a crowd of older women in the traditional white costume of Bahia.

More floats went by, and then the *bateria*, the enormous percussion orchestra drowning the city with the sound of its own *samba*. People danced on the road, in the stalls and on the balconies of the tall buildings along the avenue, singing and laughing, sweating in the heat or soaked by the torrential rains that sooner or later burst upon the city completely unnoticed, just another permutation in an ever-changing kaleidoscope.

Portela, Silvia's favourite *escola*, went past at last. Float after float in the shape of gold gingerbread ships, their silver sails and banners floating in the breeze, the Louis XV costumes of the crew echoed by the dancers crowding the avenue. As yet another wave of black women dressed as Madame de Pompadour in silver satin and blue ostrich feathers went past, it was clear to Silvia that the magnificence of this spectacle had outdone all the other *escolas*. Every year she expected them to win, but this time she was sure they would. Her shouting and dancing became frenetic, and she turned towards Ruben.

'Look, Ruben, aren't they beautiful? I love them!' She saw that Ruben was looking at his watch, a worried look on his face.

'I think we ought to go to the ball,' Ruben said, fretting.

'Why?' Silvia asked. 'It's only two o'clock. Nothing happens until three.'

'I'd rather go now,' said Ruben, taking Silvia's arm and leading her away from the front row.

They left and walked in silence for a few minutes until they came to the car.

'Why are you so worried?' Silvia asked once she had settled in the back seat, lying on it as if on a bed. She did not want to take off her headdress, and it was impossible to sit in the front while wearing it.

'I hired a security guard to keep watch on the office because of the broken safe, but I suddenly thought that the guy would probably be dancing and screwing somewhere else instead of doing his job. I just want to make sure he's there.'

'You worry too much,' Silvia said, and she began to whistle Portela's *samba de enrêdo*, the theme song of their parade.

Florinda stopped just before she reached the forecourt of the building. She could hear the sound of *samba* in the distance. She stayed still for a while, until she was certain that she was alone. Then she ran quickly across the open area outside the building, and walked along the narrow passageway at the side, her back to the wall, her eyes nervously darting in all directions. She found the small window she had unlocked that morning, and opened it. Her hands on the window sill, she pushed herself up until her head and shoulders were through. She dropped her bag on the floor inside, and inch by inch slid her body through the opening. She was glad that she had decided to wear trousers, otherwise it would have been impossible to manoeuvre her legs through the narrow opening. Supporting the whole of her weight on her arms, she brought her legs down, her feet against the wall, until they rested on the edges of the toilet seat. Sighing with relief, she stood up on the tiled floor.

She moved into the lobby next to the showroom. All the lights were out, but her eyes were now used to the dark. She scanned the empty room through the half-open door before moving on. There was no sound. Nonetheless, she tiptoed across the showroom. The sound of *samba* from distant streets was too faint to drown out the pounding of her own heart. She was terrified, but there was no stopping now; tomorrow she would be on her way to Paris.

She reached the door to Ruben's office, and tried the handle. It was open. She thought she heard the faint sound of a bell ringing somewhere, and waited for a second. Silence. She closed the door and crept over to the desk.

Florinda turned the desk lamp on. The soft light shone on the safe at the corner, under the picture of the *Nossa Senhora da Conceição*, the Holy Mother. Florinda quickly crossed herself before kneeling in front of the safe. She pulled the handle next to the combination lock, but the door did not move. She felt panic in her throat, but then the handle yielded to the weight of her hand. She opened the door.

There were two shelves inside, full of documents and files. On the first shelf, resting on top of the binders, she saw a bulging brown envelope. As she pulled it out, the revolver balanced on top of it fell off the shelf. Florinda tore the envelope open, and saw the three wads of hundred-dollar bills bound together by paper bands. It was more money than she had ever seen. She was about to take it out of the safe when the door opened, and the beam of a flashlight fell on her.

The security guard was still suffering the after-effects of the bottle of rum he had downed earlier on. He turned on the light and his hand went immediately to the gun on his belt, but not as fast as Florinda's reached for the revolver. The sound of the shot was deafening, but the guard did not hear it. The bullet went through his brain, killing him instantly. Florinda watched in shock as he collapsed to the floor, blood spurting out of a small hole in his forehead.

As Ruben parked the car in the yard outside, he and Silvia heard the shot. They ran into the building, saw the light coming through the open door of his office, and rushed in. The horror of the scene froze them: the dead man on the floor and Florinda next to the open safe, a vacant look in her eyes, the gun in her hand pointing straight at them.

'What have you done!' Silvia shrieked as she walked towards her sister.

'Don't move, or I'll shoot you!' Florinda screamed.

Silvia leapt forward and tried to grab the gun while Ruben attempted to restrain Florinda. Silvia gripped the handle and felt her finger slip over the trigger, Florinda's hand on top of hers, forcing her finger backwards. Their frantic struggle came to a sudden halt when the blast of the gun deafened them.

They recoiled away from each other, their eyes fixed on Ruben. He opened his mouth, but his lips froze before he could utter a sound. He collapsed to the floor. Blood squirted over Silvia's gloved hand and slowly spread over his chest, soaking his shirt. Silvia let go of the gun, and fell to her knees by Ruben's side. She leaned down to kiss him for the last time.

Her world had been shattered. A moment ago, she had two protectors to keep the world at bay, and she had loved both of them. Now one was dead, and the other had betrayed her.

She was filled with sudden rage. Ruben had died because of Florinda. It was her greed, her envy, that had been the cause of both his death and her misery. Silvia's savage scream echoed in the empty building as she hurled herself towards her sister.

Florinda did not hesitate. Someone may have heard the shots, and the police could be on their way. Survival was her only priority now. As Silvia drew her hand back to slap her face, Florinda picked up the heavy glass paper weight from the desk and brought it crashing down on Silvia's skull with all her strength. Stunned by the blow, Silvia stumbled, and Florinda struck again and again, until her sister fell to the ground, her feathers spread around her as if she was a dead white bird.

Then Florinda ran. She did not stop running until she joined the Carnival throng in Avenida Presidente Vargas, far away from the little room where three bodies lay together on the floor.

119

9

PARIS
April 1967

Silvia came out of the Metro at the Place de la Porte d'Auteuil. She stopped at the ornate iron archway at the top of the stairs, and looked about in all directions. It was not really necessary. She was no longer in Brazil and the nightmare was behind her, but the habit remained.

The streets were deserted. It was too late at night for the respectable *bourgeoisie* of the *Seizième* district to be anywhere but in bed; only Silvia and her kind walked in the Bois de Boulogne after midnight. She crossed the square and began to amble down the Avenue into the Bois, towards the Allée de la Reine Marguerite. After three months, it had become a familiar routine.

Silvia had fled Rio over a year ago, leaving behind the horror of that Carnival night. She had regained consciousness the following morning, and left the room without looking back. Her only thoughts were to get away from the bodies and the memories, and to remove any evidence of her presence there. If she were found, the police would charge her with Ruben's murder. She had to leave Rio at once, so she had picked up Florinda's bag and run.

After a few minutes she stopped, suddenly realizing she had no money, and that she was still wearing her costume. She did not dare to go back to the showroom to take some money from Ruben's wallet; the police might have arrived. She had to go to the apartment, even at the risk of finding Florinda there. Not only did she need clothes, but she had to get her bag, with her wallet and her identity card.

As Silvia approached the apartment building she saw the smoke coming out of the windows and the fire engine outside, surrounded by a crowd of onlookers. Florinda had obviously been as keen as she was to remove all traces of their presence. She fled before anyone noticed her.

Only then did she check Florinda's bag, and find the dress inside. She put it on, dropping her blood-stained gloves and her feather headdress into the gutter. She fumbled again, and discovered Florinda's passport and the ticket to Paris in her name. She decided to keep them. The passport was specially valuable. She closely resembled Florinda, and someone was bound to ask for her papers sooner or later.

Clutching the bag in her hand, she walked all the way to the Northern part of the city, until she stopped at a roundabout. She did not have to wait long for a lorry driver to offer her a ride to São Paulo. What she had to do to humour him once they were away from Rio was yet another memory she had erased from her mind.

In São Paulo, it soon became clear to Silvia that there was only one way she could earn a living: Florinda's way. She could not apply for a proper job. She had no work experience, no references, and she did not dare to produce Florinda's passport as proof of identity.

After two nights, she had made enough money for the deposit required on a room in one of the many seedy hotels to which her clients took her. The owner had seemed friendlier than the rest, and had made it clear that no questions would be asked as long as the rent was paid.

It was not long before Silvia realized that her period was late again. She had suspected as much in Rio, but now she was sure. She was carrying Ruben's baby. She tried not to think about it. She could not have the baby. It would mean going back to the *favela*. When they had moved to the apartment in Rio, she had promised herself that she would never go back there, no matter what. No, anything but that. She confided in one of the girls she met regularly on her rounds, who gave her the address of a reliable woman she knew.

The abortion did not take much time, but the woman warned her that there could be some bleeding afterwards. When she eventually reached her room it took four towels to soak up the haemorrhage. The owner of the hotel called a friendly doctor who attended to the ravages of the old woman's knitting needle in the best way he could, gave Silvia a massive supply of antibiotics, and informed her

121

that he would come by the following day to see her. She would pull through, he said, but she would never be able to have children. Silvia cried the whole night, thinking about Ruben and what her future might have been.

The next day she began to believe that the news was a relief in some ways. She gradually convinced herself that she did not want children anyway. It also helped her to overcome her guilt about Ruben's death. She knew that it had been Florinda's fault, but it had been Silvia's hand, forced by her sister, that had pulled the trigger. She saw her sterility as a punishment for her action.

Now Silvia lived in perpetual fear of being caught by the police. Ruben had always been very careful about keeping her away from friends and relations, but this did not mean that the police would not be able to trace the connection between them. On the other hand, Ruben's murder might well be seen as just one of many during Carnival, another case of a burglar being disturbed at work. But she could not be sure, and the sight of any policeman made her shiver.

After a week Silvia was able to leave her bed. Most of her savings went into buying a new mattress to placate the owner of the hotel. But now her luck changed; her very first customer told her that she was too good-looking to be hanging around in the streets. He suggested that she apply for a job as hostess in the 'Papillon', a bar at the seamier end of town.

She soon had a string of regular clients, and the bar's owner only took a reasonable cut from her earnings, leaving her enough to live on. She even managed to save some money. But one evening she was told that Tuco, the owner, wanted to see her.

'The police were here today,' Tuco said point-blank. 'They were looking for a girl in connection with some murder in Rio. Does it mean anything to you?' She just managed to keep an impassive expression on her face.

'No,' she replied. 'Why should it?' She took a cigarette from her bag and lit it, her eyes shifting away from his.

'Because they gave me a description of the girl. It could be you. I run an establishment for a respectable clientele, most of them married men who don't want any trouble.

I told the police I hadn't seen anyone who looked like that, but if you're still here tomorrow my memory will start coming back . . .'

She walked out of the dingy office and left the bar straight away, fear gripping her stomach. She had been using a false name, but time was running out.

One of the girls at the bar had worked for a while in Paris, and she had told Silvia that it was easy to make a living there, at a park called the Buadeboolon or something like that. She had earned good money for nearly a year, until she was caught by the police and thrown out as an illegal immigrant. Silvia mentioned that she spoke some French, and the girl insisted that she give Paris a try. She even wrote down the address of the hotel where she had stayed, and the name of the best road in the park to pick up customers.

Silvia had kept the addresses. She also had the money she had saved, the plane ticket, and Florinda's passport. Now *she* would go to Paris, after all. It was a way out. But it was not quite as simple as going to the airport and taking the next flight. Passport control in Brazil was a risk she could not afford.

She went to the bus station and took a coach to Chuy. Two days later, she arrived at the small town on the border with Uruguay. She left the town on foot at midnight, clutching a map of the region she had bought at the local petrol station. She walked all night along country roads, until she was well into Uruguay.

It had been both exhausting and terrifying to cross open country at night, the only light coming from the stars of the Milky Way, a glowing ribbon across the dark sky. There were noises everywhere; some from creatures she could identify, like crickets and owls. There were many others she could not recognize, and she began to imagine what they might be. Soon every noise resembled the sliding of snakes across her path. Even more sinister was the silence, when the empty road across the immense countryside stretched ahead towards the blackness.

She reached La Coronilla early in the morning, and slept on the bus to Montevideo. Once there, she spent some of her treasured savings on two mini-dresses, a pair of white boots, a small suitcase and a complete beauty treatment at a hairdresser's. She then went to the Air France office, and presented Florinda's ticket. The girl at the counter told her it was valid for just another two weeks, and Silvia booked herself onto the Paris flight that evening, paying extra for the Montevideo—Rio leg. She arrived in Paris the following day, with fifty dollars and a desperate will to survive. She told the immigration officer that she was on holiday. As he stamped her passport Silvia suddenly realized that, from now on, her name would have to be Florinda.

The thought filled her with revulsion at first, but as she began her work, she was glad of the disguise. It gave her a fragile shield against the reality that she was forced to earn her living through men. Three months had passed, and now at last she knew that it was going to work.

Her thoughts were interrupted by the lights of a car driving towards her. The car was cruising very slowly. Silvia stopped and took off her raincoat. She was wearing nothing but stockings, a suspender belt, and a thin chain around her slim waist. She stood in the light, displaying her breasts to the driver, the length of her exquisite legs emphasized by her very high heels. But the driver didn't stop and she let out a stream of her best French insults, her breath turning into vapour in the cool April air. She caught a glimpse of the man at the wheel. He was heavily made up, with dyed blond hair and a long white scarf around his neck. He needs one of the studs at the Avenue de Saint-Cloud, Silvia thought, quickly pulling her coat back on. She shrugged; there was trade for everyone in the Bois at night. She would be luckier next time, but she decided to try another spot. She turned into an alley where she came across an extraordinary sight.

Pregnant women were standing under the lights, their coats open to display their bulging bellies and their swollen breasts. Two or three cars were parked next to various lights along the road; trade was obviously good. Some men have really sick taste, Silvia thought. While she surveyed the scene one of the girls left the kerb, and began to walk a few yards ahead of her. A car stopped by her side. The girl kept on walking, and the car followed her, the driver addressing her through his half-open window.

'I'm going home now, leave me alone,' she said.

The man got out of the car and grabbed her arm. The girl screamed, and he punched her in the face. She stumbled, but he hauled her up and twisted her arm behind her back, pushing her towards his car while she moaned, calling faintly for help. Her lip was bleeding badly where he had broken it.

Silvia found a discarded bottle on the roadside, and did not hesitate. She picked it up and rushed towards the struggling couple. The man never saw her. He heard the tip-tap of approaching high heels, and then a flash of light exploded inside his skull. He collapsed on the road. Silvia helped the pregnant girl regain her balance and guided her away, an arm around her shoulders. They left the Bois, and Silvia stopped a taxi at Boulevard Lannes.

'Where do you live?' Silvia asked. 'I'll take you home.'

'Near Pigalle,' the girl replied.

'So do I,' Silvia smiled.

The girl took a second look at Silvia and realized they were both in the game.

'I thought you wouldn't live around here.' The girl gave the address to the driver.

The incident created a momentary bond of companionship between them, something missing in Silvia's life for too long, and she suddenly hoped they would become friends.

'I'm Silvia,' she said, using her real name for the first time.

'I'm Arianne,' the girl replied, and smiled wanly. 'Thank you for helping me. You know what some of these shits can be like.'

'You shouldn't be working if you are – like that,' Silvia commented.

Arianne laughed.

'You get a lot of money when you are pregnant, it's a speciality.' She paused for a moment. 'But you are different too. Where are you from? You're much too good-looking to be working the Bois. You should try the Avenue Foch.'

'I'm from Brazil. I've been in Paris for only three months.' Silvia looked at Arianne's broad face. Her features were coarse but her eyes were kind, and there was warmth in her smile. She liked her.

Arianne laughed. 'Yes, I've heard that you Brazilians are very popular, but I'm not jealous. I have my clients, and you have yours.' She tapped her belly. 'We may be in competition when I've had the baby, though,' she said with a mischievous smile.

'When is the baby due?'

'In June, three months from now. I hope I don't get too big, so that I will be able to work until the date. You can charge a lot during the last two months.'

'Do you have to?' Silvia asked. She felt sorry for the girl and disgusted at the same time. She would never have children, and part of her longed for a baby. In spite of herself, she felt envious of Arianne, and disturbed at the risk she was taking.

'I have to support my mother, and I won't be able to work for a while after the baby is born. The rent doesn't stop when you have a baby, love,' Arianne explained, her hands on her belly. She had taken off her shoes, and was flexing her swollen toes. 'We are nearly there, thank God,' she said, struggling to control her dry retching.

Silvia noticed that Arianne's face had lost colour as she spoke. The taxi pulled up outside a miserable-looking building facing the railway depot. Arianne pulled a fifty-franc note from her pocket, and gave it to the driver.

'Take my friend to her home, and give her the change.' She stumbled out of the car, and held on to a lamp post. She was suddenly very sick.

Silvia rushed to her. As soon as she was out of the car, the driver slammed the door and drove away at high speed.

'Go to hell, whores!' he shouted through his open window.

'Anyone with a prick is a shit,' muttered Arianne.

'Not always,' replied Silvia. 'You may have a boy. Come on, I'll help you to the door.'

She pressed the bell, and pushed the door open. She found the light switch in the hallway. The naked bulb threw harsh light on the dirty cream paint flaking off the walls. The place reeked of ammonia, and urine stains were visible on the grey tiled floor.

'How far up do you live?' Silvia asked, holding Arianne by the arm as they began to climb the rickety stairs.

'The top floor, of course. And the lights are gone from the second floor up.'

After a few minutes, they reached a door at the top of the stairs. Arianne opened it, and turned on the light. The only furniture in the room was a table, three pine chairs and a mattress on the bare floor, near the wall. A curtain track ran across the ceiling. Arianne quietly closed the door to an adjacent room.

'I have some *pastis* here. I can't offer you anything else. The kitchen is in my mother's room, and she can't go back to sleep if she wakes up in the middle of the night,' Arianne said.

'I don't want anything. I'll go now,' Silvia replied.

'You can't go. It's nearly four o'clock, and you're not going to get a taxi around here.' She glanced at Silvia's naked body under the raincoat. 'Anyway, the police are going to ask you what's happened to your dress. They look the other way in the Bois, but not here. My mother's bed is wide enough for two. I'll sleep with her, and you can sleep in my bed.'

After living on her own for more than a year, the offer delighted Silvia, and she readily accepted it.

'I'm beginning to feel better now,' Arianne said. 'Let's have some *pastis*.' They sat down at the table. Arianne poured the Ricard into two glasses, and added some water. She handed a glass with the cloudy mixture to Silvia.

'*Santé*,' Arianne said, taking a large gulp from her glass. Silvia sipped her drink, and grimaced. The taste was not unpleasant, but she was not used to it.

'Don't make faces, it tastes better than most clients!' Arianne teased. 'Now tell me about yourself.'

Silvia gave her a highly edited version of the last three years of her life. She explained that her mother had died, and she had moved away. She went into more detail about her years in the *favela* and the great sadness of her mother's death.

Arianne then told her about her childhood in the country. Her father had died during the war, and her mother had never recovered from the blow.

'The *boches* did it, dirty pigs. He was a good man, and they shot him in front of my mother. I was a few months old. She was like a zombie for years. She had to leave the farm after a while, and we came to Paris. She thought it was going to be easier . . .' Arianne laughed bitterly.

'*Merde*, it's nearly five o'clock, and I wanted to go to bed early,' she said. 'Let's hit the sack. The toilet is out there, on the landing. Goodnight.' Silvia went out to the lavatory. It was filthy, but no more so than the one at her hotel. She returned to the room and found a long T-shirt on the makeshift bed, left there for her by Arianne. She nearly cried at the idea of someone looking after her, concerned about her well-being. She got into bed and was instantly asleep.

She woke the following morning to the smell of fresh coffee and warm bread. She could hear the noise of crockery as the table was being set on the other side of the curtain. She pulled on her coat, and drew the curtain open.

'Ah, there you are!' Arianne greeted her. 'You had a good sleep, I hope. Nana has just been downstairs, and we've got fresh bread. Breakfast will be ready in a minute.'

When Silvia came back from the bathroom, there was a middle-aged women in the room. She was frail, and at first glance seemed older than Silvia would have guessed Arianne's mother to be. Her almost white hair was pulled into a bun, and she was dressed entirely in black.

'Silvia, this is my mother. You can call her Nana, that's what she likes to be called.'

'*Bonjour*, Nana.' Silvia felt ill at ease. There was something about Nana that reminded Silvia of her own mother. She was the first person Silvia had met outside her trade to whom it was clear that she was a whore, and she was embarrassed by the old woman's understanding look.

'*Bonjour*,' Nana greeted in return as they sat down to breakfast. Arianne's chit-chat bridged the awkwardness between the three people, and by the end of breakfast Silvia felt more relaxed.

'I'll deal with the dishes, and then we must do some shopping – I hope you will stay for lunch with us. You pay for your share,' Arianne said as she cleared the table.

Silvia was delighted. At last she had made a friend. 'I'll buy the food,' she offered. 'I'll cook you *vatapa*, it's my favourite Brazilian dish. I think you'll like it.'

'You cook,' Arianne countered, 'but we split the cost.' She was also delighted. Silvia was exactly what she had been looking for: someone with her heart in the right place, who would help and, if necessary, deal with whatever problems had to be faced. It was not easy to find someone like that in the Bois.

When Arianne and her mother had first moved to Paris, and things did not work out the way she had expected, Nana had lost her will, unable to face the world. Arianne had been forced to earn a living for both of them. There was only one way in which a girl of fourteen could make enough money to keep two people in Paris. Her mother had numbly accepted her choice, or at least that was what Arianne had assumed, because nothing had ever been said.

Her pregnancy came as a surprise, and Arianne thought briefly about having an abortion, but as soon as Nana discovered her condition it became impossible. For the first time, Arianne saw a glimmer of hope in her mother's eyes.

Nevertheless, she also recognized the problems. Life had been difficult enough with one dependant. It would be much harder with two: the burden had to be shared. A man was the obvious choice, but Arianne could not face it. Men were her work, not something she wanted to take home. Now Silvia had unexpectedly come into her life, and things would be easier.

While they did the shopping at the local market, Arianne asked Silvia if she would like to move into a bigger place with them. It would cost her less than the hotel, and she would only have to pay her share of the expenses. Silvia agreed immediately.

The Brazilian lunch was a great success. In the afternoon, Silvia brought her few possessions to the apartment. The girls went together to the Bois that night. As time went on, they were both certain that the arrangement was a good one.

Arianne found a bigger apartment almost immediately, not far from where they lived. It had four rooms, enabling each of them to have a bedroom. Silvia tried to use the bathroom on the ground floor the day after they moved in, but the door did not lock, and the resident drunk burst in as soon as she had taken off her clothes. She managed to push him out and jam the door with a chair, only to discover that there was no hot water. She remembered the bathroom in her Rio apartment with nostalgia; now she had to make do with a quick wash in the kitchen sink, and a visit to the Municipal Baths as often as she could manage it. But she enjoyed the two women's company, and she longed for the baby to be born. At last she was beginning to find her stride again.

Florinda entered the darkened bedroom on tiptoe, and waited by the door for a moment until she confirmed that she had not disturbed the sleeping couple. She was still wearing her maid's uniform, just in case she came across somebody on her way to the master suite, but she was wearing her own clothes underneath, ready for her flight to Rio.

She walked swiftly to the dressing table. As she expected, her employer had not put her jewellery away in the safe. Florinda, the newest member of the staff, had been in the house for nearly five months already and had managed to impress her employers soon after her arrival by engineering the disappearance of a valuable gold bracelet during the night, which she then returned the following morning, claiming to have found it while plumping up the cushions of a sofa. No, there was no reason for the lady of the house to bother to open the safe again after a long dinner party. Her staff was reliable, the burglar alarm was on, and three Alsatians roamed the grounds of her villa in one of São Paulo's richest neighbourhoods. Florinda put the jewels in

130

her pocket, picked up the master's key ring from the top of the chest of drawers, took one last contemptuous look at the sleeping rich pigs, and walked out of the bedroom.

She went to the entrance hall to turn off the burglar alarm before returning to the staff wing. She paused for a moment to make sure that the rest of the staff was asleep, then went to the kitchen and tore off her maid's uniform, dropping it on the floor. She suddenly felt an urgent need to go to the lavatory.

She squatted over her crumpled uniform and relieved herself, wiping her arse with the Venetian lace tablecloth she had removed from the dining room table after the party. It would be a nice parting gift for her mistress.

Picking up the case she had left by the kitchen door, she walked out of the house. The dogs would be no problem: they knew her. She crossed the garden, opened the side gate, and looked up and down the empty street. Not a soul in sight.

Santos would be waiting for her in the car, two blocks away. By the time the bastards woke up and called the police they would be in Rio de Janeiro. She was used to the routine by now. Two or three weeks of sun and fun on the beaches with Santos, then another 'honest' domestic job in Rio for a few months, at which she would behave impeccably. Her mother would then become suddenly ill, and she would have to leave. The glowing references from her Rio employers would get her a job with some really rich pigs in another town, she would clean them out, Santos would fence the stuff in Rio, and the cycle would start again.

As always after a successful job, Florinda found her thoughts drifting to her sister and that night at Ruben's office. She hated Silvia. It was because of her that Florinda had been forced to become a thief, to support them both when their mother had died. It was all her sister's fault, otherwise Florinda would have been a nice girl, married to a rich man, living like any of these rich women she was now forced to wait on. Yes, her sister had a lot to answer for.

Florinda's only consolation was knowing that, without

her, her sister had no hope of getting anywhere. She was probably living in a hell-hole somewhere. Perhaps she was dead – she ought to be dead, it would be fair punishment for ruining Florinda's chances.

She saw Santos' car parked ahead and ran towards it. As they pulled out, she put her sister out of her mind. She had better things to think about: the beach tomorrow, then the evening celebration of yet another success. Santos would probably get drunk and beat her up before screwing her, but Florinda didn't mind. She liked it, in fact. She was proud that he was a real man, and she considered herself a lucky girl to have found him.

10

Silvia scanned the *Allée* in both directions; she could see no cars. It was a bad night; the spring showers and the blustery wind made it unpleasant to be outside, and the clients did not like coming to the Bois in bad weather. She had thought of staying at home, but Arianne had not been able to work lately, and money was badly needed. The baby was due in two weeks.

Her thoughts were interrupted by the roll of thunder. Shit, it was going to rain again. She had just decided to go home when she saw the lights of an approaching car. She stood by the kerb, her arms akimbo, her raincoat open. Her black vinyl corset pushed up her breasts, and emphasized her narrow waist. The car stopped by her side, and the window rolled down.

She had seen many men's faces, but this one was unusually unpleasant. He was not bad looking, but his eyes were cold, and there was something cruel about the thin lips. He wore a black silk polo shirt, and he drove an expensive car. She had seen worse, she decided.

He looked at her appreciatively, ignoring the other whore who had suddenly appeared from behind a bush.

'Do you suck?' he asked.

'Yes,' she answered, glad that he wasted no time in embarrassed conversation. It had begun to rain hard, and she wanted to get into the car as soon as possible.

'How much will it cost me?'

'One hundred francs,' Silvia replied. The man will bargain if he has any sense, she thought.

'Get in,' he said, opening the door. She sat next to him and held out her hand, palm upward. He paid her, and then started driving towards the lake, making conversation about the weather and the unpleasantness of the night. At last they reached a lane into the wood and he stopped, parking the car out of sight from the road.

'Here,' he said. He reclined his seat until it was almost horizontal, and unzipped his trousers. 'Now do a nice job,' he muttered, lying back.

Silvia lowered her head onto his lap, closed her eyes, and started work. She let out the occasional moan and exaggerated sign of pleasure, thinking about the shopping she had to do in the morning. She became aware that his right hand was moving, as if looking for something between the front seats, and then she heard a 'click'. A second later, she felt the cold steel edge of a flick blade against her throat, while his left hand grabbed her hair, pushing her head down, until she almost choked.

'Do it right, bitch, or you'll regret it,' he said harshly, moving the blade down her neck, the sharp edge almost grazing her skin. He began to utter obscenities; Silvia was terrified but she soon realized that as the obscenities became grosser, his pressure on the knife lessened. She applied all her skill to make him come as fast as possible; he shuddered briefly, and his release was followed by a long grunt. She felt the salty taste in her mouth; normally she spat it out of the window, but she did not want to risk offending this weirdo, so she swallowed it.

'That was good,' he said, zipping up his trousers but still holding the knife. She faked an admiring look.

'You are better than most men I come across,' she murmured, as if overcome by the experience.

He held the knife up.

'You like a bit of excitement, don't you?' he said, his eyes glistening in the dark. 'I have some very exciting equipment at home. You should come and spend the night with me.'

Silvia thought fast. 'In five minutes, there'll be a police car waiting for me at the *Allée*.' She smiled coquettishly. 'You're not the only man who appreciates me, you know, and the *flics* don't like to be let down. They will start looking for me if I'm not there soon. Paulette, the girl you saw next to me, will tell them which car I was in. We girls remember that sort of thing.'

He looked at her thoughtfully. 'I'll drive you back. But I really would like to see you at my home . . . I can pay you good money.' Silvia didn't answer.

'You are foreign. Where are you from?' he asked abruptly.

'Why do you want to know?'

'Because if you have any problems with your papers, we could come to a deal. I can alter any document, that's how I make a living. We could have some fun, and then I can do whatever you need.' They had reached the *Allée*, and he stopped the car. He wrote something in his notebook, and gave the sheet of paper to Silvia.

'Here's my number. My name is Pierre. Call me if you need me.'

Silvia got out of the car without looking at him. She waited until the taillights had faded into the night, and only then walked off in the same direction. She crumpled the piece of paper in her hand and dropped it in the gutter, but immediately stooped down and picked it up. You never know, she thought.

Arianne and Silvia were having breakfast. Arianne was now two weeks overdue, and Nana had gone to do the daily shopping. It was the first time they had been on their own since Arianne had become house-bound.

'Which hospital will you have the baby in, in case I have to take you there?' Silvia asked, buttering a piece of *baguette*.

'You won't have to take me anywhere. I'm going to have the baby right here,' Arianne replied.

Silvia was surprised. 'Why?' she asked. 'It's safer if there are doctors around.'

'Balls,' Arianne replied, looking cross.

'It's not fair on the baby, you know,' Silvia said sharply.

'Mind your own business,' Arianne snapped, but then patted her friend's hand.

'I'm sorry, I'm a pain in the ass at the moment. I know you're worried, but there is a reason why I don't want to have my baby in the hospital. They'll start asking questions, and as soon as they find out that I am on my own, earning my living as a *putain*, they will take my baby away and give it up for adoption. People like

135

you and me live outside the fence, and we should stay outside. Once you go inside they'll kill you.'

Silvia was not so sure, but she preferred not to argue.

'Don't worry,' Arianne went on, 'Nana knows everything about these things, and she'll be in charge. I'll just scream and shout, and you two will have to get on with it.'

Arianne stood with difficulty and walked towards the kitchen, but she stopped suddenly, letting out a shout of pain. Water gushed down her legs, soaking her skirt and forming a pool on the floor. She rested one hand on the nearest chair, while she rubbed her lower back with the other hand.

'Here we go, *chérie*,' she said to Silvia, 'that was a nice big pain.'

Silvia rushed to Arianne and helped her to the bedroom, where she lay on the bed. Arianne turned on the radio.

'. . . *que c'est triste Venise* . . .' the mournful voice of Charles Aznavour filled the room.

'I'm going to be the only one moaning here today, *merde*,' she said. She switched stations, and rested her head on the pillow.

Silvia began talking about her clients, in an attempt to take Arianne's mind off the pain. Arianne listened for a while, but suddenly her face contorted into a grimace of pain.

'Another one,' she said. They heard Nana coming in, and Silvia rushed to meet her.

'Nana, thank God you are here. Arianne is in bed; her waters have broken.'

'I can see that,' Nana mumbled, looking at the puddle in the middle of the room. Silvia went into the kitchen, and came back with a bucket and a cloth. She mopped up while Nana left her shopping bag on the table and went to Arianne.

Once she had finished clearing up the mess, Silvia washed the breakfast things and then returned to the bedroom. Nana was sitting next to Arianne, holding her hand. Silvia sat at the end of the bed. Nana's face was serious, almost solemn. Silvia had never seen her with such a look of concentration; it was as if at last her life made sense.

The day passed slowly, or so it seemed to Silvia. It was nearly seven o'clock, and Arianne's contractions were now very frequent. Instinctively, she began to push and bend up her knees, but Nana told her to wait. Nana had piled up all the pillows and cushions in the apartment behind Arianne's back. She helped Arianne move forward, so that she could stand at the end of the bed and help with the delivery.

'I can feel it coming, Nana . . .' Arianne groaned, her brow and upper lip moist with sweat. Arianne squeezed Nana's hand. 'Nana, I feel as if the baby is pushing in my ass. Please, let me push,' she screamed, as her eyes filled with tears.

'I'm splitting, Nana, I can't stand it. Please let me, Nana, please!'

'It won't be long now, love, I can see the head. Push now! Push hard!' Nana said soothingly. Silvia moved on tiptoes behind Nana, eager to see. The crown of the baby's head was visible, the hair matted and wet. Slowly, very slowly, the head pushed out until the little face could be seen, eyes closed. Silvia felt a lump at her throat when she saw it, covered in a lard-like substance and streaked with blood.

Nana swiftly picked up some gauze from the little table she had set up by the bed, and wiped the eyes, nose and mouth. She then seemed to kiss the baby's mouth and nose, and Silvia realized that she was sucking them.

Once the head was out, one shoulder soon followed, then the other. Silvia watched as the tiny hands appeared, followed by the skinny torso. Nana lifted the baby's head and shoulders up, and Arianne was able to see it between her raised knees. Her face lit up, and she stretched her hands towards her new-born child. 'My baby . . . my baby . . .' she repeated again and again.

Nana held the baby up, tears streaming down her cheeks. 'It's a girl, my darling, an adorable little girl.' Silvia was also crying, gripped by the urge to protect a being both so helpless and so wonderful.

The little girl's face was crumpled, as if in anger. Nana held her upside down, and sucked the tiny mouth and nose again. The baby began to cry, and Silvia saw the skin tone change from dark blue to a healthy pink. Nana laid the baby on a folded towel on the bed, tied the cord in two places and cut it with the pair of scissors she had sterilized earlier. She quickly knotted the cord, then wrapped the baby in a towelling nappy. The little girl was crying loudly, and her skin was bright pink. With a smile, Nana presented her to Arianne.

'Here's your daughter,' she said, handing the small bundle to its mother.

Silvia stood next to Arianne, and looked at the baby gripping her mother's little finger.

'What will you call her?' she asked.

'Gloria,' Arianne replied assuredly. 'She's the most wonderful thing that ever happened to me.'

Arianne was washing Gloria's nappies when she suddenly raised her eyes and looked out of the window.

'It's a beautiful night. Why don't we go out for a beer before work?' she asked Silvia. 'I've been stuck here for three weeks, and I want to celebrate my last moments of freedom.'

Silvia dropped the copy of the gossip magazine she was reading. She had become addicted to it because it gave her an insight into a fairy-tale world of aristocrats and castles.

'I'll be ready in a minute,' she said.

The night before, Arianne had announced that she would return to work the next day. 'I can't afford to keep on doing nothing. I'll feed Gloria at midnight, and then we can go together to the Bois. I'm sure you'll hear her, Nana. Give her sugared water if she cries, but I don't think she'll wake up. She sleeps like a log.'

'Don't worry, I know what to do about babies. It's all I really know,' Nana had said.

Now Silvia noticed that Arianne had made herself up with particular care for her first night back at work. 'Some guy is going to be very lucky tonight,' she said admiringly. 'You are looking very good.'

'I don't give a shit about the guys, but I wanted to look

nice. I've looked like a monkey for the last two months.'

As they left the building, Arianne glanced at the sky.

'We are lucky with the weather,' she said. 'It's very warm. Let's walk to Pigalle and have our beer there.'

They walked along Boulevard Barbes, and stopped briefly at a kiosk to glance at the covers of the women's magazines, all about the recent fashion shows.

'That's lovely,' Arianne said, pointing at a blue satin evening coat on the cover of a magazine. The bold caption across the picture read 'Balenciaga – Autumn– Winter 68'.

'Imagine thinking about winter clothes now, those people are crazy. Come on, let's go.' Arianne took Silvia by the arm, and led her away.

They turned into Boulevard Rochechouart. As they approached the Place Pigalle the pavements became crowded, and they had to weave their way through a throng of people, mostly men, drawn by the local fleshpots.

'In a year's time, I'm going to be out of this business,' Arianne announced. 'It stinks. Look at them, they are like dogs dribbling at food.'

Silvia did not look. She had seen the scene too many times. She saw it every day and sometimes at night in her dreams. She also wanted out, and the thought of Pierre flashed through her mind. Maybe he could get her new papers, a chance of escape.

'What will you do?' she asked Arianne.

'I want to save as much money as possible, and then try to rent a small café by the sea, somewhere in the Bay of Biscay. I've never been there, but that's where Nana grew up, and I know she would like to go back. Gloria would be happy in a place like that, playing on the beach and making sand castles. You could come with us.'

'I'd love to,' Silvia said. For a moment she imagined herself with the family, working happily together in a little café by the sea, but the improbability of the dream was horribly clear to her. Sooner or later she knew she would be thrown out of France. Even if Pierre were to get her new papers, she would have no guarantee that they would stand up to inspection.

Arianne pointed at the café across the boulevard.

'Let's cross the street. It's less crowded over there and we can sit outside.' As she stepped from the kerb, a man approached her from behind and pinched her bottom, grinning at his mates on the pavement.

Arianne turned around, rage on her face. 'You mother-fucker,' she screamed, looking at the self-satisfied grin on the man's face. She stepped back further into the street so she could kick him in the balls, but the black car with the dipped lights, driving too fast along the boulevard, didn't give her a chance. It sent her flying in the air like a rag doll. She hit the ground head first, hard against the granite kerb. Her neck was broken before she could even scream. Silvia rushed to her, and gathered Arianne's limp body in her arms. Tears rolled down her cheeks as she embraced the best friend she had ever had.

She cried first in shock and anguish, and then with rage at the stupidity of Arianne's being killed because of such a lout. Her anger overwhelmed her. She stood up, and started hitting the man, insulting him, screaming out her hatred. The crowd around them enjoyed the scene at first but then someone shouted, 'Call the police!'

Silvia heard the word 'police', and her heart froze in panic. 'People like you and me live outside the fence, and we should stay outside. If you go inside, they'll kill you,' Arianne had warned. The police would be there soon. They would take her to the station to make a statement, and they would ask for her papers. It would be just a matter of time before she ended up in a Brazilian jail.

There was no time to lose. Silvia stood up, wrenching herself away from the inert body. She was swamped by guilt: she was betraying the person who had helped her most but she had no choice. She pushed her way through the crowd, muttering 'I must get to a phone,' and rushed into the café at the corner. She walked rapidly across the café and out again into Rue des Martyrs. She ran as fast as she could along the Circus Medrano, until she reached Avenue Trudaine. She could hear the sirens in the distance, but as she looked over her shoulder she was relieved to see that nobody was following her.

As she relaxed, her grief took over. She walked on automatically, her face ravaged by sorrow and tears. Only when she reached home did she realize that she would have to break the terrible news to Nana. She thought of Gloria, left without a mother, now in the hands of a grandmother scared of the outside world. Silvia was the only one who could look after them, and as she climbed the stairs, she knew that these two helpless people were to be both her burden and her salvation.

Silvia had regained her composure by the time she reached the top. She let herself in, and went straight to Nana's room. She knocked at the door, and then walked in without waiting for an answer.

Nana was sitting on her narrow iron bed, still dressed. Her prayer book was open on her lap, and she was holding her rosary beads. She raised her eyes.

'You have bad news,' she said.

'Yes,' Silvia replied, gathering her strength. 'Something terrible has happened.' She told Nana about the accident, making an effort not to cry.

'I couldn't stay, Nana, but I assure you that Arianne was dead. You know that I have problems with my papers. If the police find me, they will throw me out of France, and I can't go back to my country.' Nana did not ask why; there was only one thing she wanted to find out.

'Do you know where they took her? I want to see her.' Nana stood up, ready to go. Silvia took a deep breath. She knew what she had to say, and she knew that it was the only solution for all of them. But it did not make saying it any easier.

'Nana, listen to me. Arianne was your daughter, and I know how you feel. You have lost the person you loved most in the world. But we have to think about the future. We have to think about Gloria. That's what Arianne would have wanted us to do.'

She paused for a moment. Nana seemed about to ask something, but then she lowered her eyes and Silvia continued.

'I know that you want to see Arianne, and you want to bury her. It's your right as her mother to grieve for her. But I don't know where they took her. The only way to find out is to call the police. At the moment, Arianne is simply an unidentified body; as soon as they know who she is, they will find you, and then they will find me.'

Silvia closed her eyes for a moment, and bit her lip. She couldn't stop now; she dug her nails into her palm, and went on, her eyes fixed on Nana's.

'Once I'm gone, there'll be no one to support you and little Gloria. It will be only a matter of time before you'll have to either give her up for adoption or worse. If you are prepared to leave things as they are, and Arianne is never identified, I swear to God that I'll take care of you and Gloria for as long as I live. I love Gloria as if she were my own daughter, and I'll look after you as if you were my own mother. I promise you that you'll never want for anything.'

She was about to continue, when she noticed the anguish in Nana's face.

'You are asking me to give up my daughter,' Nana said in a strangled voice. 'It's too much.'

'No, Nana,' Silvia replied. 'I wouldn't dare do that. I'm asking you to give up her body, for the sake of your granddaughter. And for your own sake as well as mine.'

Nana walked around the room in silence for a moment, and stood in front of an old photograph of her husband, her back to Silvia.

'I'll have to think about what you said. I'll talk to you tomorrow morning.' She didn't turn round. She just stood there, silently waiting for Silvia to leave the room. Nana already knew what her answer would be. She had lost Arianne. She would not lose her granddaughter.

As soon as she left Nana, Silvia rushed to Arianne's bedroom. She stopped for a moment to look at the sleeping baby. The sight brought tears to her eyes. She touched Gloria's cheek, then turned abruptly and began to look in the drawers of the battered old chest opposite the bed. She knew what she was looking for, and it took her just a moment to find it.

Silvia walked into her own room and slipped the dog-eared card inside one of the magazines. She emptied the contents of her bag on the bed and picked up a crumpled piece of paper and her keys. She listened outside Nana's door for a moment but could hear no noise. Gloria was safely asleep. In any case, she would be back home in a moment. The café was just fifty yards away and the phone call was going to be very brief.

The magnificent dome of the Panthéon, shining silver in the moonlight, was visible at the end of the Rue des Carmes, but Silvia did not notice. As she turned into Rue Lanneau, her thoughts were concentrated on her meeting with Pierre.

She had been to see him ten days ago, soon after her phone call on the night of Arianne's death. She had given him the card, and explained what she wanted. He inspected the dog-eared *carte d'identité*, then raised his eyes.

'I assume that this person is not going to complain about the change. Otherwise, I can do what you ask without any trouble, but it will cost more money than you can pay.'

'How do you know how much money I have?' Silvia had asked contemptuously.

'I don't, but my price will always be more money than you can afford.' He fondled her buttocks. 'Alternatively, you can pay me by spending the night here, and doing everything I ask you to do.' He stared at her, a repellent leer in his cold eyes.

Silvia realized that she had little choice.

'I accept your deal. I don't know what you have in mind, but make sure that I get home afterwards. I'll leave a note for my mother saying that I spent the night at this address.'

Pierre laughed.

'You are unnecessarily careful but I respect that. We professionals have to look after ourselves.' His face suddenly changed, a no-nonsense business look replacing his lascivious expression.

'I have to take some pictures of you,' he said, beginning to set up a white photographic backdrop. He disappeared behind a cupboard unit at the end of the room, and came back with a set of lights and a camera on a tripod. Once the lights and camera were in place, he sat Silvia on a stool. He checked the viewfinder, then shot several pictures of her in quick succession.

'Come back in ten days at the same time,' he said. 'Your card will be ready by then.'

Now she had come to pick up the key to her new life. After walking a few yards down Rue Lanneau, she came to his building. His studio was at the back of the courtyard.

Pierre opened the door with a smile and let her in. It was a warm evening, but she noticed that all the windows were closed, and the white canvas blinds were rolled down.

The room was very large, and fashionably simple. The walls and the tiled floor were white, and light wood beams spanned the ceiling. At the opposite end of the room, a huge *futon* rested against a white curtain covering the wall from end to end. Pierre led Silvia to the table and offered her a seat. He went to the kitchen, and came back with a bottle of wine and two glasses.

'I'm very pleased with the results of my work, and I am sure that you will be too. Let's celebrate.'

'I don't want anything,' Silvia said, 'except for my papers.'

Pierre's eyes hardened. 'Don't make it more difficult than it needs to be. Have some wine, and at least pretend to enjoy yourself. I'm sure you can do that very well.'

He poured the wine, then picked up an envelope from the table. He opened it, and handed an identity card to Silvia.

Her heart jumped. It was her face on the photograph, the stamp over it as good as in any other French *carte d'identité*. She read the name, so familiar and yet so odd juxtaposed with her own face. She would have to get used to it.

Pierre raised his glass.

'*Santé*, Arianne Delors,' he toasted her, and took a sip of his wine. Silvia left her glass untouched.

'There's only one problem,' Pierre said. 'How are you

going to explain your accent? Someone born in Arlanc wouldn't speak that way. I thought of changing the birth-place to Argel or Casablanca, but you would have trouble, sooner or later, if you have to produce the card together with your birth certificate. You'd better think of some explanation.'

'I already have,' Silvia replied. 'My parents took me to Brazil when I was little, and I grew up there. They died in an accident, and I only learned French when I came back here, not long ago.'

'Not bad,' Pierre said admiringly. He took her hand and led her to the other end of the room, towards the bed.

'We've done enough talking. You stand here, and take your clothes off. *Very* slowly. We have plenty of time.' He lay on the bed, his arms behind his head. She did as she was told, thinking only about the following morning, and her life from then on.

At last, she was naked. Pierre stared at her and grinned, then stood up and pulled the curtain cord. The curtain behind him opened, revealing old stone masonry. A collection of whips was neatly lined up on a purpose-built rack.

'Now we are going to have a really good time,' he said huskily, unbuttoning his shirt.

It was mid-September, and autumn was already in the air. Soon the leaves on the huge plane trees lining the avenue would begin to drop.

Silvia looked forward to the change of season. She wanted to plan for the future. A different season underlined the passage of time. What had happened in the spring was becoming the past.

Silvia had had no trouble adapting to a completely new set of circumstances. In no time at all she had convinced herself that her name was Arianne, and that she had a small daughter called Gloria. In Silvia's mind, they were now facts beyond dispute.

She just wished that Nana had some of her strength. Silvia had explained to her that she would be able to pass herself off as a French citizen only by saying that she had

145

been brought up in Brazil. If Nana pretended to be her mother, sooner or later her lack of knowledge about that country would reveal the lie; she would never be free to admit that she was Gloria's grandmother. Silvia had also insisted that they move out of the apartment immediately, to a place she had found at the other end of Paris where nobody knew them.

Nana had accepted the arrangement and its conditions, but it was obvious that she had not come to terms with it. She had given up calling her 'Silvia', and remained impassive when she introduced herself as Arianne. Nana never called her by that name. She would either address her as 'child' or nothing at all. Silvia found the habit annoying, but she preferred not to raise the issue. She hoped that in time it would go away.

Money was the priority now. Living in squalor had been the nightmare of her own childhood, and she would not tolerate it for her daughter. The day after Pierre gave her the new papers, she rushed downstairs to buy *Le Figaro*, and eagerly began to search through the employment ads. She was prepared to do anything: clean houses, be a wait-ress, any job that would take her out of the Bois would do. But she came up against the same word again and again: 'references'. That night she was back in the Bois, as usual.

She found comfort in the thought that, even there, she now had alternatives. Until then the Bois had been her only option, a place where outcasts like her knew the police would leave them alone. But she was no longer an outcast, she was a French citizen. Arianne had mentioned the Avenue Foch. Maybe she should give it a try. She needed much better clothes for that, and they cost money. She would have to work extra hours.

Her thoughts were interrupted by the lights of a car approaching her. She moved over to the kerb and stood there, her legs slightly apart, her body visible through the wide mesh of her crochet mini-dress. The car looked expensive, and she decided to up her rates.

The car stopped, and Silvia smiled invitingly, her eyes on the driver. Only then could she really see him: the man had dyed blond hair, eye make-up, gold bracelets and a white silk shawl draped around his shoulders. She could not understand why such a raving queen would bother with her.

The driver got out of the car and walked up to her. He was smiling broadly.

11

Cristobal Balenciaga was a master in his field. His whole life had been a search for perfection: the perfect fabric, the perfect cut, the perfect shape and, above all, the perfect woman to wear his masterpieces.

Now he was getting old and tired, and his world was coming to an end. His purpose had been to create dreams for swans. But suddenly there were no more swans, only common girls in mini-skirts and tight sweaters. They did not want the bore of endless fittings, an off-the-rack crotch-skimming shift in drip-dry polyester was all they needed. An air of death hung over his gilded salons, and he sensed that he was now working on his last collections. One, maybe two further shows, no more.

Because he felt it was his last year at the *Maison*, Balenciaga was determined to make it the best ever, his farewell to a vocation he had followed with a religious belief. At last, he had polished his *cabine* to perfection. Twelve models, twelve goddesses, each of them reflecting an aspect of his vision.

The showing of his winter collection in June had been as frenetic and exhausting as usual, but he had begun working on the next one on the day after. As was his custom, he had locked himself in his inner sanctum with the model who most fired his inspiration. Only by draping the fabric on the chosen one could his vision become real. Once the concept had been perfected, the rest of the collection would follow, but only then.

That season, the essence of his vision was the model Ilona, an icy Hungarian beauty whose flight from behind the Iron Curtain had captured the public's imagination. They had worked together for nearly two weeks, day and night, until Ilona had insisted on a break and had left for a brief holiday on the Côte d'Azur. The framework of his dream was nearly complete, but more work was necessary. It would have to wait until his muse was back.

Disaster struck suddenly. Ilona's lover, an Italian industrialist, walked out on her after a row. It was too much for the poor girl. Her inert body was found by a maid the following morning, two empty bottles of sleeping pills by the side of the bed. As soon as Ilona's coffin had been lowered into her grave, the other mannequins had tried on her dresses, the pearls of Balenciaga's next collection. It was no good. None of the girls had Ilona's special magic, her presence, her cool arrogance.

It was early September now, and somewhere in the world there must be a woman like that. If the collection was to be ready on time, the Maestro had to find her before the end of the month.

Jacques Villette was fed up, really and truly fed up. He had been a make-up artist for many years, and he had done the couture shows for ten seasons. He had worked for Dior and Chanel. Both of them were exacting masters, but nothing compared to his experiences with Monsieur Balenciaga.

He had been called at short notice, after the usual make-up artist employed by the *Maison* had left in hysterics, exhausted by the Maestro's demands. Balenciaga was interviewing new models to replace Ilona, and wanted them made up to resemble her. Jacques had tried everything, used every trick, but nothing seemed to please the Maestro. Two of the girls were in tears by the end of the afternoon and one stormed out of the room, swearing loudly. Jacques was tempted to give up too.

'Maestro, we have tried everything on these girls. Perhaps if you were to describe the face to me, the vision that you have in mind, perhaps then I will understand.' Balenciaga expressed his thoughts in his usual laconic manner, and Jacques listened very carefully. Suddenly, something in the description struck a cord in Jacques's memory.

Jacques Villette never forgot a face. They were his business, his passion. He knew that somewhere, some time ago, he had seen a face which corresponded with

149

the vision of the great *couturier*. He sat at home, relaxing over a glass of whisky, and tried to remember where. After a while, he decided to think about something else, to take his mind off the problem. He needed some distraction, a bit of easy relaxation. He stood in front of the mirror and fluffed up his dyed blond hair, draped the white silk scarf over his shoulders, climbed into his car and drove towards the Bois de Boulogne.

It was as he steered towards the Avenue de Saint-Cloud and its collection of male studs, that he remembered. A few months ago, driving down the same route, he had seen a whore in the road, trying to interest him. She had been naked, or nearly naked, but she had seemed as elegant in her whorish underwear as most models were in evening dresses. Her body was unbelievably long and graceful, but there was none of the exhausted air common to mannequins about her.

Jacques Villette did not give a damn about women's bodies. Her face, though, was something else. He had not seen a face so perfect for a long, long time. For a moment Jacques had thought of stopping the car and asking her to his studio for a test session, but these whores were like alley cats. He drove away and soon forgot about the encounter.

But now he remembered. He knew that girl was what the Maestro was looking for. If only he could find her. There were hundreds of tarts in the Bois. Still, he would give it a try.

He had driven only a couple of hundred yards into the Bois when he saw her, standing in his path in the full glare of his headlights, and his heart jumped. Not even the atrocious cheap dress or the exaggerated make-up could conceal her uniqueness. As he got closer, her eyes shone like topaz in the dark. He stopped the car.

The alarm clock went off at eight as usual, and Silvia woke up. She had been sleeping in this room for over a week now, but every morning she went through the same ritual. She looked around her, and hoped that one day she would have a bedroom as lovely as this.

The training had been exhausting but Jacques seemed pleased with her progress. She had moved into his place the morning after their conversation in the Bois; he had wanted her to come with him that night, but she had insisted that she would make her own way the following morning. She wanted to see Gloria before going away, and to explain to Nana that she would be staying somewhere else for a few days.

Silvia had been stunned by Jacques's apartment, at the bottom end of the Rue Henri Barbusse, near Montparnasse. Her only experience with comfortable living had been the apartment in Rio, but this was a new dimension. It had a large sitting room, a double-height space with floor-to-ceiling windows on one side overlooking a beautiful chestnut tree in the courtyard. Jacques had put Silvia up in his bedroom, and he slept on a spare bed in the gallery overlooking the sitting room.

Jacques had coached her in every aspect of modelling: her posture, her walk, her make-up. He had borrowed clothes from friends, and explained to her how to show each type of garment to its best advantage. Every moment of the day was a lesson: how to eat, how to turn her head, how to sit gracefully. Jacques had also told her, again and again, never to smile. 'Monsieur Balenciaga believes that truly elegant women have a disagreeable air about them,' he explained.

After Nana's first phone call, Silvia told Jacques that she had a small daughter who was being looked after by an old friend, but Jacques wasn't interested. 'We all have stories, darling,' he had said. 'I don't want to know about yours any more than you want to know about mine. Now let's try walking with a really big hat on,' and he had dropped the subject.

Silvia stretched her arm. Time to get up. She had a quick shower, and then dressed in the borrowed clothes that Jacques had given her. 'Wear this tomorrow morning,' he had instructed.

She walked out of her bedroom, and found him in the sitting room having breakfast. She sat down and poured coffee into her cup, adding three lumps of sugar. She then buttered her croissant and spread a lavish amount of blackberry jam on it.

'I'm amazed that you can eat like a horse, and have a figure like yours. It's so annoying,' said Jacques, toying with his box of saccharine tablets. He lit an extra-long Kent, and blew several smoke rings.

Silvia stretched her hand towards the cigarette pack but Jacques moved them away.

'Not tonight, Josephine. I wanted you to sleep well and look wonderful this morning, so I didn't tell you last night that we are seeing Monsieur Balenciaga at eleven o'clock. He hates women who smoke. You will not get the job if you stink of cigarettes.'

'*If* I get the job, I won't smoke. Ever again,' Silvia promised.

She felt a mixture of excitement and fear. In two hours, her life could change dramatically. If she was accepted, she could leave the squalor of the past behind her forever; if not she would be back in the Bois that night, pinned to a car seat by the body weight of some man. It was very simple: she could not afford to fail.

'Time to work now,' Jacques said, leading her towards the bedroom. He pointed at the dressing table, and Silvia sat down in front of it.

Jacques picked up a brush and comb from the table. A handful of hairpins in his mouth, he skilfully pulled her dark hair back into a severe knot. 'You don't need hair with a face like yours.' He gently pushed her chin up, and looked at her in the full light of the huge window.

'You are nearly perfect,' he said after a moment. 'But let's make you absolutely perfect.' Brush in hand, he leaned forward, and Silvia closed her eyes. For the next half-hour there was complete silence; the only sounds she could hear were his breathing next to her face and the rattling and shaking of bottles as he picked them up one by one. Then she felt sable brushes caressing her skin. Wide brushes, narrow brushes, some wet, some dry: they went over every inch of her face, until she finally heard Jacques drop them on the glass-topped table.

'Now look at yourself,' he said. She could hear the pride in his voice.

She opened her eyes, and her heart jumped. Jacques had shown her the possibilities of her face before, but this morning he had worked a transformation. She stood up and kissed him on the cheek.

'Careful with your lipstick!' he said, immediately retouching her mouth with a small brush.

'Let's go,' he said. 'We can always walk along the Quai to calm our nerves, but we can't be late.' As their taxi drove into the Pont de la Concorde, the magnificence of the scene in the morning sun struck Silvia as a good omen. It was as if a golden future were here, waiting for her.

They turned into Avenue Georges V, and stopped outside an imposing stone building. 'Balenciaga', read the lettering on the cornice at both sides of the huge oak door, repeated on the white awnings over the windows. Suddenly Silvia was terrified.

'Come on, you have nothing to worry about,' Jacques said, leaping out of the taxi and holding out his hand to help. Silvia gripped his arm.

'I'm scared,' she whispered.

'I can feel it, my dear, you are about to break my wrist,' Jacques said. He embraced her. 'Darling, compared to some of the things you must have done in the Bois, this is child's play.' It was his first reference to her past since they had been together, and her face made him instantly regret it. He patted her shoulder. 'If it weren't for the make-up, I would give you a big kiss.' He held her arm, and led her to the side door.

They found their way to the elevator among the bolts of fabric lining the tiled corridor, but Silvia was not particularly aware of the surroundings. Her eyes were staring ahead with extraordinary intensity, and she followed Jacques, oblivious to anything other than the back of his head.

The elevator stopped, and Jacques held the gate open.

'This is our floor,' he announced. She heard him only faintly, as if he were far, far away. She followed him out of the elevator and walked behind him until he stopped in front of a padded double door.

'I'll go in now. I'll call you when he is ready to see you,' Jacques said, and disappeared through the door.

Silvia began to shake violently. In a moment, it would all be over.

'Pull yourself together, you idiot,' she said to herself. Suddenly, she remembered Gloria's little face, and her fear vanished. She took a deep breath and opened her eyes, just in time to see Jacques holding the huge door open.

'Come on, Monsier Balenciaga is waiting,' he said with a smile.

Head high, shoulders thrown back, hips slightly forward. She remembered all of Jacques's instructions, and sailed into the huge room as if she owned it. Her eyes were fixed on the elderly Spanish-looking man sitting on a high stool at the end of the room. He was wearing a white dustcoat, as were the eleven exquisite models lined up behind him. She approached him, her eyes focused on his forehead.

'Maestro, this is Arianne, the girl I mentioned to you. I thought you might find her suitable.'

Balenciaga stepped down, and walked towards her. It wasn't his expression that told Silvia she had won; it was the hatred on the girls' faces behind him.

'I am very pleased to meet you, Arianne,' he said, holding out his hand. 'Welcome to my *Maison*.'

Part III

PROLOGUE

Hatred is a great forger of character: it shaped Simon de la Force into the man he was. It had also determined the fate of the first de la Force to settle in Argentina, two hundred years before Simon's birth.

In 1707, at the time of the War of the Spanish Succession, Louis Delaforce, a young French surgeon from the Nantes region, was drafted to the medical staff of the King's Cavalry and sent to the front. He was wounded in the battle of Almanza and given up for dead, but he was picked up by monks from the nearby convent and, after nearly a year of convalescence, he recovered his health.

He did not, however, regain his love for his country. He felt betrayed by the compatriots who had left him behind like a discarded carcass. War-ravaged Spain was not to his liking either, and he decided to try the New World. He boarded a ship in Cadiz and sailed for Buenos Aires, the first leg on his long journey to Lima, the centre of power in Spanish America, where he had been told that his skills would be in demand.

He had a very vague notion of the distances involved. After nearly two thousand miles of arduous travelling on miserable roads, he reached the area of Northwestern Argentina now known as the Province of Salta, which was then an empty land dotted with a few villages and towns in the valleys.

He was struck by the beauty of the mountainous landscape, the hillsides striped by the layers of gold, burnt sienna and red soils, their colours sharpened by the bluest sky he had ever seen. After the summer inferno of the central Argentine plain, the dry climate was a blessing, and when he reached the village of San Simon he decided to rest there for a few days.

As word went around that a doctor was staying at the inn, his services were eagerly sought by the Spanish and

Creole families who had settled in the area, and soon after his arrival he shared his bed with Maria Tupac, one of the Indian girls working at the inn. After so many months of penury and forced abstinence, both events contributed to a sudden feeling of well-being, and a few days later Louis's mind was made up.

He settled in a small adobe house rented from a patient. The Indian girl moved in with him, to the horror of the pious locals. But they needed him, and the arrangement was tolerated. In time, a baby arrived, then a second, and Monsieur Delaforce, or Don Luis as he was now known, became an integral part of village life.

In 1719 Don Gaspar Céspedes del Campo, Marqués del Alcorcón, fourteenth Viceroy of Peru, decided to inspect the lands he governed on behalf of His Most Catholic Majesty. After months of slow progress through the various regions of the Vicereign, the Marquis and his retinue reached the Valle del Oro, near San Simon. It was here, in the middle of the huge plain, that fever struck. Soon the Viceroy was delirious and fear for his life spread among his courtiers. The Viceroy's physician had been affected by altitude sickness and sent back to Lima. Soldiers on horseback were dispatched to the nearest towns to try to find a doctor, while priests knelt around the stricken Grandee, praying round the clock for his recovery.

Louis Delaforce was the doctor the soldiers found, and he was immediately taken to the Viceroy's bedside. He realized that his options were either to cure the nobleman, or lose his own life. He tried everything. The Viceroy was bled, purged, bathed in cold water and wrapped in hot blankets, while Indian herbal potions prepared by Maria were forced between his white lips.

Some part of the treatment must have worked. After two days Don Gaspar was able to sit up in bed, and by the third day he was back on his feet. His gratitude knew no bounds: the Valle del Oro was given to Don Luis and his descendants, consent was granted for his marriage to Maria, and their children were recognized as legitimate. It was at that time that the family name was formally changed to 'de la Force'.

The Viceroy also ordered that a church to the Holy Mother be built on the camp site at the top of the Yanbi hill. One fiftieth of the year's production of the Potosi silver mine was to be used for this purpose, and the six largest emeralds in the treasury at Lima were set into a gold necklace to adorn the image of the Virgin at the high altar. The custody of the church was granted in perpetuity to the de la Force family. Having thus expressed his gratitude, the Viceroy returned to his capital. He never went back to Valle del Oro to see either the church or the solid silver image of the Virgin with the six green stones around its neck.

The lavish shrine in the middle of a dry, empty plain was soon forgotten by anyone other than the local population. The vastness of the 'Valley of Gold' ensured a modestly comfortable livelihood for Don Luis and his family, but its name owed more to the optimism of the first settlers than to the nature of its soil. No gold was ever found, and the lack of water made agriculture impossible. The valley was surrounded by the Sierras del Santo, a mountainous range that stopped all rain coming from the Pacific. The Rio Dulce flowed on the other side of the mountains, boxed in by a lower range of hills, its waters cut off from the fertile but desiccated soil in the valley.

In time, the de la Forces became an established family of the province. The males prudently married rich girls as a matter of principle, bringing into the family valuable farming land, vineyards or tobacco plantations. However, by the early part of the twentieth century, the family name was at risk of extinction.

Pedro de la Force, the last male of the line, had four daughters, and his wife died soon after the birth of the youngest child. Don Pedro never remarried, but in his old age he took one of his Indian maids as his mistress. The girl became pregnant, to the shock of his married daughters. Then, to the horror of their husbands, Don Pedro promised marriage to the girl if she produced a boy, with obvious implications for the eventual division of his estate among his daughters.

The young mother delivered a healthy baby boy, christened Simon, and Don Pedro's joy was unrestrained. As soon as she had recovered, a discreet wedding ceremony took place, but the unleashed emotions took their toll. That evening, while sitting in his rocking chair in the gallery, listening to the splashing of the fountain in the courtyard and to the gurgling of his baby boy, Don Pedro felt at peace with himself. He had secured the survival of his family name. He was enjoying this thought when his head dropped, and he stopped breathing the jasmine-scented air. A heart attack had killed him instantly.

His sons-in-law used their connections, and the apportionment of the de la Force estate took place in accordance with the letter of Argentine law. The daughters received the much smaller but fertile estates in various areas of the province while Simon, the newborn son, became sole heir to the useless land of the Valle del Oro – tens of thousands of hectares graced by the occasional cactus, and overvalued for the purpose of probate. No one was there to look after Simon's rights: his mother was an ignorant peasant and his sisters had no desire to protect a half-caste bastard at their own expense.

Simon grew up hating everyone around him: his mother for being an Indian, his family for rejecting him, their friends for scorning him as the undeserving carrier of a fine name. Revenge was Simon's driving motivation; he would prove that he was better than any of them, he would make them beg for his forgiveness. But to achieve that he needed money or power – preferably both – and he had neither.

His mother had struggled to raise him. Money was always desperately short. The contents of the house went piece by piece, but she understood only one thing: the house itself and the valley were untouchable. Don Pedro had left them to his son, and Simon would receive them when he came of age. Her firmness of purpose was helped by the fact that it would have been impossible to find a buyer for the dusty valley, by then nearly empty. The young moved on to decent jobs in the new industrial belts around the big cities; only the old stayed there, to die.

In 1943 a very big force began to rise on the political horizon: Colonel Perón. Simon de la Force recognized a turning of the tide, and soon joined Perón's new political movement, adding to the scorn of his well-off relations, who were all active in the Conservative Party.

In the course of the Presidential campaign at the end of 1945, when Juan Perón and his young wife, the popular actress Eva Duarte, visited the party headquarters in Salta, Simon de la Force was among those in the front line of the reception committee. He had the honour of a brief conversation with Señora Perón. It took only a few moments for them to recognize each other as kindred souls, and Eva suggested that if there was anything she could do for him, she would be only too pleased. Simon de la Force bowed in gratitude while the Señora gave him a dazzling smile. A photographer recorded the charming moment, one of many on such a happy occasion.

Perón was elected president on 12 February 1946. On 13 February Eva started the frenzy of activity that would turn her into the most powerful woman of her time. That same night, Simon de la Force undid the padlock of the abandoned sanctuary at Yanbi, in the middle of his empty valley, and walked into the church for the first time since his childhood. Torch in hand, he climbed the altar and removed the necklace from the Madonna's neck.

As he was about to leave the church, the jewels in his pocket, he noticed that the high windows were rattling. He opened the door and realized that a violent wind-storm had descended upon the valley. He took off his shirt and tied it over his horse's head. His left arm raised to protect his eyes from the clouds of dust, spurring on the terrified horse until its flanks bled, Simon de la Force rode through the valley, the storm raging around him. The next morning he went to the bank and emptied his small savings account. That night he was on the train to Buenos Aires.

He had never been to the big city and had not realized that life in the capital came to a standstill in January, when the summer heat softened the asphalt on the streets. The summer break lasted until March, and Simon was forced to spend a significant part of his money staying in a modest hotel in Avenida de Mayo until then, waiting for the luxury shops to re-open. In the meantime he took one of the emeralds from the Madonna's necklace to the Banco Municipal, the city's official pawnbrokers, for a valuation. He could scarcely believe the figure they quoted.

He asked at the hotel for the names of the best jewellery shops in Buenos Aires, and went to look at them. He chose Ricciardi because they were the biggest. Simon put on his best suit, walked into Ricciardi and asked to see the manager. The salesman took one look at this badly dressed half-Indian peasant and felt tempted to show him the door. But there was something about Simon's presence that commanded attention, and he led him instead to the owner's office.

Before saying anything, Simon took five huge stones wrapped in tissue paper out of his pocket, and laid them on a black velvet tray on the man's desk. The jeweller was staggered by the finest set of emeralds he had ever seen. The cut was very old-fashioned but they were nearly flawless. He was about to ask for their provenance when Simon put the photograph of his meeting with Eva Perón on the desk.

'These,' he said, pointing at the stones, 'are a present from the people of Valle del Oro to the Señora, and you are to turn them into the most beautiful necklace in Argentina for her. I know nothing about necklaces, but I know about pleasing the Señora. If she's not pleased, we'll be in trouble, and I wouldn't like that at all.' The jeweller looked into Simon's eyes. The man's expertise in stones was second only to his knowledge of people.

'You will not be displeased, Señor . . .' The man hesitated.

'De la Force,' Simon said.

'Señor de la Force, we can make the most beautiful necklace in Argentina, and the Señora will be delighted. However, as I am sure you know, such masterpieces are costly . . .' Simon dug into his pocket, and placed the sixth emerald in front of the jeweller.

'This one is your payment. I know how much the stones are worth, and I will have the necklace valued at

162

the Banco Municipal. It would be unwise to double-cross me. Your profit will be the Señora's appreciation of your craftsmanship.'

The necklace was finished in two months, a spray of diamond flowers with a huge emerald at the centre of each blossom. As soon as he was notified that it was ready, Simon asked for an audience with Eva Perón.

The meeting took place at the presidential residence. Simon sat in the marble hall with dozens of other supplicants, but his name was called after he had waited for only an hour, a clear indication of Eva's recollection of their encounter.

'What the hell do you want, Simon?' was her greeting to him. Whether ambassadors or humble petitioners, Eva addressed everybody with coarse familiarity.

Simon took the folder from under his arm and placed it in front of her. 'Señora, these are the plans for a dam on the Rio Dulce. The project has been shelved for many years. If the people of Valle del Oro don't get this dam soon, the valley will die. I look forward to the day when you will come to inaugurate the Eva Perón Dam, and save us from ruin.'

Eva flicked through the dossier. 'And what is that?' she asked, pointing at the large velvet box that Simon had placed on the desk after his explanation.

'An expression of our gratitude, Señora.'

The dam was built in record time, and inaugurated by Eva Perón on 20 November 1948. By then, the Peronist Government's grip on the financial system of the country was complete, and bank credits were only available to those whom the Government favoured.

It paid to be a friend of the ruling party, and Simon de la Force was a very good friend indeed. Water from the dam and cheap bank credits gushed into the valley: irrigation and drainage systems were laid, roads and a railway system built. At last, the ground was ready, and millions of cane cuttings were planted. Fourteen months later the first crop was ripe for harvesting, the huge mills were waiting to process it into sugar, and the Government was ready to buy it at a preferential price. The profits went into the factories

163

that, using the cheap electricity from the dam, would turn the fibrous residue into paper, cardboard and fibre board, and into the distilleries that converted the molasses into industrial alcohol. The residues from molasses went into animal feeds, the filter mud from sugar juice clarification went into fertilizer production. Every leaf and every stem in the huge valley was profitable, and very soon Simon de la Force was the richest man in Northwestern Argentina.

But he did not stop there. The prices fixed by the Government for beef and grain production were kept at absurdly low levels and the value of prime land in the Pampas dropped dramatically. Simon became a significant buyer of land during the Peronist years, until he was the largest landowner in the Buenos Aires province. He expanded his business interests into steel, textiles and banking in Argentina, while making foresighted investments in post-war France and Spain.

By 1955 Simon de la Force had become the richest man in Argentina. The fall of the Peronist Government cast a temporary shadow over his activities, but by then he was too powerful to be affected by any change of government. He had settled in Buenos Aires and became a leader of the Establishment, a member of the Jockey Club and the Circulo de Armas. He had long forgotten his grudge against his relations in Salta; they were too insignificant to worry about any more. He had ruined them easily enough by choking bank credit to their businesses through his Party contacts, but now he felt magnanimous towards his sisters. When in Salta, he would send his chauffeur to distribute cheques to them. The sums were not very large, on the grounds that he did not wish to offend them.

In 1960, after fourteen years of making money, his private life reduced to the odd call girl brought in to his office at short notice between business meetings, Simon de la Force decided that the time had come to secure his dynasty. He was forty-six years old. He had not married when he was young because no woman he considered worthy of being his wife would have even glanced at him, but now he could have anyone he wanted.

The most beautiful girl in Buenos Aires society at the

time was Dolores de Anzorena. After a brief engagement, the wedding of the year took place at the Santisimo Sacramento church on 20 October. Dolores looked exquisite. Simon's gifts to his bride included the best set of jewels in every precious stone at Ricciardi's shop, and a great house in Avenida Alvear – the most elegant street in Buenos Aires – originally built by the bride's grandfather.

After a lavish honeymoon in Europe, the couple settled down to married life in Buenos Aires. Simon wanted a son as soon as possible. He wanted it more than anything in the world.

12

BUENOS AIRES
July 1967

'. . . and the future of our great nation, gentlemen, depends on you. I have no doubt that, like your predecessors, you will win that battle. The Argentine Revolution in 1966, under the tutelage of our Armed Forces, opened a glorious new chapter in our history. Now, only one year later, we can begin to see the benefits of order and discipline in our society, but much needs to be done. May God guide us in our struggle.'

The Minister of Agriculture folded his notes and removed his glasses. Rapturous applause followed from every corner of the restaurant in the exhibition grounds of the *Sociedad Rural*, the traditional society grouping Argentina's large farmers. Today, only the most successful among them had gathered for lunch.

It was the Society's Annual Show, the *Exposición Rural*, the main event for farmers in a country where farming is both the peak of the social order and the main source of exports. Today was *the* day: the parade would soon begin and the juries would choose the Great Champion bull in every breed, a moment of glory for its owner worth years of work as well as money. Nobody in that room had spent more to achieve that glory than Simon de la Force.

As he approached the restaurant's exit on his way to the parade ground, he saw Dolores waiting for him near the door. By now, Simon didn't give a damn for his wife. She had failed to produce an heir and she was as vacuous in conversation as she was wooden in bed. Still, after three miscarriages she was pregnant again. She looked very chic in her maternity panther coat, and she was flanked by Maria Carretas and Malena Hamilton, the two other reigning queens of the Buenos Aires social world.

Simon felt a surge of proprietorial pride; he slipped his vicuna overcoat over his shoulders, took a deep puff on his cigar and, wrapped in a mist of cigar smoke and Lanvin *eau de toilette*, advanced towards the elegant trio, occasionally acknowledging somebody's greeting.

'Simon, darling. I've got a surprise for you, but we *must* dash.' Dolores held onto Simon's arm, and they all left the restaurant together.

'*Adio*, darlings, I'll see you later.' Dolores rubbed cheeks with her friends and they parted. Simon glanced at his watch and frowned.

'Where the hell do you want to take me now? We ought to go in,' he said.

'It won't take a minute,' she said, steering him towards the pavilion where the Shorthorn bulls were being groomed for the parade.

As soon as they walked in, the unmistakable smell of urine-soaked straw hit their nostrils. Dolores raised her collar and breathed in the Miss Dior scent on her lapel. They turned into the first of the three aisles where the Shorthorn bulls from 'San Simon' were kept in individual pens.

'Look, Simon! Doesn't he look divine?' Dolores said proudly, pointing towards the magnificent white bull in the second pen.

San Simon Field Marshal 28, number 35297 in the Argentine Herd Book, was Simon de la Force's best Shorthorn bull that year, and a candidate for the Great Championship. His noble head stared impassively ahead, while the tip of his tail was being whipped into candy floss by the ministrations of Hubert, the star hairdresser of Buenos Aires, whose fame rested on the early patronage of Dolores de la Force. He appeared as resigned to his current circumstances as the bull, and impervious to the hatred in the eyes of the two *gauchos* whose job it was to look after the animal.

'I thought I should do my bit to help you win, my darling,' said Dolores, beaming at Simon.

He sighed, and took her arm. 'Let's go,' he mumbled before he frog-marched her towards the grandstand.

It was Simon de la Force's afternoon. By four o'clock he had picked up the Great Champion prizes in the Shorthorn, Hereford and Aberdeen Angus breeds, his bulls festooned in medals and rosettes. The Aberdeen Angus award, the prize among prizes, was presented by the Minister himself, and Simon and Dolores made their way to the ground among the cheering and congratulations around them.

As soon as they left the stand and walked into the arena, they were blinded by the photographers' flashbulbs. At last, it was time for the grand finale, the slow march of the bulls on their way out of the ring. Prince Rupert of Valle del Oro, the Aberdeen Angus champion, was waiting for his master, barely able to see through the rosettes decorating his head.

Simon gallantly offered the bridle to Dolores. The band burst into the 'Triumphal March' from *Aida* and the parade began. The spectators clapped as the procession unfolded in front of the stands.

It did not go far. Half-way to the exit, Dolores suddenly stumbled. She held her stomach with both hands, her shrill scream piercing the air as she collapsed to the ground, her New York furs smeared with dung.

'A doctor! Get a doctor quickly!' the word spread. The country's top veterinarians were on the grounds. They rushed to help, but Simon would not allow them to touch his wife. An ambulance was called, and twenty minutes later Dolores arrived at the Pequeña Compañia de Maria, the clinic run by nuns which was the usual choice of Buenos Aires' smart set.

The top gynaecological specialists in Argentina had seen Dolores within two hours, and the following day a chartered jet brought Professor Lino von Kesti from Zurich. Their opinions coincided: nothing could have prevented the miscarriage, and Dolores de la Force would never have children.

Simon de la Force had a problem. He could breed the best bulls in the world, but he could not have a son.

13

Every morning, Arianne looked forward to her walk to work. It was the one part of her day when she could be alone with her thoughts. Her time at home was either dedicated to Gloria or to sorting out domestic matters with Nana, who had become her factotum as far as the running of the household was concerned. Arianne liked to be back early to be able to bath Gloria, but this was seldom possible. Balenciaga's capacity for work was extraordinary. He could inspect one hundred and eighty dresses in one day, tearing apart a sleeve here, changing the line of a collar there, his attention never waning. These fittings could go on well into the night, and it was impossible for any of the *cabine* models to leave before he had decided that he was, at last, satisfied.

After the showing of the Collection in January, Arianne had become a star. Paris had been dazzled by her beauty, her chic, and her aloofness, and the invitations had poured in: to grand balls, opening nights, elegant parties.

A different type of invitation had also been showered on her. Rich men, important men, dashing men, they all wanted at least to be seen with her, and most of them wanted more than just that. They wanted to go to bed with the most beautiful model in Paris, if only to be able to tell their friends.

Arianne invariably rejected these invitations. Sex had meant something to her with Ruben, but then it had become only a tool for survival. Now she no longer needed men, and she was neither repelled nor attracted by them. She just wanted to be on her own.

Her reputation as an ice maiden grew, but it did her no harm. Men redoubled their attentions, eager to be the first one to succeed where others had failed. A very persistent German millionaire even sent her a heavy gold bracelet, with an invitation to dinner at Maxim's. Before returning it, Arianne showed it to her friend Cameline, a beautiful English model at Balenciaga who was leaving to marry a dashing Italian, the Principe di Sarteano.

'Don't be silly,' Cameline said. 'Why would you want to offend the poor man by returning it? It's just a present. Look at it as though he had given you a box of chocolates. I would keep it if I were you. And there is no reason why you shouldn't accept the invitation. Just have dinner and say "thank you" afterwards.' Arianne went out to dinner and kept the bracelet, but felt uncomfortable about the whole event.

The changes in her life over the last few months had been immense. Her greatest pride was that she had given Gloria a proper home. She had taken a small apartment in the smart Rue Bonaparte. Nana was able to take Gloria to the Luxembourg Gardens in the mornings, and Arianne enjoyed her daily walks up the Rue Bonaparte to the Quai and then along the river to the Pont de l'Alma.

But over the last two weeks her walks had become less pleasant. Groups of students loitered in the streets, only around the Ecole des Beaux Arts and the Ecole de Médecine at first, but over the last few days they had mushroomed all over the Quarter. She had heard on the radio that morning that thirty thousand people had marched from the Gare de Lyon to the Place de la Bastille the night before, and the police had only been able to control them with a tear gas bombardment. A group of demonstrators bearing axes, pick handles and steel bars had broken into the Stock Exchange and set it on fire.

As Arianne reached the Boulevard Saint-Germain, she realized that something had gone seriously wrong during the night. The scarring of petrol bombs was visible on the front of several buildings, and hundreds of police were patrolling the area. They had even said on the radio that the President had left Paris.

Arianne found all this disturbing. She prayed to God that the showing of the collection would not have to be postponed.

*　　*　　*

'*Número 243, "Melodie"*, evening dress in blue taffeta.'
As soon as the announcement began, Arianne swept onto
the catwalk. She paused at the centre, did a quick turn and
continued to the end of the platform, where she let the huge
shawl around her shoulders slide to the ground. Her fingers
languidly held on to one end of the shawl, and she dragged
it along with studied carelessness as she retraced her steps
on her way out. As soon as she was back inside the *cabine*,
she flung it to her *habilleuse*, and sat at her dressing table.
The hairdresser quickly restyled her chignon, while Jacques
Villette retouched her make-up and attended to the loose
end of one of her fake eyelashes.

'Don't overdo the brown above the eyelid, please,'
Arianne said, keeping careful watch on his brushwork.

'You forget who created your face, *chérie*, but I suppose
that oblivion is the reward of true artists,' he said. 'Off
you go, the final lap,' he added.

As Arianne came onto the catwalk, the applause was
deafening. She was immediately joined by the eleven other
mannequins and clapping became frenetic, until finally
Balenciaga joined his models. The faithful were astonished.
His reserve was well known and, unlike other designers,
he had always refused to take the customary ovation at
the end of the show. But now, surrounded by his girls, he
nodded to his audience, then raised one hand and asked for
silence. A sense of foreboding descended upon the crowd.

'I must announce, with great regret, that you have seen
my last collection. I have decided to retire. The shows
will continue for another month, and the *Maison* will
meet all orders placed until then, but we will close at
the end of July. I wish to thank everybody in the house,
and all my clients, for their constant support . . .' Visibly moved but maintaining his impeccable demeanour,
Monsieur Balenciaga stopped his speech. He took off
his glasses, and wiped his left eye with his immaculate
handkerchief.

'Thank you very much,' he concluded, and left the stage
abruptly. The audience's concern was articulated by the
young Duchesse de Brie-Montval, who whispered to her
companion in a strangled voice:

'First the riots and now this, *mon Dieu*, what is the world coming to?'

Unlike the Duchesse, Arianne was not concerned about the world in general, but anxiety about her own little world began to gnaw at her confidence as soon as she heard the maestro's words. Their meaning was clear: she was out of a job.

Her face showed nothing as she walked towards the exit. She stopped before the velvet curtain, turned around and, facing the audience, she sank into a deep curtsey. Her white silk skirts rose behind her, framing her head like a peacock's tail. She looked out at the audience and, for the first and last time, she smiled at them. After all, it was likely to be her farewell as a model, her last collection.

She rushed into the *cabine*. Madame Florette was there, embracing the other girls, her eyes full of tears. Arianne stood still in front of her dressing table while her *habilleuse* unzipped her dress.

Jacques stood behind her. He looked thoughtful.

'We need another job,' Arianne said to him, their eyes meeting in the mirror.

'*I* need another job. If I were you, *chérie*, I would find myself a millionaire while the going is good.' He kissed the back of her neck, and Arianne glared at his reflection.

'*You* find yourself a millionaire; I don't need anyone to keep me now. I know what I'm going to do.' Her anger subsided as she carefully explained her plans to Jacques. He shook his head, but admitted it was a good idea. He had seen many good ideas in the fashion world come to nothing, but her determination was different.

'*Au revoir, chéri*,' said the stunning-looking girl, leaning down to kiss Simon on the lips, her pearl-and-gilt chains scratching his chest. She walked towards the door, and stopped by the seat near the window to pick up her quilted leather bag. Before leaving the room she glanced at Simon lying naked on the wide bed, and smiled. Her shoulder-length blonde hair, cut straight across, followed her every movement like a curtain of heavy silk thread.

Simon took one last look at her, confirming that her legs were sensational. She made most of Dolores' friends seem coarse, and she fucked like a goddess. These Madame Claude girls were real value for the money.

They had been in Paris for nearly a week now, and he had screwed a different girl every afternoon, while Dolores went to see the fashion collections. Compared to Dolores' expenditure, his pastime was a bargain and, after four weeks with his wife on the Riviera and the Côte d'Azur, he needed a treat.

Their doctor in Buenos Aires had advised Simon to take Dolores on a long holiday to cure the bouts of depression she had suffered since her last miscarriage. Simon found it far easier to live with Dolores when she was silent for long periods of time, and he had postponed the trip for nearly a year. But the doctor had finally put his foot down, and his advice was followed by a concerned phone call from Dolores' father. The couple had left Buenos Aires early in May.

The trip seemed to have worked wonders for Dolores, and she had launched into her usual frenzy of social activity. Today she had arranged lunch at Maxim's with Zou-Zou Lobos and other Argentine friends before going to yet another fashion show.

It was nearly four now. They had been asked to tea with the Ganays, and Simon did not want to be late. He had stressed to Dolores that she ought to be waiting for him outside Balenciaga at half past four.

He had a quick shower before getting dressed. A good fuck and a clean shirt always made you feel like a new man, he decided as he picked up his cufflinks from the bedside table. Before he left he called room service and told them to change the sheets.

Inside his rented limousine, Simon relaxed and lit one of his cigars. Dolores hated them, and she always made a fuss when he tried to light one. It was easier to present her with the *fait-accompli* of a smoke-filled car.

They drove to the bottom of Avenue George V, and the driver pulled in outside the Balenciaga building. Dolores was not there. Simon looked at his watch; it was four thirty-one. He rolled down the window and shouted at the uniformed doorman:

'Is Madame de la Force waiting inside? Tell her to come out immediately!'

The doorman bowed, and touched his cap.

'I'm sorry, Monsieur, but there is nobody waiting in the foyer. Madame is probably still upstairs. The show started slightly later than usual.'

'Then go upstairs and tell her to come out, damn it! I can't wait here forever!'

'I apologize, Monsieur, but we have strict instructions from Monsieur Balenciaga not to interrupt the show. I'm sure that Madame will be here in a moment.'

It was not what Simon had expected this operetta figure to say. Nobody told Simon de la Force to wait, let alone a miserable doorman. His anger boiled over. Chomping his cigar between his teeth, he jumped out of the car, pushed the doorman aside, and rushed inside the building, a raging bull charging into the world's most exclusive *salon de couture*.

Simon stormed towards the lift. He pushed aside an elegant-looking woman, and got in.

'Take me upstairs, you asshole,' he barked at the operator. Even inside the lavishly padded cabin, all buttoned leather and red velvet, his voice was deafening.

The operator let him out at the second floor, and he found himself facing the immaculately chic *directrice* of the salon, whose job depended on her skill at assessing a client's mood. She sensed immediately that this man would be a problem. She approached Simon with a smooth smile.

'Can I help you, Monsieur?' she asked, her manicured fingers toying with her long string of pearls. Simon's arm sent her flying across the room onto one of the Louis XV sofas, and he headed towards the majestic white and gilt double doors facing him.

It was the wrong choice. Three pairs of double doors led from the foyer into the enormous salon where the shows took place, but the central pair was permanently locked, because the models' catwalk ended in a circular platform in front of them. The clientele entered the salon through the side doors, but Simon was not aware of such details. He tried the ornate door handle, but the door did not give. Without a second's hesitation, he walked backwards a few steps and then lurched forward, kicking the door with tremendous strength.

Inside the chandeliered salon, the doors burst open, splinters flying in the scented air. Shocked whispers ran through the room as Simon, eyes glaring, his tie askew, stumbled in. Dolores' face went crimson. Sitting next to her, Zou-Zou Lobos squeezed Dolores' hand in silent commiseration.

Dolores knew what would follow: a string of '*carajo*', '*gran puta*', and other appalling obscenities, shouted at the top of his voice. Her only hope was that none of the audience would understand Spanish.

But Simon did not utter a word. One yard away from him, standing on the circular podium, was a woman so beautiful, so exquisitely perfect, that he could never have even imagined her. Simon stared at this vision looking down on him, her bare shoulders emerging from a froth of white feathers. There was an amused glint in her honey-coloured eyes, but otherwise her face was impassive.

Simon's life had been about wanting, and eventually owning, everything. First he had wanted money, then power, and finally status, and he had achieved it all. But he had never wanted a woman. They were easy to have and even easier to buy. Now he wanted *this* woman. He wanted her desperately, and he knew that he was going to have her.

She towered above him like an idol on an altar, and he could not take his eyes off her. 'You are going to be my wife,' he spluttered finally.

Her hands on her hips, head held high, Arianne flicked aside the stiff petticoats of her magnificent evening gown and turned her back on the intruder, walking towards the velvet curtain at the end of the catwalk. Her face was stony; after the last show, Monsieur Balenciaga had reminded her not to smile. And she didn't. Not once.

14

PORTOFINO
July 1968

It was a glorious day, and the view from the poolside of the Albergo Splendido was almost unreal in its perfection: a small castle at the top of the hill across the bay, the pink and ochre houses around the harbour and the white yachts bobbing gently at their moorings, their size reduced to that of a child's bath toy. Cameline and Arianne were lying by the pool on two yellow and white lounge chairs, languidly catching the morning sun.

'One of the few good things about Balenciaga retiring is that we can sunbathe now,' Cameline laughed. 'He would raise hell if you appeared after your holiday not looking as white as a vampire.' She stretched her arms, and yawned. 'But I'm not used to this. Let's have a drink.' She waved her hand at one of the waiters.

'Two Punt e Mès, please,' she ordered.

They had arrived in Portofino the night before. Cameline had come to meet the old Principessa, her future mother-in-law, at her palace in Genoa. Their meeting would take place at Sunday lunch, when she would also be introduced to other members of the Sarteano family. 'Bruno told me that it would be better if we don't sleep under his mother's roof until we are married,' Cameline had told Arianne when she had asked her to spend the weekend with her. 'Please come along. You Latins have some curious ideas and I am sure that the old bag expects me to be chaperoned.' Arianne had been glad to have an excuse to get away. She could ill afford the trip, but she needed a break after her frantic work over the last few weeks.

Soon after she became a model she had begun to take an interest in high-fashion jewellery. She noticed that the craftsmanship of the imitations she wore was almost as exquisite as the real pieces she coveted whenever she walked past Place Vendôme. But Arianne also noticed that, no matter how successful the setting, the fake gems still looked like coloured glass.

Fashion was changing. After the last few years of geometrics, plastic and pseudo-space outfits, she sensed a return to romanticism. A new mood required a different type of jewellery. It was then that she remembered the enormous variety of quartz sold in Brazil as cheap trinkets to tourists, the beauty of the inexpensive stones ruined by coarse wire mounts. She realized that the combination of Brazilian stones and Paris mountings would create the most ravishing pieces of jewellery, and she knew the time was right for her idea.

This was the plan she had explained to Jacques some weeks ago, and she had immediately set to work on it. Through the Trade section of the Brazilian Embassy she had been able to trace a French importer of cheap Brazilian stones, sold in the Paris markets as hippy beads.

Once in possession of the stones, she had obtained the addresses of the few specialist firms supplying jewellery to the couture houses. They were all in the Marais, and she had spent her days rushing from one corner of the old Paris quarter to the next, testing different alloys of copper and brass until the antique gold effect she wanted was finally achieved by Refoubeille. She would never forget her joy when the final sample was at last produced, the alloy poured into the mould from the furnace, the old room reeking of acid and acrid fumes.

She had worked at home for two weeks, producing her designs at night after her work at the *Maison*, in the shape of the orchids and butterflies she remembered from her childhood. Once her sketches were ready, delicate moulds in fine clay were produced for the metal casts, which were then given to the mounters. Just before her departure on holiday she had been able to see some of the finished samples.

As she had gazed at the necklaces, pins and bracelets spread on a green velvet cloth on one of the huge wooden tables by the window, the pastel-hued stones and the mellow gold glowing in the soft Paris light, Arianne had an overwhelming sense of achievement. She had been right.

The pieces were strikingly beautiful, and the effect was almost Byzantine in splendour.

It hadn't come cheap, though. She had not been able to save any money from her salary, and the cost of the manufacture of the prototypes had added up to thousands of francs. Wearing a scarf and her biggest sunglasses, she had taken the gold bracelet from the German admirer to the pawnshop near her old home in Pigalle. After bargaining in her most seductive manner she came away with enough to meet Refoubeille's first bills.

Jacques had introduced her to Monsieur Yves Osmu, his accountant, who had made plain to her that she needed seed capital to produce the line and meet the launching costs; nothing in high-fashion could be done on the cheap. Arianne had rented a room at the Crillon Hotel for the launch on 20 September. She had also hired the most elegant glass display cases she could find for the occasion, and ordered engraved invitations which she had already sent to the buyers of all the couture houses.

The overall cost was horrific, and she had to meet her living expenses in the meantime. Monsieur Osmu had suggested she secure a bank loan before going any further, so she had made an appointment to see her branch manager next week. She refused to consider the possibility of failure and what that would entail for Nana and Gloria.

Troubled by the uncertainty of her future, she decided to enjoy the sunshine with Cameline. The waiter came back with their drinks.

'Mademoiselle Delors?' he asked Arianne. She nodded. 'The gentleman asked me to deliver this to you.' He pointed towards a man in a sailor's uniform waiting on the upper terrace.

Arianne picked up a note, threaded through a ring. It was a huge heart-shaped ruby, and she was momentarily entranced by the depth of its colour. She unrolled the message.

'I would be the happiest man in the world if you would have dinner with me tonight on my yacht. The one with the blue and white pennants. 8.30 p.m.' The note was signed

'Simon de la Force', and the letterhead read *Fortuna –
Montecarlo*.

Arianne looked out towards the harbour. The biggest
boat, at least twice the size of any of the others, was
bedecked in blue and white bunting.

'Well, well, well,' said Cameline, leaning towards Arianne
and picking up the ring. She inspected it carefully, then
read the note. She raised an eyebrow.

'Isn't this the guy who kicked his way into the show?
Apparently his wife was so embarrassed that she bought
the whole collection. Isn't that sweet of her? Monsieur
B was livid, and sent the repair bills to your admirer
anyway.'

'I don't care if he is the Shah of Iran,' Arianne replied.
'I'm not going anywhere, and I'll send the ring back right
now.' She began to raise her arm to call the waiter, but
Cameline stopped her.

'Oh, come on, you are taking this too seriously. If you
send the ring back, it will probably get "lost" in transit.
He'll never believe that you tried to return it. At least give
it back in person.' She gave Arianne a mischievous look.
'Bruno is coming to the hotel for dinner tonight. If you go
off for a long, relaxed evening, I can have a few moments
of privacy with him, away from his awful mother.'

'I don't want to go through an unpleasant scene with
that man,' protested Arianne.

Cameline turned her head towards Arianne, and lowered
her sunglasses just a fraction to peer at her friend.

'You must have a pretty good idea how to handle a guy
if he gets difficult.' She lay back on the lounge chair and
sipped her drink.

Arianne remained silent.

'Listen,' Cameline went on, 'you told me about your
financial problems. What you need is chicken-feed to a
guy as rich as this.' She paused for a moment. 'I'm not
suggesting the casting couch, just a business proposition
after a good dinner.'

Cameline had a point. She was living in the hope that
the bank manager would agree to a loan, but if he refused,
she would not be able to meet the household bills in ten

days' time. There were no modelling jobs available, and she needed money.

'Make an appointment with the hairdresser now. You've nothing to lose, and you want to knock the guy flat tonight,' murmured Cameline, indicating the yellow awning and the glass door near the pool.

Something made Arianne wish this man had not appeared in her life, but she was very aware that her bills would not go away. She was briefly torn between reality and an uneasy sense of premonition, until she suddenly stood up and walked towards the hairdresser's salon.

'I'm so glad that you could come,' Simon said, standing by the top of the gangway and holding Arianne's hand as she stepped on board.

'Please come this way.' He held her arm, leading her towards the stern. As they reached the aft deck, she sensed the throb of the engines under her feet, and the yacht began to move out of the harbour. Noticing Arianne's surprise, Simon smiled, and offered her a seat on the huge semicircular bench following the shape of the stern. He sat next to her.

'I thought that you would enjoy the view of Portofino from the sea, and we would also be free from snoopers. It is tiresome to be stared at by every tourist in the harbour.' He fixed his eyes on her body, clearly outlined by her Pucci shift.

'It may get too cold for you, but I'm sure I can do something about that.' His tone was unmistakable.

'I can always borrow one of your wife's shawls,' Arianne replied, as she watched the lights of the Albergo Splendido fade further and further away. She mentally cursed Cameline for persuading her to take up the invitation.

'My wife is not on board. In fact, she's gone back to Argentina. I stayed behind to attend to ... some business matters,' Simon explained. A white-jacketed steward appeared with a drinks trolley. He stood in front of Simon, and bowed.

'Champagne, Pepe,' Simon barked. The man opened a

180

bottle of Dom Perignon, poured two glasses, placed them on a silver tray, and presented it to Arianne.

'I don't feel like champagne, thank you,' Arianne said to the waiter with a smile.

'I'm sorry, I should have asked you. What would you like?' Simon inquired solicitously.

'Now that you *ask*, perhaps I would love a glass of champagne,' she replied, picking it up from the tray offered by the steward. Simon snapped his fingers, and Pepe swiftly pushed the trolley away, disappearing from sight. Simon raised his glass.

'To our future,' he toasted, looking into Arianne's eyes.

'I don't think we have one, Monsieur, at least not in common.'

He moved closer. 'You can call me Simon.'

Arianne pulled the ring out of her bag. 'The main reason for my being here is to safely return this to you. I'm sure it's very valuable, and I wouldn't want it to get lost.' She placed the ring on the cushion between them. The stone glowed like an ember in the half-light.

Simon stared at her. An almost evil aura emanated from his deeply hooded eyes, but it was impossible to ignore their hypnotic appeal. He was several inches shorter than Arianne, and under the Lacoste shirt and the white linen trousers his body was clearly barrel-like, yet the glow of power around him was overwhelming. She found him physically repulsive, but she knew that for the first time in her life she had come across a man whose every whim could instantly become reality. A man like that could solve all problems, make life a Garden of Eden. He was repellent though, the snake in his own Garden. Anyway, she had had enough of men.

'You are making a mistake in not taking me seriously,' he told her. 'I have never wanted anything or anyone as much as I want you, and I always get everything I want, whatever it takes to get it, no matter how long I have to wait.' Simon paused for a moment, then raised his glass.

'To our future,' he repeated, taking a long sip.

Under his spell for a moment, Arianne followed his

181

example without thinking, but the taste of the cold champagne brought her back to her senses. She was annoyed with herself for having involuntarily shared his toast, and she decided to shift the conversation to less personal matters.

'This is a lovely yacht,' she said lightly. 'Have you had it for a long time?'

'I chartered it yesterday evening, when I heard that you were in Portofino. If you want it for the rest of your holiday, please let me know.'

She pretended not to have heard his offer. 'How did you know that I was here?' she asked.

'I have my ways,' Simon said with a smile. He pulled a sheet of paper out of his trouser pocket, unfolded it, and began to read it.

'Monday. 11.00: Hair appointment at Alexandre. 13.00: Lunch with fashion editor of *Elle*, Brasserie Lipp. 15.30: takes daughter to Jardin du Luxembourg . . .' He raised his eyes. 'Do you want me to read you the rest of your week's activities?'

Arianne was outraged.

'Are you having me followed? You must stop it immediately!' She stood up, glaring at him.

The soft fabric of her long shift clung to her body in the breeze, her hair shone like a halo around her perfect face, and her nipples, hardened by the cool wind, were just noticeable under the multi-coloured silk. He leaned forward and looked up at her, his face inches away from her body.

Simon was overwhelmed by the urge to make love to her. It would take one second to rip the flimsy dress apart. He had killed pumas in the Salta mountains with just his bare hands and a hunter's knife, and he knew that he could force himself on her. But he also knew that he wanted her beyond mere physical possession, and he wanted her more than once.

'I'll do whatever you ask me,' he said at last. 'I'm sorry if I upset you. You must understand that I wanted to know you.' Simon picked up the ring from the cushion.

'Shall we go in?' he asked. 'It's getting cold. I don't

know about you, but I'm hungry, very hungry.' He led her towards the door.

Arianne remained silent until they were inside the dining room. A small round table had been set for two in one corner of the room, by the huge window framing the distant view of Santa Margherita, the city lights shining on the sea.

'It was getting cold,' Arianne agreed. Simon pulled out her chair, and helped her to her seat.

As Arianne unfolded her napkin a pair of diamond and ruby earrings, the stones even bigger than the one in the ring, slid out and clinked against her plate. Simon pulled out the ring from his pocket and laid it next to the earrings.

'There is a saying in Spanish that you can't have two without a third. It usually applies to calamities, but I thought that it could have a positive side as well.' Arianne looked at her plate, at the gift that could solve her financial problems for the rest of her life, until she was suddenly aware of the steward waiting by her side, and she quickly put the jewels aside. The steward set in front of her a crystal bowl of Beluga caviar resting on a bed of crushed ice, and a small pile of blinis in a silver dish. Beside her plate was a small bowl of sour cream, a dish of sliced lemon and another of finely chopped raw onions.

Simon waited until the steward had poured iced vodka into small tumblers, then asked:

'Do you like the earrings? Otherwise I will exchange them when we are both back in Paris. You could come with me to Van Cleef and choose something you would like better.'

Arianne pretended to be transfixed by the jewels, waiting for Simon to pick up whatever was required from the endless array of cutlery at the side of their plates.

'I don't know if I like them or not,' she answered. 'Whenever I wear something like this, I have to return it after the show. It's foolish to like what you cannot have.'

'You can have whatever you want from now on,' Simon mumbled, his mouth full. Arianne followed his example and used the small horn spoon to scoop some caviar onto a blini, then some sour cream, but she did not touch the onions. She took a sip of vodka.

'I hear that you are Brazilian,' he said suddenly, changing the subject.

'No, I'm not. I was born in France, but I was brought up in Brazil.'

'I love the way you talk. Brazilian women always sound as if they are making love,' Simon said, helping himself to more caviar.

'I wouldn't know, I don't make love to women,' Arianne retorted.

Simon laughed. 'You are difficult, but I like that.' He drank his vodka in one gulp. 'Maybe it's just that, like most Brazilians, you don't like Argentines.'

'I've told you that I'm French, and you are the only Argentine I have ever met. But I don't like people who kick their way into rooms or into other people's lives.'

'I wouldn't be able to give you rubies if I didn't.' Arianne noticed the instant rage in his eyes. Perhaps it was better not to anger him unnecessarily.

'I told you that I'm not used to presents like these,' she murmured coyly. Their eyes met for a second, then Arianne lowered hers. 'I did not mean to offend you,' she finished. She put on the ring and then the earrings. 'I'll wear them during dinner, and I will give them back to you later.'

Simon leaned across the table, and patted her hand.

'You can never offend me,' he said soothingly, ringing the bell to call the steward. He wanted to finish dinner as soon as possible.

Arianne felt more relaxed now. She did not like the man, but he had tried his best to be charming, asking questions about her work while clearly enjoying the flamboyant main course, lobster à l'américaine. She told him about her business, and her plans for the launch.

'How are you financing your business?' Simon had asked point-blank. It was the opening she had hoped for, but she hesitated.

'Through a bank loan,' she said at last. 'I have no

184

finance problems whatsoever.' She could always approach him later if necessary.

'Do you have a date for the launch?' he inquired, pouring more wine in her glass.

'September 20th. At the Crillon,' she said proudly.

'Presumably you'll only know what your commitments are, once you start taking orders,' he said.

She stared at him.

'I thought this was a dinner party, not a business meeting.'

Simon laughed.

'You're right, it's just that I like talking about business. But I know nothing about this fashion stuff; we ought to change the subject.' From then on he carried the conversation, mostly about his recent travels.

Dinner over, they moved to the saloon. Simon took Arianne's arm, and led her towards one of the sofas.

'Would you like a brandy or a liqueur?' he asked, snapping his fingers at the steward.

'No thank you, I don't want anything else. It was a delicious dinner,' she replied, sitting at one end of the long sofa. The steward brought Simon a large brandy. He sat down next to her, their legs almost touching. Arianne noticed that the yacht was rolling gently.

'I hope that the boat does not move too much,' she said. 'I'm a very bad sailor.'

'You have nothing to worry about,' said Simon, resting his hand on her thigh. 'The sea is quite calm.'

Arianne stood up and walked towards the wall to inspect a portrait of a young woman.

'What a beautiful painting,' she said, her back to Simon. 'Is she your wife?'

'No, she is not. I don't know who the hell she is. I told you it's not my yacht. I wouldn't hang a portrait of my wife anyway. She is one of the few mistakes I have made in my life.' Simon took a sip of his brandy. 'I hear that you have a lovely daughter. How old is she?'

'She was one year old last week,' replied Arianne, without turning round.

'Who is her father?'

Arianne did not move.

'Not you,' she answered calmly.

Her rebuke hit home. This woman had to be put in her place. Simon gulped his drink. The brandy was burning in his stomach, and he wanted her now. He stood up and walked towards her.

He embraced her from behind, his arms crossed over her stomach, his hands on her breasts. He turned her around and pressed his lips on hers.

She offered no resistance. On the contrary, her body went soft, and her arms encircled his waist as her legs almost gave. The warmth of her body pressed against his was unbearable. Simon began to undo the buttons at the back of her dress while forcing her lips open with his tongue.

Her sudden burp sent a gulp of her breath, redolent of semi-digested lobster, down Simon's throat. Arianne pulled away, ran across the room, opened the door to the deck and leaned over the railings, retching violently. Simon ran after her and helped her to stand up. He could see the saliva trickling down her chin, and there were tears in her eyes.

'I'm so sorry,' she murmured, as he helped her back into the room, his arm around her waist. 'I told you that I am a very bad sailor.'

'Please relax. Come over here and lie down on the sofa,' he said. He slipped a cushion under her head, then stood up and bellowed:

'Pepe! Giovanni! Come here!'

The stewards rushed into the room.

'Bring a glass of water to Mademoiselle immediately, and get some Dramamine. Tell the captain to go back to harbour as fast as he can, and put out a radio call for a doctor to be waiting at the dock. Now get going!'

Arianne, her eyes closed, moaned softly. Simon sat by her side, holding her hand and squeezing it every now and then. None of his previous seductions had ended quite like this. Arianne opened her eyes at intervals, only to close them immediately, as if exhausted by the effort.

The lights of Portofino harbour were soon visible

through the windows and the rolling stopped. After a few minutes, the boat came to a standstill.

Simon put his arm behind Arianne's head, and helped her to sit up. 'Come on, we have arrived. The doctor will see you in a minute. I'll help you to the dock.' He struggled to the door, carrying her almost dead weight with both arms around her waist. As they climbed down the gangway, he noticed an ambulance and a medical team waiting nearby.

As soon as her feet were on the ground, Arianne pulled herself away from Simon, and faced him.

'Thank you for dinner,' she said firmly, swiftly taking off the earrings and removing the ring. 'If you are so desperate for a fuck, try screwing the rubies.' She pulled at the waistband of his trousers, dropped the jewels into the gap, and walked away. Her long-forgotten ability as a child to burp at will had been useful, and she smiled with glee. It was dark, and it was a long walk uphill to the hotel, but she didn't mind.

The bank manager looked at the papers in front of him, Arianne's account statements and the business projections prepared by her accountant.

'How much money do you need?' he asked at last.

'I need three thousand francs for my expenses, and ten thousand to produce the collection.' Arianne kept her eyes on him as she spoke.

The bank manager shifted his eyes away, his hands fiddling with the pen in front of him.

'I can see no problem in lending you three thousand francs; I can do that on the basis of your account. But I would not be able to lend you the rest. It is not our policy to grant unsecured loans.'

Arianne concealed her disappointment, but at least she would be able to live until the launch. She had already thought Jacques might be a willing backer if the bank turned her down.

'That will be very helpful,' she said. 'I think I can raise the rest of the money from . . . other sources.' She sensed the man's relief; he obviously had expected her to plead her case, but they both knew it would be a waste of time.

'I'm delighted to be of help,' he said unctuously. 'If you see Monsieur Raspard now, he will complete the paperwork for you and the money will be credited to your account tomorrow.' The manager stood up, holding out his hand. Arianne did not move.

'There's something else I want to discuss with you.' The man sat down.

'I know the business will work in the long term,' she said, 'but I will have a cash flow problem once I start taking orders. I cannot count on advance payments for first orders. It is unusual in the trade, and it wouldn't meet the production costs anyway. If, as I expect, I get substantial orders, I will have to finance part of the production cost until delivery.' She had agreed with Refoubeille that they would not invoice her for her sample collection until September, but any money coming in from the orders would have to go into settling that debt. And Refoubeille would not produce anything until she paid for the samples.

'What sort of figure are we talking about?' the manager asked. Arianne paused for a moment before replying.

'I have calculated between twenty and thirty thousand francs,' she said as if it were a small matter. The man wrung his hands.

'We have already discussed the problem of unsecured loans, Mademoiselle Delors.'

Arianne smiled.

'But I will have firm orders from reputable couture houses by then. The loan would no longer be unsecured,' she said briskly. The man thought for a moment.

'As a matter of practice, I would have to refer the request to my superiors. If the orders justify it, I can't foresee any problems, but the decision will not be up to me,' he said.

'It all depends on the orders then?' she asked.

'Yes.'

She had no doubts about the orders. It was her turn to stand up and hold out her hand.

'Then I'll come to see you in September,' she said. 'Where do I find Monsieur Raspard?'

Jacques rolled his eyes. They were sitting outside 'Les Deux Magots', under one of its red awnings facing the church of Saint-Germain-des-Prés. Arianne crossed her fingers under the table and raised her eyes towards the church spire.

'The things I have to do for you ...' he sighed. 'Ten thousand francs is all the money I've got in the bank. I saw the most divine pair of Art Nouveau lamps the other day. They were going to be my birthday treat, but I'll have to live without them, I suppose.'

Arianne felt her tension fade away as she heard him. She leaned across the table and kissed him.

'One day I'll buy you any damned lamp you want,' she murmured. Jacques smiled.

'You are ruining your eye make-up, *chérie*, there is no point in getting emotional in front of the tourists.' He took her hand. 'But you'd better make sure it works. I won't be able to bail you out next time.'

She wiped away her tears.

'There won't be a next time, Jacques, I know it. I'll never look back,' she said. 'I never do.'

'I hope you're right.' Jacques called the waiter and asked for the bill.

15

Arianne stood in front of the huge window overlooking the Rue Royale. It was already dark, and the traffic lights shone on the street, varnished by the autumn rain. She turned towards the room, lit only by the small spotlights inside the glass display cases, their glow dimly picked up by the gold edges of the panelled walls behind. Inside the boxes was the jewellery, *her* jewellery. She had reason to feel proud of herself.

It had been worth every borrowed franc. After a hectic day she had firm orders from four houses, for a total of seventy thousand francs, and she had managed to negotiate partial payment in advance with two of them, amounting to five thousand francs. She had been able to pay her supplier with Jacques's money, and she had used two thousand francs to meet the hiring of the room and other launch costs. She had two and a half thousand francs left to live on until early December, when she had arranged to deliver the jewellery to her customers, and full payment would be due.

She went back to the desk in the middle of the room and picked up the signed orders. She would have no problem now in raising the twenty-five thousand francs she needed from the bank.

It was nearly seven. If she hurried, she would be home in time to put Gloria to bed. She had hardly seen her in all the rush over the last few weeks.

The bank manager smiled broadly.

'Please accept my congratulations, Mademoiselle Delors. Your business is obviously a great success.' Arianne nodded her head to acknowledge his compliment, but she was not there to exchange pleasantries. She didn't need to. It had not gone unnoticed by her that he had not led her to the chair facing his desk, as on their previous conversation.

He had shown her instead to a sofa, and was sitting beside her.

'Do you see any problems in raising the thirty thousand francs I need?' she asked abruptly.

'As I told you before, it's not my decision. I have to send these' – he waved the orders in the air – 'to head office with your loan application, but I can't imagine that there will be a problem.'

'Please let me know as soon as the money is available,' she said, picking up her bag and gloves from the side table. Taking her cue, the man stood up.

'Rest assured,' he said with a broad grin.

Simon de la Force glanced at his diary. Today's date, 20 September, was circled in red: he did not need any reminder of why he had marked it two months ago. He reached for the telephone and asked his secretary to place calls to Edouard Golbins and Celine de Merteuil in Paris. After a moment the girl called back: there was an hour delay on international calls, she told him.

Simon picked up a report on his desk, and forced himself to read it. Even he could do nothing about the exasperating Buenos Aires telephone system.

Edouard Golbins was a very successful investment banker. His success was based on simple principles: always stay one step ahead of the markets, dress impeccably and do whatever a client requires, as long as it is within the law, or untraceable. Simon de la Force had been one of his most important clients for many years; if necessary, Edouard would have climbed mountains to keep him happy. As he put down the telephone, he knew it would take far less than that to comply with Simon's latest request: just a few phone calls to trace the bank holding the girl's account and the owners of the building, then a call to the right man to ask for a favour. Edouard was owed favours by most people in the financial world.

'Your bank manager phoned while you were out,' Nana told Arianne as soon as she came into the apartment.

Arianne was already on her way to Gloria's room, where she could hear her daughter talking to one of her dolls, but she stopped half-way down the corridor and returned to the sitting room. She looked up the number in her address book and picked up the phone. 'The manager, please.' She stood still for a moment, then sat on the chair by the small table.

Nana did not pay attention to the conversation until she noticed that Arianne had said nothing for an unusually long time. She turned around and noticed that Arianne was biting her lip. She seemed upset.

'No, I understand. I'll come to see you now to get my papers.' She hung up and sat for a while, saying nothing.

'Everything alright?' asked Nana.

'Yes, everything's fine,' Arianne replied. She picked up her coat and bag and rushed out of the apartment.

Celine de Merteuil had one of the oldest titles in France. The family's financial difficulties were more recent, dating back to the French Revolution only, but several generations of making ends meet had sharpened into a fine art the skill of earning a living without seeming to work. To Celine, work was a pastime for vulgarians. If unavoidable, then it should be as invisible as possible.

Her income came from the discreet services and social introductions she performed for the *parvenus* and the *nouveau riche* who could afford her fees. Simon's call at first surprised her. However, she guessed the reason behind his instructions, and by the time she put the phone down, a wry smile came to her lips. A love intrigue. How refreshing, she thought.

Her address book was next to her on the bedside table. She opened it at C, and ran her finger down the page until she found the numbers under 'Couture'.

She dialled the first number and asked for the *directrice*, an old friend with a title almost as good as hers. After two or three minutes of pleasantries and gossip, she came to the point.

'*Ma chère*, I believe you know Arianne Delors, that ex-Balenciaga girl; I hear she's gone into the *bijouterie* business. Are you by any chance buying from her? You're not . . .' She managed to finish the conversation soon after that, without in any way giving the impression of cutting it short. When required, Celine de Merteuil's skill on the telephone was comparable to a bullfighter's use of his cape. The conversation ended in a deluge of good wishes, and Madame de Merteuil cast a weary eye back over her address book. Christian Dior was next.

She was unlucky with the next two calls, but succeeded with the third.

'. . .You are? Then I have something to ask of you, *ma chère*, but first let me tell you that Madame Sudharno is here next week. I am helping her with her wardrobe, and she spends like crazy. Of course I will take her to see your collection, Nicole. You must show her lots of furs as well, you know how she *adores* them. Now, Arianne Delors . . .' She explained what she wanted, then listened.

'Don't worry for a second, my dear. Your costs will be met, and any other expense you may incur. Just send me the bill. You know I'm good for my word, and I assure you that it will be settled without any delay. Yes, I appreciate how difficult this is for you, and I'm truly grateful . . .'

By the end of the morning Celine de Merteuil had spoken to each of Arianne's clients.

Arianne came out of the bank and paused for a moment before joining the throng in Boulevard Saint-Germain. She pulled her dark glasses out of her bag and put them on. Head down, she began to walk away. She did not care in which direction, she just needed time to think.

The bank had turned down her loan application. The manager was at a loss to explain the reason, or at least he claimed to be. 'Head office, Mademoiselle. It's a head office decision, as I warned you,' he repeated again and again. She sensed that there was more to come, and she was right.

Having considered the matter, the head office had also decided that her personal loan should be called in under the circumstances. The manager had been instructed to deduct the outstanding balance from her personal account. There were not enough funds to cover it, and she now owed the bank six hundred and forty-three francs. She already owed Jacques ten thousand, and she had to pay twenty-five thousand to her manufacturer within two weeks. But two weeks seemed a long time when she realized that she only had enough money in her purse to meet the market bills for three or four days.

She couldn't ask Jacques for more money. He had already told her he didn't have any. For a moment she thought of asking Cameline, but she had overheard enough conversations between rich women at Balenciaga to know that while their husbands were quite happy to settle any bill sent to their office, they balked at requests for cash other than pocket money. Cameline's wedding was to take place next month, and she was working hard at winning over Bruno's impossible family. She would hardly want to ask Bruno for money now.

Arianne looked around her at the passers-by. They all seemed so happy, wealthy and secure, wrapped in their silk scarves and fur coats. Poverty had been her nightmare. She had learned to live with it once. She could learn again, but this was much worse than poverty. Not only did she not have any money, she owed far more than she could reasonably expect to earn within two weeks. Unless . . . unless she went tonight to the Avenue Foch. She could ask a hundred dollars a time. If she worked long hours, in two or three weeks she could save enough to meet her bills.

She raised her head and saw her reflection in a shop window. She almost struck the glass in anger, sick at the thought of a man touching her again, hating her sudden vulnerability.

She had reacted as her old self, when she had been cornered by a world she could not handle. But now she could and would. The obvious thing to do was to phone her customers, try to bring forward the delivery dates and ask for immediate payment. As for the household bills, she would have to talk to the local shopkeepers and try to open accounts with them.

She turned and began to walk home. She had found a way out. It would be difficult, but she would make it work. She felt almost cheerful. Tomorrow morning she would phone her customers. Now she was going to take Gloria for a walk.

Nana laid Arianne's breakfast on the table, next to her mail. A moment later Arianne appeared in the sitting room. Her skilful make-up concealed any evidence of her sleepless night, and she was ready to phone her clients.

'Good morning, Nana,' she said cheerfully. She frowned at the first envelope; it was the telephone bill, and she set it aside. Then she glanced at the rest, surprised to see that, other than an envelope from an insurance company, they were all from her clients. She opened the first, placed the enclosed cheque on the table, and read the letter. Her face went white.

She tore open all the envelopes. There was another cheque with a covering note, and two letters which suggested treating the down payment as a suitable cancellation fee. Numbed by shock, she picked up the letter from the insurance company, then walked to the telephone.

'Jacques! I need to see you,' she said as soon as she heard his somnolent voice at the other end. 'Yes, now. I'll be with you in twenty minutes.'

She hung up and, without once looking at Nana, went to her room to pick up her coat. The bell rang as she was about to open the front door. It was a delivery man, almost invisible behind an enormous basket of white roses.

'Mademoiselle Delors?' he asked, holding out his pad for her signature. She scribbled at the bottom, picked up the envelope in her name attached to the pad, put it in her coat pocket and left the apartment.

'Just leave them inside, the lady will tell you where to put them,' she told the man before closing the elevator gate behind her.

'Someone must be after you, *chérie*,' said Jacques, sipping his coffee. They were sitting at the table by the huge window in his apartment, and Arianne remembered her last breakfast there, before going to Balenciaga. For a second, the memory made her nostalgic for that time of hope.

'Don't get paranoid, Jacques, it's just a run of bad luck,' she said.

Jacques shook his head.

'Your bank turns down a valid application for a loan, your clients cancel their orders for no apparent reason, your landlord tells you that they ran a routine check of your banking references and feels obliged to invoke the eviction clause of your contract all in the same day, and you think it is just bad luck? Next you'll tell me that you believe in the tooth fairy.'

'What am I going to do?' Arianne cried.

'Fight them. Go to court and fight them,' he replied.

She couldn't. It was one thing to go about everyday life with a false identity, but she couldn't take the risk of legal action and a possible investigation of her past. She shook her head.

'I don't even have money to pay for our food. I can't afford a lawyer, I can't afford the rent, and I can't afford any trouble, Jacques. I don't have a past in the Sacred Heart Convent.' She knew that she would break down if she continued talking, and she stopped. Jacques squeezed her hand, then stood up and walked over to a chair nearby. His jacket was draped over the back. He pulled out his wallet from the inside pocket, took a five-hundred franc note from it and placed it in front of her.

'You already have my Art Nouveau lamps, so you might as well have my new suit,' he said with a smile. She began to cry.

'Please stop it, *chérie*, or I'll start crying too,' he told her. 'Let's be practical. How much do you owe?'

'Twenty-five thousand francs to Refoubeille, ten thousand to you, and six hundred to the bank. The rent is due in a week's time, and the telephone bill arrived today.' She folded the note and put it in her pocket. 'And I owe you this as well. I can't tell you what it means to me.'

'Don't say it then. How much money did you get for the cancelled orders?'

'Five thousand francs,' she replied.

'So you owe about thirty-two thousand francs. Have you tried to find other customers?'

Arianne shook her head. 'The jewellery is too expensive for anyone other than couture houses, and they've all seen it. The ones who did not want it at first surely won't want it now that it has been turned down around town. You know the scene, Jacques, everyone will know about this by lunchtime.'

Jacques poured more coffee.

'Something will turn up,' he said. 'In the meantime, blow your nose and dry your eyes. You will think better if you don't let your sinuses get all blocked up.'

Arianne put her hand in her pocket, and felt the envelope inside. She pulled it out.

'What's that?' Jacques asked.

'Someone sent me flowers today. They arrived as I was leaving, I didn't even look at the card.' She handed the envelope to Jacques. 'You read it while I deal with my eye make-up.'

He pulled out the stiff white card, then he whistled softly.

'You *do* have style, my darling. I don't know of anyone else who gets asked to the best lunch in Paris when they are seriously broke.' He read the card aloud, in a mockingly solemn tone.

'I hope you have forgiven my atrocious manners. I will be in Paris tomorrow, and I would be delighted if you would join me for lunch at "La Tour d'Argent" on Thursday, at 1.00 o'clock. Simon de la Force.'

'Who is this charming man?' Jacques asked, intrigued. Arianne told him about her Portofino fiasco.

'If he put a detective on you, I wouldn't be surprised if he is behind all this. A guy like that can pull a lot of strings. I said to you at the show that you needed a millionaire. You seem to have found one.'

'I don't want to go to bed with him, Jacques. The man is repulsive.'

'I don't remember Alain Delon calling for you at the Bois, *chérie*, and the guys there don't walk around with huge rubies in their pockets so far as I know,' he said acidly.

Arianne was stung, and Jacques knew it. He leaned forward and patted her cheek.

'I'm sorry, sometimes I'm a bitchy old queen. I didn't mean that, but perhaps you ought to remember that beggars can't be choosers. Go and have a great lunch, hear what he has to say, be very nice but don't promise anything. Just get him to lend you the money. And next time, keep the rocks.'

'I never cease to be amazed by how lovely you are,' said Simon. 'You make me forget the view.'

Arianne turned her head towards the picture window behind her, framing the spires of Notre Dame across the river.

'I can't compete with a thousand-year-old church, but I'm flattered,' she replied with a smile.

After the constant fear and worry of the last few days, she could not help feeling relaxed in the warm, plush atmosphere of the restaurant. The luxurious room floating high above Paris gave her the illusion of a great liner, and she felt as if she were sailing away from her problems, if only for a couple of hours. She was glad to have followed Jacques's advice. Simon had been good company, and she couldn't help being absorbed by his anecdotes. She could understand his wilful fight against adversity. Not once had he talked about his feelings for her, but she knew that there was a purpose to this meeting. Certainly for her, and she decided to tackle the issue.

'You told me in Portofino that you would be prepared to help me with my business,' she said suddenly. He seemed surprised.

'Did I? I can't remember . . .'

'You did, but let's not argue about it. The point is that I need financial support to make it work. Would you be prepared to become my backer? The business has certainly done very well here,' she said, keeping an impassive face, 'but I have realized that Paris is too small a market. I want to re-launch my line either in New York or Germany and I need capital to do that,' she said evenly, putting off the thought that all the money she had left in the world would not even pay for this lunch.

He shook his head, and sighed.

'I would love to help you, but I don't lend money. Not to friends anyway; I learned long ago that one shouldn't mix business and pleasure. And I want to be your friend.' The polite refusal was clear enough, and his face left her in no doubt that she could expect nothing from him. But she had to keep on trying. Maybe if she sounded meek rather than self-assured . . .

'Please, I beg you . . .' Arianne began, but he raised his hand to stop her.

'Don't force me to say no. What I can say is that, as long as we are friends, you'll never have a problem. Are you free after lunch?' Simon asked thoughtfully, warming the brandy glass in his hand.

She fought the urge to stand up and leave. She hated him for making her feel cheap, for taking her for granted for the price of a lunch.

'I thought you said you would try to avoid further mistakes,' she replied angrily.

'I've apologized for my unforgivable behaviour, and I assure you that I am not trying to repeat it. It is not in my interest to upset you. But there is something I would like to show you. It's only five minutes away, and I promise you that you will be free in half an hour.'

'I have to be home by three o'clock,' she warned him brusquely.

Simon gulped his brandy, and waved at the waiter.

'No problem, my chauffeur will get you there in time.'

He signed the cheque and they left, Simon slipping ten-franc notes into the hands of any member of the staff who greeted him on their way out.

The limousine was waiting just outside the entrance. They drove along the river until they pulled in at the Quai Anatole France, in front of an elegant stone building. The chauffeur opened Arianne's door and Simon, who had leaped out of the car as soon as it had stopped, guided her by the arm towards the huge front door. He opened it and let her in.

The foyer reminded Arianne of some couture houses: the marble floor, the stone pillars, the curving staircase with a wrought iron and brass balustrade, all the features of eighteenth-century Paris at its most gracious. Simon opened the lift gate and followed Arianne into the ornate cabin.

'Where are you taking me?' asked Arianne as the lift creaked its way up.

'You will see in just a moment,' he answered blithely, opening the door and letting Arianne out into a small hall. He pulled a key out of his pocket and opened the tall cream and gilt double doors leading off the lobby.

He stepped aside, and Arianne walked into a black and grey marble-floored circular foyer, leading on one side to a drawing room with three large windows overlooking the river and the Jardin des Tuileries on the Right Bank.

She entered the room, taking in the lofty ceiling, the panelling, the superb furniture and paintings. She glimpsed a large dining room beyond the doors at one end of the salon, the rock-crystal chandelier sparkling in the sunlight pouring in from the windows.

'You ought to see the rest,' Simon called from the foyer. She went back, and he opened another double door, which led onto a long corridor. He opened door after door, into bedrooms, dressing rooms, a library, everything as opulent as the reception rooms. Through the windows framed by silk curtains Arianne could see a large formal garden at the back, the smooth lawn emphasizing the whiteness of the marble statues and urns there.

They returned to the drawing room and Simon leaned against the marble and bronze fireplace.

'Do you like it?' he asked.

Arianne did not reply. 'Who owns it?' she asked.

'Someone I know who has moved to Switzerland. I am planning to rent it for a year, and I can sign the lease this afternoon, if you like it.'

'What difference would it make if I like it or not?' Arianne asked, already guessing his answer.

'Because I would like you to live here.'

She picked up her bag from the stool next to her chair.

'I thought we had agreed that I will not sleep with you, under any circumstances.' She stood up. 'I have to be home in ten minutes and I would like to go now.'

'Please listen to me.' The urgency in Simon's tone

stopped her. 'I know that you still don't like me, but you misunderstand me. You are the most exceptional woman I have ever met, and I only wish that I had married you. But I wouldn't have reached my position if I were not able to accept that it is better to have part of a good deal rather than no deal at all. I can't stand my wife, but there is no divorce in my country and I cannot live without the company of a woman I love. I want you to become my companion when I am here in Paris, which is not often. We will go out together and, if you wish, we can travel together. I will not live here, I will not force my presence upon you, and we will never have a physical relationship unless you change your mind about it. In exchange I will pay for this apartment and all your living expenses, no matter how extravagant, and any debts you may have. I hope you will agree – you would make me the happiest man in the world.' He was so taken by his own speech that he almost believed it.

'There are only two conditions,' he added. 'First, you will not see other men, or have a lover. I am a proud man, and I could not tolerate it. Second, you must not work. I'm a very busy man, I can't say when I will be able to see you, and I need you to be free at all times.'

Arianne had expected an offer that she could turn down flat; but not this. Even his restriction on men suited her. She did not want a lover.

Work was a different matter, though: it had given her freedom at last. But she looked around the room, at the luxury surrounding her, and thought about the forty-three francs in her purse. What had she gained by her freedom? Her work had turned into a fiasco, pushing her into unaffordable debt, and she would be out on the street with Nana and Gloria in no time at all.

Her thoughts about debt reminded her that Simon had specifically offered to pay them. How could he know about them, unless he was behind her current predicament? She walked up to him and faced him squarely.

'Did you have anything to do with . . .' She realized there was no point in asking the question. He would lie to her. Maybe it was better not to know.

201

Arianne walked to the window, staring down at the river for a few moments, and then turned around towards Simon.

'I need to think about it,' she said.

'I'm going back to Buenos Aires tomorrow. Call me at the George V this evening, no later than half past seven. I'm having dinner with the Pompidous,' he boasted.

They left the building in silence. As Arianne was about to get into the car, Simon pulled out a square black velvet box from his pocket and gave it to her.

'I hope you will not push them down my trousers this time,' he said, smiling. Arianne took the box and put it in her bag. She knew what it contained. Perhaps the rubies were the answer to her dilemma, after all. She could get a lot of money by selling them, and she would not have to put up with Simon de la Force ever again.

'If you don't like them, don't try to sell them,' he warned, as if reading her mind. 'They are registered as a company asset, and you may find it troublesome to dispose of them. But we can exchange them for anything else you may prefer instead.'

Arianne got into the car, and Simon leaned down to talk to her. 'If you accept my offer you will receive the keys to the apartment tomorrow, with a letter giving you the address of my banker here. He will deal with all your bills.' He closed the door. 'Take Mademoiselle wherever she wants to go. I could do with a walk,' he said to the chauffeur, and moved away without looking back.

'Pity that he wouldn't fancy *me*,' Jacques's voice chuckled over the phone.

'Please, Jacques, this is not a joke. I can't see how I can turn him down, but there has to be a catch somewhere,' Arianne said impatiently.

'Maybe, but it's better than being broke and without a roof over your head. I don't know why you are wasting time, *chérie*, it's already quarter past seven. *Please* say yes, then phone me back. I'm dying to see that gorgeous place. Goodbye.'

Arianne put the phone down, deep in thought. Perhaps

Jacques was right. Here was her chance to have everything she could possibly want, without having to give anything, or very little, in return. Yet there was a warning bell ringing somewhere in her mind. If only she could attribute her misgivings to something more tangible than fear and intuition. If only she was not crippled by debts. If only . . .

She glanced at her dressing table, at the photograph of the family group in Rio de Janeiro, so long ago. The picture brought back her memories of the *favela*, and she instantly made up her mind. She picked up the phone.

'*Le George V, bon soir,*' said the operator at the other end, almost singing her greeting.

'Monsieur de la Force, please.' There was silence on the line, and then Arianne heard his voice.

'Yes.' She could hardly bring herself to say the word.

'I am very happy. You will not regret it,' Simon replied. She slammed down the phone. She was not so sure.

16

The triple mirror reflected Arianne from every angle, allowing her to check each detail of the cream tweed suit. She turned round and looked at the back.

'The braid on the edge of the jacket isn't quite right,' she said to the *Première d'Atelier* standing by her side. 'It should be just a bit higher on the left.'

'It is a pleasure to help a client as knowledgeable as you, Mademoiselle Delors,' said the *vendeuse*. 'So many of our clients simply don't understand clothes.'

'Thank you, Yvette,' said Arianne, as the assistant carried out the minute alteration. 'I think that the buttons should be different. I would like the same buttons as on the blue coat you made for me last month. Not the fitted one, the straight one.'

'Of course, Mademoiselle.' Yvette made a rapid note on her pad.

Arianne cast her eye over the rack at one side of the fitting room. There were four other suits to try. She glanced at her platinum watch.

'I think I just have time to try on the yellow one,' she told Yvette. 'I'm meeting a friend for lunch at the Ritz, and I don't like being late.' She instantly regretted the remark. It did not matter any more if she was late. It was somebody else's problem, not hers. There was always something to remind her that she was not entirely used to her new life.

Simon had not been back since they struck their bargain. He phoned every ten days or so, always announcing his imminent arrival, but then postponing it for some reason or other. She was free to do as she pleased.

Her debts had been settled the day after she agreed to his proposal. She was looked after by two maids and a cook, and there was a chauffeured car at her disposal. Every day began with the arrival of a bouquet of white roses with a card saying 'I love you', identical to the card attached to the black velvet box from either Cartier, Van Cleef & Arpels or Harry Winston delivered every Monday. When she received the keys to the apartment there had been a separate envelope with the key to the safe in her bedroom, and a note from Simon asking her to be specially careful with it, because there was no duplicate. The need for a safe did not appear obvious at first, although it was useful to have a secure place accessible only to her, but by now it was nearly full of jewellery. And the presents kept arriving.

She was dressed by Chanel, Givenchy and Saint-Laurent, and there was hardly any shop on Place Vendôme or the Rue du Faubourg Saint-Honoré where she had not been. The day she moved into the apartment she purchased the Art Nouveau lamps Jacques wanted, and five Saint-Laurent suits in his size, and presented them to him that evening, when he came to inspect her new home.

She had expected Nana to share in her delight at their new wealth, but instead Nana had become even more withdrawn. If a particularly extravagant toy was delivered for Gloria, she would just mutter 'It's too much,' and shake her head in disapproval. At first, Arianne had tried to explain that it was all for free, but she had given up by now. Nothing could dispel Nana's fear of life.

The fitting over, she changed into her clothes and left the room, escorted by Yvette. At the top of the stairs they were joined by the *Directrice*, who apologized on behalf of Mademoiselle Chanel, who was away at the time. She would surely have been delighted to see such a special customer as Mademoiselle Delors again. On her way out, Arianne cast her eyes over the vitrines displaying the bags and accessories typical of the *Maison*, but there was nothing new, and she already had them all.

She walked into the Rue Cambon, and turned towards the Ritz entrance. She was looking forward to meeting Cameline again, now the Principessa di Sarteano and on her first shopping expedition to Paris since the wedding. They had arranged to have lunch, and then to go and see the Balmain collection. She wondered how Cameline would fit into her new life, and how long it would last, but then realized that the same could be asked about her, and she dismissed the thought. She gave the doorman just the hint of a 'thank you' smile and walked into the hotel.

Simon de la Force glanced at the Christmas cards lined up on the mantelpiece, leaned back in his throne-like leather chair and chuckled. He had just spoken on the phone to Edouard Golbins, who had confirmed that Arianne's expenditure was doubling from month to month. Good. Simon loved that English saying about giving people enough rope to hang themselves.

He looked around his office. The mahogany panelling, the desk almost the size of a billiard table, everything in the lofty room confirmed that this was the work place of the most powerful man in Argentina. His eyes lingered for a moment on the portrait of Colonel de la Force, an early nineteenth-century ancestor who had had the misfortune of being captured by Indians. His balls had ended up as the main ornament on an Indian chief's necklace, but he had gained a place in Argentine history. Simon fully identified with his martial counterpart: he was also planning a campaign, and he had won the early skirmishes. But the main battle was still ahead.

Simon trusted his nose for human weakness, and he had sensed during their conversation on the yacht that there was something in Arianne's past that made her vulnerable to him. It was just a matter of finding out what it was. But there was no police record of Arianne Delors in France, only the registration of her birth, and the detectives in Brazil had drawn a blank.

He had stayed away from Arianne to make her feel at ease in her new life, to become so used to it that she could not contemplate giving it up. Only then would he start turning the screws, but he could not rely on anyone else for what would now be required. He would have to go to Paris himself, and he was waiting for his call to Arianne to come through. He had to fly on business to Madrid anyway, and he would tell Arianne that he was going to be in Paris within ten days.

The phone nearest him rang, and he picked it up immediately.

'I have Mrs de la Force on the line, Sir, and she says it is most urgent.' He thought of not taking the call, but then decided that it was better to avoid one of Dolores' tirades later on.

'Put her through.'

'Simon!' Dolores' shrill voice was enough to set his nerves on edge. 'I have just spoken to Jacqueline, and she told me that there is a girl who is the talk of Paris, living like a queen. Her name is Arianne something, and the gossip is that you are keeping her. I will not . . .' She was not allowed to finish the sentence.

'Shut up, you stupid cow!' he roared. 'I don't know why you listen to gossip. If I were to keep anyone other than you living like a queen, I would have to own Fort Knox. I've just seen some of your latest bills.'

'Well, don't take it like that, Simon,' Dolores whined. 'I was just asking! Don't forget that we are having dinner with Miguel and Teresa tonight – don't be late.'

He put the receiver down with a sneer. She'd better enjoy it while it lasted.

'Hello, my love, I've just checked into the George V. I'm so happy to hear your voice and know that we are in the same city,' Simon cooed.

'Thank you. Did you have a good flight?' Arianne knew that she ought to say that she was so glad too, but she couldn't bring herself to do it.

'Very good, I slept most of the time.' Stretched on the bed, his shoes on the silk bedspread, Simon noticed the time: the girl from Madame Claude would be there in five minutes. Better keep the conversation short. 'Listen, darling, I'm very tired, but could we have lunch tomorrow? We can do whatever you want afterwards.'

'Would you like to go to the cinema?' Arianne asked. That would take care of conversation, she thought.

'I don't like to sit next to unknown people,' Simon replied sharply. 'If there is anything you want to see, I will ask my office to arrange a private screening.' He looked at the time again: three minutes left. 'I was thinking on the plane that I have never met Gloria. I saw in the paper that the Budapest Circus is in town, and I thought she might like to see it.'

'Gloria is only one-and-a-half years old, but you just said that you didn't like sitting next to strangers,' protested Arianne.

'I was thinking of taking over the circus one afternoon, and your nanny could ask other children to come if you like. It would be like Gloria's own party.'

Arianne began to explain why she thought that the idea was not a good one, when Simon heard a discreet knock at the door, and interrupted her.

'I'm sorry, my love, but they are knocking at the door. I asked for something to eat. We can discuss this tomorrow. Good night.'

Simon stood up and quickly slipped the envelope from Edouard Golbins with the address of the detective agency and the duplicate keys into his bedside table drawer. He began to undo his shirt as he walked towards the door. Soon he would not need any more Claude girls, but in the meantime he had to remember to tip that helpful, discreet man at the reception desk. The hotel management would not be very pleased to find out about Simon's pastime. Like so much else about Simon's life, it was better to keep it quiet.

The box, specially built for the day, stood next to the circus ring. It was draped in pink velvet, and brightly-coloured chocolates spelt out 'Gloria' across its front. On their arrival, Simon, Arianne, Nana and Gloria, followed by a few bewildered children, their nannies, and the whole of Arianne's domestic staff, were escorted to the box by a troupe of somersaulting clowns and acrobats.

Simon had been at his most convincing over lunch a week before, and Arianne's reservations about the preposterous idea had melted away. 'I have always wanted to have children, and I long to give the nicest possible party for a child I love,' he had said. He had insisted that her staff should come: 'It will be like a family party'. Arianne

208

suddenly relished the thought of her little girl having the most wonderful party in the world. To enter into the spirit of the occasion, she was wearing her new fitted hussar coat in red wool, delivered from Saint-Laurent the day before.

As she sat down and looked at Gloria's face, her eyes shining with excitement, Arianne turned towards Simon and briefly touched his hand.

'Thank you,' she said gratefully. 'This is the best present you have given me so far.' She was genuinely moved by his thoughtfulness. The emeralds, rubies and diamonds piling up in her safe were props to his vanity as well as bribes to her, but this was different. She found that, for the first time since his arrival, she was warming to him.

'You have nothing to be thankful for, my darling,' he said. 'This party means as much to me as it does to Gloria.'

The band burst into a fanfare of trumpets, and the clowns walked into the arena pushing enormous red and yellow balls. One of the clowns, helped by the others, climbed laboriously on top of a ball. The rest of the troupe began to push the ball slowly around the ring while the clown stumbled backwards and forwards, trying to maintain his balance.

It was at about this time that a black Simca pulled in fifty yards away from the building on Quai Anatole France, and the driver got out. He walked to the front door of the building, and looked at his watch.

At the circus, the older children in the box noisily celebrated the attempts of a second clown to climb onto the ball. He succeeded at last, and pulling a water pistol from his pocket, squirted the first clown in the face.

The concierge at the Quai Anatole France building was reading *Le Figaro* when the telephone rang in his room, at the other end of the hall. He grumbled at being disturbed, and left his desk to take the call. The man outside quickly walked in, ran up the stairs silently to the first floor and pulled out a key from his coat pocket. By the time the concierge returned to his desk, annoyed by having to deal with a wrong number, the man had let himself into Arianne's empty apartment.

At the circus, the merriment reached a higher pitch when a troupe of white horses came into the ring. The clowns on foot jumped on the horses running around the ring, weaving their way around the balls scattered on the arena. The two clowns on the ball held on to each other in mock terror, until they lost their balance and fell noisily, raising clouds of sawdust as they hit the ground. They immediately stood up, and jumped onto the two horses at the end of the line.

In the apartment, the man unfolded a small plan, and found his way to Arianne's bedroom. He identified the particular picture hinged to the wall, and pulled it towards him with his gloved hand. He slipped the duplicate key into the lock, and opened the safe without any trouble.

The riding clowns now pulled out rolls of ribbon from their pockets and flung them to the rider across the ring while holding on to the end of each streamer, forming the multi-coloured spikes of a swirling wheel. A second fanfare of trumpets rang out; the clowns jumped off the horses in unison, and bowed to the rapturous applause of their little audience. The ringmaster announced the next act: from Budapest, the fabled Toncnoghy Brothers, masters of the trapeze.

In the meantime, the stranger in the apartment surveyed the contents of the safe before touching anything: he had been told that there must be no evidence whatsoever of his visit. He quickly began to open the boxes. His instructions were to disregard the jewellery and concentrate on any papers or documents he might find, but he found none on the top shelf.

The circus lights changed colour, the drums rolled, and three tall, athletic men ran into the ring, their swirling satin cloaks embroidered with their names. They swiftly climbed to the high-level platforms at both ends of the ring, and unfastened their cloaks, letting them fall to the ground. One by one, they climbed onto the trapezes, and began their act. As the Toncnoghy Brothers flew over the ring in a dazzling display of physical skill, the audience was spellbound by their prowess.

The search of the middle shelf of Arianne's safe was also unsuccessful, but the man was not disheartened. He began to check the bottom shelf, and soon found what he had been looking for: a Brazilian passport was hidden behind one of the piles of jewellery boxes. He pulled out a powerful light and a camera from his leather hold-all, plugged the light into a socket nearby, and carefully laid the passport on the dressing table.

A single beam of light shone on the climax of the Toncnoghy Brothers' act, the triple somersault and the Loop of Death, flawlessly performed, while in the apartment the man aimed his light at the open passport, photographed every page of the document and returned it to the safe. The Brothers bowed to the audience while at the other end of Paris the man made sure that there were no further documents or papers to photograph, and then closed the safe.

It took the man no longer than the first half of the performance of Geza the Fire-Eater to check the contents of the drawers in the bedroom dressing table and the desk in the library. There was nothing there of any consequence. While Geza proceeded to swallow an enormous sword, the man phoned his office from the library phone, to remind them to make the second phone call in exactly one minute. He then left, closing the door behind him without a sound, and waited in the first floor hallway.

He could hear the phone ringing downstairs, and the mutterings of the concierge as he left his desk to take another call. As soon as he heard the door closing behind the concierge, the man rushed downstairs. He was out of the building long before the old concierge returned to his desk, cursing the dialler of yet another wrong number.

By the time Xenia and the African Lions came into the ring, the man was driving away in his car, along the Quai Anatole France. He hoped that the Monsieur with the Indian face and the funny name (the man had stopped believing in his clients' names a long time ago) would be pleased with his work.

As the small black Simca joined the traffic on the Pont de la Concorde, Simon de la Force was leading his guests out of the box, holding Gloria in his arms. Arianne couldn't help being delighted by the sight of them together, Gloria struggling to pinch Simon's nose.

17

'Wasn't it a lovely Christmas, Nana?' asked Arianne.

They were on their way to the Jardin des Tuileries. Arianne did not like taking Gloria out in the cold, but Nana made it a point that Gloria should go to the park every morning, regardless of the weather. Arianne found it difficult to disagree with Nana on such matters. Gloria was her granddaughter and, above all, Nana *knew*. Not the whole of Arianne's story, but enough to bring their world crashing down around them if she chose to. Better to humour the old woman. Driven out of the kitchen by the cook and kept away from other domestic chores by the Portuguese maids, Gloria had become Nana's sole occupation. The little girl was her obsession.

'Yes, it was,' Nana answered, steering Gloria's pushchair to avoid a small hole in the pavement.

Gloria was wearing the cheap blue coat that Nana had given her for Christmas. Row after row of expensive clothes hung in Gloria's closets, and the meaning of the present was not lost on Arianne. She could not understand Nana's disapproval of their life now since she knew very well how Arianne had earned her living until she became a model.

It had been their second Christmas together. Outwardly, it had been magnificent. The enormous tree glowed at one end of the drawing room, logs burned in all the fireplaces, and Arianne had bought an exquisite Nativity scene from one of Celine de Merteuil's antique dealer friends. Gloria had become particularly fond of one of the three wise men and had played endlessly with the plaster figurine, bearing its gift of gold.

Arianne had given her staff the night off. The food had been delivered from Fauchon early in the evening, and they had kept busy making everything ready for dinner. At last, the preparations completed, the three of them sat at the lavishly decorated table.

It was only then that the grandeur of their surroundings underlined the absurdity of the situation, the loneliness of two women with little to say to each other sitting in a formal dining room. Gloria, kept awake much later than her usual bedtime, became impossibly fractious by eleven o'clock. Nana took her to bed, and the two women then finished their dinner in silence. Afterwards, as they sat by the drawing room fire, the conversation limped along until the time came to open the presents, and they were at last free to go to bed.

Simon had phoned from Buenos Aires to say that he would be able to come to Paris for New Year's Eve, and that he had arranged a most special evening for the two of them to toast the New Year. No, he would not tell her what it was, it was a surprise. Simon had also said that he would not send her a Christmas present, because he wanted to deliver it in person.

But Christmas was behind them now, and it was a beautiful morning. Although it was bitterly cold, the sun shone on the roofs and spires of Paris, outlined crisply against the blue sky. As they crossed the road towards the park Arianne raised the collar of her fur-lined coat, pulled down the edge of Gloria's knitted hat over the child's ears, and smiled. She looked forward to a better year.

As was often the case, Simon de la Force was pleased with himself. Surrounded by his usual retinue of acolytes and fawning airline staff in the VIP lounge, he was waiting at Buenos Aires airport to board the flight to Paris. It was probably his last commercial flight: his new Lear Jet was due to arrive from America early in the New Year.

After a week in Punta del Este with Dolores and her family, he was more than glad to escape. As arranged, Edouard Golbins had phoned him two days after Christmas to say that Simon must come to Paris immediately for an urgent meeting. Dolores had made the customary protests, but Simon was sure that she was as glad to see him leave as he was to go.

An airline employee approached him, and gave him his passport.

'You don't need to go through passport control, Mr de la Force. You can board the plane now. Have a good flight.'

Simon put the passport in his pocket and walked to the exit from the lounge onto the tarmac. One of his minions noticed that the passport's edge was still visible and mentioned it to Simon. As he tried to push the passport further in, he realized that it was resting on top of the small leather box at the bottom of his pocket. He moved the passport to his inside pocket.

The leather box was another reason to be pleased. Simon was glad that the gift would be more than just Arianne's Christmas present. Even Golbins had been surprised by Arianne's relentless extravagance, and it was nice to be able to save some money.

As he climbed the steps towards the smiling stewardess, he thought that, nonetheless, it was all money well spent. He was not in love. Love was an emotion that, as far as he could judge from his observation of other people in such a predicament, he had never experienced. But he wanted Arianne more than he had ever wanted any other woman. Now, at last, he was going to have her.

He had married Dolores to prove to Buenos Aires society that he could buy any of them but he knew now that, ultimately, he had merely acknowledged their superiority to him. By joining them he had flattered them. Although his money was the only reason for Dolores to stand out among her peers, she felt above him, as if she had condescended to marry him. It would not be like that with Arianne. He knew enough about her to keep her under his thumb for the rest of his life.

He fastened his safety belt, closed his eyes, and relaxed in his seat. He was going to enjoy this trip.

18

'We are nearly there, Mademoiselle.'

The chauffeur's voice could be heard through the dark glass screen between the front and rear seats, but Arianne was not able to see him. She was unable to see the outside either; all the windows at the back of the car had been papered over. When she had been collected from her apartment, the driver had explained that the windows had been obscured at the request of Monsieur de la Force.

This had been enough for Arianne to try to open her window as soon as the car pulled away, but after pressing the switch several times, she realized that the driver must have disconnected the power to the electric windows at the back. At first she was annoyed, but then she entered into the spirit of the occasion and became amused by the idea of being driven around like an Oriental princess, invisible to all. She switched on the radio above the drinks cabinet, sat back in the velvet seat and listened to the music.

She was not wearing her watch, but she guessed that she had left home nearly an hour ago when the car slowed down, then turned sharply and came to a standstill. The door by her side was opened, and she saw Simon, standing a few feet away, wearing his dinner jacket. The door was held by a footman in court uniform and powdered wig, who helped her out of the car.

'You are looking gorgeous, as usual,' Simon said admiringly, kissing her on the cheek. Distracted by the physical contact, she pretended to rearrange the folds of her full length coat, matching the white satin sheath beaded in crystal and gold she was wearing beneath it.

'That is some outfit. What sort of bill am I going to get this time?' he continued in the same tone. The remark hinted at a proprietorial role, and it put Arianne on guard.

'I hope you are not complaining,' she said frostily.

'I could never complain about you, not tonight anyway,' he said, guiding her towards the flood-lit building in the background. The red carpet muffled the sound of their steps on the white gravel.

'But this is the Petit Trianon!' Arianne exclaimed, as she stopped in front of the building. 'What are we doing here?'

'Having dinner first, and then toasting the New Year. I thought it would amuse you,' replied Simon, stepping aside as they reached the entrance.

'How could you possibly rent this place?' she asked.

'I heard through friends that there is a major restoration programme going on at Versailles, and they need money. One of my companies in France has agreed to foot the bill for the restoration of one of the State Rooms in the palace in exchange for this small favour.'

Arianne was overwhelmed. Nothing, absolutely nothing seemed beyond the reach of this man. Simon noticed her expression, read her thoughts, and relished the moment.

'I am sure you know that it was built by Louis XV for Madame de Pompadour, as her private retreat. I thought that made it quite suitable for us,' he boasted.

'I came here during the summer, for a picnic with Nana and Gloria, and the guide who showed us around said that the last owner was Marie Antoinette. I am not sure I like that thought,' Arianne retorted.

Simon smiled, and patted her shoulder.

'Don't worry, I haven't brought my guillotine along.'

The bewigged waiter offered Arianne more coffee.

'No, thank you,' she said. He poured Simon another cup. 'Is there anything else that Monsieur requires?' he asked.

Simon glanced at the corner, to check that an unopened bottle of champagne stood in the ice-bucket on a side table.

'Leave the wine on the table, and that will be all for now. We don't want to be disturbed,' he instructed. The waiter left the room.

Arianne's misgivings had faded away during dinner. They had eaten in the small boudoir off the Music Room, the oak panelling carved with the delicacy of lace. The round table in the middle, just big enough for two, was covered in pink damask, and scented candles burned in gold candlesticks. The food had been as light as Simon's conversation, which had been mostly about beautiful areas of Argentina, where he seemed to own an estate in every corner of the country. He added that he hoped Arianne would see it all one day. She had listened to his small talk, and reproached herself for her early fears. But his last remark to the waiter had aroused her suspicions again.

Simon looked at his watch.

'It's only half an hour to midnight,' he said, pulling out a small leather box from his pocket. He leaned across the table and placed it in front of Arianne. 'Just enough time for what I have to tell you.' She knew from his tone that she was not going to like what he was about to say.

She opened the box and gasped. She was staring at a square diamond the size of a large postage stamp.

'Isn't it a bit too much for a Christmas present?' she asked.

'Perhaps,' Simon answered. 'But it is just adequate as my future wife's engagement ring.'

Arianne put the box aside. 'I thought we had a deal,' she said cautiously.

'I learned a long time ago that deals can always be reviewed, if the circumstances change,' he replied.

Arianne stood up and walked towards the door.

'I wouldn't be in such a hurry to leave, Florinda. We have a few things to discuss,' Simon replied calmly. He could afford to be calm: he held all the trump cards.

Arianne froze at the mention of Florinda's name. It was what she had called herself in the Bois, whenever a man had asked her name. After more than a year, the men were as faceless to her as she hoped she was to them. Most of them had been respectable citizens, terrified of being found out in the Bois. If one of them had seen a photograph of her as a model, recognized her, and decided to make money from the knowledge, he would have approached her first. If one of the whores had found out, she would probably have gone to a tabloid paper with the story, not

218

to Simon. There were only four people in Paris aware of her connection to Simon. Neither Edouard Golbins nor Celine de Merteuil would risk Simon's wrath by embarrassing him with the revelation of her past. She cringed at the thought of Jacques betraying her, but he only knew her as Arianne. No, it couldn't be Jacques. And it couldn't be Nana. It had to be that shit at Rue Lanneau, the forger. She waited for a moment until she had regained her composure, then turned around and returned to her chair.

'I don't know who you are talking about,' she said, looking straight at Simon. She knew it was useless to pretend, but she had to gain time. There had to be a way out of what was to follow, and she needed to find it.

'I admire your aplomb. It is one of the many reasons why I think you are worthy of becoming my wife,' Simon said, unable to conceal his amusement. 'We could play cat and mouse if you wish,' he continued, 'but it might be quicker to review a few facts. I have been told that the police in Rio would very much like to talk to a girl called Florinda Souza. She is wanted in connection with a murder. Her photograph looks startingly familiar. I will not say more. We are within earshot of at least twelve servants, and blackmail can be a very profitable line of business.'

Arianne understood at last. He didn't know about the Bois. Simon must have traced her passport, Florinda's passport, made inquiries in Brazil, and now he believed her to be her own sister. She briefly considered explaining the truth to Simon, telling him that she was really Silvia, but realized there would be no point. It would make no difference to her predicament if he decided to bring in the Brazilian police: she was equally guilty of Ruben's murder in their eyes. Somehow the remaining confusion reassured her: it was as if her real self were still safely out of Simon's reach.

At least she was no longer fighting in the dark, and she was relieved by his mention of blackmail. He seemed as concerned about exposure as she was.

'I wouldn't know how profitable blackmail can be. It's not *my* line of business,' she said pointedly.

Simon's eyes flashed. 'I'm sure you understand your

position, but I'll spell it out just in case. Unless you agree to my new terms, I will reveal your name and whereabouts to the police. I haven't spent all this time and money on you to end up with nothing.'

He poured himself another glass of Château-Yquem and held the glass to the candlelight, admiring its pale glow before continuing.

'Don't imagine that your past makes any difference to my feelings for you. I don't put any moral value on what people need to do in order to survive, or simply to get something they want. But I don't believe that Brazilian prisons provide *haute-couture* uniforms for their guests, and I don't imagine that you want to change your current lifestyle.'

He stood up, undid his bow tie, and began to unbutton his shirt.

'We can continue this conversation next door. There is a beautiful bedroom and the fire is lit. We have wasted enough time.' He walked around the table and stood behind her, leaning down to kiss her neck. The feel of his wet lips on her flesh made her shiver. He encircled her waist with his arm and tried to lift her from her seat, tearing the fragile beadwork of her bodice.

She stood. She had been cornered before, but she had always managed to get away. She turned to face him.

'I'm not going to sleep with you,' she said calmly. She continued before he could react. 'I know that you want me, and you know enough about me to think that you can force me to go to bed with you. But I don't know if you love me. I know that you are obsessed with me, but there is a great difference. If we sleep together, you could get tired of me as quickly as you have become infatuated with me. Not only would I become a nuisance to you, but I could cost you a lot of money if your wife learns about me and uses me as an excuse to divorce you then. It would be cheaper for you to send me to jail. No, we are not going to sleep together. Your desire for me is my only safeguard.'

'That's your problem, not mine,' he retorted. He came closer and gripped her in his arms, his hands fumbling at her zip. Her reaction was immediate. Her hand on his groin, she squeezed his balls as hard as she could, and he screamed in pain. Gasping for air, he let her go, and she ran to the sideboard. She picked up the champagne bottle with her left hand, and the ivory-handled carving knife with her right.

'If you move, this one goes into the Fragonard,' she said, waving the bottle towards the painting facing her, 'and the knife goes right between your ribs. You can try to rape me if you wish, but I wouldn't recommend it.'

Simon stared at her for a moment, then slowly began to do up his shirt. He re-knotted his tie and sat down. He wasn't particularly worried about the knife – he could deal with that. But the prospect of a fracas here, and the headlines that would follow, was a different matter. He had expected fear and submission from her, not a fight. There was no point in enraging her further.

'I admire your spirit,' he said in a soothing tone. 'I apologize again for my obtuseness. However, you are wrong. Sit down, and I'll explain why.'

Still holding the knife, Arianne went back to her chair, relieved to have regained some control of the situation.

'You are right that I want you, but I'm not interested in you just as my mistress. You are exceptionally beautiful, and you are very intelligent. You have also shown that you can take care of yourself. I told you before that I want you as my wife, and I say it again now.'

'You flatter me,' Arianne replied, 'but what guarantee would I have that you wouldn't get tired of me as your wife in the same way that you could become tired of me as your mistress? Now you know who I really am, you can always get rid of me by sending me to jail. It would be cheaper than a divorce settlement, the only reason I can think of for you not having left your wife long ago. I can't see what difference it would make, from my point of view, whether we are married or not.'

She took a sip of water, then went on.

'Having reached this point, the only sensible thing is to part now. I'll give all your presents back to you, and you will keep silent about what you know. It's the fairest arrangement for both of us.'

He sighed.

'You still don't understand me. The main reason I want to marry you is that I desperately want a son. My wife can't have children.'

For the first time since she had met him, Arianne heard an emotion other than pride or arrogance in his voice. He leaned across the table and took her hand.

'You have a child, so you probably can't imagine how desperately I want one. I have created an enormous business from nothing and I have no one to continue it, to keep my memory alive once I'm gone. I've reached a point in my life when I can no longer take tomorrow for granted. I want a son, I want him as soon as possible, and I want you to be his mother. You already have a lovely daughter, and you are going to give me a lovely son. As many as God will send us, in fact.' He tightened his grip on her hand. 'I wouldn't want to send the mother of my children to jail, would I? Our children will be your safeguard.' His eyes locked on hers. 'Your future depends on me, and my future depends on you. I can't imagine a better basis for a marriage. I will not let you down.' His voice dropped a fraction, and there was sudden, distinct menace in it. 'And I am sure that you will not let *me* down.'

Arianne recoiled. She was trapped. She could not tell him about her sterility. Not now. He had come here this evening expecting total victory. If she were to tell him that all his efforts, all his expectations, had been for nothing, his rage would be uncontrollable, and he would turn her over to the police out of spite and humiliation. She knew him well enough by now to understand that. Still, she had to play for time, if only to delay the inevitable.

'Could I have more wine, please?'

'Of course,' Simon replied, getting up and filling her glass. 'Shall we drink a toast?' He pulled the ring from the box, and offered it to her.

'Not yet,' she said. 'It's not quite midnight.' She sipped her wine.

'You told me that there is no divorce in your country,' Arianne ventured after a while.

222

'What difference would that make? I can get a divorce anywhere else, and then marry you.'

'It would make a lot of difference to me. Our children would not be legitimate in Argentina, and I would not be your wife under the law there. It wouldn't matter while you are alive, but it could matter to our children once you are dead. You are much older than I am.'

He laughed.

'You are excessively cautious. Half of Argentina is married for a second time, and there are ways of ensuring the future of the second wife and her children.'

'Maybe, but I have been an outcast for most of my life, and I have no wish to remain one. You must understand that feeling. If you want me to be your wife, you must get a Vatican annulment, that's the only thing that would make our marriage valid in your country.'

She knew from gossip that it took years to arrange. In the meantime, she could get another set of forged papers and disappear with her jewellery, somewhere out of this bastard's reach.

Simon chuckled to himself. If that was all she wanted, his own plans were certainly faster and cheaper than appealing to the Sacra Rota in Rome.

'If what you are saying is that you will only marry me when our marriage would be fully valid in Argentina, then I will drink to that with pleasure.' He raised his glass.

'And no sex until we are legally married,' she added.

'I very much dislike that condition, but I'll go along with it. No sex until then,' Simon replied. It would take rather less time than she thought. Better to humour her now that he had almost won.

The clock struck twelve. Simon stood up and began to open the champagne bottle.

'Please go to the window. You will see my last surprise of the evening.'

It was a dark night, but the outline of the trees was just visible. The loud 'pop' of the champagne cork coincided with the first flash of bright white against the sky, followed by another and then another, until the park was lit by the dazzle of giant fireworks.

Simon stood behind her, and handed her a glass of champagne.

'Happy New Year, my love,' he said softly, kissing her shoulder and slipping the large ring on her finger. A new wave of fireworks, intertwined *A's* and *S's* this time, covered the sky in brilliant reds and blues.

Her eyes fixed on them, Arianne clenched her fist, her nails digging into her palm. The ring felt far, far heavier than she would have ever guessed.

19

Carlos Gardes owed everything to Simon de la Force. He had been born in the Valley thirty years ago. He grew up in the local orphanage until, at the age of fourteen, he was considered old enough to earn his living. He found a job on the then booming Valle del Oro estate. Four years later, encouraged by his success as a tango singer at the estate's barbecues, he decided to go to Buenos Aires to try his luck.

He soon found out that while his voice might have earned him the applause of sugar-cane harvesters in Salta, it took a greater voice and a greater stage presence than his to succeed as a tango singer in the capital. However, his Salta background did not go unnoticed by the owner of one of the many seedy cafés where he tried to launch his career, and Carlos eventually drifted into work as a courier for the profitable cocaine trade between Bolivia and Argentina. Salta was a key stage on the route.

During one of his trips to Salta, disaster struck. He was receiving a delivery at the Bolivian border when the *Gendarmeria* appeared. The other courier resisted, and was shot on the spot; Carlos was taken to jail in the city of Salta to await trial.

While in his cell, Carlos had a stroke of inspiration and wrote to Simon de la Force, explaining his connection with the Valle del Oro estate. In his letter he claimed he had been sent to collect the parcel without being told what it contained, the same alibi he had used during his questioning by the police. His letter also included a detailed account of his unhappy childhood.

Simon relished his role as a feudal lord, and his secretaries had strict instructions to pass on letters asking for help from anyone connected with his estate. Something in Carlos' letter pierced his armour, and Simon arranged for the young man to be brought to his office under police custody. This was technically in breach of the law, but Simon made his own laws in the province.

During the interview Simon sensed in Carlos the same quality noticed by the café-owner in Buenos Aires. Maybe because of his circumstances, or simply because of his nature, Carlos was one of those men who would do anything, if the order came from someone he recognized as his boss. Moral considerations were his superior's problem, not his.

A man like that could be very useful to Simon. He arranged for Carlos to be released for lack of evidence, the cocaine parcel having mysteriously disappeared from police headquarters, and he offered the young man a job within the company. He had no specific use for him, but Simon was sure that one would be found eventually.

It soon became clear that Carlos had an uncanny instinct for tracking and trapping animals of any kind. He became responsible for the success of many of Simon's hunts, which were held for Simon's friends or business contacts. This was the respectable side of Carlos' job for Simon. There had been other tasks better left unmentioned, but none that could compare to Simon's latest orders.

Dolores de la Force hated Salta. The heat was impossible during the day, and the nearest neighbour worth talking to was a hundred miles away. One couldn't even put together a decent canasta table in such a place.

She had longed to stay in Punta del Este until the end of summer, but early in March Simon had insisted that she go to Valle del Oro to ensure that the household was running smoothly by the time he arrived with some friends he was expecting from Spain.

She had been there for ten days now, and she was desperately bored. She loathed the house, Simon's palace-like interpretation of a colonial *hacienda*. It had been nearly two years since her last visit, but now she had decided that the place needed drastic re-decoration. As soon as she was back in Buenos Aires she would phone Diego, her favourite interior designer. He would understand exactly what she had in mind.

She finished breakfast, and then thought about what she was going to do with the rest of her day. Suddenly she remembered that Carlos had mentioned he had noticed some very unusual orchids growing on the rocks at the other end of the park, where the water from the artificial lake was pumped out to form a waterfall on the side of the hill. It was a very isolated area and she seldom went there, but flowers were one of her very few passions. The blossoms must have been unusual indeed for someone as experienced in the region as Carlos not to have seen them before; perhaps she could send a few divisions to her greenhouses in Buenos Aires. It would take her at least half an hour to walk to the lake, a good way to kill time and to get some exercise before lunch.

She dressed quickly, putting on a white pleated skirt and a lovely pink shirt she had bought in Capri. She usually would not have worn such clothes in the country, but after a week in Salta she longed for civilized living, and she could not bear the thought of trousers, jodhpurs, or anything that would stick to her legs in this atrocious heat. But she would have to wear boots for the walk; she put on a pair of long cotton socks and some flat-heeled walking shoes in the meantime.

She left the house by the side door and turned left, along the guest wing, towards the kitchen courtyard. As she approached the gun room she noticed Zenon, the handyman, fixing the door lock. He stood up as soon as he saw her, and took off his beret.

'*Buen dia, Señora Dolores,*' he said respectfully.

'*Buen dia, Zenon.* What's wrong with the door?'

'Someone broke into the gun room two nights ago, Señora. I had to wait for the new lock to arrive from the city.'

'Nobody told me about it! Was anything stolen?' she asked, as if she cared.

'All the boots, Señora, but nothing else. Perhaps Pancho did not want to bother the Señora about something so insignificant. It is very odd, because they left all the guns. Must be some *loquito.*'

Dolores sighed. Yes, only a madman would steal the

boots and leave everything else, but it was a damn nuisance. She would have to go back to see if there was a spare pair in the dressing room. The alternative was to send some maid for it, but these girls never found anything unless they were told precisely where to look. The need for boots was probably an old wives' tale anyway. These Indians loved to frighten intruders from Buenos Aires.

'I hope that the break-in has been reported to the police. I'll have a word with Pancho,' she said, and walked away. She wouldn't put it past the majordomo to be behind the robbery himself.

As she left the house behind her and walked further into the park, she almost reconciled herself to her surroundings. The harsh contrast of arid rock mountains and fertile valleys, of an impossibly blue sky against the ochre of the hills, was very different to Dolores' favourite countryside, the gentle green of the pampas in her family estates, but it was very beautiful in its own strange way. If only the damn heat would go away.

But she didn't think about the landscape for long. As so often these days, her thoughts turned to the state of her marriage.

Dolores had been brought up to marry well, and Simon was the best catch in Argentina. She knew that Simon had been unfaithful to her from the beginning: some of her friends had taken good care to make her aware of his peccadilloes, but it had not mattered then. She was Señora de la Force, and that was enough for Dolores. In her circle, mistresses came and went, but wives remained.

Her miscarriages, and the eventual confirmation that she was barren, had opened the first cracks. Simon's sporadic visits to her bedroom had stopped as soon as it became clear that there was no hope of a child.

This did not bother Dolores. Sex did not concern her very much. But it had hurt her pride, and she worried about her future. She knew how much Simon wanted an heir, and sooner or later he would find another woman who could give him one.

The gossip from Paris had rung further warning bells, and she became concerned about the implications for her position. As usual when really serious matters troubled her, she decided to consult her father.

His wisdom had reassured her. 'He can not divorce you. He can only ask for a legal separation. Any good lawyer, and I know a few very good ones, would make it so expensive for him that he could not seriously consider the option. He will probably end up having a baby with a maid; it runs in that family. You can then adopt the child and live happily ever after. I wouldn't lose any sleep over it, darling.' Her father had then taken her for a comforting lunch at the Jockey Club, and she had stopped worrying for a while.

Simon's sudden departure from Punta del Este after Christmas had rekindled her fears, but he had returned soon after, and had spent the rest of the summer with her, other than short business trips to Buenos Aires. Perhaps her father had been right after all, and she worried too much.

Relieved, Dolores decided to concentrate on more pleasant thoughts, and turned to the redecoration of the main house. She had to plan every room to be able to tell Diego what she wanted.

The house should look cosy, that was the word, like an English country home. By the time she reached the lake, she had decided that the chintz curtains in the dining room should match the wall coverings rather than contrast with it. She had seen it in Chiquita's London dining room, and she found it lovely. As she approached the waterfall, Dolores realized that Carlos, the idiot, had been wrong. There was nothing unusual about the orchids there, at least from a distance. She decided to have a closer look.

Carlos was hiding behind the rocks. He had already spent the previous afternoon there, waiting for her to appear. He had returned before dawn to avoid being seen, and was beginning to doubt whether she would turn up at all when he saw her walking along the lake, towards the waterfall.

Dolores stood in front of the blossoms climbing up the rocks, her back to him. Carlos unfolded a thick canvas bag, and waited until she moved further to one side, where the large boulders made her invisible to anyone walking in the park, although it was unlikely that anyone would be there at this time of the day.

He approached her as silently as he would have had she been a wild animal. He swiftly slipped the bag over her head and shoulders until it reached her hips, then he tightened the bindings before she could react. He held her with both arms and found it quite easy to lift her in spite of her resistance. He carried her to a large wicker basket he had hidden behind a rock, kicked the lid open, and placed Dolores standing inside.

It had taken Carlos two days to track a large *cascabel* snake, and he had kept it in the basket for a further ten days, to ensure that its poison sacks were full. Tormented by hunger and disturbed by Dolores, the snake struck immediately; her cotton sock offered no resistance to its needle-sharp fangs. In her blind, terrified struggle, Dolores suddenly felt a sharp pain in her left leg, followed by a burning sensation.

As soon as he saw the snake strike, Carlos pulled Dolores out of the basket, kicked the lid shut, and waited. It would not take long now. He was not worried by Dolores' screams. They would be silenced by the roar of the waterfall next to them, and she soon would be too weak to cry out.

He could feel her frantic movements slowing down until she went limp in his arms, but he did not remove the canvas bag. He had seen people dying from *cascabel* bites; there would be a lot of internal bleeding oozing out of the mouth, nose and ears, and he had to be careful not to stain his clothes. Don Simon had been very insistent about that.

After a while he laid Dolores on the ground. He pulled his cigarettes and lighter from his shirt pocket, and searched in his bag until he found his transistor radio. He connected the earphone, and looked at his watch. It was time for 'The Tango Show', one of his favourite programmes. Carlos was so absorbed by the music that he did not notice Dolores' last, spasmodic convulsions inside the bag as the poison finally destroyed her nervous system.

Carlos did not much care for female tango singers but he

had to admit that Suzy Leiva was nearly as good as a man. The lack of movement in the bag when he finally turned the radio off confirmed what he expected. He undid the bindings and uncovered Dolores' body, but he closed his eyes. He did not want to see the poor Señora's face.

He left her body lying on the ground and tipped the basket open; the snake slipped away and quickly disappeared into a crevice in the rocks. He would have liked to have killed the creature, but it would mean taking unnecessary risks to walk away from the scene with the dead snake, and he couldn't leave it there. Better to let it go, as Don Simon had said.

Carlos picked up his cigarette stubs and dropped them in the basket with the canvas bag. He erased his tracks with his poncho, and then began the long walk back to the house. Along the way he stopped at the incinerator building, and flung the basket into one of the roaring furnaces.

Carlos was very tired, but that didn't matter. He had done a good job, and he hoped that Don Simon would be pleased.

The Recoleta has been Buenos Aires' smartest cemetery for over a hundred years, the regular setting for splendid funerals. But few could compare with the burial of Dolores de la Force.

Simon led the cortège along the narrow lanes between the marble pavilions. He was flanked by Dolores' family, the Primate Cardinal of Buenos Aires and the Archbishops of Salta, Jujuy and Tucuman, the sugar provinces of Argentina. Half the Government, the best of society and more or less the whole of Argentina's business establishment followed him, rubbing their elbows against the wreaths and floral tributes piled up against the front of the tombs on both sides of the procession route from the cemetery gates to the Anzorena family vault, a few hundred yards away. The warm air was heavy with the scent of carnations.

Dolores' mother had insisted that her daughter be buried in Buenos Aires, in their vault. Simon had put up some token resistance, but the de la Force family tomb in Salta was rather modest, and it would have been impossible for the people who mattered to attend a funeral a thousand miles away from the capital. He soon agreed to her request.

Simon glanced at Dolores' mother, shaken by sobs under her thick black veil, and felt some sympathy for the woman. It must be hard to lose a daughter in such a tragic accident. But it was equally hard to lose one's beloved wife, and his face immediately regained the stern composure he had adopted when leaving his house to attend the Requiem mass at the Pilar church next to the cemetery.

Simon was beginning to feel the effect of the previous night's vigil. He had to stand for hours next to Dolores' coffin, laid out in the library. He had listened to an endless stream of 'Poor Simon,' 'Poor Dolores, so young,' 'Such a terrible accident,' and similar platitudes until the early hours. At first he had replied to the effect that 'we are all in the hands of God,' alternated with 'I can't forgive myself for not having stressed enough the dangers of walking without boots in that area.' But by two o'clock most people other than Dolores' family or his business associates had left, and he did not need to bother much about them.

Still, he could not just leave and go to bed, much as he wanted to, and he had drunk endless cups of black coffee to stay awake, with the occasional Scotch to counteract his boredom. The undertakers had arrived early in the morning to seal the coffin and load it on the hearse, and at last he had been able to leave the house.

The procession reached the vault. Simon and the family, their heads bent, stood at both sides of the ebony and silver coffin, while the Cardinal gave his last blessing and prayed for Dolores' soul. The family and the Archbishops joined in the prayers, but their voices could not muffle the instructions shouted by the undertakers from the second basement of the vault, advising their colleagues at the top as to how to manoeuvre the ropes for the coffin to negotiate the narrow openings on each floor until it reached its final resting place on one of the stone shelves, alongside several generations of Anzorenas. At last the undertakers left the tomb, the bronze gates of the vault were closed, and Dolores de la Force was left to rest in peace.

Simon had to stand at the cemetery's colonnaded portico for at least another hour to receive the mourners' condolences, but he enjoyed this part of the ceremony in spite of his tiredness. The calibre of the mourners was a homage to him, not to his wife. The end of the long line was at last visible, and soon afterwards he was free to go. He stiffly embraced his in-laws and walked to the car, maintaining his sad countenance until the limousine pulled away and the onlookers were left behind.

As soon as the car joined the traffic in Avenida Alvear for the short ride home he loosened his tie and undid his collar button, sat back and gave free rein to his thoughts. Not about Dolores, and not about Arianne either. He thought about what he would like to have for lunch. He was very hungry.

20

Arianne had just finished getting dressed when her maid announced that the car was waiting for her downstairs.

'Thank you, Rosinha,' said Arianne. She took one last look at herself in the full-length mirror, and decided to change out of the plain navy-blue dress she had just put on: it wasn't sombre enough for her mood. She went back to her cupboards, and finally chose a severe black suit and a black silk shirt. She knew she was late for her appointment with Simon, but she did not care. Let him wait.

Ever since receiving Simon's cable informing her of Dolores' sudden death, she had longed for time to stand still. All her plans, her delaying tactics, had crumbled as soon as she had opened the envelope and read his message.

Simon had phoned her the following day to expand on his brief description of what had happened, and to announce that he would come to Paris in April to make plans for their future. No matter how credible his explanation, how viable the accident, Arianne knew that Simon had killed his wife. She also knew that there was no way out for her now.

Simon had arrived in Paris the night before and phoned her from the hotel. He told her that he would move into the apartment the following day, but Arianne mentioned the need to maintain at least some decorum until their wedding was announced. He had reluctantly agreed, and suggested that they meet the following morning at Cartier, to choose a present to celebrate their forthcoming wedding. 'We don't need to hide now. I want the whole world to see us together,' he had said proudly.

She checked the time: he had been waiting for half an hour, and it would take at least ten minutes for the car to reach the Rue de la Paix. She picked up her bag and left the room without bothering to glance in the mirror. How she looked had suddenly ceased to matter to her.

'Perhaps Mademoiselle would care for sapphires?' asked the jeweller, presenting yet another velvet tray to Arianne.

'These are truly exceptional stones,' he continued in a silken voice. 'They belonged to the Maharanee of Baroda, but we have re-cut them and set them in a much more flattering style. Mademoiselle should try the necklace,' he said, picking up the sparkling piece of jewellery with both hands and holding it in front of Arianne. She barely glanced at the giant stones.

'I don't wear sapphires,' she replied, her tone as dismissive as the wave of her hand. 'They don't suit the colour of my eyes.'

'Of course,' said the jeweller, promptly passing the tray to his assistant, who laid the sapphire parure next to the numerous trays already rejected.

'Is there *anything* you like?' asked Simon, unable to conceal his exasperation.

He had started the morning in a radiant mood, his joy at the prospect of seeing Arianne doubled by the early morning call from his office to confirm that the discreet disposal of Dolores' jewellery through his Geneva contacts had been arranged. The price virtually covered the cost of the jewels Simon had so far given to Arianne and, since saving money came second only to the pleasure of making and spending it, he had walked into Cartier in a glow of self-contentment.

But they had been there for an hour. They had been shown endless sets of jewels, but nothing seemed to please Arianne. First she was nearly an hour late, and now she seemed to be in an impossible mood. Women, they could be a real pain sometimes. Simon was sure it had to be her period. Well, he would soon put a temporary stop to that small problem.

The jeweller was as puzzled as Simon by Arianne's lack of interest, but decades of experience with awkward clients ensured that none of his annoyance was apparent, although the sapphires were the last of their finest pieces. It was his

235

rule to do the utmost to clinch a sale. He whispered an instruction to the attendant and, always smiling, he turned to Arianne.

'Perhaps the answer is for Mademoiselle to have something made specially for her, with stones equal in quality to any of the jewels I have shown you so far, but to a more personal design. I have asked my assistant to bring some of the pieces we have in stock for resetting. He won't be a moment.'

The assistant returned with further velvet trays, and the jeweller picked up the top one.

'The history of this jewel would perhaps interest you, Monsieur de la Force. We recently accepted it in partial payment for another necklace from one of our American clients. The gems are magnificent, but the design, alas, is not quite fashionable now. We understand that it was made in Buenos Aires for Madame Perón, probably in the late 40s. Our client bought it at the auction of her jewellery in 1956.'

Simon recoiled at the sight of the necklace as if the tray held the bloody entrails of an animal.

'I would never buy anything that belonged to that thief!' he bellowed. 'She ruined our country, and I was a fierce opponent of that despicable government from the beginning.' Years of practice gave a convincing intonation to his outburst.

'Take it away immediately,' he continued in a slightly quieter voice, 'or I shall become very upset indeed.'

'Wait a minute,' Arianne said, placing her hand on the tray. 'It's really exquisite.' She examined the huge emeralds shining in the centre of diamond flowers. She did not know why the jewel upset Simon so much, but she did not care; it was enough that it annoyed him.

She tried on the necklace and looked at herself in the small mirror standing on the table. It was one of the most vulgar things she had ever seen.

'It's lovely, truly lovely,' she said. 'I will wear it at our wedding. Thank you, darling.' She leaned towards Simon and kissed him on the lips. The jeweller rose to the occasion and launched into an incantation about Mademoiselle's unerring eye, her superb taste, her knowledgeable disdain for conventional style. Simon took in Arianne's determined expression and knew that he was defeated.

'At least have it re-set,' he protested.

'Absolutely not, I adore it just as it is.' Arianne's tone made it clear that the matter was closed. 'Let's go,' she said. She walked towards the exit, without waiting for Simon. She smiled for the first time that morning, but there was little reason for her to smile for long these days. By the time Simon was beside her in the car her face was as impassive as usual.

It was mid-June, and the chestnut trees in the Jardin des Tuileries were in blossom. Arianne thought that it was probably the last time she would see them, and moved away from the window.

She gazed at her drawing room, the furniture shrouded by dust sheets laid by the removal men who had come that morning to take their luggage away. Seventeen Louis Vuitton trunks, God knows how many suitcases, and the enormous crate from Saint-Laurent holding her wedding dress.

When they had discussed the wedding plans four weeks ago she had insisted that she wanted a totally private ceremony, only witnessed by Nana. Simon had agreed, and told her that the wedding would take place at Our Lady of Yanbi, the colonial church on his Salta estate, far away from Buenos Aires and the social crowd. However, he had asked her to wear a white wedding dress for the occasion. 'I am very sentimental, and I am entitled to see my bride wearing a proper dress,' he had said cheerfully. Arianne found Simon in a good mood even more grating than his usual dictatorial persona.

Futile as it was, her only means of evening the score with him was to spend his money, and this she had done over the last weeks with a vengeance. Apart from her wedding dress, suitable for a Royal marriage, she had ordered seventy-five couture outfits. She had only stopped when she realized that the fittings were more exhausting for her than the bills were for Simon. She hadn't bothered to have the second fitting for many of the clothes, or even to pick up those that were ready.

Arianne had come to terms with her predicament, but she could not bear to think about what would become of Gloria and Nana because of it. She had had dinner with Jacques the night before. She had said nothing to him about what was troubling her, but at the end of the evening, when she kissed Jacques goodbye, she had given him a shoe box holding her best jewels and a letter asking Jacques to use the money from the sale of the jewellery to support Gloria and Nana. Arianne had never mentioned her friendship with Jacques to Simon, and she hoped Simon would not be able to trace him, at least for a while.

'I want you to keep this,' she had said. 'If anything were to happen to me, please open the box and read the letter inside, but only when Gloria and Nana are back in Paris. I have asked Nana to contact you.'

Jacques had taken the box.

'The wax seals are unnecessary, darling. I would not look into your box any more than I want to look into your past, but I will do what you ask me.' His eyes had shifted away. 'Better go now. I'm not as good as you are about not getting emotional,' he had said, gently pushing her out of his apartment.

That morning she had been to the Argentine Consulate to go through the formalities of the civil marriage by proxy that would enable them to marry in church in Argentina as soon as she arrived. Edouard Golbins had stood in for Simon. Officially, she was now Mrs Simon de la Force.

It was nearly dark. Nana had already retired to her bedroom, after helping Arianne to put Gloria to bed. Ever since Arianne had mentioned to her that she was going to marry Simon, Nana's attitude had changed and her tacit disapproval had vanished, as if she had sensed Arianne's difficulties. Nana was incapable of expressing her feelings, but Arianne had learned to gauge them, and she knew that in her curious, irrational way, Nana understood what was going on. Arianne had given her two return tickets from Argentina, in Nana and Gloria's name, and a power of attorney allowing Gloria to travel with Nana.

'If anything happens to me once we are there, please come back to Paris with Gloria immediately, and contact Jacques,' Arianne had told Nana.

'I will do what you ask me,' was her reply. Nothing else, but Arianne had felt relieved.

She walked into her bedroom. Everything other than her beauty case and the clothes she would wear for the trip tomorrow had been packed away. She looked at the fireplace, at the pile of ashes that had been Florinda Souza's Brazilian passport. The room reeked of Chanel No 5 and burned paper. She had poured a large bottle of scent on the passport to fuel the flames.

After the ceremony at the Consulate Edouard Golbins had handed her a letter from Simon, which she had read in the car. He had arranged for an Argentine passport in Arianne's married name to be delivered to her the next morning. 'The plane may have to make an emergency stop in Brazil, and I wouldn't want you to run into immigration problems. They can be very tiresome,' the letter said. He did not need to say more; they understood each other. 'The passport will be handed to you by the chauffeur just before you go through passport control in Paris. I want to make sure that you board the right flight,' he had added. Arianne picked up the poker from the side of the fireplace, and crumbled the ashes until they blended into the dusty pile in the grate.

She sat at her desk, switched the desk light on and picked up a few sheets of her pale blue writing paper from the stationery tray next to her. She stared at the blank sheet for a while, and then began to write, page after page. It was easier than she thought.

Her letter finished at last, she put it in an envelope, wrote 'Simon' on it, and put it away in the silk pouch inside her beauty case. She walked into her bathroom and ran her bath, but she did not linger in it. She wanted to go to sleep as soon as possible. Before getting into bed she returned to her beauty case for a bottle of Seconal, and took two pills. She rattled the bottle before putting it away, and was relieved to notice that there were still plenty of pills left.

21

SALTA, ARGENTINA
June 1969

The afternoon sun shone on the hilltop, outlining the white-washed building of Our Lady of Yanbi against the cobalt blue sky. As they began to climb towards the church, Arianne saw Simon's car parked outside it, in the shadow of a cluster of giant cactuses. The solitary car accentuated the emptiness of the landscape.

They had been driving for nearly an hour, across endless fields of sugar cane at first, and then through the stony plateau that surrounded the isolated hill. Arianne sat in the back seat, almost drowning in the froth of her wedding dress.

Arianne, Nana and Gloria had arrived in Salta the night before, exhausted by the twenty-hour flight to Buenos Aires. At Ezeiza Airport they had boarded Simon's jet for the last leg of the journey. They had landed at midnight, and they had been driven to one of the guest houses in the park, where Arianne found a large basket of white orchids. 'I'm not supposed to see you until the wedding, and we can't sleep under the same roof, since it brings bad luck. I love you,' read the unsigned card. Arianne crumpled it in her hand. Bad omens would not have made any difference to her now, but she was relieved not to have to see Simon. A maid showed them to their rooms, and Arianne fell asleep almost immediately, her tension defeated by her tiredness.

She woke up close to midday, to find that Nana and Gloria had been taken for a cart ride in the park. By the time they came back, escorted by gauchos in leather chaps and a French-speaking nanny in uniform, lunch was being served in the dining room. Arianne was unable to eat anything. After lunch, the nanny took Gloria to her bedroom for a rest, and the butler suggested that the ladies retire to their rooms to get ready for the ceremony. They should leave for the church at five o'clock. The ceremony was scheduled for six o'clock, and Don Simon hated delays.

At four o'clock the maid had knocked at Arianne's door and announced that the hairdresser from Buenos Aires was ready for the Señora. Arianne found Spanish surprisingly easy to understand. The hairdresser was shown into the room and introduced himself as Hubert, the Frenchness of his name belied by his atrocious accent. Arianne sensed his animosity, the reason for which became clear when he explained that he had been Dolores' hairdresser.

However, once he noticed Arianne's wedding dress on a dummy in the corner of the room, he launched into an ecstatic praise of Paris couture. Arianne had then told him about her life as a Balenciaga model. His enmity receded, and his passion for gossip exorcised Dolores' ghost. Even now, when time had nearly run out and everything mattered so little, Arianne was not prepared to be under anyone's shadow.

Her hair done, Hubert waited while Rosinha helped Arianne into her wedding dress, and quickly made her up. Only then did he pin the immense veil, sprinkled with hundreds of silk orange blossoms, to her chignon. Arianne asked Rosinha to bring her the black silk box on her dressing table, and she fastened the emerald necklace around her neck, throwing Hubert into further spasms of admiration.

She left her bedroom and was joined by Nana, dressed in her usual black. For once, she thought, Nana was the most appropriately attired person for the occasion. Gloria was holding Nana's hand, the nanny standing behind them. As Arianne appeared, Gloria ran to her.

'Where are you going, mummy?' she asked, trying to pick at the orange blossoms on Arianne's dress.

How could she explain to Gloria where she was going? What could she say to her two-year-old child? Arianne just stroked Gloria's head, and waited for the lump in her throat to subside.

'I'm going to a party, my darling. A very big party. I'll see you later.' Arianne pulled her veil down and turned towards the nanny. She did not want anyone to see her face now. 'Please take her away,' Arianne whispered. Gloria's light footsteps echoed on the tiled floor, until Arianne finally heard the door close behind her daughter.

They walked out of the house. The car was already waiting by the entrance. Arianne turned towards her maid, who had begun to gather the long train of her dress. 'Rosinha, please don't forget to take my beauty case to the main house after we have left, and leave it in my . . . our bedroom, on the bed.'

'Don't worry, Mademoiselle, I haven't forgotten your instructions,' the maid replied, as she carefully laid the train on the seat next to Arianne. Nana and the driver got into the car, and the butler closed the doors. The 'clunk' of the locks sounded like prison gates.

The warden pushed Florinda inside the cell, and slammed the steel door shut behind her. Florinda stumbled, then fell on the narrow bed, the dirty cotton cover soaking in her tears, new stains over the old ones. It had all been Santos' fault. She had been an idiot to fall for him, under the spell of his slow eyes and his hard fists.

If only she knew what had gone wrong at the last job. She had left the villa during the early hours, when she knew the security guard would be asleep. Either the man or the woman must have awakened while she was crossing the park, noticed the jewellery missing from the dressing table and rung the alarm. The park lights went on and the security man came out of his hut, gun in hand, just before she reached the gates. She pushed him aside and ran to the street. Santos, damned Santos, should have been there, waiting for her in a stolen car, but he wasn't and she heard the bullet whistle past her ear. She didn't have a chance; she dropped her bag on the sidewalk and held her arms up in surrender.

The police soon matched her fingerprints to those found on the gun at the scene of Ruben's murder, and she was found guilty at the trial. She would spend the next twenty-five years in jail because of Santos. Hatred was all she had left.

But Santos was not the only one responsible for this. She

242

*would have got two, at worst three years, for the robbery.
If she was going to be in jail for as long as she had been
alive it was because of her sister. She had ended up paying
for Silvia's crime. No, she didn't hate Santos most. She
hated Silvia, and she hated her more than even she would
have thought possible. Prison wasn't bad enough for Silvia:
she ought to be dead.*

Arianne walked into the cool shadow of the church's
entrance, and stood still as Nana arranged her train behind
her and straightened her veil. She could not help noticing
the unadorned wooden doors in front of her, leading into
the church, and the modesty of the architecture, the plain
white-washed walls, the terracotta tiles on the floor. She
was surprised that Simon's vanity could be satisfied by
such a humble venue for their wedding.

The music filtering through the doors was vaguely
familiar. It was not organ music. The sounds were much
fuller, much richer than any church music she had ever
heard. But she *had* heard it before, this passionate crescendo of strings, the bass accents a foreboding of something portentous yet to come.

The crescendo of strings came to an end, leading to the
melancholic sound of the horns punctuated by a solitary
violin, a moment of calm before what she now knew
would follow. The doors slowly opened in front of her,
the melody as haunting as the fear that suddenly gripped
her, and the splendour of Our Lady of Yanbi was revealed
to her eyes.

'Go, just go,' Nana whispered behind her, gently pushing
her forward.

As Arianne stepped into the nave, the National Sym-
phonic Orchestra and the one hundred and twenty singers
in the choir burst into the magnificence of Beethoven's
'Ode to Joy'. The waves of sound crashed against the
silver-covered walls, rising to the vault where silver cher-
ubs sat on silver clouds against a golden sky. The light of
hundreds of candles sparkled against silver pillars, shining
on the petals of the white lilies banking Arianne's path.

The music rang in her ears during her slow progress

down the aisle. She walked, barely able to see the high altar through her tears, which refracted the candlelight into a thousand stars.

> *Whoever has created*
> *An abiding friendship,*
> *Or has won*
> *A true and loving wife,*
> *All who can call at least one soul theirs,*
> *Join in our song of praise;*
> *But any who cannot must creep tearfully*
> *Away from our circle*

sang the choir as Simon de la Force surveyed the scene from the altar, waiting for his bride by the silver balustrade. He did not understand the words, but it did not matter. The rapturous sounds echoed his feelings.

Of all his many hours of triumph, this was the one that he savoured most. The power of the music, the silver of the Viceroy, the silks of Saint-Laurent, Arianne's beauty, they all fused into a perfect monument to *his* might and *his* glory. He cast a contemptuous glance at the silver Madonna in her niche above the altar, her jewels now adorning Arianne's throat; there was no limit to what he could achieve. As he offered his arm to Arianne, he enjoyed the significance of the gesture, and felt a flutter in his heart.

The Archbishop of Salta, in full attire, began the ceremony. As he asked the incongruous gathering of hundreds of musicians and one old woman for any reasons why this marriage should not take place, Arianne's mind went blank, oblivious of anything other than her anguish, the Archbishop's voice blending with the music into the distant din. Finally she realized the Archbishop was addressing her, waiting for her answer. The moment had come.

'I do,' she murmured.

Simon raised her veil and kissed her on the mouth, but she felt nothing. Her lips were numb. In despair, she raised her eyes to the Madonna. She had never been truly religious, but she needed to believe that there was

244

still hope. Her eyes fixed on the naive face carved by an Indian centuries ago, she asked Our Lady of Yanbi for her help, and she made her vow.

The Archbishop gave his final blessing to the couple, the orchestra burst into Mendelssohn's 'Wedding March', and the wedding was over. Simon shook hands with the Archbishop and turned to Arianne. He offered her his arm, but she did not pay any attention to him. She addressed the prelate instead.

'I want to give you this, to help the poor people in this parish. It is a vow I have made,' she said, unfastening her emerald necklace and handing it to the Archbishop. It had been a long time since he had had to deal with requests of this nature, and he did not even know who handled such matters in this diocese, but he betrayed none of his momentary confusion and blessed Arianne for her generosity. Simon remembered the Cartier bill and cursed her silently, but he felt too elated to mind. Trust a woman to get carried away by her emotions, he thought as they left the church.

A Cadillac convertible was waiting outside, the top down. They climbed in, and the car pulled away slowly. Arianne looked back, and saw Nana being led to a second car. She could not bring herself to talk to Simon, but she knew she had to say something, anything to break the isolation of her silence. She saw a plane flying over them. A moment later, she noticed another one, and then a third, far away on the horizon.

'Why are there so many planes?' she asked. 'This place can't be on the route to anywhere.'

'It is on the route to our wedding party. I chartered ten planes to bring the guests from Buenos Aires,' he replied, an amused smile on his lips.

'You promised we would have a private wedding,' Arianne said quietly. She did not have the strength to be angry, and it didn't make much of a difference. The party might even serve her purpose.

'I agreed to a private wedding, but I never said anything about the reception.' The car slowed down.

'Stand up,' Simon said. 'We are about to join the main road to the house.'

On both sides of the road men dressed in bright red ponchos with a broad black stripe along the edges lined up into the horizon, waving sugar cane stems as the car moved slowly past. Simon was already on his feet, waving to his peasants. Ahead of them, the road was white and glittering in the setting sun, as if covered with snow.

'I thought sugar would be the best possible carpet for us.' Simon pointed at the men. 'Stand up, they want to see you.' She obeyed, waving at the cheering crowd.

She had always disliked Simon, but now she hated him. He had ruined her business, denying her the opportunity to have her own life. She had justified her decision at the time with the excuse that she didn't want Gloria and Nana to face poverty, but it hadn't been the ultimate reason; poverty would have been preferable to what she had to face now. The truth was that she had been tempted by what Simon had offered her, and she had taken it. She hated him for manipulating her, and she hated herself for having allowed it.

'You are mad, completely mad. I hate you.' She said it again and again, shaken by her own sobs. Simon paid no attention. He was engrossed in receiving the homage of his people.

As Simon had planned, everybody who counted was at the party. Or nearly everybody. The President had had to cancel at the last minute because of the recent troubles in Cordoba. And Simon still rankled at the polite refusals received from the Borns, the Fortabats and a few others like them, too rich to feel the need to humour his whim. Some of Dolores' relations had also declined, but by and large all the people who mattered were present.

They were trying their best to be festive, but the conversations seemed to turn, again and again, to the escalation of political unrest in the nation. The country's leading trade union leader had been assassinated the previous day, there were rumblings in the Army, and the days of General Ongania as President seemed numbered. The guests all conveyed their good wishes to Simon, particularly when he said to whoever he was talking to that he looked forward to Arianne having a baby as soon as possible.

The Argentine situation may have worried his guests, but not Simon. One General would be followed by another; he could deal with any of them. He had sensed the crisis coming long before anyone else, and over the last three years he had concentrated on expanding his business abroad. Thanks to Bob Chalmers' advice, he was now worth more money in the United States than he was in Argentina, and that did not take into account his vast interests in Europe. Simon made a mental note to have a few words with Bob, who was somewhere in the party. He knew that it paid to be nice to useful people. He picked up a glass of champagne from a tray, and moved on to talk with the Chilean Ambassador.

While discussing the future of the mining industry in Chile, a matter in which Simon had more than a passing interest, he noticed Arianne coming towards him. Even from a distance, he could see that she was deathly pale.

'Excuse me,' he told the Ambassador, and walked over to her.

'I'm about to faint,' she whispered. 'I need to lie down for a while. I have very low blood pressure, and I think I'll pass out unless I rest.'

Simon was annoyed. He could not possibly leave the party now. It was another hour and a half to the formal end of the reception, when the planes would take the guests back to Buenos Aires.

'Why don't you sit down?' he said.

'It would make no difference, it's the crowd that affects me. I will go to our bedroom now. Please make my excuses.' Arianne walked away without waiting for his answer.

She made her way through the crowd and walked upstairs. Rosinha was waiting for her there.

'This way, Madame,' the maid said, leading her down one of the corridors. Rosinha opened one of the doors leading off it.

As she entered the room, Arianne's first thought was that it had been Dolores' bedroom. She could see the marks on

247

the walls where pictures had recently been removed. She was relieved to see her beauty case standing on the table by the side of the enormous four-poster bed.

'Please help me undress, Rosinha.'

'Already, Madame?' The maid was surprised.

'Yes, now,' Arianne replied impatiently. Without further questions, Rosinha unpinned the veil, unzipped her, and helped her out of her dress. Arianne took off her underwear, and put on the satin and lace nightdress laid out on the bed.

'Don't bother to put the dress away, Rosinha, you can do that tomorrow. Leave it on the chair.'

'Would Madame like me to brush her hair?'

'No, that will be all for now.' She wanted Rosinha out of the room as soon as possible. She knew what she had to do, and she could not wait any longer.

'Good night, Madame.' The door closed behind the maid, and Arianne was alone at last.

She opened her beauty case and searched for the letter to Simon, which she placed on the pillows at the other side of the bed. She then took out Gloria's portrait, kissed it, and put it back in the case. Before closing it, she removed the Seconal bottle and placed it on the bedside table, next to the water carafe.

She sat on the bed, poured a glass of water, opened the bottle and swallowed the pills one by one. There were twenty-two tablets, but she did not count them. She knew there were enough.

The last guests boarded the coach and Simon waved goodbye until the taillights disappeared in the direction of the airstrip. At last. He ran into the house, and climbed the steps in twos, pulling at his wing collar and his silver grey cravat. His pearl tie pin dropped to the ground but he didn't care. He wanted Arianne, and he wanted her now.

He burst into their bedroom, his face beaming. Arianne was asleep on the bed. He noticed the soft silk satin clinging to the curves of her breasts and her belly, the folds gathered between her legs. He tore off his clothes as he walked to the bed, ready to wake her.

When he came closer to Arianne, he realized there was something unnatural about her sleep, and he saw the letter on his pillow. He leaned over her, picked up the envelope, ripped it open, and began to read.

Rage and frustration burst inside him, and his animal roar echoed in the silent house. This cow, this whore, this ... this ... this *woman* had tricked him. He had spent millions to get her, murdered his wife to marry her, and she had tricked him. His dream, to which he had devoted so much of his energy, had been shattered: she could not have his child. She was right! He would kill her. But before that he was going to have her. For the first and last time he was going to screw her, as he had never screwed any woman before.

He tried to wake her but he could not, even when he slapped and then punched her. It scarcely mattered. He did not need her to be awake.

He ripped her nightgown to shreds and spread her on the bed. Holding her thighs apart with his hands, he plunged into her, his fury increasing his pleasure. He had never hated anyone so much. His hands encircled Arianne's neck, and his urge became unrestrainable. He began to tighten his grip, increasing the pressure in unison with each thrust.

Simon sensed his climax approaching as his thumbs dug into Arianne's soft flesh. He felt the rush in his balls, and squeezed her neck harder. 'Die, bitch, die,' he shouted as he pushed deeply into her.

He never felt his orgasm. What he felt was a ball of fire in his chest, an agony so great that it obscured everything else. Simon gasped for air, but he could not breathe. His eyes were open, but he could not see. He did not even realize that his hands were no longer grasping Arianne's neck, that he had raised his arms in a mortal spasm of pleasure and pain.

His sperm and his life left his body simultaneously. As he slumped forward his hand caught the bell cord by the bed, his fingers gripping it in an unconscious reflex. His face contorted by his agony, he collapsed on top of Arianne. At long last, he had made her his wife in the eyes of God and man.

Part IV

22

Pandora had been in the library for hours and she was tired. She squinted at the bright screen, her hand slowly moving the lever across the microfiche on the plate.

She had begun her search by looking up Arianne's entry in *Who's Who*: she was not listed. She then moved on to the *International Who's Who*. Again she found nothing. She tried several editions until she found Simon de la Force listed in a *Who was Who* volume, giving some general information and the date of his death. There was nothing on his marriages other than 'm. 1st 1957, Dolores de Anzorena (d. 1969), 2nd 1969, Arianne.' Just the first name, nothing else.

Then Pandora went to the microfilm library to see if any Argentine newspapers were kept. The only one was the international edition of *La Nación*. With the date of his death as a reference, she quickly traced Simon's obituary, which took up half a page. Even with her little knowledge of Spanish she was able to understand that the obituary mostly consisted of platitudes. It mentioned the sad fact that his wedding had preceded his death by a few hours, but Arianne was barely mentioned and only as Mrs de la Force. Again, no other name. Pandora carefully checked the ensuing issues through to the end of the year, but there was only the very occasional mention of Arianne de la Force on the business pages.

By then Pandora's right arm and her legs were numb from remaining in the same position at the microfiche reader and she began to hurry her research, feeding cards from the box at random and scanning the first three pages of each issue only, until she reached 1975. She found a number of reports of guerrilla incidents, but none concerning Arianne. At last Pandora concluded that the library route was a dead end. If it had just been a matter of finding facts from old newspapers, some other journalist would have picked up the story long ago. If there was one.

But she was then annoyed by her own doubts. The next step was to talk to Geraldine. She would have to go to Argentina, even Brazil, and spend some time doing research there. The prospect suddenly filled her with excitement.

'Darling, how nice to see you! I gather you are doing *won*-derful things with your section,' Geraldine gushed, leading Pandora towards the sofa with the usual clanking of bracelets. Having waited for nearly a week for her appointment with Geraldine, Pandora did not want to waste time on small talk.

'Thank you. There is something very important I want to discuss with you though,' she said as soon as they sat down. 'I've been doing some research on Arianne de la Force.'

'How clever of you! Did you find anything worthwhile?'

Pandora was chafed by Geraldine's patronizing sympathy, but ignored it.

'Yes, I found out that I am wasting my time in the library. Women like Arianne don't talk to journalists about their secrets.'

Geraldine sighed.

'You shouldn't dismiss research. You'll find out in time that it's the basis of all good journalism.'

'I'm not dismissing it, not at all. I'm simply saying I've been doing it in the wrong place. If I'm really going to find out anything about Arianne, I have to go to Argentina, and perhaps to Brazil as well.'

Geraldine looked away. She regretted having started this charade. She had encouraged Pandora when it suited her, but she was not prepared to waste time and money on stale social gossip. If she were to put people on the trail of every lurid tale about rich women, the magazine would come to a standstill. If the story was really worth it, she would put an experienced journalist onto it, not a novice. More to the point, if Pandora went off chasing non-existent leads, she would have to find somebody else able to put two words together and willing to spend her time visiting shops. It didn't make sense to waste another staff member's time for Pandora's sake. She turned towards her friend with her usual dazzling smile.

'What a wonderful idea! Why didn't I think of that? We must arrange it at once. Have you met Stephen? He's our Features editor, he will make the arrangements for you. I'll call him right now.'

Geraldine walked briskly to her desk and picked up the phone, humming loudly as her manicured nail ran along the staff directory. Pandora was slightly surprised by her enthusiastic agreement. She had expected Geraldine at least to ask what she had done so far, but it was in Geraldine's nature to be supportive, and she felt grateful to her friend. Geraldine dialled a number, paused, then put the phone down.

'I've suddenly remembered something,' she said, looking pensive. 'I have a friend at the *Sunday Times* who wanted to go to Argentina, and it took simply ages to get his visa. They can be quite awkward about visas for British journalists, you know. Those God-forsaken islands, I suppose . . .' Geraldine's voice trailed away. 'I wonder if it would be safe for you to go there, after all.'

For a second, Pandora was slightly suspicious. Concern about personal risk, her own or anyone else's, was unlike Geraldine. But she had no reason to doubt Geraldine's sincerity, and she dismissed the thought.

'I wouldn't walk around with the Union Jack, and I have an American passport as well. I wouldn't have any problems if I use it instead of my British one.'

Geraldine sighed with relief.

'Of course, silly me. Then it's full steam ahead. Leave it with me, darling, I will talk to Stephen as soon as I can. His number seems to be engaged all the time these days.' She wrung her hands. 'Goodness, I'd *love* you to stay for a chat, but I must throw you out. I'm *so* behind with my work.' Once Pandora had left, Geraldine made a quick note in her diary to ring her in three days. Then she picked up the phone and gave Vanessa a list of calls she wanted to make. By the time she put the phone down, her mind was on a million other things.

*   *   *

'I like this,' Tony Andreotti said after checking Pandora's feature on wedding parties for the forthcoming issue.

'I'm glad to hear you say so. I have an idea I want to discuss with you,' she told him. It was her third piece for the magazine and she had tried to do what was expected of her, but now she wanted to do more. Her feature on Arianne de la Force had come to a sudden end that morning, after Geraldine's brief phone call.

'Darling, it was *so* stupid of me not to have thought about it, but we are already doing a profile on Mrs Goncalves in a couple of months' time, and it would be too much exotica to have two features on South American women one after the other. Let's leave your wonderful project until the new year, shall we? You are so busy anyway . . . Talk to you soon. Bye bye.' Geraldine had hung up before Pandora could open her mouth. She thought of phoning back, but she knew it would be a waste of time. She could not give Geraldine any reason to continue the project other than her own boredom and her determination to follow up on Arianne's story; that would not be enough to counter Geraldine's plausible excuse about editorial scheduling. Perhaps it would be more sensible to grind her teeth, be patient, and find something else she would like to do in the meantime. This morning's newspaper had given her a possible idea. If nothing else, it had helped her deal with her disappointment after Geraldine's call.

'I was just reading in the *New York Times* about the hole in the ozone layer,' she said to Andreotti. 'Everybody is getting concerned about the environment. I thought we could do a feature on environmentally safe products.' The subject had begun to interest her in England a few months ago, and now she felt she could do something about it.

Andreotti shook his head. These girls were all the same. He gave them something to do, and they immediately began to have their own ideas about something completely different. This one wanted to rewrite *The Fate of the Earth*.

'We are not *The Village Voice*, honey. You just find me

nice things in nice shops. That's what our readers want, that's how we get the ads, and that's what you're paid to do. You shouldn't worry your pretty head about the world's problems.'

Pandora stood up.

'I'm glad you acknowledge I've got a head at least. We've made some progress, and I'll let you have the copy soon. Don't worry in the slightest if you find it ghastly, it would just even the score vis-à-vis your compliments.' She left his office before he could reply.

She stormed along the corridor and slammed her office door behind her. She was wasting her time here. She had to find something worthwhile to do, and all the ideas that excited her seemed to leave her colleagues cold.

She didn't fit in here. She had come to New York to give herself a break, to leave her old problems behind her. But a change of scene was not enough. Her job was routine now, and other than Geraldine and her superficial warmth, there was no one she really cared about here. Loneliness had been behind her decision to come here as well, and now she felt lonelier than ever.

But she didn't want a man in her life, not yet. She had heard plenty of friends going through a love fiasco complain that all men were the same, and she had smiled indulgently. Now she found herself sharing their view. She had thought that Johnny was different when they met, years ago.

She met him at a dinner party, just after he had started work in the City. A few months later, Pandora moved in with him, and their engagement was announced in *The Times* soon afterwards.

The thrill of finding their new home, the shared work during weekends spent wallpapering the rooms and moving the furniture from here to there, the joys of new love and equally new ownership, it all added up to the happiest months in Pandora's life. After the honeymoon in the Caribbean, real life began. Fed up with her private clients, she borrowed money from her father to open a small shop instead, at the cheaper end of the Fulham Road, selling her furniture designs and a small line of furnishing

257

fabrics printed to her patterns. She would never forget the excitement of those days, the hours spent working out a prototype chair or sofa, her relentless pestering of suppliers until the right weave or the right shade was achieved, then going back home in the evenings and telling Johnny about it.

The shop had been a small success at first, but once the novelty wore off the occasional passer-by was not enough to carry the cost of producing one-offs or small runs. After two years she had to accept that the shop had been an ill-conceived dream. Eventually she got an offer for the shop's lease, and in the meantime Johnny had moved to another job with great prospects.

Once or twice she mentioned to Johnny that she would like to take up her private work again, but he had laughed at the suggestion. 'What you did wasn't real work,' he had said. 'Why don't you think of something else?' She could not think of anything else she really wanted to do. It was at that time that Johnny's interest in her began to wane.

The cooling of their physical relationship brought to the fore a new, fundamental difference between them. They had both been brought up in the belief that the acquisition of money was distasteful as a priority in one's life. It had to be overshadowed by at least a token display of compassion towards those less fortunate than oneself. But the crises of the 70s and Mrs Thatcher had challenged the old values. The changed climate in the City was pivotal to this new world, and Johnny became first a convert, then a preacher of the new ideals. At the time Pandora thought that perhaps all men weren't the same at the start, but they became the same as time went by.

She shook her head, annoyed by her thoughts. It was silly to dwell on the past. She had to look forward. She glanced at the clock, and was about to leave her office for lunch when the phone rang.

'Hi, remember me? I'm the man who owes you lunch.' She recognized Tom Cansino's voice.

'Oh, hello, how are you?' She was trying to sound non-committal.

'I'm fine, but I have the sneaky feeling that you may not like me any more,' he said quite cheerfully.

'I haven't considered whether I like you or not,' Pandora replied crisply.

'You *don't* like me, I knew it. That's the problem with us divorced men, we put the nice girls off. We just can't help it, mother has warned you about us too many times.'

Pandora remembered her mother's admonitions about the dangers of getting close to a divorced man, and smiled.

'Maybe you are right. Listen, I'm very sorry, but I have to rush. Could you phone me another time?'

He laughed. 'It's better than don't call me, I'll call you, but you still haven't told me if you are free for lunch.'

'Unfortunately, I'm not.'

'Well then, how about a movie tonight? I hope you didn't see *My Beautiful Laundrette* in London. If you're free, we could have dinner afterwards. Please say yes,' he pleaded, 'it may not be mutual yet, but I really enjoy being with you.'

Pandora was flattered in spite of herself. She had not been out with a man for months; she suddenly looked forward to the prospect, but she was not going to sound too eager.

'Thank you very much for the thought, but I'm busy tonight too,' she lied.

'Is that the British way of giving me the brush-off?' he asked.

'No, I was going to add that I'm free the day after tomorrow.'

'OK, we can meet at the movie. It's the Quad on West 13th.' She quickly wrote down the address and the time of the show.

'See you then,' she said before hanging up.

'The check, please,' Tom said to the waiter. 'Would you like another coffee?' he asked Pandora.

'I would love one.' She wouldn't really, but she was reluctant to end the evening so soon. Although she had felt slightly uncomfortable during the film, its acid view of get-rich-quick Britain during recent years showing the down-market side of the process she had seen in Johnny, she had enjoyed being with Tom. Sometime during the film she had noticed Tom's arm next to hers on the armrest. But his conversation afterwards, both during the short walk to the restaurant and at dinner, had been friendly and not at all flirtatious.

'I've been meaning to ask you where you got your tan,' she told Tom after the waiter poured more coffee and moved off, leaving them alone.

Tom smiled. 'Why do you ask?'

'Out of curiosity, I suppose.'

'What a pity, I hoped it would be out of interest. I've just been to the Seychelles. I stayed at a wonderful place, some bird sanctuary. There's an old plantation house there where they take a few boarders. It's run by a very nice guy, a compatriot of yours who's crazy about tropical birds; I think he is writing a book about them. The house is beautiful, with bare floorboards and large verandahs. You can have your evening drink watching the sun set over the sea.'

'Sounds idyllic,' Pandora said.

'Do you have tropical fantasies?'

She smiled, and shook her head.

'No, my fantasies at the moment are slightly more practical than that. I just want to concentrate on my work, and enjoy it.' She told him about her latest project for the *Shopping* section.

'I don't think that Tony will make anyone's fantasies come true, but I wish you luck,' Tom said, briefly squeezing her hand and releasing it before she had time to react.

'I hope you haven't been bored,' he said as he slipped his credit card inside the folded bill and handed it to the waiter.

'Not at all. I've really enjoyed myself,' she replied eagerly. Tom settled the bill and they walked towards the exit, where he picked up her coat from the girl by the door. They began to walk along 14th Street and Tom looked at his watch.

'It's not too late,' he said. 'Would you like to come to

my place for a drink? It's quite near here and since you told me you were an interior decorator, you can give me your professional opinion.'

Although Pandora had half-expected it, his invitation jolted her. She did not want the evening to come to an end, but neither did she wish to encourage him. To accept might lead to awkwardness later on, but to turn him down would be acting like a frightened fifteen-year-old.

'I can't stay for long. I have some things to do at home,' she said at last.

'That's OK, I'm just a minute away,' Tom told her.

They turned on Seventh Avenue, then into a side street, and he stopped outside a run-down building, its front criss-crossed by metal fire stairs. Tom opened the door and let her into the lobby, harshly lit by a bare fluorescent tube.

'Not the kind of place Geraldine would take you to,' he said. 'And don't look for the elevator either,' he added, guiding her towards the stairs.

'Having seen the outside, I wasn't expecting one. As long as you have running water and electricity I'm not complaining,' she told him.

'Are you planning to move in then?'

She laughed.

'No, I just wanted to make sure you can make a cup of coffee.'

When they reached his floor, Tom took out a fistful of keys and began to undo a succession of locks, until the door finally opened and he let her in. It was the first loft she had seen, and she looked around while Tom hung their coats on a steel hook near the entrance. The setting was similar to the interiors used for beer commercials in London but here it was real. She immediately began to think how she would rearrange the furniture to maximize the impact of this wonderful space.

'Your chairs are too tall, the table is not big enough, and you need a longer sofa,' Pandora said.

'The problem is that my wallet is too thin,' Tom shouted from the other end. She could hear the hiss of the espresso machine.

She walked around while Tom was busy in the kitchen,

then absentmindedly glanced at the pictures lined on a long shelf along one wall, until her eye caught a series of framed prints. She recognized them, her vivid reminiscence catching her by surprise. Her memory telescoped over the years, to a particular moment during her father's last visit to England.

It had been a glorious summer evening at Glyndebourne. They had their picnic near the ha-ha among the other opera-goers, the scene framed by the mellow brick and stone house behind them. She remembered looking at her father, with whom she had made her peace after so many years of bitterness, and then at Johnny, the setting sun reflected on their faces. She had wished the perfect moment would never fade away, and now she remembered every detail: the food in the hamper she had prepared, the pink champagne Johnny had bought, her new dress. Her father had asked them to *The Magic Flute*, and she had particularly admired the sets designed by David Hockney. Now she found herself, years later, in a New York loft, in front of framed prints of the sketches for those very sets.

It was a stark, unexpected reminder of what she had lost, and she moved quickly away. Tom found her sitting on the sofa when he came back.

'Why are you so pensive?' he asked, sitting next to her.

She shook her head. 'I'm sorry. I was . . .' She stopped. There was no point in brooding. 'Maybe I'm just tired. Black coffee for me, please,' she said, anxious to change the subject. 'Have you ever been to South America?' she asked.

'I might go there soon, to follow the old Inca trail from Peru to Northern Argentina. Are you planning a trip?'

She smiled.

'I was,' she replied. 'I wanted Geraldine to send me to Argentina to research a piece on Mrs de la Force, a very glamorous lady I met here, but Geraldine turned me down. In the nicest possible way.'

Tom chuckled.

'You should know that your friend does not like spending money if she is not sure about the result. Sometimes she makes the wrong judgement, but it is difficult to prove it unless you can write the piece and it comes off. The old problem of chicken and eggs.'

Pandora sipped her coffee. 'She certainly doesn't think I'll lay the golden egg.'

'And what do *you* think?' he asked.

Pandora raised her eyes.

'I would have phrased it differently if I didn't believe I could,' she said sharply.

'It's her loss then, and please put your gun back in your holster.' He leaned back against the cushions, and she could feel the warmth of his arm through her silk shirt. She did not move. After a while she glanced at him, noticing for the first time the golden flecks in his brown eyes, and then she moved forward to place her cup on the coffee table, ending the brief physical contact between them. He got up and walked towards the corner, searching through a pile of compact discs. After a moment, the sound of Nat King Cole filled the room.

The slow music put her instantly on her guard. He returned to his seat next to her. She stood up.

'I'm sorry,' she said, 'but I really should go.' He followed her towards the door, and helped her put her coat on. Then he turned her towards him, his hands on her shoulders. She kept her eyes on the open collar of his shirt, on the skin of his neck only inches away from her face.

'I hope I'll see you again,' she heard him say. She pulled herself away and opened the door.

'I'd like that. I'll call you,' she replied without stopping. The door closed behind her.

She rushed down the stairs, glad to find herself free at last. It had all been too sudden, and she needed time. She liked him, but there was no need to rush things. She forced herself to think about what she had to do at work tomorrow. She walked rapidly away from the building and scanned the street for a taxi. As she waited at the corner, her thoughts went back to Tom.

She had felt uneasy in his loft, but now she was angry with herself. She felt trapped by her memories, the memories triggered by the prints on the wall, and she had behaved as if it were possible to go back to that time. Her reaction had been her way of preserving the illusion that nothing had changed, that there was no room for anyone else in her life. The empty street was a reminder of her true situation. She was here now, not in London. Johnny had left her and her father was dead. She turned back and began to walk fast.

'It's me,' she said when Tom answered the entry phone. She pushed the door open without any hesitation.

23

'Good morning, Miss Gloria.'

The uniformed maid rested the tray covered by a pink linen napkin on the table next to Gloria de la Force's bed. She walked to the window, drew open the silk curtains and returned to the bedside. Gloria leaned forward, and the maid plumped up the huge pillows behind her.

The girl laid the breakfast tray in front of her mistress, and uncovered it. 'Thank you, Corazon,' Gloria said. The maid bowed her head, the morning sun briefly shining on her blue-black hair, set off by the starched white pique toque.

'Do you want me to run your bath now, Miss Gloria?' Corazon asked, while her mistress opened her mail.

'Yes, Corazon, but run it very hot because I have to do my exercises after breakfast. I wouldn't want to have to ask you to run it again if it gets cold.' Early in life Gloria had been taught the importance of consideration to servants. She spread marmalade on her croissant, brought fresh by messenger every morning, and looked at her mail: invitations to the Gigli and Versace shows in Milan next month, the weddings of two school friends, one in Geneva and the other in Caracas, and the Wyndham-Stewarts' dance at Highbury Castle just before Ascot. She sighed deeply; she just didn't have the energy to do so much.

She took a sip of black coffee, picked up her pen from the bedside table, and wrote 'No' on the Caracas invitation; there was no way she could go there at that time of the year. She was fond of the Geneva friend, so she wrote 'Yes' on the card. She hesitated for a moment about the English dance. It was during Ascot week. She could wear one of those wonderful Lacroix things. She would drop Christian a line, and ask him to make her something really special. On the other hand, the Royal enclosure seemed to be full of rather dreadful people these days.

She wrote 'maybe' on the English card, and turned to the Milan invitations.

She found Italian designers amusing for everyday wear but Milan in summer was so hot; it would be easier to see the clothes here. She wrote 'No' on the Italian cards, piled her mail on the tray, and rang the bell. A minute later there was a knock at the door, and Corazon came in.

'Corazon, please take this to Kayzie. I'll phone her in a moment to tell her what I want,' she said.

Corazon picked up the tray. 'I'll leave it on her desk, Miss Gloria, but François told me that she phoned early to say that she was ill.'

'Did she say when she will be back?' asked Gloria, her impatience showing in her voice. 'I can't wait forever to have my mail dealt with.'

'I don't know, Miss Gloria, I can ask François if you want me to,' Corazon replied.

'No, just leave it, I'll talk to her tomorrow,' Gloria waved her hand towards the door, dismissing her.

Gloria raised her eyes towards the window, which framed a perfect view of Central Park, its trees covered with a blanket of new leaves. She adored New York at this time of the year, and she adored it even more when her mother wasn't around. Anywhere in the world could be adorable if her mother wasn't there. Sometimes she felt guilty about it, but it was very hard to be the daughter of a woman like Arianne, someone who seemed to have been born with an invisible spotlight on her. Her mother's money would have been enough to guarantee her the world's attention, and her beauty was at least as remarkable as her fortune. Gloria guessed that anyone meeting her would automatically compare her with Arianne, and she knew what the outcome of such comparisons was likely to be.

Gloria had not inherited her mother's looks, although some day she would inherit her money. She was a de la Force only because the change of name had been arranged after Simon's death. Her claim to his fortune was as indirect as her right to his name. She had pressed her mother again and again for her real name, until one day she told her that it was 'de Souza', a Portuguese name common enough to be untraceable. Her mother had been even more vague about her father. According to her he had just walked out one day, and she had never heard from him again. As Gloria grew up, she began to ask more questions, and eventually she asked for a photograph of her father.

At first her mother had said that she had none, because they had all been destroyed in a fire at their home in Brazil before she had moved to Paris. Then one day her mother appeared with the photograph of a dark-haired man, neither handsome nor ugly. She told her that she found it among some old papers, but Gloria was sure that it had been obtained from some casting agency. She tried to believe in the picture and put it in a silver frame, but it took only one look at Nana's face when Gloria showed it to her to realize that the man had nothing to do with her at all. The photograph ended up in a drawer, and her mother never asked after its whereabouts.

Gloria set aside her breakfast tray. She stretched her arms languidly and snuggled up for a moment under her feather-filled duvet, covered in the same apricot silk as the walls, enjoying the warmth of her bed, the smooth freshness of the linen sheets rubbing against her bare skin. Her body was many things to Gloria: a prop to her vanity, a tool for her pleasure, and a weapon to use against her mother. Through sheer dedication she had turned an indifferent figure into a superbly fit machine. It took endless time and money to achieve it, but Gloria had both.

Long before her body had become a source of pride, Gloria had discovered the unique, spine-tingling delights of a good fuck, particularly with an older man. A further *frisson* was added when she found that her mother was hurt by the voracity of her precocious sexuality, and further mortified when it involved the staff, as Gloria realized at the age of fourteen, when Nana found her in the pool house at 'La Encantada' straddling the hips of one of the gardeners. It was the first in a long list of similar episodes.

It was at that time, five years ago, that she had begun to sense Nana's rejection; it had hurt her more than any of

Arianne's terse admonitions. Nana had been with her for as long as Gloria could remember, the only one to come to her when she cried in bed at night. The old woman would stay with Gloria until she went back to sleep. Her mother had never been there; nannies, mademoiselles, frauleins, a whole collection of them studded the early years of Gloria's life, but only Nana had been constant.

She remembered an episode a long time ago, when she must have been only four or five years old. Her mother was away, and Gloria had remained in Buenos Aires, in the enormous house on Avenida Alvear. It must have been late in the spring, in November, because the jacaranda trees in the garden were covered in lilac blossoms, forming a deep carpet on the lawn. It was early in the afternoon, and the house was under the usual blanket of silence at that time of the day. The staff were either resting in their rooms or doing work in the kitchen area, far away from the family quarters.

After lunch Gloria had been taken to her room for her usual nap, but she couldn't sleep. She left the nursery, and nervously ran along the length of the gallery overlooking the main hall. The nursery was at the back of the house, facing the garden, while her mother's rooms looked out to Avenida Alvear. She was not allowed there. She tried the double door, the curlicued door handle almost too big for her tiny hand, but she managed to open it, and she found herself in a long pillared corridor. The white double doors between the marble pillars had overpanels painted with fruits and exotic birds.

She opened the door facing her, and walked into the shoe room. Three shelves formed by paired brass rails ran along the walls holding her mother's shoes, padded-silk shoe trees inside every pair. They were grouped by colour and aligned by tone, from light to dark, the evening shoes on the bottom shelf. Further up the walls, a triple row of pigeon holes in polished mahogany held the handbags, matching or corresponding with the shoes below.

Gloria was fascinated by the room. She began to inspect the shoes, picking them up and then dropping them on the carpeted floor. An arched opening led to the next room

268

where dozens of evening gowns were stored, each on a wide shelf of scented cedar wood. A pair of enormous floor-to-ceiling mirrors faced each other across the room: Gloria stood in front of one of them, admiring her reflections, making faces until she got tired of the game and moved on.

Two further dressing rooms followed, clothes hanging on all sides, with large shelf units in the middle. Gloria found these rooms less interesting than the shoe room, and opened yet another door.

At last, she found herself in her mother's bedroom. Gloria walked across the vast chamber and reached the four-poster bed, slowly running her hand over the embroidered bedspread. The photograph on her mother's bedside table caught her eye, a young woman with two children, and she picked it up. It was then that a side door opened, and Nana came in.

She rushed across the room, took the photograph away from Gloria, and began to admonish her in a harsh voice. Frightened by her tone, and overwhelmed by the shame of having been found, Gloria burst into tears, and the old woman's face changed. She hugged the little girl, patting her head and saying 'It's all right, my baby, your Nana will always be here.' Gloria was carried back to her room and nothing more was said. Much later, when she was allowed to move freely around the house, and she was able to walk into her mother's bedroom any time she wanted, she noticed that the photograph was gone.

But as Gloria grew up, Nana had become increasingly distant. Occasionally, Gloria had tried to ask questions about the past, but Nana's answer was to say that she did not remember, or know about, such things. If further pressed, she would claim an urgent task and leave the room. Nana's increasing introspection eventually turned her into a virtual recluse, until she refused to leave 'La Encantada'. Gloria saw her only during January or February and even then Nana endeavoured to make herself invisible, her only concern to keep the tower inaccessible to anyone other than Arianne and herself. Gloria felt sorry for the dotty old woman obsessed with her little kingdom in the tower, but she seemed content enough. It had been a long time since Gloria had felt really close to Nana . . . She looked at the clock. Shit, Milka was coming to wax her legs in an hour's time. She jumped out of bed, slipped into her dressing gown and walked to the gym, at the other end of the apartment.

As she came into the room she saw that Charles was already there, working out his arms and pectorals on one of the Nautilus machines. She thought of leaving again, but it would mean conceding to Charles' superior claim to the room. She stayed.

He stopped and smiled at her, his arms pushed back by the padded flaps, the damp T-shirt clinging to his broad chest. 'Good morning,' he said cheerfully.

'You shouldn't do exercises if you are not feeling well,' said Gloria, ignoring his greeting.

'What makes you think I'm ill?' Charles asked. He was surprised at her concern, but it pleased his vanity and suited his plans.

'It's so unusual for you to get up early that you must be ill,' she answered, her back to him. Charles grinned and said nothing. Gloria took off her bathrobe and threw it on the floor. She was wearing only her panties, almost as small as a G-string, and she sensed Charles' eyes on her body.

'Don't get excited, you've seen it before,' she said as she stepped onto the treadmill. She turned the control knob and began to run. Charles moved to the bench next to her. He set his digital timer at twelve-second intervals, and interlaced his fingers behind his neck. He counted 'one' aloud, raising his head and shoulders off the bench, then counted 'two', and lifted both feet. He was able to look at Gloria in the mirrored wall facing them.

'Gloria, I want to apologize for our little fight.' The timer bell rang. He stopped talking and, mentally counting to four, returned to the starting position while breathing in, and then repeated the start of the exercise.

'I hope you understand that there was nothing I could do, I . . .' the bell rang again, and he went through the second half of the exercise. 'I would have had trouble with your mother otherwise,' he continued.

Gloria turned up the speed knob. The machine's humming became noticeably louder.

'I can't hear you,' she shouted.

Charles stopped talking and completed his fifty-exercise cycle, while Gloria began her warm-up schedule. They remained silent, absentmindedly listening to the tape of Elgar's Cello Concerto playing on the sound system.

The first part of her routine completed, Gloria put on her ballet shoes, then moved to the bar on the opposite wall. One hand loosely placed on the bar, her arm almost straight, she pulled her stomach in and stretched her neck upward. As Gloria started her *pliés* and *demi-pliés*, Charles left the bench and moved towards a large ball on the floor, a couple of yards behind her. He began to jump sideways over the ball, raising his arms when he was up in the air.

'You must understand my position,' he gasped between jumps, watching her in the mirror all the time.

'The only position someone like you understands is the missionary one,' Gloria retorted, sliding her foot backwards and forwards in a *battement tendu* movement.

Charles managed to contrive a sad face, and stopped jumping.

'You really hurt me, Gloria. We have known each other for twelve years. I know you don't think much of me but I love you, and I wish we could be friends.' He really could not delay the cool-down sequence any longer; he stopped talking, and began his side-bends.

Gloria stopped half-way through a *grand-battement*. Charles' conciliatory manner was a surprise to her; there had to be a reason for it. It might be useful to humour him, and find out what he was up to. She waited until he had finished with his bends, and then came over to him.

'I'm glad to hear that, Charles. It's no good to fight. After all, we are almost family.' She leaned against the mirror, her arms slightly spread, hands on the bar. 'I *would* like to be friends with you,' she said, looking into his eyes. She couldn't believe that this shit was so desperate for a screw that he would risk it with her. But it would be an excellent way of getting rid of him. Once and for all.

'Then we are friends,' Charles said. He returned her gaze for a second, then looked down. No need to rush anything, and he'd better be careful. 'Great. I'm going to have a sauna now,' Charles took off his T-shirt, and walked to the shower cubicle behind a marble screen. Taking off his shorts, he stood for a while under the high pressure jets, then walked out, picked up a towel from the pile on the marble shelf and opened the heavy wood door into the sauna cabin at the opposite end of the shower area.

Gloria was already there, stretched along the bench on one side, her panties carelessly dropped on the wooden floor. She slowly moved her leg on the inner side of the bench, bending it slightly at the knee. Her body was in full view, and her position emphasized the flatness of her stomach and the firmness of her breasts. She smiled at Charles.

'The sauna's a really good idea,' she said.

He moved his eyes over her body, taking in the gentle sloping of the belly, the softness of her inner thighs, the silky skin glowing under a dew of fresh sweat. He removed the towel from around his waist, spread it on the seat opposite her, then turned and faced her.

'I'm glad you did. It really does wonders for the system,' he said, before sitting down and closing his eyes.

Gloria suddenly understood why he had kept her mother under his spell for twelve years: his prick was sensational. It would be nice to play with that toy for a while before letting mummy know, she thought. Then bye-bye, Charles.

'Charles, would you mind giving me an oil rub?' she asked in a languid voice, her hand waving towards the tray on a side table, covered by a damp cloth.

'It would be a pleasure. Which oil would you like?' he asked.

She rolled onto her stomach and let her arm drop down, her hand languorously resting on the floor palm up.

'Jasmin de Chypre is my favourite, but I really like them all,' she murmured.

'Jasmin de Chypre it will be,' he replied, holding up

the bottles to the light until he found it. He stood next to Gloria, close enough to feel her breath on his leg. He pulled out the stopper and leaned down, his broad chest over-shadowing her body. He tilted the bottle and let a trickle of oil drip onto Gloria's shoulders and back, the scent of jasmine rising in the hot dry air. She turned her face away from his legs, and closed her eyes.

He laid his hands flat on her shoulder blades, his palms pressed against her skin, and rubbed in a circular motion, very gently at first, then applying just a fraction of pressure, a hint of the weight of his body on hers. Every now and then he would move his fingers and, for a second, the edge of his nails would glide over her skin.

He rubbed gently downwards until he reached the hollow in her lower back, where he could feel her vertebrae under the thin layer of firm flesh. He pressed both his thumbs on the bony ridge, and pushed hard. Her bones cracked, and Gloria moaned softly. He paused for a moment.

'Did I hurt you?' he asked solicitously, his hands still on her.

Gloria raised her head from the bench and looked up towards him. The massive head of his penis was just inches away from her eyes, dangling above her like forbidden fruit. Nothing was more exciting to Gloria than what she should not have.

'No, not at all, I like it,' she said, clearly scanning his body. 'It's hot in here,' she moaned. Gasping for air, she aimed her breath straight at his balls. Her eyes were fixed on his prick, waiting for any stirring of his flesh, but there was none.

'We can make it cooler,' Charles paused for a moment, his hand sliding down her back. 'Or we can make it even hotter.' He dripped some oil onto her buttocks, and then let a thin trickle drip between them, the oil slowly slipping between her legs. 'What would you prefer?' he asked in a low voice.

She let her head rest on the bench. 'How could you make it hotter?' she murmured, spreading her legs just a fraction.

'Easy,' he answered, picking up the wooden pail by the heating coil, and pouring some water on the stones at the top. The water sizzled on the hot rocks, and a cloud of eucalyptus-scented steam enveloped them. 'But you have to be careful with these things, sometimes you can get badly burned.' He had just begun to rub her buttocks, cupping them in his hands, when the extension phone on the wall next to him rang. He continued rubbing her bottom with his left hand, his thumb gently digging into the crack between her cheeks as he answered.

'Hello, darling!' he said, moving his hand to the upper thigh, his thumb now sliding between Gloria's legs. 'How are things there? I miss you!'

'Gloria? She's here in the gym, doing her exercises.' As he said this, Gloria let her arm slide down the wooden side of the bench until her hand rested on the top of his thighs, her wrist touching his smooth foreskin. Charles did not move.

'Yes, I got up early,' he continued. He looked at his watch. 'The time here is nearly ten now . . .'

Gloria jumped up, and rushed out of the sauna. She had completely forgotten about her leg-waxing, and she still had to have her bath. Milka did not like to be kept waiting, and she was much in demand. After all, she was the best in New York.

'I have to go to the airport now. I'll be there tonight. Goodbye.' Arianne put the receiver down, took one last look at her favourite room, and then left.

On the landing, she caught sight of the sun shining on the still waters of the Laguna del Sauce in the distance, through the narrow window in the thick stone wall. She did not want to think of this trip as a farewell journey, but in many ways it was.

Gloria, once the most important thing in the world to her, had become a time bomb. In another year she would be of age under Argentine law, the sole heiress to her mother's estate in Argentina. She would not be hampered by guardians, trustees, or any other legal arrangements available elsewhere to protect the property of rich parents from their

274

offspring's mistakes. Arianne knew Gloria. She also knew the way Charles' mind worked, what his reaction would be to her refusal to marry him. She had no illusions as to how far Gloria would go in order to hurt her.

She had to remain in total control, and the first step was the disposal of the Argentine part of the de la Force estate, denying Gloria any automatic rights to a significant portion of the fortune. It had taken her over three weeks of round the clock negotiations, but at last terms had been agreed for the sale of San Simon, the holding company for all the de la Force agricultural business in Argentina, other than the sugar company.

It had not been easy to find a buyer at short notice for nearly a million acres of prime farming land scattered among thirty-seven estates, plus the innumerable assets of an enormous agricultural company. Her options had been further restricted by her wish to sell for a token sum in Argentina; most of the price had to be paid abroad, outside the stiff restrictions on foreign currency transfers imposed by the Argentine Government.

Over the years there had been approaches from a number of prospective buyers. Once her mind was made up to sell, Arianne had quickly sounded them out. The choice had finally come down to two: a Japanese company with vast interests in South America, and an Italo-Argentine concern.

Negotiations with the Japanese had been unsuccessful. The Italians had offered less money, but discussions had proceeded rapidly. Forty-five million dollars were to be paid in Argentina, and three hundred and twenty-seven million transferred into a company incorporated in Liechtenstein. The transfer would take place through an agreed third party in the Cayman Islands. Arianne's ownership of the Liechtenstein business was as untraceable as the transfer of funds itself. San Simon owed the Argentine Government twenty-three million dollars in taxes, creative accounting showed a loss for the year of approximately twenty million, and lawyers and accountants' fees would take care of the last two million. The balance of the transaction that would be accessible to Gloria in the event of Arianne's death was precisely nil.

275

However, her plan was pointless unless she sold Valle del Oro as well. She could justify her hesitation on financial grounds, but it was not the main reason. She had come to see the Valley as a symbol of her triumph, her ability to rise to Simon's challenge and beat him at his own game, against the odds. To sell it now could forestall Charles' plans, or what she imagined his plans to be. But it also implied giving up what she valued most, to acknowledge that Gloria had become her enemy. Perhaps it was wiser not to rush into a decision just yet.

Nana was waiting for her at the bottom of the stairs, dressed in black as usual. Arianne embraced the old woman. 'Take care of yourself, Nana. I'll try to come back soon.'

'May God be with you,' Nana replied. She walked away from Arianne, who turned round and slipped into her coat, held by a maid. Arianne was suddenly struck by the foreboding that it was the last time they would see each other, but she quickly dismissed the idea, the maudlin thought undoubtedly triggered by her own emotions.

She briskly walked to the waiting car and got in without looking back. As they drove down the hill, she wasn't thinking about Nana any more. In a few hours she would be in New York, facing Gloria. And Charles.

24

'Of course I can do something for your nephew, Rodney. I'm delighted to hear he wants to become a journalist, and I'm offended by you even considering the possibility that I wouldn't help him. There's nothing I wouldn't do for you, darling.' The ensuing exchange of gratitude and compliments brought the conversation to an end, and Geraldine put the phone down. She had a problem.

Rodney Gibson was chairman of one of the largest cosmetic corporations in America, and they took forty pages of advertising in the magazine every year. It would be foolish to upset him. It would be equally foolish to ignore the fact that Connie van Naalt sat on the same ballet committee as Mrs Greene, the owner of *Chic*. Like all rich people, Mrs Greene had pet obsessions, and the slightest indication of over-staffing was one of them. She would not blink at the magazine spending tens of thousands of dollars on a party, but she regularly checked the personnel list and asked probing questions about each employee. Connie would love nothing better than being able to go to Mrs Greene with evidence of Geraldine's recklessness in that respect. Geraldine was not prepared to waste one minute of her time explaining the reasons, and it usually took longer than a minute to convince Mrs Greene. But she had to please Rodney.

Pandora struggled for a moment with the unfamiliar lock, until she managed to let herself into the loft. Tom had gone to Vermont with the children for a few days, and he had asked her to keep an eye on the place and water the plants. Although saddened by the thought of his temporary absence, she had jumped at the offer. She preferred not to admit it, but she was growing fonder of him every day. They were still at the stage of keeping each other at a distance for the sake of self-protection, but she had begun to face the possibility of loving Tom. What had started as her acceptance of the fact that she did not want to be alone had almost become the certainty that she wanted him.

She went slowly around the empty space, checking that everything was switched off. It was unnecessary, she had already done it during her first visit, but it pleased her to have a reason to play a proprietorial role. She moved to the kitchen and put away the few dishes she had left in the drainer, Tom's breakfast things which she had washed up after he was gone. She filled a jug, making sure that the water was not too cold, and watered the small pots along the window sills, leaving the biggest task for last. Then she refilled the jug, walked across the room and emptied it into the huge planter holding a thriving ficus tree under the sky-light. Tom was very proud of the tree. He had told her that he bought it four years ago. 'It was this size,' he had said, his hand in line with his waist. Its foliage now brushed against the soot-smeared sky-light; she would suggest to Tom that they climb to the roof and wash the glass next weekend. The soil was almost dry, and she had to pour three further jugfuls of water into it. The watering finished, she thought of leaving but decided to stay for a while. She liked it here.

She moved to the bed at the opposite end of the loft and stretched herself along Tom's side, her head on his pillow. She brushed her cheek against it, the faint trace of his after-shave confirming how much she missed him. She remained still for a moment, her eyes closed. Enough of this, time to go, she decided. Tom would be back soon.

She sat up and absentmindedly glanced at the bedside table, her eye caught by a blinking pair of red lights. Probably she wouldn't have noticed the pin-point flashes if it had been still light, but it wasn't, and she had not turned on the lamp. Without thinking, she pressed the 'play' key on the answering machine.

The unknown woman's voice sounded as angry as Pandora would feel in a few moments, demanding to know where Tom was. The next message was from another woman, giving a loving description of what she would do to Tom's body next time they were together. Pandora stood up and switched off the answering machine. She was too numb to move, and tried not to cry. All Tom's apparent caring, everything had been a lie. She had been cherishing the possibility of loving him while he had been seeing other women, and she had probably slept in the very same sheets as they had.

Suddenly she was filled with a rage more intense than any she had ever experienced. She had been betrayed by Johnny, but at least she had had years of growing awareness prior to that, and she had had few illusions left by the time it happened. Tom's duplicity was unexpected, grit rubbed into a not yet healed wound, and she wanted to hurt him as much as he had hurt her. She looked around through her tears at the place where she thought she had been happy until a minute ago. Then she ran to the kitchen, picked up a bottle of bleach and dashed towards the ficus tree. She was about to empty the contents into the pot, but she couldn't. She thought for a moment, then walked towards the cupboard and opened it. Very slowly she sprinkled the bleach over Tom's clothes. Then she flung the empty bottle away from her and rushed out of the loft.

'Would you like some scrambled eggs?' Geraldine asked, nodding at the butler standing by the Regency sideboard. Compton uncovered the silver chafing dish.

'No, thank you,' replied Pandora. Compton replaced the lid, and returned to his post.

'I don't know why we have scrambled eggs at breakfast,' Geraldine continued, sipping her coffee. 'I don't eat it because it's fattening, Solly doesn't eat it because he is terrified about cholesterol, none of the staff eat it because it's cold by the time it gets back to the kitchen, and the dog doesn't like eggs. Must be my nostalgia for England.' She laughed. 'And it's very like us to worry about wasted food. Why should I care? I don't even pay for the damned eggs.'

It was obvious to Pandora that Geraldine was making small talk before tackling whatever was on her mind. Pandora had been surprised to be asked for breakfast at her house, but Geraldine had explained that they had not talked for a while, and her daily schedule was simply impossible. 'Breakfast tomorrow morning is the only time I have to see you until the end of the month. You can come to the office in the car with me. Don't worry about Solly, he's going to Madrid until Saturday, and we'll be free to talk.'

Geraldine glanced at her watch and then spread sugar-free jam on her toast.

'Darling, I must ask you this, and please believe me that I do it only because I want you to be happy. Are you planning to stay in New York?'

Pandora was startled. It was the last question she had expected, and she could not guess the reason behind it.

'I appreciate your concern. The answer is I don't know. Why do you ask?'

Geraldine peered at Pandora over her glasses.

'As Elton John would say, it seems to me that you live your life like a candle in the wind. I will be here when the rain sets in, but it might be wiser if you buy yourself an umbrella in the meantime.'

'What do you mean?' Pandora felt uncomfortable, and she was in no mood for lectures.

Geraldine leaned back in her chair, and crossed her arms.

'Darling, I worry about you. If you don't grab the bull by the horns, nobody is going to do it for you. You married that idiot Johnny, and you thought that all you wanted to be was a nice wife. Then the roof caved in and now, rather than try to make the most of your work at the magazine, you get yourself entangled with Tom Cansino, a good-looking jerk who lays every girl in the building for a maximum of two weeks each. I could staff another magazine with the girls who have left in tears because of him.'

Pandora was irritated by Geraldine's well-meaning intrusiveness. What she did with her life outside the magazine was not her friend's concern.

'What are you trying to tell me?' Pandora asked angrily. For once, Geraldine was not taking the trouble to blunt her knife.

'We are not in England, sweetheart. I'm not trying, I'm telling you that what you ought to do is concentrate on doing what *you* want to do, what would help *you*, rather than trying to find another miracle man to solve your problems. I fear that you may be wasting your time here. You can write, but I wonder if that's what you really like to do. You were an interior decorator once, maybe you should try that again. But you need contacts for that, and probably London would be a better place to start.'

'Everything you say is perfectly reasonable, and I've been thinking about going back to London. But there is one thing I would like to know before we go any further. Are you firing me? If so, I want to know why.' At least now Pandora had some grasp on Geraldine's motives, and she felt more at ease.

'Darling, how can you even think that! Of course not, I only want to help you. But I think you ought to seriously consider if New York is the best place for you. I don't want you to waste your time.'

'That's very kind of you, and I wouldn't want you to waste yours either,' Pandora snapped. 'If you want me to leave my job, just say so.'

Geraldine looked at her pensively.

'I'm so sorry that you misunderstand me. I just want you to do what you really want. I would be terribly sad if you decide to leave, but I can't force you to stay against your will. It's you who mentioned the possibility of your leaving, not me. The decision is yours, and that's what I think you have to do: make decisions. But don't rush into anything.' She turned towards Compton. 'Let's have another coffee, and then we should go to the office. It's getting late.'

Geraldine fluffed her hair with her hand and smiled at Pandora endearingly, as if nothing had been said other than warm chit-chat between old friends.

'Guess who I saw last night at the Mortons. Arianne de la Force! She is just back from Argentina, and she looks ravishing, as usual. Have you heard from her?' she asked, as if Pandora and Arianne were inseparable. Pandora waited until Compton had finished serving them.

'Amazingly enough, her secretary called me some time ago to ask me to lunch tomorrow, on Arianne's behalf, then she called again two nights ago. Arianne was still abroad and apparently the cook is ill, so the lunch has been changed from her apartment to La Côte Basque. I have no idea why she asked me any more than I know why you asked me here today, but I hope I'll enjoy seeing her as much as I always enjoy seeing *you*,' she said pointedly, but she got no reaction from her friend. Geraldine finished her coffee and stood up, Pandora following her.

'I love La Côte Basque,' Geraldine said glibly as they crossed the entrance hall. 'Give my love to Arianne. It's such a shame you won't do her profile now, but I must confess that I never thought Arianne was a good subject.'

Pandora was tempted to remind Geraldine that a few minutes ago she was supposedly waiting for Pandora's decision, but decided not to. She was still uncertain about Geraldine's motives, but the conversation had helped her crystallize the thoughts she had been having ever since she had left Tom's loft, and she was beyond needling – or needing – Geraldine now.

Compton held the door open, and they left the house. As they reached the waiting limousine, Pandora stopped.

'Do you mind if I don't come with you? I feel like walking,' she said.

'Of course I don't mind,' Geraldine replied, brushing her cheek against Pandora's before getting into the car. Pandora waved as the car pulled away, but Geraldine had opened her briefcase and was already studying her papers.

Pandora began to walk towards Park Avenue. Puzzled as she still was by the conversation, it had touched on an issue she could not postpone any further. When Geraldine had appeared in London, Pandora was adrift after a shipwreck, and she had climbed onto the first boat she could find. A few months ago, she would have followed wherever Geraldine led. Now she wanted to make her own choices.

She had come here partly to try to live by her father's

values in his world. But it wasn't her world, and she did not want to become like Geraldine. She had hoped that her choices would somehow sort themselves out for her. New York had been, in essence, her way of leaving her old world behind her, of running away. It was a negative reason. If she really wanted to change her life, it was possible anywhere; if she didn't, then no place would do it for her. Tom was the evidence of that. She had seen him as a new beginning, but only her unconscious wish to fall back into the old pattern, her hope of finding another man as the centre of her life, could justify her reaction. He had never promised her anything, and she had expected too much.

Upset by her thoughts, she glanced at the store window on her left. It was a small art gallery-cum decoration shop, a few pieces of furniture elegantly displayed against the white walls, and skilfully lit. She could not help admiring the simple beauty of the furniture, and her eye was caught by a discreet notice next to the entrance: 'The Shaker Style'. A week ago she would have gone in, because this was good material for her section. It no longer mattered now, and she kept on walking.

But she was glad to have come to New York. She had seen a different world, and learned more about her own. She was not going to be a candle in the wind. Not any longer. It was probably one of the few true things Geraldine had said over breakfast, and it had hit home. She had to find her own way, and she would.

As she walked past the newspaper stand near the office, she noticed the cigarette ad on it, showing a beautiful girl confidently walking ahead. 'You've come a long way, baby,' was boldly printed across the white background. No, not yet, Pandora smiled to herself, but at least she was at the starting gate.

Charles removed his earphones and switched off the cassette deck. He had listened to the tape early in the morning, but he wanted to check the facts before talking to Gloria. He congratulated himself on his wisdom in tapping Arianne's phone while she was away. It was nearly one o'clock. Arianne would have left for her lunch party at La

283

Côte Basque by now. He had checked Kayzie's diary an hour ago, and Gloria was having lunch with her friend, Paola Santa Coloma, at 1.30 p.m. Knowing Gloria, she was unlikely to leave before then, but he would take no chances. He went to the library and left the door open. He sat in the armchair closest to the door, giving him full view of the entrance gallery. Then he opened the *New York Times*, and waited.

Half an hour later, he heard Gloria's footsteps on the marble floor. He dropped his newspaper, and walked towards her.

'Gloria, have you got a moment?' he called.

She stopped by the front door and faced him.

'Not now, Charles, I'm in a hurry.'

'I'm sorry, but it's important, something vital to your interests.'

Gloria was perplexed for a moment, then dropped her bag on the marble console by the door, the chain straps clinking against the stone.

'What is it? Please be quick. I'm late,' she said impatiently.

'Let's talk in the library. What I have to tell you is highly confidential,' he said, leading her by the arm.

Gloria sat by the fireplace, and Charles stood next to her.

'Before I say anything, I want your assurance that you will never mention me as the source of your information. It would put me in an impossible position with regard to your mother, which you may not mind, but it would mean that you would never be able to find out anything else about what is going on from me. I am only taking this risk because you know that I always have your best interest at heart,' he said.

'Fine, I promise not to mention you. What is it?' she asked.

He told her. He described Arianne's phone conversation with Bob Chalmers, almost word for word. He had a very good memory.

'. . . which means that, very soon, there will be no de la Force property in Argentina. If your mother dies, under

284

Argentine law you would be entitled to her estate, but if there is no estate in Argentina, then you will only receive what she leaves you in her will. She is disowning you, Gloria.' He glanced at the mirror above the fireplace, to check that his expression was suitably aghast at the pain of what he had just disclosed.

Gloria stood up. Her face was white, and she was shaking. Charles embraced her, holding her tightly against him, and kissed her forehead.

'I know how painful this is for you, my darling, but you know that you have a friend. I'm on your side,' he murmured. He felt her arms tighten around his waist. For a second, he considered whether to kiss her on the lips, but decided against it.

After a moment, he let her go. She ran away, slamming the apartment door behind her.

Charles paused for a moment, then went to Gloria's bedroom. He walked in without bothering to see if the room was empty. The maids would be having lunch now. He searched Gloria's bedside table drawers and then moved to the medicine cabinet in the bathroom, concealed behind one of the mirrors, where he found what he was looking for. He took one of the many boxes piled on a shelf, put it in his pocket, and went to his room to make a phone call.

Gloria left the building and walked into the waiting limousine. She did not hear the doorman wish her a good day as he touched his cap. She must have told the driver where she was going because he took her to the restaurant, but it did not register, nor did her friend Paola's kiss after she was shown to her table by the maître d'. Paola's voice was a million miles away, as blurred as the writing on the menu in front of her eyes.

She said 'yes, fine' to the waiter's first suggestion, without hearing it. Every now and then words from Paola's conversation would briefly pierce the fog around her, but they did not sink in. She was only aware of her fury at her mother's betrayal. She had always lived in her mother's shadow, and now her mother was making sure that there would never be any light for her. Choked by her despair, she knew that she could not wait a moment longer.

She suddenly stood up, her chair crashing to the ground, and ran away from the table, not looking at Paola's startled face, not even bothering to pick up her bag.

'. . . and she told her husband that she wanted to go to Rio to stay with Elizinha. What she did not tell him was that she wanted to have *everything* lifted by Ivo. He did her face, the tits, every bit between her hairline and her toes. The husband was at home in Geneva, and he became quite restless because he thought that she'd found a toy-boy. He started sending her ultimatums. She got really worried when she got a 'come back, or else' wire. Ivo warned her she was in no condition to fly but she paid no attention, and discharged herself. By the time she landed in Geneva the poor darling looked like a Halloween pumpkin! She was in the hospital for a few weeks, but I saw her not long ago and she's fine now.'

Arianne caught a waiter's eye and nodded towards the silver wine cooler. The waiter refilled their glasses while her guests laughed at her amusing tale.

Desserts were offered and declined by all but Pandora, who asked for a Grand Marnier soufflé with raspberry sauce.

'That sounds delicious. I think I'll keep you company,' said Bob Chalmers, sitting on Pandora's left. Arianne confirmed the orders to the waiter, and asked for coffee.

'I'm very glad to see you again,' Bob said. 'I've been meaning to call you and ask you out for lunch ever since I met you with Geraldine, but I could not face the embarrassment of you not remembering me.'

'Of course I remember you. You were interested in my work, which is unusual. Most men can only talk about theirs,' Pandora replied.

He laughed and raised his glass to her.

'I really enjoy your company. I would be delighted if you enjoyed mine,' he added smoothly, after a brief pause.

Pandora now understood why she had been asked to the lunch, and she decided to stop his interest from going any further. A few weeks ago it might have been amusing, but now it was tiresome.

'Thank you, but I won't be able to have lunch with you. I'm going back to London soon.' The Principessa di Sarteano had finished talking to the man on her left, an up-and-coming fashion designer, and Pandora addressed her across the table.

'I gather from what you said earlier that Arianne and you worked together as models in Paris. Do you ever miss your work?'

Cameline raised her hand to her throat and toyed with her multiple strands of pearls.

'My dear, that was so long ago that it's almost embarrassing to remember it. We both have grown-up children . . .' Cameline never finished her sentence, because the door of the restaurant burst open and Gloria stormed in, her eyes blazing.

She stared at her mother at the head of the table. Here, everywhere, her mother was the centre of attention, her beauty and her money guaranteeing her the spotlight. Now she was scheming to deny Gloria her only chance of recognition. Her rancour burst forth.

'You shit! You bitch! You are stealing my money! I hate you!' she screamed.

Arianne stood up. Her face was very pale.

'Gloria! I don't know what's come over you. I have no idea what you are talking about, but whatever it is we will discuss it at home. I'll be there soon. Please apologize to my guests and leave now,' she said, her voice very low. All conversation in the restaurant had stopped, and everybody's eyes were fixed on Arianne's table. The maître d' hovered in the vicinity, anxious for an opportunity to bring the ghastly scene to an end.

'You are the one who ought to apologize. You're trying to cut me out of my inheritance. *This* is what you deserve!' Gloria shouted. She picked up Pandora's dessert from the table and flung it at Arianne, but she was so shaken by her own sobs that the soufflé landed on the bosom of a woman sitting at a table nearby, splashing the jacket of her white suit. It was Maria Dimitrescu, who had been unsuccessfully trying to catch Arianne's attention all through lunch. She shrieked as the raspberry sauce stained her outfit, and the maître d' rushed to her, napkin in hand. He uttered apologies in French as he tried to pacify his hysterical customer and her escort, who was threatening to sue him.

Bob Chalmers stood up, put his arm around Gloria's shoulder, and firmly led her away. She was now overcome by her tears and went without resistance.

'I'll take Gloria home. Thank you very much for a wonderful lunch. I'll call you later,' he said to Arianne over his shoulder as he pushed Gloria towards the door. The fashion designer muttered some excuses about an urgent engagement, and left behind them. Cameline conspicuously looked at her watch while Arianne apologized to Maria, who regained her composure only when Arianne asked her to send the bill for a new outfit to her secretary.

'Dear me, it is terribly late. We must go, Bruno.' Cameline stood up, followed by her husband, and kissed Arianne.

'Darling, it's been lovely to see you. It was the most marvellous lunch, but we have to go. Do call us next time you are in Rome.' Bruno kissed Arianne and followed his wife towards the door.

Arianne smiled at Pandora, but her sorrow showed in her eyes and her voice.

'You're the only one left. I'm very sorry for all this trouble. Gloria seems to be at her very best whenever I see you.'

'Please don't apologize, it wasn't your fault.' Pandora moved up the table and sat next to Arianne. She didn't know what else to say, but Arianne was obviously distressed, and she thought it would be unkind to leave in a hurry like everyone else.

'It's my fault, but maybe not in the way you mean. Let's go, anyway. I think that I have provided the audience with enough entertainment for one day.' She nodded at the waiter, and smiled gratefully at Pandora. 'Thank you for staying, I wouldn't have liked to be seen leaving on my own.' The waiter returned with the bill, and Arianne signed it. She briefly made her excuses to the maître d' before leaving the restaurant. Her car was waiting outside, and the driver opened the door. Arianne paused for a moment.

'I was thinking of going for a walk in the park before going back home. Would you like to come with me?'

Pandora hesitated. Three weeks ago she would have seen it as a God-sent opportunity to probe into Arianne's life, to find out as much as possible. Even yesterday, it would have boosted her ego to be able to puncture Geraldine's condescension by casually referring to her budding friendship with one of New York's richest women. All that was behind her now, yet she sensed that, for some reason, Arianne did not want to be left on her own. She could understand the fear, and felt sympathy for her. She had never imagined she could feel sorry for Arianne de la Force.

'Thank you. I'd love to come with you.' The driver held the door open for her and she climbed into the car, Arianne following her. As soon as the car pulled away, Arianne turned towards her.

'I'm ashamed to have to ask you this, but I hope you will not write anything about what you just witnessed. It would hurt me to see what Gloria said in print,' Arianne said, in a very low voice.

Pandora was astonished. 'It would not cross my mind to write about something like this. I may be a journalist, but I'm not a muck-raker.' She was suddenly annoyed by the fact that the reason behind Arianne's invitation had not been her wish for company but her fear of scandal.

'You shouldn't worry, in any case,' Pandora added coolly. 'I'm no longer a journalist. I resigned yesterday, and I'm going back to London next week. Even if I wanted to, which I don't, there is no longer any reason for me to write about anything at all. Certainly not your life.'

'I'm sorry. My behaviour is unforgivable. Anyone else would have sold the story of what happened at my apartment to the tabloids, but you didn't.' Arianne looked at Pandora thoughtfully. 'You are very unusual,' she added.

'I always thought my problem was that I am so very ordinary,' Pandora replied.

'Not in my circle,' said Arianne. 'I'm beginning to realize that you may be that rarest of creatures, a normal human being.'

'Maybe it's just that I haven't had the opportunity to be anything but normal.'

'You devalue yourself. What we make of our lives has less to do with the opportunities we have than how we use them,' Arianne said, her face turned towards the window. 'Few people have had Gloria's opportunities in life, and yet she's a mess. I blame myself for that. I was too busy being Mrs de la Force.'

'I've been busy over the last eight years being Mrs Lyons, and I have achieved nothing. Zilch. At least you have something to show for it,' Pandora said bitterly.

Arianne seemed surprised.

'Is money what you want? I wanted it desperately because I thought it would take me away from everything I wanted to leave behind. It has helped me, but I wish that Gloria would set herself a higher aim than just being my daughter.'

'No, money is not all that I want,' Pandora explained, 'and I would guess that neither do you, since you have all the money you can possibly need, and yet you still work. I want to do something I care about, and not as a dilettante. One of the few things I've learned is that being somebody's daughter, or somebody's wife, or somebody's anything for that matter, is not the answer.'

Hearing Pandora's words, Arianne couldn't help thinking about Gloria again. Arianne's power only allowed her to alter the course of future events. It could not undo the last fifteen years, nor place Gloria where Arianne would have liked her to be, making decisions about her own life, like Pandora. There was something about this girl that touched her.

The car drove into the park and slowed down as they reached The Mall. Arianne tapped on the glass screen, and the driver stopped the car. 'Please wait for us here, Mike,' she told him.

The driver opened Arianne's door and they got out, Arianne briskly climbing the stone steps towards the fountain, Pandora following her until they reached the balustrade overlooking the lake. Arianne pointed at the view across the water. 'I love coming here, it reminds me of an

English park,' she said. Pandora glanced at the scene, and she felt homesick for a second.

'When are you leaving New York?' Arianne asked. They began to walk along the path bordering the lake, joggers rushing past as they talked.

'Next Saturday. I used to be an interior decorator. I want to start again, but on a completely different basis. I had my own business for a while, and I'd like to take that up again. But times have changed, and I need to do some thinking about it, about the right approach.'

'I had my own business in Paris, a long time ago. I was a costume jewellery designer very briefly after I gave up modelling.' There was a wistful edge to her voice.

'Why did you give it up?'

'Because . . . I got married,' Arianne replied. 'Why did you give up your business?'

Pandora laughed. 'Same reason. But at least your husband gave you a chance to prove yourself later.'

'Maybe, but I wouldn't advise you to marry a man like my husband.' There was bitterness now in Arianne's voice.

'I'm not planning to marry anyone, don't worry,' Pandora said jokingly, trying to dispel the sudden change of mood. 'I've just had an . . . unfortunate experience, and I think it's put me off men for a while.'

'That's wrong, don't let it happen,' Arianne murmured.

Pandora was nonplussed by her comment. Perhaps Charles meant more to Arianne than she had thought.

'I know, I suppose I'm just convalescing. Probably I'll marry again. I'm almost thirty now and I know I want children.'

'I also wanted children. Perhaps my real problem is that Gloria is not . . .' Arianne suddenly heard her own words and stopped mid-sentence. She had almost been carried away by her introspection, but she was not going to give hostages to fortune. She knew nothing about this girl, and making her party to her problems would only add to them. She was not going to throw away the defences painstakingly built over twenty years of her life in one second of weakness. '. . . my favourite person at the moment,' she finished, staring at Pandora to gauge her reaction.

Pandora was thunderstruck. It could not possibly be that Arianne had tried to tell her that Gloria was not her daughter, but it would explain what Pandora had seen of their relationship. Yet there were less far-fetched explanations for a daughter's hostility towards her mother. In any case, she did not want to know. She had come here spurred by sudden companionship, not to dissect Arianne's life.

'But she is your daughter, and you can't change that,' she said. 'Sometimes it is better to start from a difficult relationship. I used to think that I was just like my mother, only to find out that we had very little in common at all.' She glanced at her watch. 'I'm sorry, but it's getting late for me.' Arianne did not seem to hear her last words.

'You have begun to find your way, Pandora. Gloria hasn't got a clue. After what you have seen, you can understand that I blame myself for it.' She shook her head. 'But enough of Gloria. You're right, we ought to go back.' They turned and began walking towards the car, Arianne's eyes fixed on their long shadows ahead of them.

'What have you done with your painting?' Pandora asked after a while, to break the uncomfortable silence.

Arianne raised her head, and Pandora noticed that once again she seemed her usual, confident self.

'You may see this as another indication of my terminal extravagance, but it is in storage. I've been thinking where I would like to hang it, but I haven't made up my mind yet. Too many choices, perhaps. At least now you know one of my secrets.' Their eyes met and they smiled, their faces warmed by the dappled sunlight filtering through the leaves.

25

Pandora walked into her office. It was her last day, but she had finished her work yesterday. The only thing left was to see Geraldine. By now she was in no doubt about Geraldine's motives for the breakfast invitation. Pandora had bumped into Tony yesterday, and he had told her during the short elevator ride that her replacement had already been hired. 'He's the nephew of one of our big advertisers. You need a rich uncle, honey.' The comment had been meant to hurt Pandora, but it didn't. On the contrary, it ended any lingering doubts she might have had about leaving. But she still had to say goodbye to Geraldine, if only for old times' sake. It was too early to call her; Geraldine was probably looking at her mail, and Vanessa would not disturb her.

She decided to get herself a cup of coffee and read the paper to kill time. She was about to leave the office when the phone rang. She didn't bother to pick it up, and went to the coffee dispenser at the end of the corridor. The phone was still ringing when she came back. It was Vanessa.

'Pandora, Miss Freeman would like to see you right now, if you have a moment.' Obviously Geraldine was as concerned as she to keep to the forms. Pandora left the weak brew in the plastic cup on her desk without much regret. She would go home right after seeing Geraldine, and have a decent cup of coffee on her way.

Vanessa showed her into Geraldine's office. In spite of what had happened, Pandora realized she still held some affection for the place, if only for the sake of her earlier illusions. Geraldine walked towards her with both hands stretched out, as if she were holding an invisible hank of wool.

'Darling, I'm *so* glad to see you! I was worried that I wouldn't be able to find you. We must talk, right now.'

'I wouldn't have left without saying goodbye,' Pandora said tersely.

Geraldine waved her hand in a dismissive gesture, her wrist clanking with gold bangles in the shape of crocodiles.

'I'm sorry I didn't phone you as soon as I got your note, but you know what my life is like. I simply haven't the time to do what I really want any more, it's *ghastly*. But we must talk about this nonsense. I can't believe that you could have misunderstood me so dreadfully! Would you like some tea or coffee?' Geraldine asked as they sat down.

'No, thank you.' Pandora did not want to prolong the conversation a moment longer than necessary. Whatever Geraldine could say would make no difference to her decision, but she was mystified by her tone. It made no sense to reopen the issue once it had been settled to everyone's satisfaction. Geraldine toyed with her bracelets for a moment.

'Darling, I know how hard it is for you now after your disappointment with that Cansino creep, but life goes on and you must think about work.'

Pandora knew that she had not been summoned to discuss her personal life. She waited.

'I believe that you have come across a wonderful opportunity.'

'What do you mean?' Pandora was suddenly perplexed.

'I heard at dinner yesterday that there was the most spectacular row between Arianne de la Force and her daughter at Côte Basque. You were there. You can write your profile of Arianne around the incident. Here is your chance at a feature article at last,' Geraldine's voice was full of excitement.

Pandora almost expressed her disbelief, but then thought better of it. It wasn't outrageous, it was just amusing. It could be *very* amusing, in fact.

'But you told me you were running another feature on a high-powered South American woman. I agreed that my piece would clash with your editorial policy, and I have to bow to your experience,' she replied sweetly.

'Forget about other boring pieces, this is *really* exciting.' Geraldine's enthusiasm was plain to see. Pandora pretended to think for a moment.

'You're right. After lunch I spent some time with Arianne, and she told me the most *fas-cinating* things about her life. It's really incredible!' Pandora replied, mimicking Geraldine's excitement.

'Then write about it, darling! We could knock the pants off *Vanity Fair*. You will be famous!' Geraldine clapped her hands in glee. Pandora looked at her. She found Geraldine absurd and had had enough of this charade. She stood up.

'I can't do that,' she said quietly. 'I gave Arianne my word that I would not write about what happened.'

'Did you put it in writing?' Geraldine asked, clearly perplexed.

'No, of course not, but I said that I wouldn't, and that's that.'

Geraldine sighed. 'Darling, please listen to me. We are no longer at school, and there is no house-mistress here to make you a prefect because of your impeccable behaviour. This is the real world, where you told me you wanted to be. Honour is admirable, but it doesn't get you very far. Don't waste your big opportunity! I might even say don't waste your life.'

'I don't intend to, and that's why I'm going back. I'm sorry, but I have no intention of writing anything else,' Pandora said. It was clear from her voice that she meant it.

Geraldine's face hardened for a moment, then she realized that she had lost the battle and flashed her best smile at Pandora.

'I think you are hopelessly wrong, but I wouldn't dream of forcing you to do anything, my darling.'

Pandora returned her smile. 'I'm not wrong, and I'm sure you wouldn't force me to do what I don't want to, aside from the fact that you cannot. I'm leaving for London the day after tomorrow.' She began to walk towards the door, then stopped and turned back to face her oldest friend.

'Thank you for everything. I really mean it.'

Geraldine came to Pandora and threw her arms around her.

'I only wish you'll find your own way. I'm sure you will.'

'I hope so,' Pandora said. She kissed Geraldine on the cheek and left.

Arianne looked at herself in the elevator mirror. She removed her heavy diamond earrings, put them in her evening bag, and rubbed her aching earlobes. François was waiting for her in the vestibule. He opened the elevator door, and followed her into the apartment.

'Would Madame require anything else tonight?' the butler asked.

'No, François, thank you. Tell Rosinha that I will not need her tonight either. She can put my clothes away tomorrow morning,' Arianne replied, walking towards the far end of the entrance gallery.

Alone in her bedroom, she took off her evening dress and flung it on the nearest chair. She kicked off her pumps and put on her dressing gown. The touch of the cool silk felt pleasant to her skin. It was a warm evening, and she was glad to be leaving for the yacht the following day. She was cheered by the thought of being on her own, lazily cruising around the Aegean.

Gloria had gone to stay with Paola in Cap Ferrat. She had left the previous afternoon, soon after their row. With hindsight, it might have been preferable to have kept quiet after the fracas at Côte Basque, but she couldn't. The memory of the scene that followed when she returned to the apartment would live with her for a long time.

Gloria had poured out her venom as only Gloria could. She had accused Arianne of denying her a father, of lying to her about him, and then she had launched into a tirade about Arianne's new machinations to deprive her of her money. 'You want it all yourself. You want me to have nothing so there can be no other Mrs de la Force, only you, the legend, the one and only *you*.'

Other than the accusations about the money, Arianne had heard it all before. Many, many times. But like cliffs continually beaten by the sea, her resistance had begun to crumble. For a second she thought of telling Gloria the truth about herself and her past, but she recoiled from it, for her own sake as well as for Gloria's.

At the time she wondered how Gloria could have found out about the sale of San Simon. Arianne was sure that it had not been through Bob. It had to be Charles, but how did he know? After a while, it dawned on her that Charles must have tapped her telephone. He had left the night before, saying that he was going to Capri for the rest of the summer. She had the apartment checked that morning by an expert sent by Bob, but the man could not find anything.

She had been relieved to see Charles go, although she guessed that he was following Gloria. His allowance enabled him to travel as he pleased and she was glad to be rid of him, if only temporarily. Her dearest wish was to get him out of her life for good, but she knew the price for that. Her money.

Her money, her money, her money. It all came down to that. Aladdin's lamp had become Damocles' sword. Gloria wanted it, and Charles wanted it too. Through Gloria, she assumed.

Her money had given her power and everything she had wanted. It had been the ruling element during all these years. Whom she saw, what she did, where she went, it had always been determined by that one priority, her money. She had lost sight of many things in the process, Gloria foremost among them. She had the best jewels, the best sables, the best pictures. She had palaces and yachts. She had everything – too much, in fact. But it was not enough.

Her thoughts drifted to her conversation in the park with Pandora Doyle. Maybe it was just her fantasy, but she had sensed in Pandora qualities she would have liked Gloria to have, a determination to find her way concealed by her quiet manner. A sudden impulse overtook her, and she went to Kayzie's office. She looked up 'Doyle' in the card index, and dialled the number.

*   *   *

Seat belt fastened, Pandora was ready for landing. She looked out of the window at the lights of London, and suddenly recognized the unmistakable roof of the Albert Hall. A few moments later the plane began its final descent into Heathrow Airport. She stretched her legs. She had not been able to sleep on the plane but she was not tired. She was too excited for that. She was about to begin the next stage of her life.

Her thoughts went back to her conversation with Arianne the day before. Pandora had been packing her bags when Arianne phoned her. She had been tempted to decline her invitation, but then thought better of it. Their unlikely acquaintance had turned out to be one of the pleasant surprises of her stay in New York. For whatever reason she enjoyed Arianne's company, and the thought of seeing her again suddenly cheered her up. If nothing else, it would break the solitude of her last day in New York.

It had not been a long conversation. Arianne was leaving for the Turkish coast the following morning, and Pandora noticed through the open doors that the furniture in the enormous drawing room was already shrouded in white dust sheets, and an assortment of expensive trunks stood in the entrance gallery. 'I'm sending a few things to Venice, I always go there in September,' Arianne had explained as she welcomed Pandora. Pandora remembered the first time she had been to the apartment, not long ago. She had been both overwhelmed by Arianne's grandeur and aware of her condescension. It felt different now. At first she put it down to the piles of luggage somehow breaking the formality of the place, but she realized as soon as they moved into the immaculate library that it was something else. The inexplicable rapport established at the park had not faded away. Arianne prepared the drinks herself and made small talk about her forthcoming trip. Then, suddenly, she changed the subject.

'I have been thinking about what you said yesterday about going back to London to set up your own business. I know that what I'm about to say is perhaps easier for me than for you, but I would advise you not to start small, if the business can carry it. I don't know how you are planning to finance your company, but I know from experience that it can hinge on being able to convince a bank to lend you the money. If so, it takes the same effort to convince most bankers about the viability of any loan, irrespective of size, and you will be less vulnerable if you are a bigger customer. I learned that many years ago.'

A discussion with Arianne about financial vulnerability seemed extraordinary to Pandora at first, then embarrassing.

'Thank you for the advice. I learned from my first business about the problems of being small, and it's one of the things I told you I was planning to study in more detail in London. I have to see what the options are,' she replied rather vaguely.

'Please let me know if you have any problems with your bank about raising the money. I can put you in touch with other bankers.'

Pandora smiled. 'One of the few advantages from my marriage is that I met quite a number of bankers. If I decide to start on a larger scale I'll approach them, otherwise I can just finance myself, but I'm grateful for your concern.' However much she warmed to Arianne, she didn't want to be beholden to her – or to anyone.

'I just want to let you know that, if you have any trouble, I'm prepared to help you if I can.' Arianne was as surprised as Pandora when she heard herself make the offer. She decided to put it down to her earlier feeling of gratitude, but Pandora did not quite know what to make of it. She thought for a moment.

'It would be disingenuous to say anything other than that I'm astonished by your generosity. Thank you very much for your offer, but I can't accept it. We hardly know each other, and I don't know yet if I will need help or not. It may sound foolish to you, but our conversation yesterday meant more to me than you think. We were just two people talking without ulterior motives. I hope we will become friends, but to accept your offer would probably make that very difficult.' She kept her eyes down as she spoke, suddenly embarrassed by the personal turn of the conversation, as unexpected to her as Arianne's offer had been a moment ago.

Arianne was deep in thought for a while. 'I was going to say that it is unwise to question somebody's offer of help if you need it, but you are right. I have my reasons, but they don't concern you. Also, I remembered while listening to you that I once accepted an apparently irresistible offer without much thought about it. I've regretted it ever since. I understand what you are saying; I can only add that I enjoyed our conversation yesterday as much as you did. I'll be away until September. Let's talk then; I'll make a note of your London number.' She walked to her desk and picked up her address book, then opened a drawer and pulled out a stiff white card edged in gold before returning to her seat.

'I hope you are free in September,' Arianne said as she handed the card to Pandora. 'I give a big party every year, and I am giving a costume ball in my palazzo in Venice this time. I would love you to come. It's on September 14th.'

Pandora smiled gratefully.

'My diary is far less busy than yours. I'm sure I'm free, and I would be delighted to come.' She gave Arianne her London phone number.

'Don't forget you are a businesswoman now,' Arianne said cheerfully. 'You may find that you are too busy by then.'

'Even if I become wildly successful, I hope that I'll still have time for my friends,' Pandora replied.

Arianne looked at her affectionately. 'I truly hope to see you in Venice,' she murmured as she kissed Pandora goodbye.

On her way home, Pandora tried to find an explanation for Arianne's unaccountable kindness towards her. The last thing she had expected as she was about to leave New York was this extraordinary, unlikely . . . well, friendship. Perhaps there was no need to look for reasons. In any case, she had an invitation to Venice, and it sounded wonderful. New York had made her feel like Cinderella sometimes; now she would be going to the ball. But there was work to do first.

Part V

26

BUENOS AIRES
June 1969

Arianne felt extremely weak. She looked around at the
unfamiliar room, wondering where she was, glad to find
her curiosity returning. She had been conscious for a little
while but indifferent to anything, even to the doctor's visit.
Until this moment, she had just felt like closing her eyes
and going back to sleep, but now she struggled to stay
awake.

There was a knock at the door, and the nurse came
in.

'You have a visitor, Señora,' she announced. 'A Señor
Chalmers.'

The name meant nothing to Arianne. 'Show him in,' she
murmured. She probably looked ghastly, but she didn't
care. After a moment, a man walked in, and the nurse
left the room.

'I'm very glad to see you,' the man said in French. He
had an American accent. 'I came as soon as the doctor
told me your condition was no longer critical. I am not
allowed to stay for long, though,' he added.

'Who are you?' Arianne asked, horrified at the weakness
of her own voice.

The man smiled.

'I'm sorry, I should have started by introducing myself.
We met at your wedding, but I wouldn't expect you to
remember. My name is Bob Chalmers. I advised Simon
on his business. I am a director of the de la Force holding
company.'

Arianne wondered why he was here, but there were more
pressing questions on her mind.

'Where is my daughter?' she asked anxiously.

'She is at the house, with her governess. Don't worry,
they are perfectly fine.'

Arianne was at first confused by the reference to the
governess, then realized that he meant Nana.

'Where am I?' she asked.

'At the Pequeña Compañia clinic in Buenos Aires,' Chalmers replied.

'Who brought me here?' Now that her strength was returning a little Arianne found she wanted answers to a string of questions.

'I arranged for an ambulance plane to bring you from Salta to Buenos Aires. I thought it would be unwise for you to stay in a critical condition in a local hospital. The de la Force family must have many doctor friends there.'

Arianne was thoroughly puzzled now. 'Please tell me what happened,' she said weakly. 'I can't remember.'

'May I sit down?' Chalmers asked.

'Of course.' She tried to indicate the armchair in the corner, but couldn't find the strength to raise her hand.

'Simon had asked me to stay at the house after the party. I don't like going to bed early, so I stayed in the library doing some work after you all went to bed. Suddenly I heard this great commotion, and I noticed the staff running around like headless chickens. Someone had gone to your bedroom to answer a bell, and found you unconscious. You were taken to the hospital in Salta, and I arranged for your transfer here.' He tactfully avoided any reference to the doctors pumping her stomach in Salta. Until then he had never come across a woman who had attempted suicide on her wedding night. He had expected a neurotic wreck, but other than her pallor she seemed perfectly normal and calm.

'Where is Simon?' Arianne forced herself to ask the question. She had tried to push him out of her mind since regaining consciousness.

Bob's face showed his surprise.

'Haven't the doctors said anything to you?'

'No,' she replied.

He left the armchair and stood near her. She became anxious at his obvious hesitation.

'I'm very sorry to have to tell you this,' he said at last, 'but Simon died that evening. His family immediately asked for an autopsy. It showed that he died from a massive coronary.' He did not tell Arianne that they had also asked for evidence that the marriage had been consummated, in a desperate attempt to find some reason to have it declared null so they could claim his inheritance. The doctors had confirmed to them that the evidence was there.

Arianne leaned against her pillows, tears running down her cheeks.

'It is very hard for me to have to disclose such bad news to you. I didn't know they hadn't told you yet. Simon was buried in Salta yesterday,' Bob said.

Arianne remained silent. She could not tell him that her tears were tears of joy. Her nightmare was over. She would soon be back in Paris, with Gloria and Nana. She would sell her jewellery, and get on with her life as she wished.

'When will I be able to leave Buenos Aires?' she asked.

'In accordance with Argentine law, you will inherit the whole of Simon's estate. He may have made provisions in his will for other beneficiaries, although I think it is unlikely, but he can only dispose of one fifth of his estate. The rest will be yours in any case. You will have to stay here at least until the estate is settled.'

Arianne's reaction was immediate.

'I don't want it,' she said.

Bob stared at her in surprise. She looked as if she meant it.

'The night before your wedding, Simon gave me a letter for you which I was to take back to New York for safekeeping, and only give to you after his death. Nobody could have guessed that it would become relevant so soon. I don't know its contents,' he said, pulling an envelope out of his inside pocket. 'It might be better if you read it before making any decision.' He handed the envelope to Arianne.

She tore it open and unfolded the letter. It was in Simon's unmistakable jagged handwriting. Her face became even paler as she read it.

Valle del Oro, 15 June 1969

Dear Arianne,

In accordance with the provisions of my will, you are to be the beneficiary of my estate. If we have children,

*the estate will be apportioned in equal shares between you
and them, and you will be their trustee until they are of
age. If we do not have children, you will then be the sole
beneficiary.*

*I do not wish the estate dispersed or disposed of in
any way until my children can take control of it. To
ensure this, I have left a sealed envelope with a lawyer,
holding the photocopy of your Brazilian passport and
an explanation addressed to the Brazilian police with
regard to your identity. His instructions are to refer the
envelope to the Brazilian Embassy as soon as he is aware
of any significant disposal of the estate by you, or any
evidence that you are not willing to take control of my
business.*

*This restriction applies for a period of ten years after
my death or until the children are of age, whichever is
the soonest. Once these conditions are met, the lawyer has instructions to return the sealed envelope to
you. If I were to die childless, I have set the ten-year
limit in the knowledge that, once you have become
used to running the business, you would find it very
difficult to relinquish control. I have also made it a
condition that you do not re-marry during that time.
I am sure that after ten years of absolute power you
would not wish to share it, and thus put my estate
at risk.*

*I have taken this action because I trust my judgement
of people, I am only seeking to ensure your willingness
to execute it. My estate is my monument, and my family
its keeper. I wish to ensure its survival in my name after
I'm gone.*
    Simon

She slowly folded the letter, stunned by Simon's machinations to trap her even after his death. Ten years. It was
difficult for her to encompass the implications. Ten years
ago she had been living in the slums, with Florinda and
their mother. Ten years from now . . . It was futile to think
about it: she had no choice.

She sat up in bed and turned towards Chalmers.

'Simon's letter explains what he expected of me. I will take over the business,' she said firmly.

'I'm very glad to hear that, Mrs de la Force. There is a board meeting scheduled for next week, and key decisions have to be made.'

'No, it's not going to be like that. If I'm in control, then I set the rules. I don't know anything about the business, and I will not approve anything until I do. And please call me Arianne.' There had to be a reason behind Chalmers' concern for her. 'Why are you here anyway? I'm sure this is not just a courtesy visit.'

He smiled.

'Not entirely,' Chalmers answered. 'I just wanted to let you know that I hope I can be of assistance in these difficult times. It could be in your interest as well as mine,' he added.

Arianne liked his frankness. She knew he hadn't come to see her out of kindheartedness only. He needed an ally, and so did she. Her instinct told her that she could trust him.

'How much did Simon pay you?' she asked point-blank.

He hesitated for a moment. 'I'm on a percentage fee. I don't think it is the time to discuss it.'

'You are wrong,' Arianne countered. 'I will double it for this year. I'm going to check out of here tonight. You will find me the best language teacher in Buenos Aires, and I want him in the house tomorrow morning at 9.00 o'clock. He has to teach me Spanish in two weeks, mornings only. In the afternoons, you will explain the business to me. The board meeting will take place only when I know both the language and the rules.'

'But . . .'

'No "buts". That's the way it's going to be from now on. There will be no decisions on *anything* other than day-to-day matters until I know what I'm doing. I'm tired now. I will see you tomorrow at the house.' She didn't know where the house was nor the phone number. 'Please leave me the number where I can phone my daughter,' she added. Bob wrote it on the note-pad on her bedside table, said goodbye and left.

As he walked down the corridor towards the elevator he thought about his conversation with this woman who had been nearly dead three days ago. Simon had obviously met his match when he had chosen her as his wife. But she was in the hospital while the board was planning to get rid of her. Bob hoped that he had made the right choice.

The car turned into Avenida Alvear, and Arianne noticed the enormous *gomero* tree, its top overshadowing the corner like a giant's umbrella. Her eye caught the name of the side street in white letters on the blue enamel plate fixed to the ornate railings of a big house at the corner, lit by the white glass street light at the top of a gilded steel column. Everything, even the street names, were alien to her, but the French-style mansions along the avenue reminded her of Paris. It was like Paris with tropical trees.

The car slowed down and turned right, stopping in front of a pair of massive wrought iron and brass gates. The gate were opened by a uniformed porter, and Arianne looked at the house through the car window as they drove towards it.

The house front was at least two hundred feet long. It was built of pale grey stone, an obvious copy of the façades of the Place de la Concorde. The car drove slowly up the wide gravel pathway and stopped under a massive stone portico. The driver opened Arianne's door, and she got out of the car. She paused for a moment in front of the huge glass and iron doors. A liveried footman opened them for her. Head high, she walked into her new home.

The staff were lined up on both sides of the wide stone stair leading from the entrance to the foyer, the red carpet held in place by thick brass bars. Arianne went up, nodding her head to acknowledge the bows of the servants as she walked past them. When she reached the top, a short, plumpish woman dressed in black, her dark hair pulled into a roll at the back, came towards her.

'I am Nelly, the housekeeper, Señora. It is an honour to meet you,' the woman said, her bow almost becoming a curtsy.

'Thank you, Nelly,' replied Arianne, walking into the

large square room at the top of the stairs. The dark oak panelling carved with garlands of fruit reached the coved cornice and a massive crystal chandelier hung from the ceiling, nearly fifteen feet above Arianne's head. She noticed the huge painting hanging between the doors on one of the walls. It was a full-length portrait of a beautiful young woman in turn-of-the-century clothes, her strands of pearls reaching down to her waist.

'Where is my daughter?' Arianne asked.

'She was very tired, so she was put to bed at seven, Señora. Her governess is waiting for you upstairs.'

She was eager to see Gloria and talk to Nana but realized that, as the new master, she had to go through the motions of this handing-over of the keys. She walked up to the portrait and glanced at the small brass plate at the bottom of the ornate frame. 'Josefina A. de Anzorena – Giovanni Boldini – Paris 1911', she read.

'Who is the lady in this portrait?' she asked.

'It is Mrs de la Force's grandmother, Señora. I believe it is a family heirloom. It is by a famous painter,' Nelly answered proudly.

Arianne cast an icy look at the housekeeper.

'I appreciate how sudden all this has been, Nelly, but I am Mrs de la Force, and this lady is no relation of *mine*. Have the portrait taken down and returned to her family, please.'

Nelly's face went crimson. She could sense the silent satisfaction of the staff behind her at the rebuke.

'Of course, Señora,' Nelly said humbly. She would have to be careful with this one.

Arianne walked through the double doors on her left, and rapidly went through a succession of reception rooms, crammed with exquisite French furniture, until she reached a small oval salon. Nelly caught up with her at last, and opened the doors on one side.

'This is the dining room, Señora. It is a copy of one of the main rooms in a French palace.' Arianne found her 'helpful' comments grating, but decided to say nothing. She had to make some allowance for the housekeeper's pride. There was no point in making an unnecessary enemy.

Arianne walked into the vast chamber, her steps echoing on the Versailles parquet. There were fireplaces at both ends of the marble-lined room, with huge painted hunting scenes above them. A set of silver tureens had been placed in the middle of the polished mahogany table.

'I would like to see the silver and the china,' Arianne said.

'There are seventeen sets of china, Señora. Would you like to see them all?'

'Show me the silver now. I'll look at the china another time,' Arianne replied tersely.

Nelly went to the side door at the far end of the room, and opened it with one of the keys hanging from her large key-ring. They walked into a vast pantry lined with glass-fronted cabinets, the china stacked in neat piles on the shelves on one side of the room, crystal glasses on the other. She opened one of the cutlery drawers, the silver gleaming against the green baize lining the compartments. She then moved to another cabinet, and opened a number of drawers.

'The silver-gilt is kept here, Señora,' she said. Arianne picked up a fork from the first drawer, and inspected the monogram on the handle. 'dlF' read the ornate cipher.

'If there is any silver with a monogram other than this, send it to the silversmith to be altered. If it can not be changed, then I will sell it. The same applies to the linen and the china, Nelly. I'm tired now. I would like to see my bedroom.'

The housekeeper closed the drawers, and locked the door behind them. She then walked across the dining room and opened the double doors leading into the main hall.

Arianne had been able to conceal her amazement at the grandeur of the house, but now she found it impossible. She stopped in her tracks, her breath caught in her throat, overwhelmed by the splendour of the room.

The Renaissance-style hall was sixty feet square and forty feet high. Five massive brass chandeliers hung from the carved oak ceiling, matched by the oak gallery at high level. Enormous tapestries hung on the stone walls, and medieval statues in wood and stone stood on the chests lined up against the wainscot. The gold background of the Siennese religious paintings glittered in the half light, matching the embers of the fire in the hearth on one side of the room, between two cathedral-size windows with stone mullions.

Arianne regained her composure and rapidly walked across the hall, back into the foyer dominated by the rejected portrait. Nelly opened the wrought-iron gate near the staircase and followed Arianne into the elevator.

They came out and walked along the first-floor gallery in silence, until Nelly stopped in front of one of the many doors and opened it.

'Were these Señora Dolores' rooms?' Arianne asked before entering.

'Yes, Señora. They are the best rooms on this floor,' replied Nelly defensively.

'Please show me my husband's bedroom,' Arianne said. 'And show me the way to my daughter and her governess's rooms. I would like to see them. I want breakfast at seven thirty. Black coffee, orange juice and toast. That will be all for now, Nelly,' she added.

The housekeeper did as she was told, made a short speech about how honoured she was to have had the opportunity to meet the Señora, wished her goodnight, and began to walk towards the stairs. Arianne called her back.

'I am most impressed by the superb job you have done in running this house, Nelly. I just wanted to thank you, and let you know that I will double your salary as from this month.' From the expression on Nelly's face Arianne knew that she had achieved her aim. She did not care if she had the best-paid housekeeper in South America; the house was a white elephant and she wanted this woman to be on her side.

Once she was alone, Arianne suddenly felt weak and sat on one of the throne-like chairs set at intervals along the wall. Still, she could feel the excitement rising inside her.

Until this day, she had been at the receiving end of Simon's largesse. He had bought her a life of inconceivable luxury, but now she realized that what she had had

311

so far had been only the dividends. Before, she could buy anything in any shop. Now she could have anything in the world. Everything that Simon had owned she now owned, everything that Simon had been she now was. *She* held the power.

She stood up and went to Nana's room. She paused for a moment before knocking at the door, and smiled. Perhaps she was going to enjoy being Mrs de la Force after all.

27

BUENOS AIRES
July 1969

Bob Chalmers held the large door open.

'This way please, Mrs de la Force,' he said politely. Arianne had noticed he had stopped calling her by her Christian name as soon as they had walked into the building. Tact was obviously one of his virtues.

The memory of a similar moment flashed in her mind. Less than two years ago, Jacques Villette had held a door open for her at Balenciaga. She had not failed then, and she was not going to fail now.

She walked into the room, taking in the full-length portrait of Simon on the far wall facing the door. The twelve men sitting around the long table stood up as she entered. The man sitting at the head of the table, under the portrait, came towards her. She recognized his hawkish and slicked-back black hair from the photographs she had studied at the house. He was Simon's Vice-Chairman.

'I'm very pleased to meet you, Mr Massera,' Arianne said, before he had time to introduce himself. He started to address her in heavily accented French, but Arianne interrupted him.

'It is very kind of you to speak to me in French, but it is unnecessary,' she said in fluent Spanish. The man escorted her around the table, trying to introduce Arianne to the members of the board, but she addressed each of them by name, and Massera remained silent after his second attempt. The introductions completed, he then pulled out an empty chair in the middle of one side of the table.

'Please sit down, Señora,' he said courteously. Arianne paid no attention and walked to the top of the table, sitting in his seat. Massera was startled but he collected his papers, and returned to the seat he had just offered to Arianne. As soon as he sat down, she spoke to the table at large.

'Gentlemen, I'm extremely pleased to meet you today.

These have been very difficult times for all of us but I hope that, with your help, I will be able to make this transition period as short and as smooth as possible. My husband's sudden disappearance undoubtedly creates problems, and I understand your position at the moment.' She rested her elbows on the table. 'I'm sure that you understand mine,' she added, her right hand toying with her enormous engagement ring in full view of her audience. She paused for a moment, her silence underlining her point.

'Now let's get down to business,' she finished.

As soon as she ended her speech, Massera stood up.

'It is a great honour for us to welcome you today as a visitor, Señora, and were it not for the tragic loss we all share, it would be a joyful occasion. We were delighted to hear of your wish to come here, and we sincerely appreciate your interest in becoming acquainted with us. It is the duty of any board to take the shareholders' interests to heart, and we will endeavour to run Valle del Oro SA along the same path of growth and prosperity as during the days when Don Simon was our Chairman. Please rest assured that we will keep you informed of our activities, even when you return to Europe. You are more than a shareholder, you are Don Simon's widow, and as such you are very dear to us all.' He sat down, taking the mute approval of his fellow directors for his tactful speech.

He now waited for Arianne's reply, hoping that it would be as short as his welcome. She surely had better things to do with her time than sit here. He hoped that he would not be forced to remind her that she really had no right to attend the board meeting at all. He had to admit that she was the most beautiful woman he had seen in his life, though. No wonder the old bastard had died trying to perform his marital duties.

Arianne looked around the table.

'I'm touched by your kind welcome, gentlemen. I appreciate your concern, Mr Massera, but I would like to put your mind at ease on several scores. I will live in Argentina from now on, and it will not be necessary for you to keep me informed, since I will be party to all your decisions. In fact, I intend to make them myself.'

314

A stony silence fell on the scene until Massera spoke again.

'Señora, I fully appreciate how distressing these times must be for you. It may also be that your relative inexperience of business matters has led you to several well-intentioned, but misguided, assumptions. One of the purposes of the board meeting later today is to confirm my appointment as Chairman and Chief Executive Officer of Valle del Oro SA. Only members of the board can attend a board meeting.' He smiled indulgently. The poor girl was obviously out of her depth, and he felt sorry for her. He hoped that this nonsense would not go on for much longer.

Arianne returned his smile. 'You are one step ahead of me, Mr Massera. I was not thinking of the board meeting yet. I came here to call an extraordinary shareholders' meeting, which it is my right to do. Since I hold 100 per cent of the shares, we have a full quorum. The purpose of the meeting is to dismiss the current board, and the motion has the shareholders' approval. The second item on the Agenda is the reappointment of the board, with myself as Chairman and Chief Executive Officer. Before casting my vote on this second motion, I would like to ask the ex-members of the board if they would have any objections to their reappointment under such conditions, otherwise I will have to find suitable replacements.'

She glanced around at the well-dressed, well-paid men, clearly dumbfounded by her speech. She was sure that they were quickly thinking about the implications of fighting a legal battle against her, the immediate loss of income and the slim chance of success. She knew the likely outcome, but Massera spoke before any of them could open their mouth.

'Señora, I must warn you of the possible consequences of the course of action you seem to be considering. I have a contract ensuring my position as Vice-Chairman of Valle del Oro SA,' he thundered.

Arianne enjoyed the mounting tension in the room, which reminded her of a poker table when the stakes are impossibly high. She knew she held a Royal Flush.

'Mr Massera,' she said at last, very quietly, 'I know about your contract. It was signed twelve years ago, and it is understandable that the small print may have slipped from your mind. However, there is a copy among my husband's papers, and I have read it. Your appointment is conditional on the shareholders' approval every year. I'm sure that my husband had no reason to revoke your appointment, but I'm the only shareholder now, and I take a different view. Your appointment has not been confirmed this year. There is a termination clause in your contract, and I assure you that it will be honoured in full. Since you no longer have anything to do with this company, I would be grateful if you would leave us so that the board can continue with its business.'

Massera's face went crimson, and he held the edge of the table with both hands. He stood up forcefully, overturned his chair, and grabbed his papers.

'You will hear from my lawyers, you bitch!' he screamed.

'Good afternoon, Mr Massera. Before leaving, please put your chair back in place. I don't like untidy rooms.'

The directors on both sides of Massera rushed to pick up his chair as soon as he left, slamming the door behind him.

'Now, gentlemen,' Arianne said with a captivating smile, 'let's continue with our meeting, shall we?'

'Thank you very much, Rosinha, that will be all.'

'Good night, Madame.' Carrying her mistress's evening gown and her opera cloak, the maid left the room. It was nearly two o'clock in the morning.

Arianne had been sleeping in this room for almost three months, ever since the decorators had finished removing every trace of Dolores' presence. It was her room now.

Not that she had been in it much. After a month of mourning which had been nothing but an alibi to keep people away until she was sure of her ground, she had begun to accept the inevitable invitations arising from her new position, and she had immediately found herself at the centre of the Buenos Aires social whirl. Everybody wanted to meet her, and it was useful for her to make contact with all the people who mattered.

But she found being the focus of so much attention disturbing. For many years she had lived under the fear of being found out. She had begun to outgrow that feeling in Paris, when first her modelling career and then her lifestyle had brought her to the attention of a small circle of society. But now she was a focus of interest for the whole country, and it worried her. She half-convinced herself that her power was her shield. Even if someone were to find out about her days in Brazil or the Bois de Boulogne, she reasoned, no one would dare to follow up on the story, let alone divulge it. The consequence would be the wrath of Arianne de la Force.

The fear nonetheless remained, but she had to learn to live with it if she were to survive because, as she soon realized, the public attention would be constant. Tonight, when she had appeared in her box at the Teatro Colon for the gala performance of *Norma*, she knew that thousands of eyes were on her as soon as she took her seat. Everything about her was commented upon, as it had been from her earliest public appearance here.

It was unnerving, but by now Arianne relished it. Her position ensured admiration from everyone, even from those who were themselves in an enviable position, and she found it irresistible. Money no longer mattered to her; she had very quickly got over the brief thrill of possession, dulled by the knowledge that she could have anything she wanted. But there was no end to the excitement of undisputed ascendancy.

She was about to get into bed when she decided to look in on Gloria, asleep in her room. She hardly saw her daughter these days. She left the house early, came back late in the evening to change her clothes, and her weekends were spent visiting the de la Force estates all over the country. She had taken Gloria with her on her first visits, but soon realized that the child was upset by the change of surroundings. There had been too many upheavals in Gloria's life recently, and it was better for her to stay at home with Nana.

She turned off the lights as she left the room, leaving only her reading light on. It was enough to make the diamond bracelets she had carelessly dropped on her bedside table sparkle, their glow picked up by the polished silver frame of the photograph of a woman and her two children in a Rio de Janeiro square, years ago.

28

BUENOS AIRES
November 1969

'We are now flying over the *estancia*, Señora. We will be landing in ten minutes. Please fasten your seat belt,' the captain's voice said over the loudspeaker. Arianne gathered her papers from the table in front of her, and looked out of the window as the steward folded the table away.

In preparation for her visit, she had read a brief history of the 'San Simon' estate, which was located in the South of Buenos Aires province. It had been settled in the 1840s, after General Anzorena's efficient elimination of the local Indian tribes. His successful campaign opened up the region, and the General's reward was half-a-million acres in the area. The estate was christened 'El Fortin de Anzorena', and became the backbone of the family fortune. But the relentless division of the original estate among three or four generations of a large Catholic family had led to the decline of the family wealth. By the time Simon married Dolores, her father had just a small holding in the area. The *casco* of the original estate, the main house rebuilt in 1907 and the vast park around it, belonged to a relative, and Simon bought it from him soon after his marriage. It was still called by the original name of the estate then, but Simon changed it – predictably – to 'San Simon'.

Within a few years, he bought surrounding land until he had put together one hundred thousand acres of the original estate, making it once again the largest holding in the area. It became the flagship of his agri-business in the Pampas region. The house, an idiosyncratic interpretation of Scottish-baronial style as understood by Dolores' grandfather, was returned to its original grandeur by her. The long-neglected park was restored, and an eighteen-hole golf course was added, a birthday present from Simon when Dolores briefly took up the sport. 'San Simon' became one of the most visible props to Simon and Dolores' leading role in Buenos Aires society, a monument to both Simon's money and Dolores' lineage.

The estate's close association with Dolores had delayed Arianne's visit. She finally scheduled her trip for September, but the wave of labour unrest during that month, aggravated by the Government's fierce repression of the strikers, meant that most of her time had to be spent in urgent meetings with management and trade union leaders to try to minimize losses in the de la Force factories.

There was a further, personal reason for the delay. Soon after taking control of the business she had made her first visit to a de la Force *estancia*, where the harvest of winter corn was taking place. She left her plane dressed in her severe suit and high heels, only to face the estate manager and a stable boy, both on horseback. The stable boy was holding a third horse by the bridle, a horse for the boss. It had been Simon's pride to ride across his land.

The boy was sent back to the house at great speed and a car soon appeared, but Arianne was embarrassed by the episode. She imagined the sneering jokes after her departure about the foreigner, the woman, the city doll now playing at being the boss. It would not happen again.

As soon as she was back in Buenos Aires she arranged for daily riding lessons at the crack of dawn. After three months she felt confident enough in the saddle; no one would be able to say that the *patrona* could not ride. And she was not wearing Chanel but her riding breeches and boots now, sufficiently worn to look acceptable to a countryman's eye, together with a white shirt and an old jacket.

The ostensible reason for her visit was to inspect 'San Simon's' recently completed silos and grain-drying facilities, the latest stage in a massive investment programme. Storage capacity, drying temperatures, planted areas, size of lorries, all the figures were at her fingertips.

The Lear Jet began its descent onto the airstrip, and Arianne lay back in her seat, closing her eyes. As she felt the wheels touch the ground, she quickly reviewed the resumé of the estate manager who would be waiting to meet her: Paul Liehr, thirty-six years old, graduated from the University of Kansas, employed at 'San Simon' since his graduation.

The steward opened the door. Arianne picked up her briefcase and walked towards the exit, into a rectangle of light cast by the bright sunshine on the red carpet.

'I am very pleased with the results so far. I hope you are as well, Señora.' Paul Liehr was referring to their inspection of crossbreeds between Charolais dams and Hereford and Aberdeen Angus bulls. Arianne had been able to see for herself that the results were indeed encouraging. Their tour over, Paul Liehr had driven her back to the house and they were now standing outside the main entrance.

'If it suits your plans, Señora, I will be here at four o'clock to continue our inspection.' Arianne would have liked to carry on immediately after lunch, but she had to make allowances for rural working hours. People woke up before sunrise, and the midday heat made work unbearable at this time of the year. To disregard the fact would make her unpopular among the staff, but she did not relish the prospect of a few hours in the house on her own. No matter how much she glossed over the fact, she still saw it as Dolores' territory. The answer came to her in a flash.

'Why don't you stay for lunch?' she asked. 'Then we can talk about other aspects of your work,' she added, uncertain about the justification. It was unnecessary, certainly on his behalf. Paul Liehr hesitated for a moment, obviously surprised by the invitation.

'Let's go inside, it will be cooler,' Arianne said, not waiting for his reply and walking up the steps towards the studded oak door. Paul rushed ahead and held the door open for her. They walked into the hall, and Arianne noticed the butler waiting for her nearby. 'Mr Liehr will be staying for lunch, Oscar.' The butler nodded his head in a discreet bow, but not before Arianne noticed the fleeting disapproval reflected in his eyes. Neither Don Simon nor Señora Dolores would have invited any member of staff, no matter how high his position, to lunch with them. But she was the boss now, whether the butler liked it or not.

* * *

Arianne was about to order more coffee when she saw Paul surreptitiously glancing at his watch. It irritated her at first, because she had found lunch in his company more enjoyable than she had anticipated, and she was no longer used to people showing signs of anything other than enraptured interest towards her.

'Please let me know if I'm boring you,' she said curtly.

'On the contrary, Señora. I was wondering if I hadn't taken too much of your time already.' His embarrassment was genuine, and Arianne felt sorry. Paul was telling the truth, and she had probably kept him past the time of his afternoon nap anyway.

'I've really enjoyed our conversation, but it's time we broke off for siesta now.' She was briefly amused by his possible misunderstanding of her remark, but decided not to look at his face just in case. She stood up, and Paul followed her to the hall, where they quickly made their goodbyes at the foot of the stairs, Paul confirming that he would be back at four o'clock. She stared at him as he walked away, then turned around and swiftly climbed to the upper floor.

Arianne wandered along the corridors for a while, opening door after door until she glimpsed a room larger than the others, with a four-poster bed covered with a lace bedspread. It probably was Dolores' bedroom, and she shut the door. She walked to the other end of the corridor and opened another door. A tweed jacket still hung on the clothes stand by the mirror. It was Simon's bedroom, and she walked in.

To her surprise, she felt like an intruder at first. It had been different in the Buenos Aires house, perhaps because she had gone there desperate to establish her position as Mrs de la Force, pushing aside any other feeling. But the need was no longer pressing, allowing her to acknowledge her true feelings. Arianne was tempted to leave the room, and for that reason she forced herself to stay. She began to glance at the pictures, without really taking them in, until her eye was caught by the silver-framed photograph on Simon's bedside table. It was her own portrait, and she was strangely touched by the discovery. Simon must have placed it there when Dolores died. Perhaps he had loved her, after all. She had always thought that he was unable to love, but finding her photograph where she had least expected it to be made her wonder.

She shook her head, and looked at the time. It would be almost an hour before Paul came to meet her. She stood by the window and gazed at the park under the full glare of the afternoon sun, the sky almost white and the trees standing in pools of black shadow. After a moment, she turned away and sat in the leather armchair by the empty fireplace. She felt restless, without being able to focus on the reason.

Her thoughts went back to the earlier part of the day. By now she was familiar enough with most aspects of agri-business, and her task had been made easier by the fact that Paul Liehr, unlike her other estate managers, had not made a point of impressing her with his knowledge whenever the opportunity arose. He was passionate about his work, and they had spoken about it at length, but at no point had he made her feel out of her depth.

Arianne had reassured him that she would maintain the current investment programme in the estate, and Paul had obviously been pleased by his employer's support. Arianne suddenly reproached herself for her rashness at the end of lunch. She had to be more thoughtful about the difference in their positions. The man was just a farmer in the middle of the country, not an ambassador at a dinner party in Buenos Aires.

The clock on the mantelpiece struck four. She rushed downstairs, surprised by her own enthusiasm.

Paul was already waiting for her outside, his Land Rover parked in the forecourt. As he greeted her, a stable boy approached them, leading two horses by the bridle, one of them a magnificent black Arab stallion. The silver trimmings and decorations on its saddle and reins glistened in the afternoon sun. The other horse, a bay, recognized its master, and nuzzled against Paul's shoulder.

'The horses are ready, Don Paul. I was told that you would need them at four o'clock,' the boy said. Paul was visibly annoyed.

'I sent a message with Don Segundo that we would not need them,' he said brusquely. The boy shuffled his feet, uncomfortable now.

'He didn't tell me anything, Don Paul,' he mumbled, his eyes on the ground.

'I'd love to have a ride. I've been sitting all day,' Arianne said, approaching the Arabian.

'That is . . .' Paul was going to add 'Don Simon's horse', but he stopped mid-sentence. '"Azucar" is a very nervous animal, Señora. He doesn't like riders he doesn't know.' Paul turned towards the boy. 'The tail is too long. What have you been doing over the last month? Not much, by the look of it,' he admonished.

Arianne took the reins from the chastened stable boy and swiftly mounted the horse.

'"Azucar" will soon learn to know me. Let's go,' she said with a smile.

As Arianne and Paul approached the gate into the park, the gables and pinnacles of the house were visible in the distance, their brickwork almost orange in the setting sun. Their tour was over, and Arianne realized she might be home in time to see Gloria.

They were on their way back from the stud farm, which had been the last item on their schedule. Arianne's interest in horses did not go beyond turning herself into an accomplished rider for the sake of her image, and before coming to 'San Simon' she had considered the possibility of closing down the stud farm as an unnecessary extravagance. But having listened attentively to Paul's explanations of the work in progress, she was not so sure. She wondered if he had guessed her thoughts, because time and again he stressed the fact that, although small in the context of the overall business, the stud farm was profitable.

Towards the end of the inspection she had kept her eyes on his face. The vivacity of his features and the enthusiasm in his eyes made her realize that he was a good-looking man. The thought briefly disconcerted her, and she decided to make an effort to concentrate on his talk. She had not come here to inspect *him*.

324

Intrigued by her silence, Paul suddenly interrupted his explanation and looked at Arianne. Troubled by his awareness of her unnecessary scrutiny, she glanced at her watch, avoiding his gaze.

'I ought to go back soon,' she said. Paul apologized for taking so much of her time, and they left the stables. They had barely exchanged a word on the way back, and she thought it would be counter-productive to leave Paul with the impression that she had been less than pleased with his work.

'I am truly impressed by everything I've seen today. You're doing very good work here.'

He smiled. 'I am relieved, Señora. I have heard that you fire people on the spot otherwise, and I love what I do.' She looked at him sharply for a moment, but she realized there was no malice in his words, he was just being honest. She smiled at him.

'Only when necessary. You have nothing to worry about, Paul.' It was the first time she had addressed him by his name, and she wondered why she had not done so earlier. They stopped by the gate and Paul leaned down from the saddle to unhook the lock, pulling it open. Arianne steered her horse onto the grassy bank of the road to get out of his way. Paul was waiting for her on the other side now, and she spurred her horse on, unaware that a dry thistle on the ground had become entangled in the horse's long tail. As they went through the gate, the thistle pricked the horse's hind legs. Startled, the animal jumped towards Paul, who swiftly moved his mount to block the way. Stretching his arm, he encircled Arianne's waist and pulled her out of the saddle. He held her tight against his side, her legs in the air. Relieved of her weight, the horse ran around in confusion for a few seconds and then came to an abrupt halt nearby.

Her face pressed against his shoulder, Arianne automatically flung her arms around Paul's neck to regain her balance. For a second she was only conscious of the feel of his shirt on her cheek, his heartbeat, and the smell of soap and warm leather. Paul jumped down, still holding her. As soon as they were on their feet he released her and

325

walked calmly towards her horse, until he had hold of the reins. Very quietly, he moved along the horse's side. Its tail within his reach, Paul gently disentangled the thistle. He then led the horse back to Arianne.

'Are you all right, Señora?' he asked with concern. 'I told that boy the tail was too long. He's going to get the rough edge of my tongue now,' he muttered.

Arianne nodded her head.

'Thank you very much for your help. I'm perfectly all right.' She wasn't. Her legs were shaking, and she walked slowly towards her horse so Paul wouldn't notice. She climbed into the saddle, hoping he would not attempt to assist her. He didn't, and a short while later they arrived back at the house.

The lights of Buenos Aires spread in every direction beneath her, and Arianne was delighted that she would soon be at home. The visit had unsettled her. She told herself it was because of her discovery in Simon's bedroom, but she did not allow herself the luxury of personal ruminations. Whatever Simon may or may not have felt towards her was in the past.

The plane landed smoothly, and her limousine was waiting for her on the tarmac. As she was driven away, she was pleased to see that it was still early. She would indeed be home before Gloria went to bed.

The jacaranda trees lining the street were in blossom, huge puff-balls of lilac-coloured blooms carpeting the sidewalks with their bell-shaped flowers. It reminded her of the streets of Rio de Janeiro, a long time ago, which had also been covered in jacaranda blossoms at this time of year. But personal memories were as painful as personal feelings, and she endeavoured to push them both out of her mind.

Her thoughts returned to Paul. She couldn't deny she found him attractive, but there was nothing inexplicable about that. He had the figure and glow of health of a man who spent his life in open-air pursuits, and he had the quiet authority of a country man with none of the arrogance of her city executives. But it only meant that one of her managers was more handsome and better company than most of his colleagues, nothing more.

Yes, he was attractive, but she was not going to do anything about it. She had had enough of men. Ever since Ruben, she had seen men as nothing other than a tool for survival. They wanted her, she needed their money. Since she could not afford to respond to her emotions, she ignored them.

Before Simon appeared in her life, her looks were still her livelihood, but now she would be well paid just for being herself. No longer an inevitable imposition, sex became a cherished denial, to be able to refuse it as much a part of her vanity as the knowledge that she could trigger the need.

Perhaps Paul was the first attractive man she had come across since the roles had been reversed, since she was the one who could make things happen. Or maybe it was because *she* could now dictate the terms, that she allowed herself to notice the attraction. It didn't matter, she thought as the car stopped outside the house. It was the one luxury the all-powerful Señora de la Force could not afford.

She ran upstairs and rushed into the nursery. Gloria was already in her nightgown, riding the enormous rocking horse Arianne had bought for her. Nana was sitting in a chair by her side, oblivious to the vitriolic glances from the uniformed nanny standing in the far corner of the room.

'Hello, my darling,' she said, picking Gloria up and kissing her. As soon as she put her down, Gloria ran back to the wooden horse and climbed on it again. The nanny left her corner and came over to Arianne.

'I'm resigning, Señora. I don't like any interference in my work. I have been offered a job by Mrs Lobos, and I have accepted it,' she said disdainfully.

Arianne thought of placating her, but took one look at Nana and realized that it would be unwise.

'Fine,' Arianne replied tersely. 'Have a word with Nelly. You can settle up with her.' The nanny left the room without a further word. Arianne did not like the woman, but her departure was a nuisance. She was the third nanny she had engaged since their arrival in Argentina, and Arianne was desperate to create a stable environment for her daughter. She knew that the reason behind their huffing and puffing and eventual departure was Nana, whose role in the house was impossible to explain to the staff, but equally impossible for Arianne to control. She knew that Nana wanted to be in charge of the child, but Arianne wanted Gloria to learn Spanish and to grow up with other children, not be isolated in a nursery with Nana. At least Gloria had begun to speak the language; it might even be possible to humour Nana now.

'I want to look after Gloria,' Nana said as soon as the nanny was gone, as if she had read Arianne's thoughts. 'I have that right.'

Arianne was about to speak when Gloria fell off the rocking horse. Both women ran to the crying child.

'My darling, are you all right?' Arianne said, kneeling down and holding out her arms. Gloria stood up and ran straight to Nana, who took her up in her arms and rocked her gently. Arianne stood in silence for a while. She suddenly felt too tired, too distressed by the scene: there had been too many similar episodes recently. She leant forward and kissed Gloria on the forehead.

'Good night, my darling. Nana will put you to bed. Sleep well,' she said before turning and leaving. It was much easier to deal with business problems, she thought as she walked towards her rooms. She had some urgent papers to read tonight in preparation for a Valle del Oro meeting. She went to her desk, turned on the reading light, and sat down. Five minutes later, she was completely absorbed by the problem of sugar export quotas to the US and the rigidity of the Argentine market.

Arianne put down the phone, deep in thought. The problems, anticipated for a long time, were now reaching a crisis. She knew who she was dealing with, though, and it would have been foolish to expect anything other than a lukewarm response at first. The Russians were wily negotiators, and Madame Sherbatiev, the woman in charge of their sugar trade, was the wiliest of them all. But Edouard Golbins, whose network of contacts never ceased to amaze Arianne, had confirmed that Madame Sherbatiev would be in Paris tomorrow, ostensibly on an unexpected courtesy visit. Arianne decided to fly to Paris immediately.

Encouraged by the Government's tax incentives fourteen months ago, Arianne, like most other producers in Argentina, had increased sugar planting to record levels, and conditions in the Valley had ensured a bumper harvest. But, against the expected trend, domestic demand for sugar had remained static. Exports were her only hope. Arianne needed a substantial sale now, but production costs in Argentina had remained above the spot market prices in London and New York for a long time.

In the tightly knit sugar market, word soon spreads about a possible supplier troubled by over-production. She had been approached by London brokers a number of times, but she had turned down their loss-making offers, waiting for an improvement in market conditions. But the sugar was in her fields now, losing her money every day.

Hurricane 'Eliza' was her chance. It had been expected, but it had changed course the day before, sparing other Caribbean islands but devastating Cuba. The implications for their sugar crop were obvious and, judging by their record grain purchases in America, the Russians were no longer prepared to accept the consequences of food shortages. They would have to come to the market soon. Or at least that was Arianne's guess. She would find out in Paris tomorrow.

'Madame Sherbatiev doesn't want to see you,' was Edouard Golbins' opening line to Arianne after they sat down on the sofa in his large office, overlooking the Champs-Elysées. 'I wouldn't take it personally, she's not seeing anyone at the moment.'

'I *have* to see her. Can she be persuaded?' Arianne asked.

Golbins smiled. 'If you are suggesting sending her to Christian Dior at your expense, she is not the type. However, these Russians like to be entertained, and I spent a lot of time last night with some members of her entourage. It was exhausting, but useful,' he said with a smile. Arianne noticed the dark rings under his eyes. She had some idea of the type of entertainment which would appeal to Russian negotiators abroad.

'The problem is that Argentina is not significant for them. They are looking for deals, but they can get them in the Caribbean, or in Africa. If the Russians were to consider a deal with you, it would only be because you offer them something you shouldn't, if you have any sense. I was told they are not interested in deals under two hundred thousand tons, they will only consider offers below the spot market price, and they want the price fixed now. A bad deal of that calibre will cost you a lot of money.'

It would. Two hundred thousand tons was about double Arianne's surplus. She would not only lose on her own sugar, but she would lose much more in securing the additional tonnage they required.

'Are you saying they are open to offers?' she asked.

'They haven't said that. But they haven't said they would not listen either. I can contact them. I would say it's up to you to make an offer, but if you decide to go any further don't blame me for the consequences,' Golbins warned.

'I have a deal to offer that I don't think they will turn down.' Arianne went to his desk, quickly wrote a few lines on a piece of paper, and gave it to him.

'You're mad!' Golbins said. 'You're not only losing millions on the deal, you are compounding the loss.'

'Maybe,' Arianne replied. 'But I have a lot of sugar sitting at home, and I *have* to get rid of it. Sometimes one has to play Russian roulette. Phone them now.'

Six months later, twelve cargos of sugar, amounting to three hundred thousand tons, were unloaded in Vladivostok. Scrupulous as ever in the observance of their contracts, the Soviet Government released payment under the unusual terms agreed. Arianne de la Force suffered a loss amounting to many millions of dollars in the transaction. As in everything else she did, she took it gracefully.

Three months after the deal was completed, OPEC's dramatic increase of the price of oil sent fear of inflation rippling through the world markets. The price of gold, depressed for years, began to climb beyond anyone's expectations, until it reached record levels. The Russian gold Arianne had received in payment for her sugar was stored in a Zurich vault; its swift disposal resulted in a net profit equal to four times her loss on the sugar deal. Madame de la Force was very pleased, but not surprised. The markets had simply behaved as she had expected.

Her marriage had made her known in business circles. Her Russian deal made her a legend.

Fuck the nun, fuck the nun, fuck the nun, Florinda repeated mentally with every stitch of bright thread into the stiff white cloth, the pattern of flowers she was embroidering at the edge slowly taking shape as the afternoon faded into evening. Soon it would be time to go back to her cell. A shadow fell on her work and she turned her head. Used as she was to it, she still found the old nun's ability to walk about without making any noise unnerving. Maybe she had also been a thief before deciding to become a saint, she thought.

'That's very good work, Florinda,' the nun said approvingly.

'Thank you, Sister Rosario,' Florinda replied humbly, a smile of gratitude on her lips.

'You ought to put your things away until tomorrow. It's almost time now.' It was Florinda's turn to sweep the room and she rushed to the cupboard in the corner, picking up the broom and dustpan as if they were tools of pleasure. She meticulously swept every thread off the floor into the pan, giving a beaming smile to Mother Rosario in the process. She was careful not to include Palmira, the warden, in her smile: the ogress needed less encouragement than that to check whether a prisoner had washed properly in the showers later. It was Florinda's good fortune to be small-breasted, making checks on her personal hygiene less interesting for Palmira, but she had endured a few with the same beautiful smile she now gave to Mother Rosario.

She thought of the years still ahead. Twenty-two years, or seventeen if she became eligible for parole because of good conduct. She had jumped at the chance when the pasty-faced nun had asked for volunteers. She was prepared to embroider every shitty tablecloth in Brazil for the sake of five years of her life.

Five years of what would be left of her life. By the time she got out of jail she would be forty-five, an old woman. She would be finished. No man would want her then, not even her scrap dealer. No money, no men, she would be ready for the scrap heap herself. As she stomped down the cheerless corridor, she kept her eyes on the back of the woman in front of her and closed her ears to the shouts of the warden. But she did not close her mind to the only thought that mattered to her: one day she was going to find her sister. Imagining what she would do to her then was the only source of joy left in Florinda's miserable life.

Part VI

29

LONDON
July 1987

Pandora piled up her suitcases in the entrance hall. During the cab ride from the airport into London she remembered the first time she had returned from New York, many years ago, and how small the buildings and roads had seemed by comparison. She wondered if the city would look any different to her now, but she soon realized it was as familiar, as reassuringly known, as when she had left. She was home.

She hesitated for a second before the door to her flat, then she turned the key, pushed the door open and quickly walked across the hall into her sitting room. There, in the most personal of her environments, at its best in the morning sunlight, she was confronted with the evidence of how much she had changed.

Pandora took in the pale yellow stippled walls, the chintz curtains in soft Vermeer-blue with their pattern of cream magnolia blossoms tied back by silk ropes and tassels, the facing sofas upholstered in eau-de-Nil chintz in a contrasting yet harmonious pattern to the curtains, the woodwork and the carved fireplace glazed to an ivory tint. She sat on a needlepoint stool, her eye caught for a second by the small medallion pattern of the carpet, and stared at the room for a while. She had been inordinately proud of it six months ago. Now she found it almost asphyxiating in its predictability.

She picked up her address book, and quickly flicked through it. Then she went to the telephone.

'Hello, Mr Howard. I'm sorry to phone you at home. It's Pandora Doyle. Yes, Mrs Lyons, but I now work under my own name. I wondered if you could send a couple of men round to re-paint my flat as soon as possible . . . Yes, I know you did it only six months ago, but I want to change it. Of course I appreciate that you're terribly busy, but I really need this done immediately . . .'

*　　*　　*

The girl switched off the hair dryer and put it aside, then held up a small mirror behind her customer's head. 'It's *so* much more attractive, it really suits you.'

Pandora raised her eyes to the mirrored wall in front of her. The short, brushed-back style brought out her high cheekbones, and the new streaks in a subtle shade of copper underlined the blue-green of her eyes, complementing the make-up she had adopted in New York. She looked at the back of her head in the girl's mirror: the haircut also flattered the long graceful line of her neck, and she smiled her approval.

'I like it. You've done exactly what I wanted.' She stood up and the girl helped her out of her pink kimono-like robe, then began to brush Pandora's shoulders meticulously, but Pandora moved away, too impatient to wait for her to finish.

'Please don't bother, it's fine. Thank you so much for your help,' she said as she opened her purse to tip the girl. She was eager to leave.

She had spent her first Sunday in London taking down curtains and packing away pictures and ornaments. A few pieces of furniture could be auctioned, the rest would go to a house-clearance dealer. Then she had gone through her wardrobe, weeding out her old outfits to make space for her New York clothes. It had been then, while briefly holding up her new clothes against her body in front of the mirror, that she decided she needed a new haircut. That morning she had waited impatiently until nine thirty-one to phone her hairdresser for an appointment. After a long discussion with the receptionist, she had managed to cajole an appointment for ten o'clock. Now it was done, and she wanted to get on with the rest of her day.

A few yards away from the hairdresser she was approached by a smiling young man holding a green box.

'It's for Friends of the Earth,' he told Pandora, and she stopped. During the flight from New York she had read a *Newsweek* cover story on the devastation of the Amazon rain forest. She had felt both concerned and powerless about it. This was her chance to do something. She pulled a ten-pound note from her purse and slipped it into the collection box.

'Thank you *very* much. Would you like to become a member?' the man asked.

She thought for a moment.

'Yes, I would. I admire what you do.' He leaned down and rummaged through his satchel, propped against the wall behind him. He produced a clipboard, asked for her name and address and filled in a form, which she signed. It took less than a minute, and Pandora was once again on her way, her head feeling light and free without the accustomed weight of her hair.

Sitting on her drawing room floor, Pandora checked her notes. There were a few shops she had not covered while wandering around different areas of London, and she would still have to visit them. But she was already able to form a picture of the interior design market.

The corollary was clear. There was a mainstream modern style, epitomized by designer matt-black, expensive fabrics and Italian furniture at the top end of that market. Then there were endless variations on the Victorian period, from cheap to high-price. Both styles were ready for retirement: they had been around for a decade. She had to find a new angle.

She glanced at her empty sitting room, and realized there was an equally urgent, although less momentous priority. She had to buy new furniture for her own home. She had seen a few modern pieces she would like to have in various shops, but there was a four to six weeks wait. Old furniture, however, was immediately available.

'I'll take the kitchen table and that pair of Welsh chairs,' Pandora informed the lady at the antique shop. 'Please arrange for delivery as early in the morning as possible. I live just around the corner.'

The starkly simple furniture, of old wood stripped of any polish, had been the only items that had appealed to her. Not only did Pandora like them, but there was something pleasantly familiar about them. She wrote a cheque and left, glad that the whole operation had taken very little of her time. She was now ready to start her tour of the few remaining shops she had listed the night before.

It was when she reached the railings around the Kensington Church yard that she suddenly remembered why her choice of furniture had seemed so familiar. The old Welsh chairs and the plain table were very similar to the Shaker furniture she had glimpsed briefly in New York, on her way back to the office after breakfast with Geraldine. Pandora felt a rush of almost uncontrollable excitement. She had found *her* theme.

'From what you've said, I think I know someone in London who could be very useful to you. His name is Chris Outram, and the firm is Outram Cullinan. They're business and management consultants, and they advise me on certain aspects of my business in France. They are excellent. I'll phone Chris, and tell him to expect your call.' Arianne's voice came very clear over the occasional satellite blip.

While going over her figures the day before, Pandora had decided to phone Arianne on impulse, partly in genuine need of advice, but also for some much-needed support after her latest conversations with her worried accountant. She had been told that Mrs de la Force was away on her yacht and she had been relieved when she put the phone down. Her problems were her own concern, after all. But Arianne returned her call, showing genuine interest in Pandora's ideas. It was wonderful to have somebody's support for a change.

'I'm really grateful for your help,' Pandora said. 'I need an objective view as to how viable my project might be. I'll call Chris Outram and mention your name.' The conversation had reached its end; Arianne had given no indication that she wanted to discuss anything else, but Pandora decided she ought to give her the opportunity to do so, if she wanted to.

'I hope everything's well with you,' she said.

'Yes, thank you. The weather is glorious and I'm having a very relaxing time. You mentioned you're drafting a

338

report on your proposal for your bankers. Please send me a copy as soon as you have it, I would like to read it. I'll see you in Venice, I hope.'

Pandora took her cue.

'I'll certainly send you a copy and of course I'm coming to Venice. I couldn't possibly miss it. It will be marvellous,' she replied enthusiastically.

'Good,' Arianne said. 'I look forward to seeing you. Call me if you need anything else. Goodbye.'

Pandora put the phone down, and inspected the figures in front of her once again. There was only one way to go, only one viable strategy. But it was better not to think too much about the consequences if it didn't work.

It was a beautiful morning, the large plane trees filtering the sunshine into patterns of light and shade. The pale grey stonework of the twin towers of St John Smith Square seemed almost white in the midday sun as Pandora left the building on the corner.

Chris Outram had asked her some piercing questions at first, but once she had explained her project to him, and he had realized that she knew what she was talking about, he had been extremely supportive, although carefully underlining the risks. After a while he had called in one of the firm's experts on the retailing sector and had made his excuses, leaving them to go through the proposal in detail. They had spent the whole morning discussing every aspect of it. Both Pandora's hopes and her fears had been confirmed.

After her revelation a month ago, she had put together the designs for her Shaker-inspired furniture and fabrics. One morning, while working at home she received a thick envelope from 'Friends of the Earth'. Inside she found a folder holding literature on ecology and guides to environmentally safe products, as well as confirmation of her membership. She read it all, and it sparked a further refinement of her idea: she would use renewable resources and natural dyes. It made sense to her personally and it would also be a valuable marketing angle: 'A gentle style for a gentler world,' she thought.

Pandora then approached her old suppliers for manufacturing prices and colour-test runs on the fabrics. It had meant several trips to the North of England and many hours in East End workshops. She had stressed the urgency of the project, and she had begun to receive estimates over the last week.

As expected, the cost difference between large and small runs was staggering. Small-scale production meant opening a shop similar in size to her former one, and she already knew the dangers involved. The investment would not be beyond her means, but she could not afford another failure.

There was a further danger. While it would have been possible a few years ago to open a small shop on the strength of a fresh idea, and expand carefully on the basis of its eventual success, the retailing scene had become ferociously competitive. It did not take long these days for the established chains or large retailers to pirate any successful idea from the more adventurous small outlets, killing it off in no time with lower prices and market saturation. Pandora's concept was her main weapon, and if she was to exploit it to the full, she had to appear on the market with a presence strong enough, and prices low enough, to overcome the inevitable copy-cat competitors. She had a new angle, she had the designs, and she sensed it would work. But at a price.

Several outlets, central locations, and sizeable stocks were essential, plus capable staff, a warehouse, vans for distribution, and a large promotion campaign. Pandora remembered Arianne's advice about the dangers of starting small. It was sensible, and easy from Arianne's perspective. It just meant money, lots of money. Pandora did not have it.

She had spent most of the previous day on the phone to people she knew, making preliminary inquiries about property. The response was identical in all cases: it was very difficult to find suitable space in central London in the middle of the current retail boom; space was at a premium, and landlords preferred to let to established chains rather than unknown newcomers. Pandora would have to pay significantly over the odds to be considered as a suitable tenant. She would need to pay not less than three quarters of a million pounds per shop, before she even began to think about the refurbishment costs. It would require millions to go ahead.

Pandora had phoned her broker to sell some of her shares, but she had already used the proceeds for the prototypes and trial runs she had commissioned. Even if she sold the whole lot in the currently buoyant market, she would only raise about two hundred thousand pounds. She could mortgage her flat for a further hundred and fifty thousand, and her father had left her money in trust which she could borrow against. She could sell the New York apartment. But even counting every penny she could lay her hands on, it was still a fraction of the total she needed. She would have to borrow the rest. It was not yet possible to quantify the precise figure, but her guess last night had been between five and six million.

At least one of Pandora's worries seemed to have been taken care of. She had mentioned the question of competent management to Chris Outram. 'I can work seven days a week, but I can't do everything myself. I will need efficient managers, and it takes a long time to put a working team together. Ideally, I ought to find an existing team, and poach it.'

'I know for a fact that Martha Bradley's management is very unhappy,' Chris had told her, 'and a few of them are looking for an opportunity like this. They are the best team around. We can arrange informal contacts for you.' Martha Bradley had been one of the great success stories in the decorating world during the early 70s, but she had sold her company last year and had retired to Barbados. Pandora would definitely contact the Bradley team, but she needed a secretary now. She would phone some agencies once she was back at the flat.

The first massive hurdle was to raise the money, though. Nothing would be possible without it. Pandora remembered Arianne's offer, but decided she had been right to refuse it. She did not need a friend to do her a favour, she needed a banker willing to invest in a viable business.

* * *

'I did not have dinner in my room that day. Young man, I have not had dinner on my own for the last twenty years, and I find it intolerable that I should be presented with such a mistake at a hotel with the reputation of La Reserve,' the old woman said. She had been complaining about her bill for the last five minutes in the nasal tone peculiar to the French aristocracy. Charles Murdoch was tempted to interrupt her and ask the concierge for the key to his room, but he had recognized Celine de Merteuil. He had never asked why, but he knew that Arianne disliked her and, as with so many of Arianne's foibles, he had made it his own. He preferred to avoid her.

It had been an enjoyable holiday, or rather he had made constructive use of his time. Holiday was a word that had long ceased to have any meaning for Charles, but the purpose of his visit here was accomplished, and he was now leaving for St Tropez.

As soon as Gloria had left New York, he had found out from Kayzie that she had made last-minute arrangements to stay at Paola Santa Coloma's villa in Cap Ferrat, and he had immediately booked himself into La Reserve in Beaulieu. At Nice airport he had toyed briefly with the idea of renting a small Renault, less noticeable than a bigger car, but he was not able to overcome his reluctance to squeeze his 6'3" frame into it, and settled for a two-door Mercedes.

It had taken him three days of waiting outside the gates of Paola's villa before he was able to make contact with Gloria. The first day he saw the two girls drive in Paola's Ferrari to one of the villas nearby, where they spent the afternoon. On the second day Charles followed them to Montecarlo harbour, where they boarded one of the big yachts moored there. His opportunity came on the evening of the third day, when the girls left the villa with a couple of young wimps dressed all in white, both with slicked-back dark hair.

He tailed their car until they stopped outside Les Hirondelles, and went into the restaurant. Charles waited for a moment then he followed them in.

He told the man at the door that he was joining some other people. He quickly scanned the room: Gloria and her friends were sitting on the terrace overlooking the harbour. He stepped outside and walked around the tables, as if searching for someone. His eyes met Gloria's, and he approached her.

'Gloria! What on earth are you doing here? You're the last person I was expecting to see.' His tone matched the surprised expression on his face.

Gloria raised her eyebrows.

'What are *you* doing here?' she asked in return.

'Oh, I'm trying to have a few days of peace and quiet on my own. New York was a bit hectic,' Charles said, his voice conveying the significance of the last sentence. 'I'm at La Reserve. I bumped into the Cliffords earlier today, and they said that I could join their party for dinner, but I must have misheard the restaurant they mentioned.'

He sensed Gloria's hesitation. If their conversation went on for much longer, she would have to introduce him to her friends or, even worse, she would have to explain to them who he was.

'I'd better go back to the hotel and have dinner there. I'm enjoying my solitude, but I would love to spend some time with you. Give me your number, and I'll call you tomorrow.' Gloria dithered for a moment, then asked Paola for the number. Charles wrote it down. He sensed Paola's eyes on him, but he did not return her look; he had to be careful now. He said goodbye to Gloria, smiled sweetly at the table at large, and sauntered out. He truly enjoyed his dinner at the hotel that evening, particularly the half-bottle of very fine Chablis suggested by the wine steward.

The rest had been easier than he had expected. He went to Paola's villa for a drink the following evening, and he was at his most charming. As he was leaving, he managed to take Gloria discreetly aside for a moment to tell her that he would like to have a quiet word with her as soon as possible, because he had something very important to tell her. He got up early the following morning, and notified the desk to transfer any calls for him to the poolside telephone.

343

He only had time to improve the tan on the left side of his face before Gloria called.

She told him that she would be on her own in the house later that day, as Paola had arranged to go sailing. She suggested that Charles spend the morning with her by their pool. As he was let into the house the servant asked him to wait in the drawing room. He left Charles alone for a moment while he went to tell Gloria that her guest had arrived. Charles quickly returned to the hall and slipped the brown envelope he was carrying into the top drawer of a chest close to the staircase. By the time Gloria appeared he was standing in the drawing room, absorbed in the contemplation of Warhol's portrait of Paola's mother.

Although it was very hot, he did not follow Gloria into the pool straightaway, but announced that he was going inside to the bathroom, and walked briskly towards the house. He took the envelope from the drawer in the hall and rushed upstairs. Earlier on, he had asked Gloria if her room had a view of the sea. She had pointed to her room's window, and he had no trouble now in finding it. He went into the bathroom, and locked the door. He saw Gloria's beauty case on the marble vanity. He opened it, and discovered what he wanted. It took him only a moment to make the swap. As he left the room he noticed a pile of discarded shopping bags by the door, waiting to be removed by the maid. He put the brown envelope and the box he had removed from Gloria's case at the bottom of one of the bags, covered it with crumpled sheets of tissue paper, and ran downstairs again.

Gloria was still in the pool when he returned. Feeling on top of the world, Charles rushed down the broad staircase linking the terraces, flung his Lacoste shirt onto one of the chairs by the pool and dived in, pausing just long enough at the edge to give Gloria a full view of his muscular body, his tan emphasized by his white swimming trunks.

He swam a few lengths and then stopped in the shallow end, waiting for Gloria to join him.

'Your breast-stroke could be improved. You don't spread your arms wide enough,' he said. 'I'll show you; just swim towards me.'

As she came close, he slipped his left arm under her belly, holding her weight. The tip of his fingers slid under the edge of her bikini top, barely touching her nipple. He held her hand with his right arm, their fingers intertwined, and gently guided her strokes.

'There, you see, a wider reach makes it much more powerful,' he murmured. He repeated the motion a few times, his left arm thrust forward by Gloria's body movements, until her breast was cupped in his hand. A white-jacketed waiter appeared, carrying a tray. The man briefly surveyed the scene, left the tray on a table by their seats, and returned discreetly to the house. Charles sensed Gloria's confusion, and decided it was time to stop. The prize was within reach now, but a little more work was necessary.

'This is lovely, but I still need to talk to you,' Charles said, helping her gently to the pool steps. They went back to their chairs, and he poured two glasses of orange juice from the iced jug on the tray. He handed a glass to Gloria. His eyes on hers, he began his long-rehearsed speech.

'Gloria, this is very difficult for me to say . . .' he paused briefly, to underline the significance of the moment. 'I have decided to leave your mother. All relationships run their course, and it would be foolish for me to pretend otherwise.' As he expected, her face betrayed a mixture of suspicion and interest. He stood up and continued talking, his head down as if overwhelmed by the burden of what he was saying.

'I know what you are thinking – that I am a worthless gigolo, only interested in money. You are partly right, as far as the past is concerned. I was a carefree young man when Arianne and I met. Your mother's money overwhelmed me, as I know it has overwhelmed you in a different way.' He hoped that the frank admission of guilt would pass for sincerity, and the reference to their shared predicament might stir Gloria's sympathy.

'But I am a different person now. I know that money is just an illusion. Other things are much more significant, at least on a personal level. I have changed, and I need the help of someone who believes in me to keep me honest.'

He knew from experience that few women would not respond to such an appeal from an attractive man. For someone as lacking in self-confidence as Gloria it would be irresistible.

'I have long accepted the fact that your mother does not love me,' Charles went on. 'In fact, I think she would be glad to get rid of me. Our relationship has been just an arrangement for years.' It was the first true statement he had made so far, and it helped to maintain the sincerity of his tone. 'My pride stopped me from confronting the problem, but what has happened now, your mother's machinations against you, made me face the fact that you are the one that really matters to me.'

He sat down and hid his face in his hands. He sighed deeply, then carried on.

'As you became a woman, I realized that you meant much more to me than I wanted to admit. I knew that you did not like me, and I don't blame you for that. More to the point, I also knew that you could think I was after your fortune, and even I had doubts in that respect. But your mother's duplicity towards you has made things much clearer for me. She might make you penniless, but I still want you. You are the only woman in the world for me.' He stood up abruptly and walked away, as if embarrassed at having bared his feelings. As soon as he disappeared from Gloria's sight behind the poolhouse, he stopped and waited.

At last able to gather her thoughts, Gloria was puzzled. She had been tempted to stop Charles in the middle of his platitudes: she found it insulting that he could believe she would fall for such a pack of trite lies. But he was not a fool, and the only possible reason for him to make such a ridiculous speech was that somehow he meant it. She had noticed before that a man trying to be sincere about his feelings usually made an ass of himself. He was not there because of her money; he was the only man in the world who knew her mother was disowning her.

Gloria wanted him. She found Charles physically very attractive, and he could be useful as an ally. Her original plan had been to taste forbidden fruit, have a good time, and then embarrass her mother by revealing their affair, getting rid of Charles in the process. Now it would be more productive to join forces with him, at least for a while, and have a spy in her mother's camp.

Whatever the reasons, Charles was there now, and the sun always stirred Gloria's appetite for good sex. It would be fun to humour him. She stood up, adopted her sweetest expression, and walked after him, hoping that the fool had not left the villa.

Behind the poolhouse, Charles heard her approaching steps and left his cover, walking towards her. One look at her face was enough. He opened his arms, and drew her tightly against him.

'My darling, my darling,' he murmured, stroking her hair. His hand under her chin, he gently raised her head and kissed her, softly at first, then his tongue pushed into her mouth.

Charles picked her up in his arms without breaking their kiss and walked into the poolhouse. He undid her bikini strings and laid her gently on the pile of sun mattresses, her golden skin shimmering in the blue half-light reflected from the pool. Staring at him, Gloria yanked down his swimming trunks and pulled him on top of her.

His hand moved slowly down her body, his teeth gently gripping first one nipple, then the other, his fingers and his tongue making Gloria's longing for him unbearable. Guiding him with her hand, she moaned as he entered her, her nails clawing his back. She was overcome by her pleasure. She needed him now, and she would need him again.

'I love you, I love you,' Charles said, in rhythm with his long, deep thrusts. After a while he began to count them. Premature ejaculation was not one of his problems, but he needed to take his mind off what was going on. Even for him, what he was about to do required unusual control.

As he counted 'forty', he suddenly pulled away from Gloria, and stood up. 'No,' he cried, 'no, this is not right! I'm forcing you to do what I want, without any consideration for your feelings.' He picked up his clothes and quickly slipped on his trousers. He knelt by her side;

her face was covered by the flush of her imminent, and now suddenly truncated orgasm.

'I want you to come to me when you are sure of what you are doing, not before.' He kissed Gloria deeply and walked away, then he stopped by the door and looked back longingly at her.

'I'm driving to St Tropez now. I think that we both need to be alone for a couple of days. I'll be staying at Byblos. We have to think very seriously about this, my love,' he said, then he turned and left. He ran to the gate, got into his car and drove away.

As soon as he was out of sight of the house he stopped the car, slapped his thigh, threw back his head and roared with laughter. Charles knew that Gloria would come to St Tropez even if she had to walk on water to get there. But he needed to pick up a girl fast. His balls were aching and he felt randy as hell.

30

LONDON
August 1987

Pandora did not like the restaurant. The food was too rich, and the décor attempted to suggest elegance and class by piling up brass-framed hunting and racing prints on its Ultrasuede walls. She found it crass, although it probably worked for the clientele, mostly Far Eastern businessmen escorting expensive call girls with streaked blonde manes, and a few local Mayfair men with exotic-looking young women. Pandora lost interest in the scene, and tried to concentrate on her companion.

He was not very interesting either, but he could be useful. She hoped he would be. She had not seen Peter Wentworth-Briggs for years. He had married a girl who had been at school with Pandora, and she and Johnny had bumped into them a few times at cocktail parties or City functions.

Things had moved fast since Pandora's meeting with Chris Outram, and they had met a number of times to develop the business strategy. Pandora had developed her design concepts at the same time, discussed production and delivery schedules with suppliers, and had talks with her prospective management team. Her enthusiasm was contagious, and soon she had the core of a first-class management group. They were ready to jump on board as soon as she was ready. But she still had to find the money.

Pandora had phoned every friend, every relation with a banking connection. It was always the same story. A very interesting concept, the figures appeared good on paper, but they were either fully committed to their existing clients, or they were hesitant about increasing their exposure. One of her second cousins said charitably, after turning down her proposal with the utmost tact, that he hoped she would find another husband soon.

In the course of one of her many conversations someone

had mentioned to her that Peter Wentworth-Briggs was in charge of venture capital at Tomkins & Cruikshank, a long-established merchant bank. She phoned him the following morning.

It took him a moment to place her, but he sounded encouraging over the telephone. He was about to go on holiday, but he suggested she send him the papers. If he thought that her proposition made sense, he would call her. Pandora would have preferred to see him in person first, but she had no choice. She sent him the documents by courier as soon as she put the phone down.

He called her two days later. He was interested, but there were a few points he would like to discuss with her. He suggested dinner the following day, the only time he could see her before leaving for Nice in the morning to join his family. She agreed.

The situation was critical. An estate agent had phoned her ten days ago. A small chain of retail outlets in Central London were for sale: four shops of the ideal size, located on the King's Road, Long Acre, Kensington Church Street and Brook Street. They were excellent locations, and the agent told her that it would be a waste of time to offer anything under four million. It was almost impossible to find properties like these for sale in the current climate, and it was a unique chance to set up her London chain in one go. She could not miss it. But after inspection she realized the shops would need substantial alterations for her purposes, adding a further million to her costs. She would need five million *now*, without taking into account any other commitments.

Pandora had walked into the restaurant with the conviction of the desperate. She *had* to get the money. She put up with Peter's small talk while they had a drink, but as soon as he ordered the food she pulled her papers out of her briefcase and spread them on the table.

Once she began to go through the proposal, she realized that Peter seemed to have forgotten most of the facts, and she carefully went over each item, point by point. Half-way through her explanation about her marketing strategy, she noticed that his eyes were wandering around the room.

'There you have someone who could solve your problem very quickly. He can't stop looking at you, and I can't blame him. You look gorgeous tonight,' he said.

'Who are you talking about?' Pandora asked, annoyed by his interruption.

'Ted Carson,' Peter replied. 'His eye for women is obviously as good as his eye for business.'

Like most people in England, Pandora knew who Ted Carson was. He had built a large conglomerate in Australia from nothing, and had now settled in Britain, where his audacious (some said buccaneer) approach to business kept him in the newspapers every day. She would not have glanced in his direction, no matter how many breweries or newspapers he was trying to buy, had it not been for the fact that she remembered he was supposed to have been the underbidder for the painting on the night she first saw Arianne. She was curious to see what he looked like.

In fact he looked exactly as she would have imagined. He was big, not fat, the white hair at his temples emphasizing his leathery tan. He had just enough lines to give character to his face, but he was not old, probably in his mid-forties, and his casual clothes added to his youthful appearance. He was not handsome but he was attractive in a coarse way, and he smiled broadly as he caught her eye. Pandora immediately turned her face away, and carried on doggedly with her explanation.

Peter made occasional comments in response, but by the time Pandora reached the last page it was obvious that he was not really interested in anything she had been saying.

'The short of it, Peter, is that I need five million at least. As I've shown you, the market is there, and the return would be well above average retail profits. It will work, and you know it,' she finished forcefully, in a last ditch attempt to capture his attention.

The waiter cleared their plates away.

'Would you like some coffee?' Peter asked.

'Yes, please,' Pandora replied impatiently. It was about time he committed himself either way.

'The bill, please,' Peter said to the waiter. 'We can have

coffee at my place,' Peter continued. 'We can talk in peace and quiet there. Miranda is already in France with the children,' he finished, giving Pandora a meaningful glance.

She felt outraged, but restrained herself from showing it.

'I can't imagine what we can discuss at your home that we can not discuss right now. Since we are already here, please ask the waiter to bring the coffee.'

A quizzical expression briefly came to Peter's face, then he called the waiter back and ordered. As the waiter left, Peter leant forward, his hand almost touching hers.

'I like your business proposition. I like it a lot. But as you can appreciate, I would have to convince my people about its merits. It would help my enthusiasm if *you* were as convincing as possible tonight.'

'Are you saying that you would consider lending me five million pounds if I go to bed with you? In other circumstances it might be almost flattering, but certainly not now,' Pandora said point-blank. She felt enraged at his easy assumption about the outcome of the evening.

'You are putting it rather crudely,' Peter replied, clearly uncomfortable at Pandora's directness. 'What I would say is that there are plenty of takers for five million pounds, all with viable propositions. You ought to be flattered that I might be prepared to consider yours. I told you that you are a very beautiful girl. I remembered you as soon as you phoned me,' he said, touching her hand. Pandora began to gather her papers and put them in her briefcase, then she stood up. She noticed she was attracting attention to herself, but she didn't care.

'Why don't you buy yourself a calculator and strap it to your prick? It will make your approach to business meetings a great deal clearer to prospective clients.' Impervious to the commotion around her, Pandora stormed towards the exit.

She did not even notice that Ted Carson's eyes were on her. It would not have mattered if she did. The only thing on her mind was that she had to find five million pounds within three weeks.

*   *   *

Lying by the side of the hotel pool at the right angle to maximize his exposure to the sun, Charles waved his hand at the waiter nearby.

'Campari and soda, please,' he ordered.

He had been in St Tropez for ten days now, and he was bored. More than that, he was worried. He had expected Gloria to turn up the day after their meeting, but she hadn't.

After four days he rang Paola's villa. The butler told him that Mademoiselle de la Force had departed the day before.

Charles had no choice but to stay put and wait for Gloria to appear. He had scored with a couple of girls during his enforced stay, but casual pickups were no longer much fun. Both girls had insisted on safe sex.

The waiter returned with his drink. Charles sipped it slowly, watching the crowd around the pool. Most of the women were lean and fit, their gold jewellery and white bikinis showing off their tanned skin, but a few of them had slit-like navels, the unmistakable sign of a belly tuck, the surgeon's scalpel creating a navel where none used to be. He wondered if Arianne had had a few tucks here and there. She still was as beautiful as when they first met, even more so. She was a bit of a wreck then, but even at her worst she had looked better than most women. Still, that had been twelve years ago, and the clock ticks for everyone.

It was perfectly possible that she had had a face-lift during one of her many trips on her own, but maybe she didn't need it; maybe money and power were her Elixir of Youth. People would say that she was gorgeous even if she used nitric acid to take off her make-up. Arianne did not need to worry about her looks, and not worrying about something was probably the best way to ensure that it would not become a problem.

Maybe he should listen to his own wisdom and stop worrying about Gloria, Charles thought. He *had* to believe that she would turn up, sooner or later.

It was past one o'clock. Charles didn't feel hungry but he decided to have a light lunch. Anything to kill time.

He walked to the poolside terrace, where the maître d' showed him to one of the best tables in the shade. He had just finished ordering when he saw Gloria. His heart jumped. He immediately stood up and walked towards her, an adoring smile on his face.

'My darling, you don't know how worried I've been for you. I called the villa, but they couldn't tell me where you'd gone,' he said, taking her hand.

'Oh, I've been here and there,' Gloria replied rather curtly.

'Would you like to have lunch?' Charles asked solicitously as they sat down.

'No, thank you. I have to tell you something.' She seemed distracted.

Shit, Charles thought. This was not what he had expected, and it didn't sound as if he would like whatever Gloria had to say. His only chance was not to let her speak, not at least until he had had time to work on her. Life always looked better after a good orgasm.

The waiter placed a lobster salad in front of Charles. It looked delicious but he couldn't afford to sit here now and give her time to say whatever was on her mind.

'Take it back, I'm not hungry. Just put it on my bill,' Charles told the waiter, handing him a hundred-franc tip. He stood up.

'We can't talk here,' he said, nodding towards the occupied tables nearby. 'Let's go to my room. We'll have more privacy there.' He walked away before she had time to reply, but was relieved to notice that she was following him.

Once inside the lift, he embraced her.

'You don't know how I've longed for this moment,' he murmured between kisses. She seemed to respond, but guardedly. He was seriously worried now.

They walked into his room, Charles' arm around Gloria's waist. He kicked the door shut, and kissed her again before she could say anything at all. He lifted her and carried her to the bed, his hands all over her body. She was wearing just a long T-shirt. He endeavoured to roll it up without breaking their embrace.

354

'Not now,' Gloria managed to say twice, but her conviction was noticeably weaker the second time.

'I love you, I love you,' Charles said again and again, kissing her constantly to shut her up. Occasionally she was still trying to speak, and he briefly thought *soixante neuf* might be a solution. It would certainly silence her, but on the other hand it might be counterproductive if tried so soon. This was supposed to be romance, not fun. At last he heard Gloria moan and decided that it was safe to take off his clothes, but as soon as Charles shifted his weight from her she sat, bolt upright.

'I must tell you this now,' Gloria said, avoiding his eyes and clearly embarrassed. 'I've got herpes. I had a flare-up at the villa, and I'm very contagious at this stage. That's why I did not come to you immediately.'

Charles was thunderstruck. He knew from friends that it was an extremely painful and incurable condition, but he could not risk delaying making love to her any longer, giving her time to change her mind. He could not wear a condom either. He had no guarantee she would stay with him; he needed to score a bullseye. He had no choice.

He managed to conceal his fear. He also managed to regain his excitement, momentarily deflated by Gloria's sudden revelation.

'My darling, it doesn't matter to me. There's nothing in this world I want more than you, and I want you now,' he said, taking her in his arms.

'Do you really mean that?' Gloria asked. He sensed hope in her voice.

'Making love to you, being with you, is all that matters to me,' Charles reassured her.

He slowly pushed her down on the bed and, after a few moments, resigned to his possible fate, he gently parted her thighs.

The things one has to do for money, he thought.

31

Pandora held the cheque up for a few moments, staring at the figure in the box immediately above the dotted line. It was the largest cheque she had ever written, and now she had to sign it.

She looked at the stream of zeros, which reminded her of the jackpot of a television game show. She could imagine the presenter, probably wearing a lurid tuxedo, holding his hand up and shouting to the audience: 'Give me a four!' 'FOUR,' they would roar. 'Now give me a zero,' the man would bellow, only to be dutifully obliged. 'Now give me another zero,' he would plead, the figures going up in lights behind him, one after the other. '. . . and another one . . .' At last, his silhouette outlined against the wall of lights, he would chant 'Ladies and gentlemen, we have FOUR HUNDRED THOUSAND POUNDS!' At the mention of the figure the audience would applaud wildly, the chorus girls would launch into a dance routine displaying their highest kicks, and the band would burst into . . . what? Pandora thought for a moment; maybe any of the disco versions of the Beatles' 'Money' would do. She not only wanted it, she needed it desperately.

Since her fiasco with Peter Wentworth-Briggs at the restaurant she had tried every other possible source of venture capital. She was still waiting to hear from a couple of people she had seen two weeks before, but events had finally overtaken her. The offer for the chain of shops had to be submitted tomorrow, and a cheque for an amount equivalent to 10 per cent of the offered price had to be included as a deposit with the tender documents. It would take months, maybe years, to find similar properties, and she could not afford to lose her team or her suppliers, neither of which would accommodate an indefinite wait. Her only chance was to send in the tender documents with the cheque, commit every penny she had

356

and hope that the rest of the money would materialize from somewhere.

Having gone this far Pandora could not back down. It was not just that she could not tell anyone she wasn't able to raise the money. What she really and truly could not do was to face yet another personal failure.

She was starkly aware of her recklessness. She was about to sign a commitment to pay nearly half a million pounds, and a promise to pay a further three and a half million on completion, plus legal fees, plus . . . money, money, money. She had been advised to pay well over the odds to get the shops, and she was likely to succeed – if she found the money. The adjustment to the estimated starting cost had pushed the figure she needed now to six million pounds.

Well, it's *only* money, Pandora thought. Either she would find it, or she would not. She picked up the pen, swiftly signed the cheque, and clipped it to the other documents. She sealed the huge envelope carefully, and left it on the other desk in the tiny temporary office she had rented a month ago. She had asked Sophie, her new secretary, to send the envelope by courier first thing in the morning.

She looked at the envelope for the last time and left the room. She still had to pack. She had thought of cancelling the trip at the last minute, but the invitation to Arianne's ball in Venice had arrived with a first-class plane ticket and a note that a room had already been booked at the Gritti. She would only be in Venice for the night, and she badly needed a break.

One last fling in Arianne's glamorous world, and then back to reality. Next week she would either get a phone call saying that the money was available, or all hell would break loose.

Lying on her bed, alone in her suite at the Hassler, Gloria stared at the ceiling. The huge box from Tirelli holding her costume was in one corner of the room, next to the rest of her luggage, ready to be collected by a porter. But she couldn't think about her costume, or anything else. Not since the phone call she had received about an hour ago.

During her last days in the South of France she had

noticed that she was feeling nauseous in the morning. The smell of cooking fat in restaurants made her feel sick, and there was a metallic taste in her mouth. Just before she left for Rome, she had noticed that her breasts had become fuller, and sometimes she felt a tingling sensation around the nipples. If it weren't for the fact that she was on the pill, Gloria would have worried about being pregnant. The alternative was that she was ill, a thought which frightened her. She had asked Paola for the address of her doctor in Rome, and had made an appointment to see him the day she arrived there.

She now knew that she was pregnant. Charles' child, of all people. Her first reaction was to curse her bad luck, then the damned, useless pill. Next she thought of having an abortion, but after a while she realized that she could not do it. Her child was the first thing in her life to be truly her own, something which she did not owe to her mother. She suddenly had a role, to be somebody's mother, and she did not give a damn about the implications or what other people would say. Some years ago she would have been terrified of Nana's reaction to the news, of her displeasure, but even Nana's feelings did not matter much to Gloria now. Nana had been the only person who had really loved her, but in the end she had been as unsympathetic to Gloria as everybody else.

Obviously she would have to tell her mother, and Gloria would do it as soon as possible. But Arianne did not need to know who the father was. It was unlikely that, having kept Gloria's own father a secret for so long, she would have the nerve to press Gloria on the subject. As for Charles, it would suit him to keep the matter quiet. Disclosure would mean the end of his meal ticket.

The news had forced her to think about Charles and what she felt about him. It had all begun as a lark, but she had to admit that the sex had been great. It was hard to spend nearly a month having torrid sex with an attractive man who talked about love without somehow entering into the game yourself. She did not know what she felt for him, but whatever it was it no longer mattered. What mattered to her now was her baby.

She heard a discreet knock on the door. The porter was there; time to go. Gloria got up, picked up her bag from the dressing table, and walked to the drawing room to let the porter in. She was ready to go to Venice.

Charles liked his reflection in the mirror. The shaving lather brought out his deep tan, which in turn accentuated the luminous blue of his eyes. He smiled at himself, but quickly dropped his smile when he realized that the white foam made his teeth look yellow. He began to shave instead.

He was glad to be back in New York, temporarily out of Gloria's reach, although his time with her in the South of France had been better than expected. After a few days, the little vixen had owned up that the herpes story was a complete fabrication, her way of checking the sincerity of his feelings. He was greatly relieved to know that he was not at risk, and that his courage had paid off.

Gloria had been good company at times, and certainly enthusiastic about sex. They had been together for nearly six weeks, with sporadic breaks for Gloria to keep up with part of her schedule of invitations to yachts and villas. Charles dissuaded her from disappearing completely from sight, because it would trigger Arianne's concern. The last thing he wanted was a private detective on Gloria's trail.

Gloria could already be pregnant, but maybe not. There was always the possibility that he had been sold genuine birth control pills at the ludicrous price of fakes, but he preferred not to consider that possibility.

Charles had contacted Louis Morello in New York as soon as he found out what pill Gloria was taking. Although he had bargained hard on the strength of their long-past association, it had cost Charles three thousand dollars a box to have the duplicates made. It was an outrageous price for sugar pills, but a bargain in the context of what they would do for him. It was pointless to agonize about what might have gone wrong.

Before leaving the room, he stood in front of the full-length mirror for a final inspection. There was no doubt in his mind that he was a fine-looking man, but there was one thought that had been worrying him for a short while. He went closer to the mirror and smiled. Charles was immensely relieved to notice that, the shaving cream gone, his teeth were as white as usual: he would not need to make an appointment with the dental hygienist after all.

Her arms resting on the railings, her hair blowing in the lagoon's breeze, Arianne could see the distant outline of Santa Maria della Salute in the summer haze. The yacht had just dropped anchor, and the motor boat was being winched down to the sea to take her ashore.

Over the last ten years she had looked forward to her annual ball, but not now. It had started as a business tool, a way of building up her profile and strengthening her contacts. After a while, the original purpose became clouded by habit, and she simply enjoyed the pomp and glitter of the occasion. But Arianne had gone through the process many times, and the game had lost its edge.

Now that she sensed that she was about to lose Gloria, Arianne wondered if it had been worth it. Her problem was not really Gloria though; there had been troubles between them before. Her problem was Charles. It was true that he was able to hold her to ransom for his silence, but any ransom is payable in the end. Arianne had thought a lot about Charles during that summer, and she had thought about herself.

She had agreed to Charles' terms originally because of fear, but once her fear had subsided, as time went by, she could have made him an offer he could not refuse, and see him off. If she had not made it, it was because the arrangement had suited her. Charles' presence by her side had been her shield against other men, and it had only taken money to keep him around. It would only take money to throw him out. She had plenty of it, but she was not going to settle on his terms. While in Argentina, she had heard that Ines de la Force, the last member of Simon's family, was seriously ill. Charles' threat could soon come to an end.

32

VENICE
September 1987

'Who is the father?' Arianne asked. She felt a mixture of love, rage, and pity. Her daughter's capacity to make a mess of her life would never cease to amaze her.

'It's none of your business,' Gloria replied angrily. 'It could well turn out to be my own father, for all I know about *him*. Frankly, I hadn't realized that fathers mattered in this family. Anyway, I couldn't possibly guess – you know that I screw around,' she added acidly.

'I can't do anything about nymphomania, but I wish you had taken precautions, at least,' Arianne snapped. She regretted her remark as soon as she had uttered it, but Gloria had a way of needling her until she was beyond control.

'I took the pill if you must know, which is more than you did when you had me. I'm sorry, I always forget that you were legally married, and all that. You can sue the pill company, if you wish. You've always been very good at making money out of everything, haven't you, Mummy?'

Arianne decided not to explore the subject of the child's father any further. It opened up a scar that ran along the length of their years together, and it served no purpose. It was better to be practical about it. Cameline had told her she had a similar problem with one of her daughters last summer, and how she had dealt with it.

'I'm glad you are at the beginning of the pregnancy. The plane is here. We can fly to London tomorrow and you can have an abortion. It can be arranged very quickly there.' She realized from Gloria's face that she had made another mistake. She had tried to handle this as if it were a business decision, by assessing the problem and coming up with the speediest solution.

'Is that what you thought of doing when you were expecting me? It might have made your life easier, but not mine,' Gloria said, nearly in tears. She stood up and walked to the door. 'I don't know why I decided to tell you. I should have guessed what to expect. But there is one thing I do know: I'm going to have this baby, whether you like it or not. Even better if you don't,' she shouted before slamming the door behind her.

Arianne went to the window. As usual, crowds of tourists were walking along the Riva on the other side. Some were staring at the marble façade of her palazzo, probably wondering who the lucky person was who lived there.

Arianne was sure that Charles was the father, but Gloria had said that she was on the pill. Gloria had told her that she was the first person to hear the news. Perhaps Charles had no reason to suspect what had happened, and didn't know yet. If so, there might still be time to make him an irresistible offer. She left her room and ran up the broad stairs to the next floor. Walking decisively down the central hall, she knocked at Charles' door. She waited for a while, then opened it. He wasn't there.

Enraged by the thought that he could be with Gloria, Arianne dashed to the stairs, on her way to her daughter's room, but she suddenly stopped in her tracks. If she were to find him there it would not help matters, it would only increase her fury. She paced up and down the hall; she felt humiliated by having to wait, but nonetheless she stayed.

The clock struck the hour. Her hairdresser would be here any moment now, she had to check the last details in the reception rooms below, and she still had to get ready for her party. Perhaps it was better to give herself some time. She needed to be calm to confront Charles.

Standing in front of the mirror, Pandora adjusted her lace jabot, its ruffles spilling over the edges of her gold-braided satin jacket. She was dressed as a Louis XV courtier, and she was pleased to notice that the line of the outfit emphasized her slim figure. The powdered wig had startled her at first, but she got used to it after a while. She grimaced at the mirror, wrinkles forming on her forehead and around her eyes, trying to imagine what she would look like when she was old. Her hair was unlikely to be as white as this, and she would certainly wear it in a different style, but it

362

gave her an idea of her future. She was comforted by the thought that white hair seemed to bring out the green in her eyes; perhaps it would be better not to dye it when the time came.

She wished it could be as easy to fathom the future of her business. She had phoned her secretary earlier: the envelope with the tender documents had been delivered that morning, and there were no messages. She felt a moment's panic: the cheque would probably be deposited on Monday.

If only time could stand still. She would soon be taken by gondola to the world's most glamorous party, and she enjoyed the feeling of anticipation. Pandora had thought of herself as Cinderella when Arianne invited her to the ball. The comparison had turned out to be more apt than she had imagined. It would probably all turn to rags in the end, with no crystal slipper to bring about a happy ending.

Her thoughts were interrupted by a knock on the door. It was room service, bringing in her omelette. The ball did not start until ten thirty, and supper would be served late. A rumbling stomach would not enhance Pandora's temporary marquess persona. She took off her jacket and sat down to her solitary meal.

'Ferruccio told me that you wanted to see me,' Charles said as he walked into Arianne's dressing room. She was standing in front of a gilt-framed mirror, and Rosinha was on her knees next to her, fluffing up the ruffles of her train.

'Please knock on the door before coming in. Yes, I wanted to see you,' she added, adjusting some crystal beads on her huge headdress. 'It's all right, Rosinha, you can go now.'

'You look gorgeous all in black. Who are you supposed to be?' asked Charles with a smile.

'The Queen of the Night,' Arianne replied curtly. 'And cut the crap. I don't need it, and we don't have much time. I have to go downstairs in a moment.' She moved to her dressing table, and fastened her long ropes of pearls around her neck.

'You don't seem to be in a party mood,' Charles said, crossing his arms and leaning against the damask-covered wall.

'I find it difficult to be in a party mood with you around, but that is not what I wanted to tell you.' She turned and faced him.

'I have been thinking about our conversation in New York, and I have decided that it might be better if you and I part company,' she said briskly.

Charles raised an eyebrow.

'Have you thought about suitable compensation?' he asked.

'Fifty million dollars,' Arianne said. 'On two conditions: you keep your mouth shut, and you will never be anywhere at the same time I happen to be there. The world is big enough, and you will be able to afford a lot of plane tickets.'

Charles whistled softly, and then chuckled.

'You are a very good business woman. I appreciate your trying to get things as cheaply as possible, but you ought to know me better than that.' He came close to her and took her hands. Arianne tried to pull away, but he tightened his grip.

'I have already explained this to you, but I will try again. Fifty million would not even buy me that nice picture we bought together last April. I couldn't possibly face a future of commercial airlines when you've got me used to a private jet. You know you have to come up with a better offer than that.'

'Eighty million,' Arianne said, raising her voice.

'Try again. You really disappoint me,' Charles replied calmly.

'A hundred million!' she shouted, nearly out of control.

Charles was astonished. Nobody, probably not even her, knew her precise worth: hundreds of millions, perhaps billions. He could make her lose everything, and yet she kept coming up with these ridiculous offers. On the other hand it was unlike Arianne to increase her offers so readily, even if it was almost petty cash for her.

He was about to tell her the sort of figure he would

consider reasonable when he realized that, other than on their first night together many years ago, he had never seen her like this. She was out of control. It could not be because of confronting him, nor could the bargaining have that effect on her. She had learned long ago to live with her dislike for him, and bargaining was part of her life. No, it had to be something else, something that mattered much more to her. Could it be . . .? His heart jumped at the possibility, but he had to make sure.

He flung his arm around her waist and pulled her against him.

'Arianne, my darling, this is nonsense. You and I can not part like this,' he murmured, trying to kiss her.

The feel of his body, the thought that those hands had touched Gloria not long ago, revolted her. Arianne pulled away from him and slapped him hard across the face.

'Stay away from me, you bastard!' she screamed.

He didn't need to know any more. His suspicions had been accurate. There was no point in discussing his price any further. He wanted it all, he wanted it now, and he knew he was going to get it. He turned around and left the room.

Pandora was helped out of her gondola by a liveried servant, one of many assisting guests onto the small pier outside the floodlit palazzo. There was a crowd waiting to go into the building, and the Grand Canal was almost completely covered with gondolas, their lanterns bobbing like huge fireflies in the night.

She joined the crowd, moving with it until she found herself in the foyer. The scene was breath-taking. The huge double height space was lit only by candles, their glow reflected on the marble walls. The gothic pillars and arches were outlined by ropes of orchids, which were also banked at both sides of the huge staircase leading to the main floor. Arianne was standing on the landing at the top, greeting her guests.

'You look gorgeous!' *'Bellissima!'* *'Ravissante!'* The compliments showered on her like tropical rain, in many languages and in every possible accent. Arianne greeted them all with a dazzling smile, her face the face of a ravishing woman without a care in the world.

'I'm delighted that you could come,' she told Pandora as their cheeks brushed against each other, the otherwise standard greeting accompanied by Arianne's hand affectionately squeezing Pandora's for a second. Their eyes met briefly, and Pandora thought she saw a shadow in Arianne's, but she was pushed forward by the crowd behind her before she could take a second look, and she went through an archway leading into the main salon.

It was at least eighty feet long, and the whole width of the building. Full-size 'brunus' trees in full bloom stood in the corners, yellow silk ribbons threaded through their foliage, their pale blue blossoms glowing in the candlelight from the gilded chandeliers. The huge carved beams and coffers in the ceiling were also bordered by orchids, forming a thick floral grid high above the sparkling crowd. The din of hundreds of voices was muffled by the sound of an orchestra playing in the minstrels' gallery.

Pandora took a glass of champagne from a tray and walked aimlessly around the room. Everybody seemed to know each other except her. She was startled to hear her name.

'Pandora!' cried a familiar voice. She turned around and saw Geraldine wearing a huge Spanish comb, a lace shawl and yards of black ruffles. She had not expected to see Geraldine here. Now that she was facing her she realized that what had happened between them, awesome as it had seemed a few months ago, now mattered very little to her.

'Geraldine, how nice to see you! Who are you supposed to be?' Pandora asked as if she cared.

'Goya's *Maja*. Can't you tell?' Geraldine asked with a giggle. 'I thought of coming as the naked version. I would have stolen Arianne's thunder for sure, but I don't think that Solly would have approved.'

'Where is Solly?' Pandora inquired.

'Oh, he's somewhere over there, talking to some very grand French woman. She is la Duchesse de Brie-Montval. I can't resist name dropping, and Solly is trying to buy some land she owns near Paris. I probably won't see him until he's made her sign a contract on a napkin. How are you, anyway? I haven't seen you for *a-ges!*' It had been less than three months since they had parted company in New York, but anything over a couple of days counted as *a-ges* in Geraldine's calendar.

'I'm very well, thank you.' After a moment, Pandora realized that she couldn't leave her answer at that, if only for old times' sake. 'I'm setting up my own business,' she added.

'Oh, I'm so glad to hear that. Are you still in New York?' Geraldine asked, scanning the room over Pandora's shoulder.

Pandora wondered if that was a barbed remark, but it was obvious that Geraldine was distracted by the crowd, her mind not focused on their conversation. Pandora felt tempted to say that she was living in Bangkok, but realized that the joke would not register anyway.

'No, I'm back in Lon ...' she began to say, when Geraldine interrupted her.

'I'm sorry, darling, but I've just noticed Paloma and Rafael over there. I simply must say hello to them. I'll see you later. I'm delighted to hear that you're doing so well.' She grinned toothily at Pandora for a second before dashing away.

Pandora shook her head and smiled. She should have known better. She took a sip of champagne and continued her tour of the room until she reached the windows overlooking the Grand Canal. She leaned against the marble sill and surveyed the scene. It astonished her. She had been to many dances in England, some in houses as magnificent as this one, but she had never seen wealth so carelessly displayed. Her current difficulties came to mind, and she couldn't help thinking about how much it had all cost. Throwing in the clothes and the jewels, probably much more than she needed to start her business. Perhaps it was better not to know the figure.

'Many millions.' Pandora heard a man's voice next to her. It was Bob Chalmers, wearing a pirate's costume.

'Are you talking about your loot, or the cost of the party?

367

If the latter, I'm amazed by your intuition. I'd better watch my thoughts if you can read them,' Pandora said.

'I always try to read the thoughts of attractive women,' Bob replied, almost whispering in her ear.

'Then you're going to have a very disappointing evening if you stay with me for long. But how did you know what I was thinking about?'

'Whenever I find myself somewhere like this, I always think about how much it costs. But I'm a business man; maybe you were just thinking about how beautiful it all is. I'm very glad to see you again.' He leaned forward, and kissed her on the cheek.

'I tried to phone you in New York after our lunch, but there was no reply,' Bob went on. A few months ago his attention would have been flattering, but now it simply amused her.

'I'm back in London. I'm setting up my own business,' she said.

'Are you?' he asked, a new note of interest in his voice. 'Let me know if there is *anything* I can do for you . . .'

Pandora had learned to recognize what that tone and that expression meant. His approach was more credible than Peter's, but only because he was a more intelligent man.

'Actually, there is something you can do for me. I'm having some problems financing my company. Do you think you could find me five million pounds? I would be truly grateful,' she said, not a hint of guile in her voice.

His face froze.

'Are you serious?' he asked at last.

'I'm never anything but serious, particularly if I'm talking business,' Pandora replied with a deadpan face, enjoying his brief bewilderment. Bob thought for a moment.

'This is not the best place to discuss business. We could have lunch at my hotel tomorrow. I'm staying at the Cipriani. My wife is having lunch with a friend here in Venice, and we would be able to talk in peace and quiet,' he said.

'I would love to talk to you in peace and quiet,' Pandora agreed, giving him a Geraldine-like grin, 'but I'm flying

368

back to London first thing in the morning.' She took in his disappointed face. 'I wouldn't have thought about millions if you hadn't mentioned them. Don't blame me,' she added before walking away from him, into the next reception room.

It was a smaller room and it was not so crowded. She noticed Gloria in a group at the centre of the room, pointing towards the ceiling. Pandora looked up and saw the oval fresco, Tiepolo's famous *Triumph of Venus*. Gloria's dress was a copy of the goddess's. Pandora also noticed a masked man dressed as Zorro approaching the group and exchanging a few words with Gloria. The tall, athletic figure seemed familiar, but she couldn't place him. After a moment she saw Gloria and the man leave the room together.

Standing in the middle of the Great Gallery, glittering in the soft-hued light from the golden *torcheres*, Arianne held court. She took compliments and returned them, her small talk polished to a mirror finish. She was glad that the incessant parade of guests gave her an excuse not to think about Gloria. She knew that she had made a mistake, but this was not the time for recriminations. She would talk to Gloria tomorrow.

Arianne realized that her attention was slipping, and focused on the conversation around her, on the rumoured marital difficulties between the Prince and Princess of Wales. Arianne turned to greet some newcomers to the group when she noticed Pandora Doyle in the distance, talking to Cameline Sarteano.

Arianne was briefly struck by the change in Pandora since she last saw her in New York. There was an air of apparent confidence about her, and she remembered their recent phone conversation. She was about to make her excuses and break away from her group to join Pandora and Cameline, when Ferruccio, almost unrecognizable in his Court uniform instead of his usual butler's outfit, came through the double doors in the middle of the Gallery. He tapped his long silver and ebony stick loudly on the marble floor three times before

369

making his announcement in a voice that silenced all conversation.

'Your Royal Highnesses, Ladies and Gentlemen, dinner is served,' he boomed.

Arianne gathered her train and, on the arm of her dinner companion, Prince Wenceslas zu Liechtenstein und Krantz, led the procession of her guests down the marble stairs. The orchids on the sides still looked as fresh as if they had just been cut.

The shimmer of the crumpled silks on the floor was just visible in the moonlight, Zorro's black cloak lying next to Venus' shell-pink dress. Both naked, stretched across the bed in each other's arms, Charles and Gloria did not pay much attention to the muffled sound of music and conversation from below. At least Gloria didn't; she had no reason to take notice of anything other than her sudden peace of mind. Charles had given her a new certainty.

'We ought to get dressed and go downstairs. It's getting late,' he murmured.

'Not yet,' Gloria replied, rolling on top of him. 'Plenty of time for that.'

He tightened his arms around her waist.

'Tonight you've made me . . .' Charles began to say, but her kiss silenced him. Her hand slid down his body, and they did not hear the noise from below any longer. Not for a while, at least.

'. . . and I've heard from someone who knows her very well that she is the illegitimate daughter of a Brazilian plantation owner and one of his maids, and . . .' Pandora had listened attentively to the first part of her dinner companion's virtual monologue about the secrets in Arianne's life until she realized that it was all gossip, most of which she had already heard from Geraldine. The man was a bore, and she was relieved to notice that people were standing up at Arianne's table, at the far end of the enormous room.

'Excuse me, please,' she said as she got up, then walked away. She wandered around the ground floor. There was a discotheque in one of the salons and it was already packed.

In the laser-lit crowd she caught sight of Maria Dimitrescu and a few other faces she had seen at Geraldine's party in New York. A man dressed as Othello asked her to dance. It was one of her favourite 'Pet Shop Boys' songs, and she was pleased. She was a good dancer, and she enjoyed it.

> *We never calculate the currency we spend,*
> *I love you, you pay my rent*

The crowd cheerfully chorused the key lines of the lyrics. Her partner suddenly leaned towards her and placed his hand on her forearm, slowly rubbing it up and down.

'Do you shoot?' he murmured close to her face. Pandora stared at him, hardly believing her ears at first. English was obviously not his first language, and she couldn't place his accent.

'Yes, oh yes, I love it,' she humoured him.

'Great. Let's find somewhere quiet. I have some heroin, and really good coke. What would you prefer?' he asked, his arm around her waist.

'Grouse, if you have it, but we would have to be very careful with Arianne's ceilings,' Pandora replied, pushing him away and moving on. After a while, she looked back and saw him busily talking to a blonde girl nearby, dressed in a few ounces of feathers. Some of Arianne's guests were more surprising than Pandora had expected.

Pandora went back upstairs to the saloon now returned to its original use as a ballroom. The orchestra was playing Cole Porter music, a crescendo of songs leading up to 'Anything Goes'. Arianne was dancing with Bob Chalmers, and apparently having a good time. As Pandora continued her inspection, she was surprised to notice the man dressed as Zorro standing on the side of the orchestra balcony.

The music became faster and faster, until a blast of trumpets underlined the final line, and it came to a sudden end. The dancers paused, waiting for the music to start again, but the pause seemed longer than usual. Like many others in the crowd, Pandora raised her eyes to the minstrels' gallery and noticed that Zorro had come to the front. He had removed his mask.

It was Charles. He clapped his hands loudly three times, and all conversation stopped. Gloria suddenly appeared by his side.

'Ladies and gentlemen,' Charles' voice boomed across the expanse of the room, 'tonight is the happiest night of my life, and I hope of Gloria's too. We just wanted to let all our friends know that we are going to get married.' As he finished, he gave a signal to the conductor, and the orchestra launched into 'I get a kick out of you', drowning the astonished murmurs of the guests.

Gloria's expression was a terrifying mixture of triumph and hatred. She was staring at someone in the crowd and Pandora followed her gaze.

Gloria's eyes were fixed on Arianne, whose face reminded Pandora of the stone sphinxes in Uncle Harold's garden. It was impossible to read anything in it. She remained impassive for a few moments, then a smile came to her lips. It was not the joyful smile of a mother at the announcement of her daughter's happiness, nor the plastic smile of a polished social performer for the benefit of the audience. It was the calm smile of polite pleasure at an event which, pleasing as it may be, does not have much bearing on one's own life.

Arianne raised her hands slowly, and began to clap. She was followed by the crowd around her, hesitatingly at first, until the applause spread across the whole room, encouraged by Arianne's visible approval of the match.

'These South Americans are incredible,' Pandora heard somebody say behind her. The extraordinary announcement had not broken the party mood. There would be plenty of time to dissect the news, to examine the implications over lunches and dinners. But that could be done tomorrow. Now they were having fun. As Charles and Gloria joined the crowd on the dance floor, the first wave of well-wishers burst forward, following Arianne's example. Her congratulatory kiss to her daughter was enchanting to see.

'. . . we are going to get married.' As she heard Charles' words, Arianne's first instinct was to scream in rage and pain. She thought of bringing the party to a sudden end, to say exactly what she thought to Charles and Gloria and then throw them out of her house for ever.

But she couldn't. Not when she had so many newspaper owners, magazine editors, and social columnists under her roof. The story would make the columns, there was no doubt about that, but as it stood now it would be today's wonder and tomorrow's old news. Any hint of a feud and it would run for weeks, encouraging the gossip columnists to probe, to become interested in her past, to find out more than they already knew. There was no way of guessing what Gloria would do if Arianne publicly humiliated her. Gloria did not know enough to bring the house of cards down, but she knew just enough to put a newspaper hound on the right track. But Charles certainly knew enough. Arianne didn't know what he may have disclosed to Gloria to strengthen his hand.

At least Charles now had to be on Arianne's side. If she were to antagonize the couple, it could encourage Charles to try and strike a deal with Simon's family before it was too late. She wondered if he knew his time was running out on that score.

She needed to gain time. There were eight hundred people around her waiting for her shocked reaction. Gloria certainly was. Her face said it all when she stared at Arianne from the orchestra balcony. Arianne's pain was Gloria's victory, and she wanted her spoils. Well, she was not going to have them.

She was going to give them the last thing any of them was expecting: her public approval. As she raised her hands and began to clap, the diamond on her ring shone brightly in the candlelight.

'. . . we are going to get married.' Staring at her mother as Charles, standing next to her, said the words, Gloria was overcome by joy and fear.

She had expected Charles to shy away from her once he heard about the baby, to take Arianne's view, to give her a speech about the most sensible course for all concerned. Meaning whatever would make life easier for him.

But he hadn't. He had been delighted at the news, and suggested that they marry immediately and move away together. 'I have always wanted to live quietly in the country. I have saved some money, and we can manage on that. Just the two of us and our baby, far away from all this.' Gloria would have her baby, a way out of her mother's grip, and her revenge on Arianne.

The reasons behind her fear were equally obvious to her. She was tying her fate to Charles. But Charles could not be marrying her in order to wait for her to inherit whatever Arianne cared to leave her, if anything. There were plenty of rich, bored women around, and he could take his pick. Everyone, her mother most of all, had always seen Gloria as a worthless, spoilt brat, and treated her accordingly. She knew differently; perhaps she ought to extend Charles the same credit she was granting herself.

As he put his arm around her waist, her fear seemed less and less justifiable, until it faded away in the warm applause that surrounded them.

At three o'clock in the morning, the chimes of seventeen clocks around the reception rooms ran simultaneously. Hardly anyone heard them because the party was in full swing. Pandora was one of the very few who took notice. Less jaded, or maybe less indifferent than most of the other guests, her festive mood had been punctured by the scene in the ballroom two hours ago. In other circumstances, Pandora would have left soon afterwards. She thought of going back to her hotel to try to catch some sleep before her morning flight, but she knew that reality, her reality, was waiting outside Arianne's bronze gates, and she did not want to confront it. Bothered by the noise, she climbed a second flight of steps, leading to the top floor of the palazzo.

As on the floor below, the stairs led to a central hall, a row of Gothic arched doorways at the far end opening onto a terrace. The moon cast the pattern of the marble clover-shaped lights above the doors onto the bare floor of the hall. One of the doors was open, and Pandora decided to look at the Grand Canal in peace. But someone else was already there, leaning on the balustrade. She recognized the remarkable headdress at once. It was Arianne.

The moon shone on her face as she smiled at Pandora. Although there were no tears, her distress was plain to see in the tension around her mouth and eyes. By the time Pandora greeted her, however, Arianne's perfect mask was back in place.

'I'm glad to see you. Please come and join me. The view is marvellous at this time of the night,' Arianne said calmly.

Pandora stood next to her. She could not take Arianne's cue, and embark on a banal discussion of the view to avoid the subject that was really on their minds.

'I shouldn't say this, but I'm really sorry. I hope you don't feel responsible for Gloria's actions. It's her mistake, not yours, although you might not see it that way.'

Arianne looked at Pandora with a sad smile. It was the first honest thing anyone had said to her that evening.

'Maybe you're right, but let's not talk about Gloria. Not now. I've read the report and the proposal you sent me. I'm truly glad that things are going well for you in London. Tell me about it.' Pandora doubted that Arianne could be really interested, but at least it would make their conversation easier, and she launched into her speech with the enthusiasm rehearsed time and time again for her London meetings.

'Things are going *really* well. I've finished all the designs, which will soon go into production, and I've found a chain of shops in perfect locations. I am in the process of negoti-ating the lease; in fact, I'll complete the deal as soon as I go back to London. I have every confidence . . .' She was talk-ing as if on auto-pilot, and she could hear herself uttering lies, or at least hopes rather than facts, as she had had to do in London so many times. She suddenly felt immensely tired of it all, tired of lying, tired of keeping up appearances for no reason. It was half past three, probably she would never see Arianne again, and she might as well go to bed.

'I'm sorry,' Pandora said, mid-sentence. 'It's very late. I think I'd better go. Thank you for a marvellous party and a most generous invitation.'

Arianne stretched her arm out and held Pandora's wrist for a second.

'I don't want you to go,' she murmured. 'Now just tell me the truth.'

'What makes you think I'm lying?' Pandora asked, concealing her embarrassment under a shade of quiet, polite indignation.

'I'm not saying that you *are* lying, but you're not telling me the truth. After twenty years of dealing with . . . let us say non-truths, one learns to recognize them. I'm sorry if I have offended you, but I'm genuinely interested.' Arianne wanted to take her mind off what had happened earlier, and this girl was a window into something else, something different.

Pandora leaned on the balustrade. It would be better to say nothing and just go, but she couldn't. There was nothing ahead of her now other than her own problems. She had to speak to someone about them.

'I've made a mistake, a big mistake. You told me in New York that I ought to start my business on as big a scale as I could. When I went back to London I thought you were right, and you probably are. But I have run into serious difficulties raising the money, and I can't help questioning my motives. I wonder if I am just driven by the wish to prove to myself, and everyone else, that I'm not a failure. It seemed a good motivation at the time, but now I'm facing the biggest failure of my life.'

'It's simply called ambition, and it's rather pointless to question your motives,' Arianne interrupted her. 'Are you unhappy about your decision?'

Pandora thought for a moment.

'No, I'm just doubting my motives, though I admit that if things had turned out differently, if I were all set, I wouldn't be. I thought that work would give me my own certainty, but maybe I was naive.' Absorbed by what she was saying, she did not notice that Arianne's eyes were also fixed on the middle distance.

Arianne was not looking at the churches and palaces on the other side of the canal, she was looking back over the years, to her conversation with Simon in the

Paris apartment when they had gone there for the first time, when she had thought the same things as Pandora about her own work. Her doubts had pushed her into accepting Simon's offer. She had also had dreams then – the urge to prove to others, and to herself above all, who she was and what she could do – only to give it all up because the prospect of failure had seemed intolerable. Her fears made it seem a difficult time, but it wasn't, not when compared to the present, when everything was possible but very little was true. When her own daughter cared more about hurting her than for her own happiness.

'Never doubt your motives if they lead you to something you want to do, something which is yours and yours alone. You may question the results, you may even give it up, but at least try as hard as you can to make it work first. You'll regret it forever otherwise.'

Pandora thought for a moment. 'Maybe you're right, but even this conversation is becoming a self-indulgence – at least as far as I am concerned. I have no right to bore you with my troubles.'

Arianne smiled. 'You are too British for your own good, Pandora. All conversations on personal matters are self-centred, otherwise they would serve no purpose. You call it self-indulgence, but it isn't. It is a perfectly valid way to work out what you really want.'

'But that's the whole problem,' Pandora sighed. 'I'm no longer sure if I want what I want because *I* really want it, or because I want to prove myself to others. I took the easy option by marrying, I wasted those years, and now I'm trying to make up for lost time. Perhaps I can't.'

'Of course you can! You can't afford to think otherwise.' Pandora was surprised by the sudden urgency in Arianne's voice. 'I think you're questioning the consequences, not your motives, and I think you're talking about fear of failure, nothing more. Nobody likes it. In any case, why do other people matter so much to you? They are not important.'

Pandora stared at Arianne.

'You wouldn't have come out here on this terrace, alone,

if Gloria didn't matter to you. She probably matters more than anything else to you, and rightly so. It doesn't matter in the end if "others" are just one person or a hundred people.'

'I thought we were talking about work. Now you are talking about love. It's a different subject.' The strain in Arianne's voice showed that she was now as uncomfortable as Pandora had been during the early part of their conversation.

'Not really,' Pandora persisted. 'Meaning something to other people is what we, or at least I, ultimately want from work *or* from love, and only because other people matter to me. If it's no longer a question of survival, one works because one loves the work, but also because it is a way of proving one's worth. I failed to get that out of my marriage, and now I'm trying to get it out of my work. It's probably going to cost me everything I have. When we began this conversation I thought that it was pointless, but now I wonder.' She paused, and laughed softly. 'Otherwise I should jump into the canal right now.' Suddenly she felt less anguished. 'And it's not true that the conversation has been pointless, far from it. You've taught me a few things. I've been talking like a spoiled brat, trying to justify the easy option and giving up.'

Arianne was not listening. While Pandora spoke she had felt an indulgent benevolence towards her naivety, the self-assurance of cynical knowledge when facing guileless candour. But in the same way that the earlier reference to doubts had reminded her of her mistake in accepting Simon's offer out of fear, what Pandora had just said touched her more deeply. This girl, in her ultimate innocence, was right, and she had helped Arianne perceive something more important than anything they had discussed so far. Much, much more important. She turned towards Pandora.

'You haven't yet told me what the figure is that's causing you so much trouble,' she said.

'Five million pounds at least. It's an awful lot of money,' Pandora answered. Arianne leaned forward, her eyes on the water below, her pearls dangling over the balustrade.

'It is an awful lot of money,' she agreed. 'But it all depends on your view point. It is everything to you, yet it would be far less than the cost of another painting on my walls for me.'

'I'm not asking you for a loan, and I hope you are not taking this conversation as a request. We discussed this in New York. There is no reason why you should lend me any money, let alone a figure like that,' Pandora said defensively.

'I don't lend money,' Arianne replied, briefly taken aback by the realization that she was using the very same words Simon had used during their lunch in Paris. 'I give it to charities, but I don't lend it. I do make investments. Sometimes in people, sometimes in businesses, although I'm not sure that there is much difference. Both turn either good or bad in the end, but perhaps people can let you down to a greater degree.'

The implications of her last sentence hung over them and the two women lapsed into silence.

'In the end, it's all a matter of making a choice, of making the right decision,' Arianne said at last. 'You are trying to prove something for the sake of others as much as for your own sake. I can understand that; I just hope you are clear about *your* reasons. In any case, I intend to help you.'

Pandora recoiled as she heard her. Her heart beat faster, her perplexity mixed with budding excitement. She could no longer afford to turn down Arianne's offer. She had no other options left, and the alternative was to give up. But she could not yet believe the offer was there.

'But why? It means everything to me, but why on earth would you do something like this?' she murmured, choked by her emotion. Arianne adopted a matter-of-fact expression.

'You're reading too much into it. I asked you to send me your proposal, and your business seems a very viable proposition. Let's say that I want to invest in a good prospect. I know that you only succeed from a position of strength. You say that you need five million, which probably means that you need six. I'll back your company as an investor, but you will be in complete control of the business. I'll talk

379

to my bankers in London tomorrow, and everything will be arranged on Monday. Now go back there, give hell to the competition, and good luck.'

Pandora was overwhelmed, her relief bringing tears to her eyes. 'You are making everything I want possible. I know it can't be just a business decision. I don't know how I can thank you for this,' she whispered.

Arianne smiled. 'By making a success of it. I only hope that what you think you want is what you really need. And don't think that there is anything else to this other than my business judgement. Please go now. I would like to stay here for a moment before going back downstairs.'

As she walked away, Pandora felt a surge of energy. It was no longer very late, it was the morning of the best day of her life, and she ran down the stairs, towards the light and the music below.

Alone again, Arianne stared at the gondolas lined up by her pier that would soon take her guests away. Time would tell if she had made a wise investment. The risk was worth taking, but any business could go sour. Nonetheless, it had been worth it for tonight's sake. The girl had a purpose, as she herself had had once, a long time ago, and she had shown her something about herself which mattered more than money. Pandora's mention of belief in others took her back to her days in Rio, when her love for Florinda and Ruben had been the centre of her concern. She had been happiest then, she realized, and she had never found such happiness again.

Pandora, so outwardly different from everything she had ever been, so transitory a presence in her life, had triggered something in her when they had first spoken in New York. She had thought then that it was simply that she saw in Pandora the girl she would have liked Gloria to be, but it was more than that. She had reacted unknowingly to Pandora's essential values, which had burrowed through Arianne's defences because she had protected herself against an attack from the opposite direction. She had learned to deal with malice or calculation as they had become part of her everyday life. But she remained vulnerable to someone still willing to trust others.

Once that kind of trust had also been the most important quality in Arianne's life, but she had been forced to shed it in order to survive. She had pushed honesty and trust out of her life a long time ago, until they seemed irrelevant, but something in her had withered in the process.

If she had failed with Gloria it was because she had refused to trust her with the truth. She had lied to Gloria, as she had lied to everybody else. But while lying to others had been inevitable, she had *chosen* to lie to her daughter. Her lies had secured her a fortune, everything she was, but they had caused her to lose the one person who was most important to her. She had not lied to Gloria to make Gloria's life easier, but to make *her* own life easier. She had feared that Gloria, armed with the facts, would be a potential enemy, like everybody else. If Gloria now saw her as such, it was her own fault.

Their rift had begun many years ago, when Charles had appeared in her life and Arianne had sent Gloria away to boarding school. She had told herself then that it would be best for Gloria to stay away from a home which had become hell, and she genuinely wanted to keep Gloria away from her life with Charles, but her decision had been equally based on her fear of Gloria's questions, Gloria wanting to know the truth about her father. The truth could mean losing everything Arianne had.

But love became impossible without truth. She had considered love as a Trojan horse, something which, if allowed into her life, would push her back to what she had wanted to leave behind, that love was only possible for someone like Silvia. It wasn't. But love was a choice, and she had made hers long ago. Silvia had chosen to become Arianne, and now Arianne wanted what Silvia once had. It was ironic to discover it through Pandora, someone who, until moments ago, had been nothing more than a pleasant acquaintance. Arianne had not been able to explain to herself why she had felt inclined to help her in New York; now she knew. She had not really invested in Pandora's business, she had invested in herself, in what she had once been.

The clock struck four. Breakfast would be served downstairs any minute now. Arianne's ruby earrings felt heavy on her earlobes, and she removed them. They were Simon's gift to her in Portofino, the beginning of a long journey leading to this awful night.

She stared at the earrings. She had not liked them when she had first seen them, but she had changed her mind as time went by. Now she looked at them anew. She weighed them in her hand for a short while, then raised her arm with slow deliberation and flung them out into the canal. They glowed like red fireflies flashing in the moonlight before disappearing into the murky water. A moment later she joined her guests.

Part VII

33

Her hands in the pockets of her Barbour jacket, her green
Wellington boots and thick cable-knit socks protecting her
feet from the damp coldness of the Norfolk soil, Pandora
started out across the wood, the short cut between her
mother's home and the Hall, when she remembered that
she would disturb the pheasants, the most frequent reason
for Uncle Harold's scoldings during her childhood. Uncle
Harold was senile now, and beyond such preoccupations,
but Pandora imagined it would trigger a similar reaction
from Harry, her cousin and Uncle Harold's heir, now in
charge of the estate, including the shoot. She backtracked
and began the long walk across the fields, skirting the
wood, when she heard a helicopter flying above her head.
She caught sight of it briefly before it disappeared in the
distance.

The success of 'Doyle' during the first three weeks of
December had been beyond anyone's wildest expectations.
The general prosperity had created a new mood in the
country. Spend, spend, spend, was the rule, and it kept
Doyle's tills ringing in an incessant crescendo.

Pandora's designs had also been proved to be exactly
right for the market. After a decade of designer black at
one end, and chintz nostalgia at the other, her natural
look reflected the new mood of the times, a style both
distinctive and desirable at a price most people could
afford. The Green, environment-friendly angle had been
a further boost to the public's reaction. On the evidence
of the sales figures it had been possible to raise the money
for expansion immediately, and new shops were scheduled
to open in the Greater London area within two months.

It was all thanks to Arianne. She had kept her word, and
since Venice everything had become possible. Pandora had
tried to phone her after her return to London, but she was
told that Madame had left for Tokyo that morning. Then

she tried to phone Arianne in New York two weeks later, but a secretary told her that Mrs de la Force was in Zurich. Then Pandora had written her a long 'thank you' letter, but she had received no reply. Geraldine phoned her three weeks ago, during one of her lightning visits to London, and told her that she had heard that Charles and Gloria had married, 'very privately', and had disappeared from sight. 'Arianne's probably sent them to Mongolia. Can you imagine her position, poor thing. But she *is* admirable. She carries on as if nothing had happened,' Geraldine said. At first Pandora had ascribed Arianne's silence to her ever-busy schedule, but after hearing Geraldine's information she thought that a combination of embarrassment and pain because of Gloria was the more likely cause for it. The only communication Pandora had received from Arianne had been an elegant Christmas card, with a hand-written seasonal greeting.

Partly because of pressure of work, and mainly because she found the prospect of three or four days of enforced coexistence with her mother daunting, Pandora had not decided to come to Norfolk until the last moment. When her mother had phoned earlier in the month to ask if Pandora would be coming home for Christmas, she had said she probably wouldn't be able to get away. But as the date approached, she found the option of being alone in London for Christmas even worse, and she phoned her mother at the last minute to tell her she would spend the holiday at Walsham after all. Besides, she suddenly felt a surge of nostalgia for her old habitat, the flat landscape of her childhood under the mackerel-grey sky.

It had been a mistake. Pandora's mother was as bitter as she had always been, the roots of her dissatisfaction so deep in the past as to make it impossible for her to identify them. Life had passed her by, and she blamed everybody else for it. Unlike the landscape, her mother had not changed at all over the years.

The estate as Pandora remembered it had been a Beatrix Potter-like setting of small fields, fruit trees, kitchen gardens and semi-derelict greenhouses, their rusting frames and broken panes the shelter for many games of hide-and-seek with the other children living at Walsham. Not any more. Spurred on by Harry's enthusiasm for profit, the estate had become an efficient concern, the hedges gone to create enormous fields better suited to the new agricultural machinery. The fruit trees, no longer profitable, had been uprooted, and the land was now allocated to grain production. The kitchen garden and the greenhouses were also gone in the relentless drive to reduce staff and maintenance costs. The shoot, once Uncle Harold's favourite pastime, was now a thriving enterprise let to London companies for business entertainment. The estate was profitable again, but at a cost. Pandora had been warned by Camilla, Harry's wife, to drink only bottled water at her mother's house because the local wells had become contaminated by the intensive use of fertilizers.

Pandora had been glad that Camilla asked her to help her with the catering for the shoot, giving her an excuse to leave her mother for a while after the gloom of Christmas and Boxing Day. She had planned originally to return to London the next day, but had now decided to leave that evening if there were any trains running.

At last she reached the house and noticed the large number of cars parked outside, Harry's mud-splattered Range Rover an oddity among the BMWs and Mercedes. A second Range Rover, much newer than Harry's, was parked next to the main entrance, its golden metallic finish dulled by the flat morning light. A uniformed driver was polishing it, and Pandora noticed the licence plate: TC 1. She was amused briefly by its vulgarity and went on around the side of the house. She came into the kitchen yard and walked past the kennels. She was expecting the noisy welcome of the dogs, but they were already out with the guns. They would not have recognized her anyway. The Labradors she remembered had probably died and been replaced a long time ago.

As she went into the house through the staff entrance, she felt the warmth on her cheeks after the numbing chill of her walk. The door on one side of the room, leading to the larder, was open, and she saw Mrs Thomas, the cook, rummaging through the shelves. Mrs Thomas had worked at the house for as long as Pandora could remember, but the old woman had not changed much from the last time Pandora had been there. She was just a bit stouter, a shade greyer than before. Pandora was glad to see her, and waited until Mrs Thomas came out of the larder, holding a dusty jar of Branston pickle in her hand, probably already well past its 'sell by' date.

'Hello, Mrs Thomas! How are you keeping? I always miss your Yorkshire pudding, it's the best in the world,' Pandora said cheerfully.

'My you've changed, girl. Must be marriage,' the old woman replied, without acknowledging Pandora's effusive greeting. 'How's that husband of yours? Haven't seen him since your wedding. I haven't seen *you* since your wedding, come to that,' she added in a reproachful tone.

'I know. I never seem to find the time to come here any more,' Pandora said, not answering the uncomfortable question. 'Camilla asked me to come and help. Where is she?'

'Mrs Temple-Stewart is in the kitchen,' replied Mrs Thomas. Pandora followed her along the broad corridor, the stone flags eroded into dips and mounds by generations of servants' feet. Mrs Thomas' respectful reference to Camilla had not passed unnoticed. Pandora and Harry had never been equals in the cook's eye when they were children, and Camilla took precedence now as Harry's wife.

They went into the vast kitchen, where endless pots and pans lined up on deep timber shelves. Camilla was standing by the old-fashioned Aga, taking trays of sausage rolls out of one of the ovens. She laid them on the huge table in the middle of the room, and took off her quilted oven gloves.

'How lovely to see you!' Pandora said after kissing Camilla in greeting. 'You seem to have a pretty flash lot here today. I've just seen the cars outside.'

'You should see the owners. I'm amazed they remembered to take the price tags off their clothes,' Camilla laughed. 'They must have all been to Purdey's to buy the whole kit just before they came. We got a call out of the blue ten days ago, someone from London desperately trying to book a shoot at the last moment. Harry was planning to keep the day for himself, so he asked for thirty pounds per pheasant. It's twice the going rate, but they didn't seem to mind. I only hope they don't shoot each other when they try to hit the birds. Worse still, they could shoot one of the beaters. They haven't a clue how to behave.'

Camilla wrapped the baking trays in large tea towels, then turned back towards Pandora.

'They'll come to the house after the last drive for a late lunch, but they are having elevenses at the lodge by the lake. Why don't you give me a hand putting these in the car? Don't worry about what we do at the other end. I've managed to convince Harry to part with some money, and we've just put a microwave oven in at the lodge.' Camilla rushed out of the kitchen for a moment, and returned wearing a Barbour jacket identical to Pandora's.

'Let's go,' she said. Mrs Thomas followed them with a huge thermos of coffee in her arms.

'I hear you're running a shop now. How *splendid*,' Camilla said as they drove down the narrow lane towards the lake. Pandora sensed the patronizing undertone and was about to correct her, but realized that the difference between running a shop and managing a business would probably be lost on Camilla.

'My cousin, Pandora Lyons,' said Harry, introducing Pandora to the big man at the centre of the group standing by the fireplace in the lodge. 'Ted Carson,' he added, almost as an unnecessary, embarrassing formality.

Ted Carson held out his hand. 'Pleased to meet you,' he said.

'The name is Doyle now, Pandora Doyle. Harry and I haven't seen each other for years,' she replied as Carson's hand gripped hers firmly. For a moment she worried that he might remember her from her scene with Peter Wentworth-Briggs at that ghastly restaurant, but he gave no indication of recognizing her.

389

'As far as I can see, it's his loss,' Ted Carson said cheerfully.

Pandora smiled. 'I'm flattered, but Harry might not agree with you.'

'I've read about you in the papers. If you're as successful as they say you are, I may be tempted to take *you* over,' Ted chuckled. Pandora noticed both his Australian accent and his blunt charm. He spoke like a man who was used to being the centre of attention, and he expected his own attentions to be more than merely acknowledged.

'You wouldn't be able to take me over. Mine is not a public company, and I can't imagine that four shops would interest you. Are you involved in retailing?' she asked.

'No, but I'm always interested in good opportunities. I wish they were as plentiful as people seem to think, but I know one when I see her,' Carson said, smiling.

'It might be better if you concentrated on the pheasants today, instead. A small business is a very personal occupation, and mine is not for sale, anyway,' Pandora answered casually.

Everyone else in the group was now focused on their conversation, and Pandora was glad to see Mrs Thomas approaching, holding a tray of sausage rolls. Harry indicated to Ted that he ought to have first choice.

'After you,' Ted said to Pandora.

'No, thank you. I'm not hungry,' she replied.

'They're very good,' Ted said to Harry after taking a large bite.

'My wife made them, but I believe Pandora helped her.' Pandora was surprised by Harry's obsequiousness, so unlike him. She put it down to his thirty-pounds-per-pheasant coup, but she was annoyed by the implication that she was somehow part of the all-inclusive deal.

'There are some things women can do better than men. And vice versa, of course,' Ted Carson said, smiling. The men around him nodded in approval of his remark.

'Maybe you're right, Mr Carson,' Pandora replied. 'But I've found that the difference between men and women, as far as men are concerned, is usually *much* smaller than men would like it to be,' she added.

The men suddenly went quiet, and Harry glared at Pandora. After a moment's silence Ted began to laugh.

'You give as good as you get,' he said at last. 'I like that. Please call me Ted.'

'Thank you. I think that Camilla and Mrs Thomas need some help with the coffee. Excuse me, please.' As Pandora passed a window, she saw the beaters and the loaders outside helping themselves to coffee from the thermos flasks, the dogs around them, their breath visible in the cold air.

She was helping Camilla unpack the coffee mugs when she sensed somebody standing behind her. It was Ted Carson.

'I want to apologize for what I said. I've spent too long in the outback. I would like to ask you to come with us and stand with me for the next drive. You could stay for lunch later, if you want to,' he said.

'It's very kind of you, but I've got to go back home to pack,' she answered. Pandora continued to line the mugs up on the table. Maybe she was being foolish. She liked to walk with the guns, and it had been a long time since she had done so. More to the point, it was flattering to have his attention. She had learned that anyone might prove useful in the future, particularly someone like Ted Carson. 'But I'd love to see some shooting,' she added.

'Good,' Carson said with a smile. 'I can take you back to London later if you are in a hurry.'

'That's most kind, but I don't like to sit for hours on the road. I take the train when I come here, it's quicker,' she replied.

'I'm going back in my chopper. You'll be in London in no time,' he said gleefully.

Pandora smiled her sweetest apologetic smile.

'What a shame. It would have been so nice to go back with you, but I *hate* flying. I think I'll stick to the train, but thanks for the offer anyway.' She suddenly remembered the golden Range Rover outside the Hall. 'I thought I saw your car outside the house. It's difficult not to notice it.'

'My staff and my dog came in the Range Rover. I came

in the chopper. I don't like to waste time,' he replied with evident pride.

Standing by their numbers, the guns formed a line across the open field between two woods, facing the trees one hundred yards away from them. They stood in silence, and they could hear the beaters coming through the trees towards them. The sounds of shouts and wood on wood grew louder, and then the birds broke in front of them, suddenly taking flight. The firing began.

A few steps behind Ted Carson's left shoulder, Pandora took in the scene. It was as bad as Camilla had anticipated, most of the guns firing when the birds were too low or aiming at somebody else's bird, either in brash eagerness or because of ignorance of the rules. Not Ted Carson, though. He was an exceptional shot, as good as Harry.

But his display was so ostentatious it was almost embarrassing to watch. He had three men standing behind him: his two loaders and his butler, dressed as though he had stepped out of a book by P.G. Wodehouse and holding a portable phone, something Pandora had never seen before in shoots. The purpose of the second loader became clear as Ted handed his gun back after firing his second barrel. One of the men broke the gun and held it while the other reloaded. During the quick manoeuvre Pandora caught Ted's eye briefly shifting towards her, checking if she was taking in his performance.

He was trying to impress her, and it amused her. She had realized something else. In many ways, she was now as much a stranger in Walsham as Ted and his group were. She was not part of this life any more. Her visit had underlined how far apart she had grown from Harry and Camilla, from what they represented, from their confidence based on who they were rather than what they did.

During the walk the men had talked eagerly about their work, as eagerly as she would talk about hers in London. They were slightly ill at ease in their brand-new country clothes, but no more than she had been at first in her designer outfits. They were learning the rules of the world she had left behind, as she was now learning the rules of theirs.

Pandora was no longer 'one of us', she had become one of 'them'. But she could not help finding the brashness of Ted Carson and his friends almost as irritating as the relaxed, and unjustified, self-confidence of the likes of Harry and Johnny. She knew she could not carry on with one foot in each world, yet not entirely at ease in either of them.

Now Ted Carson was standing with a pile of birds in front of him, clearly pleased as his dog kept adding dead pheasants to the heap. Most of the birds shot by the other guns had dropped behind them, winged but not dead. Familiar with inexperienced guns, Harry had doubled the number of men to pick up behind them, and their dogs were now fetching the wounded birds.

'Not bad,' Ted said to Pandora with a grin, obviously expecting admiration.

'You are a very good shot. Have you been shooting for long?' she asked. She guessed he must have attended one of the many shooting schools around London.

'Long enough. My father had a small farm in Australia. I learned as a boy,' was his reply, and she felt chastened by it. She had found out that there were alternatives to being a housewife in Fulham. Equally, being a young squire in the shires or a city type at a shooting school were not the only ways to learn to handle a gun properly.

'It's four pounds thirty, young lady.'

Pandora gave the taxi driver a five pound note. 'Keep the change,' she told him.

'Thank you, love,' he said, looking closely at her.

'I've seen your face before, haven't I? You are a famous person!' he exclaimed.

Pandora smiled. 'Not really,' she answered. The press coverage arranged by her public relations agent was obviously working.

'Don't say it, don't say it, I know who you are,' he went on, closing his eyes. The tip of his tongue was just visible between his teeth as he strained to place her.

'I know, you're Selina Scott!' he said triumphantly after a pause. He leaned down and picked up a piece of paper and a pen from the luggage compartment by his side.

'Could I have your autograph, then? It's for the kids, you know,' he said, both pleased and awed by his discovery.

'Of course,' Pandora said. She signed herself 'Selina Scott' and gave the paper back to the man. He waved cheerfully at her. 'You're more beautiful than Lady Di!' he shouted as he drove away.

Amused by the incident, Pandora walked up the steps to her front door. She felt tired after the long walk with the guns, but there had been a late train, and she was glad to be home. She was looking forward to her bath, and then going to bed.

As she slipped the key into the lock she saw a man get out of a small van parked in front of her building.

'Are you Miss Doyle?' he asked.

'Yes, I am,' Pandora replied cautiously.

'Please wait a minute, miss. I've got something for you,' the man said.

She thought it odd that someone was delivering anything so late at night. There was nobody else in sight and Pandora was suddenly frightened, but if the man were a burglar surely he would not have given her time to open the door and get into the building.

After a moment, he approached her again, this time carrying a huge basket of lilies.

'Thank you,' Pandora said after she had opened the door. She pulled the crisp white envelope from the huge white bow on the basket, tore it open and read the card as she went into the hallway.

I hope you have forgiven my brashness, but I am a rough Australian after all. I am flying to Sydney tomorrow morning, and will be there until February. Would you like to have dinner with me on Friday 12th in Paris? My plane will take us there, and we can come back the same evening. My secretary will call you to confirm. I hope you are free.

Pandora did not need to read the signature to know who it was from. Only one man could offer an invitation like that, and she decided to accept it. She was flattered by his interest; no one had ever asked her out to dinner six weeks in advance. She would tell his secretary that Mr Carson should phone her in person when he was back. It wasn't just his shooting style that could do with some polishing.

34

Los muchachos peronistas
todos unidos triunfaremos ...

The opening lines of the Peronist Anthem filled the room. The screen showed the enormous crowd at Ezeiza Airport, twenty miles outside the city, waiting for Perón's return after his eighteen-year exile in Spain.

Disgusted by the circus-like atmosphere, Arianne picked up the remote control and switched off the television set. She glanced at the *Buenos Aires Herald*, a habit she had acquired during her crash course in English two years ago, but threw it aside after a moment. She picked up the house phone and called the kitchen to ask for a cup of tea. After a long while, Rosinha answered. Arianne was surprised, but then she remembered that the Government had declared a national holiday for the day. Rosinha, being Portuguese, did not care much for these events, but the rest of Arianne's staff was probably at Ezeiza, chanting and shouting the imminent end of the stinking rich – of people like her, in fact.

Perón's return was as celebrated by most of Arianne's friends as his departure had been in 1955. They had cheered his departure out of hatred, and now they cheered his return out of fear. But their enthusiasm did not compromise the safety of either their money, wisely deposited abroad, or their children, sent to the country in anticipation of the turmoil in the city once Perón arrived. Arianne had sent Gloria and Nana to one of her estates, a hundred miles from Buenos Aires. She was on her own in the almost deserted house, and missed the familiarity of Gloria and Nana's presence.

She felt lonely. Gloria and Nana were the only two people she could count on. Her friendships now were merely a matter of practical interest. Even Jacques, once so close to her, had faded from her life. She had seen him in Paris last year and sensed the difference. Not simply because of her money – she had lived like a very rich woman towards the end of her time in Paris. They had both been on the same side then though; what she had was by the grace of Simon. It was difficult to maintain a friendship with a make-up artist when she crossed the Atlantic in her own jet, and was supposed to dine with a Cabinet minister.

Many men had courted her since Simon's death, but Arianne was not interested. Besides, they would want to marry her sooner or later, either because of her money or because of the prestige attached to catching her. Simon's letter to her had put an end to that prospect, and there was no point in starting fires that she would have to put out.

Living as she was in the small circle of Buenos Aires society, Arianne's love life or lack of it became a popular topic during her early days in the city. The venom of some of the men she turned down, the vanity of those who claimed success for the sake of their image, and the envy of some of the women, had given her a reputation as both a *femme de glace* and a nymphomanic. The lack of firm evidence of the latter dampened the interest, her evident disinterest in men enhancing the former. Failure is not an enticing prospect, and men stopped asking Arianne out after a while. She found herself having to rely for male company on a small circle of rich homosexuals who provided her with regular escorts to the theatre or the opera, but did little for her feeling of isolation, a feeling that overwhelmed her today.

Weakened by her introspective mood, she allowed herself to think about Paul Liehr. After her visit to 'San Simon' three years ago, Arianne had found herself eagerly waiting for reasons to visit the estate. When she began inventing them, she realized that she was close to making a fool of herself. From then on, Paul reported to her on the phone when necessary, and she had learned to dismiss her feelings on the rare occasions when personal contact was unavoidable. She sensed that attraction played no part in his respectful attitude towards her. Everybody took notice of the fact that she was a woman, of her attractiveness, bar the one person whom she would have liked to. In a way, Arianne was glad he didn't. Life was easier if she was in full control of everything, her business as well as her emotions.

But it wasn't easy today, and she suddenly felt a compelling need to see him. She walked around her home for a while, forcing herself to look at her tapestries and paintings. Then she went to the library and picked out a book at random. She sat in one of the leather armchairs and began to read, but flung the book down on the coffee table after a while.

It was absurd. She was fretting like a schoolgirl because she felt like seeing one particular man. Her mind was instantly made up. She picked up the phone again and called her pilot. Half an hour later she was at the *Aeroparque*, and then she was airborne, oblivious to anything else other than the fact that soon she would have her wish.

At the opposite end of the city, many miles away, the Peronist rally had reached fever point, scuffles breaking out everywhere between right-wing and left-wing supporters. 'Perón, Evita, the country is Peronist,' chanted one side. 'Perón, Evita, the country is socialist,' replied the other. The noise was deafening, but even the roar of a million voices could not drown the firing of automatic weapons when the shooting finally broke out.

Nobody would ever know which side started it, nor how many died in the massacre that followed. Men, women, and children ran in all directions, but the bullets came from all directions, mowing them down. Hundreds of white doves escaped from the huge cage at the side of the main stage. They were to have been released when the leader, the hero of the day, made his appearance in front of his cheering supporters, but now they flew over the carnage.

The volcano of violence, rumbling for so long, had erupted. It was to burn the country for nearly ten years.

As the plane landed, Arianne realized that she had forgotten to warn the staff that she was coming. There would be no car to take her to the house. No matter. The house was not quite a mile away from the landing strip, and it was a fine day. She would enjoy the walk through the park.

After a while she began to catch glimpses of the house in the distance, and only then did she wonder what she was going to say to Paul. She ran through possible topics for discussion in her head, but they had already discussed them all. As Arianne reached the casuarina wood she thought of a possibility, its implications both tempting and frightening.

She had to fly to America next month. She would tell him that she was thinking about introducing new bloodlines to the stud farm, and he should come with her to advise her.

The possibility of a few days away with him, if only for part of the time, made her heart beat faster. She decided to take a shortcut to the house by walking through the fountain garden, hidden from view by a circular yew hedge. She wanted to see Paul as soon as possible.

She saw him sooner than she expected. As she walked onto the broad white gravel path around the fountain, she noticed a couple sitting on one of the stone benches at the far end of the garden, the man's arm around the girl's shoulders. It was Paul.

He jumped to his feet, as did the girl.

'Nobody warned me that you were coming, Señora,' he said apologetically. The girl realized who Arianne was, and looked fixedly down at her feet.

'May I introduce Anna Rauch,' Paul went on after a pause. 'She is . . . a friend.'

Arianne nodded to him graciously, ignoring the girl.

'I'm only here for a moment, Paul. I suddenly decided to come to 'San Simon' because I urgently needed . . . some papers I left in my bedroom last time I was here. I'm going back now.' She left abruptly without saying goodbye. It was not the awareness of her obvious lie, heightened by the fact that she held nothing in her hands, which made her walk away. It was worse. Her violent trembling confirmed to her that she was hopelessly in love.

*　　*　　*

The front page of the company's July newsletter was largely taken up by a message of welcome to General Perón, accompanied by a photograph of Señora de la Force, the Chairman, greeting the General at his home. The announcement of Paul Liehr's elevation to the main board after his brilliant management of 'San Simon' was one among many others on the second page.

The announcement said that Mr Liehr would now take up residence in Buenos Aires.

35

The wine waiter carefully poured Château Margaux, just enough to fill the bottom of the glass. Ted took a sip of his wine, closing his eyes and pursing his lips. Pandora had seen wine experts go through similar motions, reminding her of mouth-wash commercials on television. Ted nodded his approval, and the waiter began to fill their glasses.

'How much is your turnover these days?' Ted asked suddenly.

Pandora toyed with her *Emincé de Veau et sa Chartreuse de Poivrons Rouges* until the waiter went away.

'Is that what you usually ask girls you fly to Paris for dinner?' Ted's question took her by surprise, since he had not mentioned business, either his or hers, until then. She found his abrupt change of tone as gauche as it was direct, almost as gauche as she had found the air hostess in his plane, her pale blue uniform buttoned with golden 'T's.

'Answering with another question is an obvious tactic,' Ted said. 'I can try to seduce you, or we can discuss business. Either would suit me. I would prefer the first option, but I suspect that you might be the kind of woman who does not succumb on the first date. I like you enough to be prepared to wait.'

'You seem to take for granted that there is something to wait for.' However blunt he might be, Pandora could not avoid being flattered by Ted's rough-edged admiration, although she was not going to acknowledge it. 'I can't see why you should be interested in my line of business, though. I thought you were mainly into brewing.'

'I'm involved in other things as well. I've just bought a computer company in America. They distribute a range of office furniture on the East Coast, and they own a string of large showrooms in most major cities. The business is a dead duck, but it's not the right time to sell it and I'm thinking of alternative uses for the showrooms.'

Pandora was not interested. Expansion into America, or any other country for that matter, was out of the question for a business the size of hers, at least at present. But she could not help thinking how effortless Ted could make it sound. Perhaps it was, in his scale of things.

'I might be interested one day, but not now,' Pandora replied. 'The food here is too good to let it get cold for the sake of your empty showrooms and my turnover. I'll only say that it is certainly less than yours but more than you think,' she added.

Ted chuckled. 'You are right. This is not the place for hard talk. I should have said it earlier, but you look gorgeous tonight. I like your dress – I hope I'll see the label someday.' It was the dress she had bought for Geraldine's party, her most glamorous evening outfit, and it was clearly making an impression.

'You don't seem to waste time. Perhaps we should go back to our business conversation,' she replied with a weary smile.

'I've already told you that I have little time to waste and I'm going to New York for a week tomorrow. But let's change the subject if you like.' Ted took a sip of his wine, and embarked on a knowledgeable explanation of the merits of this particular vintage.

'Unfortunately, all good things are expensive, but it's just a matter of preference. For instance, I'm sure you don't find what you pay for scent outrageous. What would you imagine a bottle of scent this size would cost?' he asked, holding up the wine bottle. The patronizing tone in his voice grated on Pandora.

'I wouldn't know. I don't drink my scent,' she said curtly. Ted was visibly nonplussed. 'The only reason I can think of for your comparison,' Pandora went on, 'is that you want to find a way to let me know that this bottle costs hundreds of pounds.' His embarrassment was immediately obvious, and she regretted her catty remark.

'I love the Place de la Madeleine, it always reminds me of an Impressionist painting,' she added hastily, looking out of the window next to their table. 'I'm very grateful for your wonderful invitation.' She smiled at him. He was now sitting in stony silence, but after a while he smiled too.

'You *are* a classy lady. It shouldn't surprise me. I hear you are related to the Earl of Felmingham. I met him shooting not long ago.'

It would have been simpler to refer to him as Lord Felmingham, but Ted's tone showed that he liked the full title rolling off his tongue. It made Pandora feel awkward on his behalf, but he was trying to make up for his *faux pas* by taking pride in his social progress.

'He is my second cousin, on my mother's side. I hardly ever see him.' It occurred to Pandora that he must have carried out some pretty thorough research on her background if he was aware of such a distant relationship. 'Use what you've got, that's the secret,' had been Geraldine's advice. He found her attractive, and aspired to what she represented. She did not find him unattractive, and he could be useful. Perhaps there was more common ground here than she had been prepared to admit at the beginning of the evening.

Pandora talked for a while about the English side of her family and her days as a deb. At first she was pleased by Ted's interest, until she realized she was playing up to the role he expected of her. There was not much difference between his earlier, coarse boasting, and her seemingly casual display of social connections. They served the same purpose, but at least he had made his reasons for displaying his power absolutely clear. She knew what her own motive was, and she didn't like it. It was one thing to see the point in Geraldine's advice, quite another to start behaving like Geraldine.

'All this talk about friends and relatives must be very boring for you. They aren't very interesting, really,' she said, hastily trying to bring the conversation to an end.

'Are you being sincere, or just patronizing? It's the easiest thing in the world to emphasize what you've got, and then dismiss it as if it's of no consequence. If we're going to play games, then at least let's play by the rules,' Ted replied.

Pandora thought for a moment.

'You're right to ask the question, but wrong about the

reason. I just wanted to change the subject. But since you mention rules, perhaps we ought to clarify who's laying them,' she retorted.

Ted laughed. 'It's too complex a question for our first evening out. But the fact that you ask it gives me hope for the future, and there's no need to play games tonight. I took your point earlier, and I'm not trying to seduce you.' He looked away for a moment to catch the waiter's attention, and she felt both relieved and disappointed by his words. He turned back to her.

'Not yet,' he added with a smile as the waiter presented the dessert menu.

It was nearly seven o'clock, and almost everybody else in the office had gone home. Pandora was still rattled by her last meeting.

Soon after Christmas, one of her friends from her school days had come to see her, to ask for a job. She had said that now that her children were at school she wanted something to do, and Pandora had offered her a job as an assistant in one of her shops. The manager had phoned her in the morning to tell her that Mrs Harrison had been caught stealing goods from the stock room. 'I would have handled the problem myself, Miss Doyle, but I know that Mrs Harrison is a friend of yours . . .' Pandora asked that Mrs Harrison should come to her office at the end of the day.

Dismissal was the only option. Even if she were to move Charlotte to another branch, the problem would arise again. The fact that the outcome was inevitable had not made the conversation less difficult. Charlotte had been tearful at first, then angry, then tearful again, and Pandora could not help feeling sorry for her. Charlotte had gone at last, but the scene had been very unpleasant. From now on it would be wiser not to get involved in dismissing staff if it could be done by somebody else. She understood why generals stay away from the front. Her own battle had just begun; she wouldn't last long if she made a point of walking among the casualties and getting upset by their wounds.

404

Her phone rang, and she answered it. She recognized the Australian drawl immediately.

'Hello, I'm back. I'm glad you haven't gone away yet. Does that mean you are free this weekend?'

'Why?' Pandora asked.

Ted chuckled. 'No questions. You have to tell me now if you are free or not.'

Her first inclination was to say no, but it dawned on her that she was glad to hear his voice.

'Yes, I am free.'

'Good. I'm having some friends to stay in my house in Hampshire. I would love you to come,' he said. 'I'll pick you up at half past nine tomorrow morning. We're going in the chopper.' He had not waited for her to accept, but she decided to let it pass.

'I've told you I don't like flying in helicopters,' Pandora replied.

'You'll learn to love it. I'm looking forward to seeing you. Oh, and I've bought something in New York for you. Sorry, there's somebody else on the other line, and I can't keep him waiting. I'll see you tomorrow,' he said before ringing off abruptly.

As Pandora put the phone down, she wondered if she had been wise to accept. After a while, she switched off the lights and left the office. At least she was no longer worrying about Charlotte.

'That's my home,' Ted shouted in order to be heard over the roar of the helicopter, pointing at the spread of slate roofs and gables below them. As soon as he heard him, the pilot tilted the helicopter slightly towards Pandora's side, to give her as full a view of the ground as possible. 'It's very beautiful, it reminds me of Blickling,' she said. She noticed Ted's blank look at the comparison. 'Blickling is a lovely house near Walsham. It is one of the great stately homes of England,' she added.

Now pleased by the effect the house seemed to have on her, Ted tapped the pilot's shoulder.

'Let's have a quick tour of the estate from the air, Freddy,' he said. 'I want Miss Doyle to see everything.'

405

The unexpected extension of the flight made Pandora regret her admiration.

Once they landed, Ted insisted on walking around the house before going in: he clearly wanted to show off his domain. It was said to have been built for Anne Boleyn, and had had a succession of distinguished owners ever since. Ted had bought the estate from the Duke of Barnsbury and had immediately embarked on a massive restoration programme. 'I employed only the best people,' he boasted. The Victorian wing had been demolished, and the park restored at great expense. 'I've added a couple of polo fields,' he told Pandora as they finally went inside the house.

The other guests were already waiting for them in the Great Hall, some playing backgammon while others read the *Financial Times* or the *Daily Telegraph*. The women were all blonde, or had become so, and were dressed in designer slacks and silk shirts, their chunky gold jewellery as new as the bags they had casually flung on the sofas. The men wore either City shirts with the sleeves rolled up, a pale yellow cashmere sweater thrown over their shoulders, or brand-new country tweed jackets over Viyella shirts. They all wore trousers pressed to a razor-sharp crease. Pandora had upgraded her usual country wardrobe of jeans and a sweater for the occasion, but she now realized that she had underplayed her hand. Everybody else seemed to have just arrived from a very sunny corner of the world by way of Sloane Street.

Ted introduced Pandora to his guests. There was a Greek man whose name Pandora was not able to catch, accompanied by Melissa Harvey, whose name she did not need to catch because her life was permanently featured in the gossip columns. Her last marriage had been to a very rich industrialist who had been knighted before their divorce. 'I'm Lady Harvey, but do just call me Melissa,' she told Pandora with a smile.

There was also Norman Bragg and his wife. He was a property developer originally based in the North of England. His roaring success in shopping mall developments had triggered his equally successful move to the London Docklands, where 'Bragg'-emblazoned cranes were now an everyday sight. His wife looked as perfectly suburban as a golf-course, and equally well-groomed.

Pandora was surprised to see a face from her old days. Nick Aston-Jones used to be the boyfriend of one of the girls at Mrs Ogilvy's shop when Pandora worked there. She had lost touch with both of them. He was accompanied by Olivia Treadwell, the notorious journalist, whose ability to outrage her readers was second only to her skill in infuriating those she wrote about. She was now riding high on the success of *Seduction*, her latest novel. Pandora was puzzled by the unlikely pair.

'Nick! It's been such a long time! What are you doing these days?' she asked, as Ted led the other guests towards the seats around the monumental fireplace, where his butler waited by a huge refectory table, the top almost invisible under the bottles and glasses on silver trays.

'I'm a publi-*shah* now.' His career might have changed, but his accent had not. Pandora instantly understood his connection with Olivia. Authors and publishers, wheelers and dealers, we all have something to sell to each other these days, she thought. They chatted for a while, and then joined the others at the far end of the room.

'You're very lucky to have caught a man like Ted,' Melissa suddenly said to Pandora.

They were leaning on the white painted rail around the polo field, while Ted and Vlasos Kalomeropoulos rode up and down, practising their cut and pulled strokes. Pandora had learned the Greek's name during lunch, at the same time she had learned that Melissa was a well-coiffed viper.

'You are wrong on two counts. I haven't "caught" Ted and, if I had, it would be *his* good luck as well as mine,' Pandora replied tersely, her eyes fixed on the riders. Melissa seemed absorbed in checking her nail polish.

During lunch Pandora had worked out the reasons behind the gathering. Norman Bragg owned a hundred acres of redundant docks on the Thames, and Ted and Vlasos were joining him in re-developing them. Nick was there because his publishing house had recently been taken over by one of Ted's companies, and Nick was being considered for a top position in the larger group. He had presumably brought Olivia along as a party decoration. Pandora glanced at the ancestral portraits hanging on Ted's panelled walls, unlikely to be members of the Carson family; she wondered what the elegantly dressed squires and ladies would have made of the group under their painted eyes. Perhaps they had been as concerned to get their hands on somebody else's property during their time as the crowd beneath them, who were laughing too loudly.

'I think I've sorted out that planning problem we discussed last week, Ted,' Norman Bragg had announced in the middle of lunch. 'I've engaged Sheridan Crabtree as Senior Design Consultant for the project. The bloke is a bit weird and he charges as if he were Boris Becker, but the geezer knows his way around the Prince of Wales. He even *knows* the Prince of Wales, can you believe it? He has stuck columns on everything, so it's going to look *really* posh.'

Ted turned towards Pandora.

'Norm is talking about our Docklands project. It's a very big development: flats, houses, offices and a shopping mall, all first class. Maybe you could do the show houses.' Pandora noticed that he had chosen to explain the project to her before replying to Bragg, making her party to the conversation. It could be sheer politeness, but it pleased her nonetheless.

'I'm glad to hear that, Norm. We don't want any more hiccups, and we don't want to rub the planners up the wrong way. Will you do the show houses for us?' he asked Pandora.

She smiled.

'I'd love to, but I met Sheridan Crabtree in New York and we may not be on the same wavelength. So far as I can tell, he does not even approve of electric lighting in houses. In any case, it would only be worth my while if I open a branch in your shopping mall. Otherwise it's too far away for potential clients.'

Ted leaned towards her, and patted her hand.

'That's the spirit,' he said approvingly, almost possess-
ively. Pandora remained still for a moment, then moved
her hand away and turned towards Bragg.

'What stone will they be using for your columns?' she
asked. Bragg seemed surprised, then he laughed.

'. . . The lady has expensive taste, Ted. We don't use
real stone, glass-reinforced plastic looks the same and it's
cheaper.'

Pandora did not like either his tone or the fact that he
had obviously forgotten her name. She was about to reply
but Ted spoke first.

'The lady is called Pandora, Norm. Don't forget it,' he
said sharply. 'I guess you don't like our plastic columns,'
he said to her, as Norm joined in the conversation at the
other end of the table.

'I wouldn't know. I haven't seen them,' she replied. 'But
if you're going to bother, you might as well do the thing
properly.'

He seemed amused by her comment.

'Are you talking about the columns or about you and
me?' he said very quietly, so that only she could hear
him.

She smiled.

'About the columns. Truth is always better, in either
case,' she replied.

'But much more expensive, in *this* case.'

'Are you still talking about the columns?' she asked in
mock innocence. He laughed.

'I was, but I've suddenly remembered I've got a present
for you, and now I'm not sure. I hope you'll like the present
at least.' He turned to the table at large.

'We'd better get a quote for real stone, Norm,' he said
loudly, his hand over Pandora's. This time he moved it
away before she could react.

Afterwards they all sat in the library, where the Braggs
soon announced that they were going for a walk around
the park while Nick, who had polished off an extraordinary quantity of claret during lunch, stumbled up the stairs
towards his bedroom for an urgently needed nap. Olivia
said that she had some work to do and also went upstairs,

probably to transcribe everything that had been said during lunch for future use in her next novel, and Pandora found herself stuck with Melissa. After ten minutes of listening to her monologue on travelling and shopping, Pandora guessed that Melissa's sex life would be the next subject. She was about to say that she would also like to go to her room for a while when Ted asked them to come along to watch him and Vlasos practise.

Once Vlasos and Ted left them by the edge of the polo field and the two women were alone, her fears about likely topics of conversation were proved accurate. Melissa launched into an account of her colourful experiences during the time between her ex-husband and Vlasos, whom she had met last summer in Sardinia. 'I *adore* Vlasos. He would do anything for me, but we had our moments. After the Stock Market crash last year he went limp on me, darling. As limp as cooked rhubarb! I tried *everything*, but it was no use. Luckily the market picked up after a while, and so did he.'

Pandora remained silent.

'I hear that Ted is like a tiger in bed,' Melissa said quietly.

Pandora decided that she was not going to be an item in next week's columns.

'You should ask Ted, because I certainly haven't got the faintest idea,' was her terse reply.

Melissa raised her eyebrows.

'You mean . . .?'

'Yes, I mean that,' Pandora said shortly.

There was genuine puzzlement in Melissa's voice now.

'But darling, why not? Ted is a terrific guy . . .'

Ted and Vlasos had dismounted, and they were handing their ponies to the grooms. Pandora climbed under the rail and began to stride across the field towards them. It would have been difficult for her to answer Melissa's last question. She had a point.

Sitting at the dressing table in her room, Pandora finished taking off her make-up. She was ready to go to bed when she noticed that she had forgotten to bring the book she was reading from London. She looked at the books neatly piled on the bedside table for an alternative, but they were the standard issue for guest rooms in English country houses: a biography of Lord Mountbatten, a novel about the last days of the Raj, a best-selling thriller, somebody's boring account of the Second World War, and Joyce Grenfell's diaries, resting on an equally neat pile of out-of-date issues of *Country Life* magazine. She had put together many rooms like this during her early time as an interior decorator, and she could remember the last minute rush to the bookshop to achieve a lived-in, comfortable atmosphere.

After dinner, Olivia had given Ted a signed copy of her new novel, followed by a hard sales pitch about how riveting it was, and how horrified booksellers had been by the sexy bits. 'Dynamite, *real* dynamite,' she stressed. Olivia had stopped only when Nick had reminded her that they were reprinting it, and the book was momentarily unavailable in any bookstores. Pandora was curious about it, and remembered that Ted had left his copy on one of the library tables. She decided to go downstairs to fetch it.

It had been straight after dinner when the main reason for her reluctance towards Ted, the answer to Melissa's question, became clearer to Pandora. Ted had asked her beforehand to act as his hostess tonight, and as soon as coffee was finished Pandora stood up, the signal to the other women around the table to follow her to the drawing room, leaving the men to drink port and smoke cigars. Olivia protested loudly at what she called a troglodite custom, but followed the others after a moment. The loftiness of the room underlined the awkwardness of their situation, a small group of women waiting for the men to grace them with their presence.

They did not have to wait long, because soon they heard riotous laughter from the dining room, followed by Ted's voice booming across the hall, calling them to come and see. As they re-entered the dining room Pandora noticed that the men had taken off their dinner jackets and Nick was squatting on the floor, his head thrown back, an open bottle of port clenched between his teeth, his arms

411

stretched out to keep his balance. The men began to clap their hands and Nick started his Cossack dance around the table, gulping down the port at the same time. The shouting grew louder and louder until he completed his round, the bottle now empty. His bet won, he stood up and grinned, only to pass out immediately on the floor. Ted beckoned his butler and told him to carry Mr Aston-Jones upstairs. Amid much laughter, they all moved to the library nearby for coffee, but the scene made Pandora wonder if her main role here, Nick's role as well, was to give credibility to a coarse, high budget replica of the world she was trying to leave behind.

She had just switched on the lamp and picked up Olivia's book when the door opened and Ted came in. He was still in his evening clothes. She had not bothered to put on her dressing gown, and felt embarrassingly vulnerable in her thin nightdress.

'How did you know I was here?'

'I realized I had forgotten to give you your present, and went to your room.' Ted was holding a small rectangular blue box. He gave it to her, and she opened it. It was a bracelet, a simple line of square diamonds. She saw the name Tiffany's in gold letters on the white lining of the box. He had bought it in New York. She closed it, and gave it back to him.

'It's wonderful, but it's too much. I can't possibly accept it. It would make me feel . . .' She was going to say 'cheap', but it would offend him, and she didn't want to do that. He put the box on the table and looked at her.

'From my point of view it's a little thing, but there you are. As I told you in Paris, it all depends on one's values. But it wasn't meant in the way you think.

'You don't like my friends,' he said after a pause. There was no reproach in his voice. It was a matter-of-fact statement.

'You're right, I don't.'

He didn't seem to find the conversation uncomfortable, but she did.

'Is it because you don't like them, or because they show you something about yourself that you don't like?'

412

'I thought we were talking about your friends,' Pandora said angrily.

Ted smiled.

'I like it when you are angry. I wouldn't miss my sleep just to discuss my friends, though. You know what we are really talking about, and you've seen enough to know if you want me or not. Since you're in business, you must know that it pays to make up one's mind quickly. I'm not the waiting type.'

'We are not talking business here,' she retorted.

'Maybe not, but we are talking about personal decisions. I've never seen any difference between them.'

It was what Arianne had said to her in Venice, and he had been right on one score. She had not liked his friends because they showed her what she could become, maybe had become already. But her stay at Walsham had equally shown her that she no longer belonged in Harry and Camilla's world. At least Ted represented the future.

The question was whether she wanted him around her. She was not interested in a fling for the sake of it, and she could not go back to being an appendage to somebody else's life, as she had been with Johnny. But the frantic pace of her work life contrasted with her loneliness outside the office. She would be thirty soon, and she could not spend the rest of her life trying to avoid the issue. She could not deny that it was flattering to have a man like him by her side, and if there had to be somebody, well, it would not have to be on his terms alone. Not any more.

Her mind was made up, but she still found it difficult to give an answer.

'What are you expecting me to say?' she murmured at last.

'You've said it.' His arms around her waist, he kissed her. She was beginning to return his kiss when they suddenly heard a loud buzzing.

'What's that?' she asked.

He laughed.

'That's my butler setting the burglar alarm. There are

sensors under every door, and we won't be able to leave this room until seven in the morning, when he switches it off. Don't worry, there are plenty of sofas around.' He took her hand and led her away from the bright light, towards the comfortable half-light beyond.

36

BUENOS AIRES
June 1975

The limousine, escorted by a Ford Falcon in front and a second Falcon immediately behind it, made slow progress in the busy traffic. The escort cars were chauffeur-driven, each carrying three men armed with sub-machine guns. The mirrored windows blocked all sight of the limousine's interior, where Arianne de la Force sat in the back between two bodyguards, their Magnum 44s on their laps. But those were dark days in Buenos Aires, a city scarred by violence, and the rich and powerful took elaborate precautions to protect themselves, especially after the spectacular kidnapping of the Born brothers by guerrillas a year before, followed by a sixty million dollar ransom demand. It was the first in a wave of abductions, against the background of open war between right- and left-wing paramilitary groups.

Like others, Arianne had been forced to surround herself with bodyguards in order to maintain a semblance of normal life. A false sense of security spread at first, and some party givers took pride in the fact that the number of bodyguards gathered outside their houses often exceeded the number of guests inside, the evidence of their social standing. But pride was soon overwhelmed by the dreadful suspicion that the bodyguards, an unrivalled source of inside information about security arrangements, could be bribed by the guerrillas. It was unnerving to rely on the loyalty of men for hire.

After the Born kidnapping, Arianne's security advisers had insisted that Gloria be sent out of the country. Arianne had refused point-blank, but she had made the mistake of mentioning their suggestion to Nana, who became obsessed with the possibility of risk to the child. Again and again Nana told Arianne that she would hold her responsible if anything were to happen to Gloria, and after two months of relentless pressure, Arianne finally gave in. Gloria had been sent to Paris with Nana, and she was now at a convent school. Arianne missed her, but once she got used to it she realized that it was a relief to know that Gloria was out of danger. She was looking forward to her trip to Paris tomorrow. For the first time, business was not the only reason behind her going away. She had taken a villa in Cap d'Ail for the summer. Gloria and Nana would spend the school holidays there, and she would stay with them for as long as possible.

As the convoy approached its destination and the limousine slowed down, the bodyguards in the escort cars jumped out and formed a double line on both sides of the entrance to the building. Arianne got out of the limousine without any delay, and walked swiftly into the relative security of her office. She paid no attention to her grim guard of honour. She had become accustomed to them.

Her mind made up, Arianne returned the papers on her desk to the leather folder in front of her. It was time for the board meeting. She would announce her decision then. It would hurt Paul, but she had no choice. In spite of so much time having gone by, she still found it hard to make decisions she knew would upset him, but the business must be her priority.

After her initial impulse, Arianne had half-convinced herself that nothing but business reasons were behind her decision to bring Paul to Buenos Aires. He had run a very large estate brilliantly. It was only natural to promote him, and she had expected him to live up to her expectations. Soon after he joined the board, though, it became clear to Arianne that while he was a very good leader of people, he was a very poor manipulator of them. A board position required the skill of planting ideas in the minds of fellow directors so that they took root and developed as if they were their own, the ability to form alliances, to leave markers to be called up when necessary. Paul was an open character, incapable of dissembling, and soon he had found himself isolated from his colleagues.

For a while Arianne had expected that, thrown into close proximity by his move to Buenos Aires, their personal relationship would develop. She could not but believe that, once they were in daily contact, it would be a matter of time before he was attracted to her. She had endeavoured to consult him at all times, to be together as often as possible, until people in the company began to talk about her favouritism towards him. This did not worry Arianne nearly as much as Paul's lack of inclination to validate the gossip. She was forced to accept that she had been misled by a silly fantasy, and his lack of response was perhaps the best outcome.

'The problem is that you don't understand the point!' Paul Liehr said angrily to his colleague. Everyone's eyes turned to the top of the table, waiting for Arianne's reaction, but she remained silent.

The board had been discussing future policy for the 'San Simon' estates, in view of the country's plummeting economy. The more general view was that the time had come to trim down, liquidate cattle stocks and cancel any plant expansion projects, which would only create hard currency commitments at a time when the peso was going through the floor. Paul had been advocating the opposite: land prices had fallen dramatically, making it possible to expand stocks at very low real cost. It would take only a small upturn in international beef prices, which would generate additional dollar earnings to absorb the initial losses.

'. . . and you will have to sell the dollars at Mrs Perón's official rate of exchange. At the present rate, even this company could not afford it,' another director said from the far end of the table.

Arianne decided to put an end to the squabble. There had been too many similar episodes in the past, and there was no point in delaying the outcome.

'Gentlemen, I've listened carefully to what you've all said. Paul has made his point very well, but I must agree with what is clearly the general view.' She avoided Paul's eyes as she spoke. She knew that her perfunctory compliment would not have made any difference to him, and she knew how strongly he felt about anything concerning 'San Simon' and its future.

She looked at him at last, but he was not looking at her, and it didn't matter any more.

'Let's move on to the next point,' she said to the table at large. Tomorrow she would go away, and she would leave all this behind her for a while. She looked forward to it.

Arianne had just finished taking some of her jewellery out of her bedroom safe and packing it into her travel case when the phone rang. She would be leaving the following morning, and her luggage had already been taken to the airport. As she picked the phone up, she caught sight of the photograph of herself as a child in Rio on the bedside table, and slipped it into her case as she tucked the receiver under her chin. It was the housekeeper.

'Security just phoned to say there is a gentleman at the gates to see you, Señora. His name is Paul Liehr, and he says it's very urgent.'

'Please let him in and show him to the library.' Arianne was momentarily dumbfounded by Nelly's announcement. She could not think of any possible reason for Paul's visit, and she dared not imagine one either. She rushed to the mirror for a last-minute check before going downstairs.

Paul was standing by the fire, his back to the door, and she paused before entering the room. She was used to seeing him, but it had always been in the neutral surroundings of her office, where she could pretend that he was no different from the hundreds of others she employed. But now he was in her home, and they were alone. His presence here suddenly turned her tapestries and paintings into a lifeless collection of woven and painted figures, only underscoring the reality of the man quietly waiting by the fire. She forced herself to go into the room.

'This *is* a surprise,' Arianne said with a perfectly gracious smile. 'Please sit down,' she added, pointing to the nearest sofa as Paul turned round.

'Thank you, but I won't be long. I know that you are busy, and I don't want to keep you. I'm sorry to drop in like this, but I had to see you. I have something to tell you.' He spoke faster than usual, rushing out his words, as if he were embarrassed. No, it wasn't embarrassment, it was as if he were almost overcome by what he had to say, she thought, and her heart jumped in anticipation of what she wanted to hear. Arianne stood next to him. She was too close to the fire, but she didn't mind.

'What is it?' she asked anxiously.

'Here is my resignation,' Paul answered, pulling an envelope out of his jacket pocket.

Arianne felt as if the ground had suddenly given under her feet. It was work after all that had brought Paul here. She had assumed too much from his manner, but there was only anger behind it, and it now occurred to her that her position had shielded her from other people's anger to the extent that she was no longer able to recognize it. She looked away to conceal her disappointment, then took the envelope. She was about to open it but suddenly changed her mind.

'I want to know why.' She endeavoured to speak with her chairman's voice.

Paul turned his face away from her, and leaned on the mantelpiece.

'You know why. I've been very unhappy since I came here. There's no reason for my staying with the company any longer. It was only you . . . your support that kept me.' His voice was almost inaudible now. 'I've accepted a job in Patagonia.'

'Are you saying that you've stayed here only because of me?' Arianne was now more aware of his physical presence than her own. She had heard him, and she wanted to be sure. She could not face another disappointment.

'You don't need to ask that question. You know . . .'

Arianne didn't know. Or at least not until now. Wrapped up in her own concerns, too aware of her own situation, she had failed to understand his. She had remained on high, and had expected him to climb to her. She had moved him to Buenos Aires as a way of bringing them together, without realizing it only made him more aware of the difference in their positions. Arianne suddenly felt angry, bitter about the time they had wasted. She had waited for *five* years to hear what he had just said, only for him to say it when it was too late.

419

'No, I don't know!' she shouted. 'If you're saying what I think you are, then why didn't you tell me before?'

'Before what?' Paul asked quietly. 'You will always be Mrs de la Force, and I am who I am. Nothing can change that. I can't be the queen's favourite. I'm too proud for that, and it couldn't have lasted anyway. I love you too much to face losing you.'

Arianne felt tears in her eyes. It had been pride, nothing but bloody pride that had kept them apart, hers as well as his. But it was not too late. She came to him and held his face in her hands, as gently as if she held the most valuable object in the world. She saw herself in his eyes, and the fire behind them.

'What makes you think you'll ever lose me?' she murmured just before he kissed her.

She had waited years for this kiss. It gave her back many things she had long chosen to forget: mornings at the beach, when she had leaped and tumbled in the sea until she screamed with laughter, and evenings under the moon, when she had danced until tiredness went away. It brought back the joy of innocent surrender, of complete trust. His kiss gave Silvia back to her, and she gave him Silvia, not Arianne, in return. She had waited years for this moment, and now she knew it had been worth it.

Daylight was breaking, and Arianne was at last able to see the clock on the table: it was quarter to seven.

Unable to sleep, she had spent the night watching Paul's face, his mouth, following the line of his shoulder and then his arm, the contour of his fingers, the rise and fall of his chest as he breathed. Common features to every man, to any man. Nothing in particular was special about him, yet everything was. Arianne stared at him again, trying to comprehend when everything had been clarified, a mystery understood but still an enigma. Maybe she, not he, was the answer to her own riddle.

It was morning now, and there wasn't much time left. Arianne gently woke Paul up. Half-asleep, he began to kiss her but after a moment she stopped him.

'You're coming with me. Now. Give me the keys to your

apartment, and tell me where your passport is. My driver will collect it, and we'll go to the airport. You don't need anything else.'

Paul was suddenly wide awake. He sat up and leaned against the carved headboard, deep in thought.

'No,' he said after a while. 'It's no use, and you know it. It's better for both of us if we part now. But we might as well say goodbye properly.' He began to kiss her.

It was not what Arianne had wanted to hear, but she was encouraged by his hesitation. She threw her arms around Paul and returned his kisses, seemingly as carried away as he was now, as she wanted him to be. She suddenly pushed him away and jumped out of bed.

'We are wasting time,' she told him. 'My yacht is in Montecarlo. We can cruise the Mediterranean for a week, just you and me alone. We both need a holiday. Let's not think about the future. Let's just have some time together and then you can come back. I won't put any obstacles in your way.' Arianne knew that after a week together there would be no need for obstacles. She picked up his jacket from the pile of clothes on the floor, and took his keys from his pocket. She faced him, fully aware of her nakedness and the effect it had on him.

'Now tell me where your passport is.'

He told her.

As their convoy drove away from the house, Arianne glanced at the huge gates closing behind them, and squeezed Paul's hand. A new, wonderful stage of her life had begun. She moved closer to him and rested her head on his shoulder. Paul pointed at the back of the driver's head.

'I don't give a damn,' she said, kissing him on the ear.

She didn't. As the convoy moved down Avenida Alvear, she couldn't care less about what anyone would say. They would talk, of course they would. Little else would be discussed at Malena's or Zou-Zou's dinner tables for weeks. The almighty Arianne had fallen for her employee.

It did not matter to her, not one bit. Not when they were about to spend first a week together, then as long as she dared to hope. Simon's wealth had weakened her own defences. Her money combined with her love would be irresistible.

They crossed Avenida Callao and were now heading towards Recoleta. She could see the tower of the Pilar church in the distance, its white and blue tiled top gleaming in the winter sun. Suddenly, a group of policemen diverted the traffic, and forced Arianne's convoy to turn into a side street, along the flank of the Alvear Palace Hotel. As they slowed down on the steep incline towards the River Plate, Arianne saw a procession coming up the road towards them. It was Corpus Christi day, a carefully observed religious event in Buenos Aires, and the full-size image of the Crucifixion carried by devout men surrounded by priests and nuns was just one of many to be seen around the city that day. The street was too narrow for the cars to bypass them, so they pulled to the side to allow the procession to continue towards the church.

As the nuns approached, Arianne saw their sun-tanned faces, but it was too late. The image of Christ crashed to the ground as the terrorists disguised as priests and nuns suddenly pulled their guns out of their wide sleeves.

'Look out!' The driver managed to shout. Paul pushed Arianne to the floor and fell on top of her. Unable to see, she could only hear the roar of machine guns and the shouting around her.

If Arianne's bodyguards had been less professional, the outcome would perhaps have been different. Three of them held the advance of the bogus policemen from the rear, while the others fired their automatic weapons at the guerrillas before they could break into Arianne's car and snatch her away. The gun battle went on for a short while, until the attackers ran towards their get-away cars.

Almost suffocated by Paul's weight, Arianne kept her eyes tightly shut until she heard the gunfire cease. Just as she was opening them, a shattering of glass cascaded on top of her and Paul, as one of the bodyguards smashed the window on her side to release the lock. The door was opened, and she could see the horror of the scene outside. What had been an elegant street just a moment ago had become a panorama of destruction. The marble shopfronts were scarred by bullets, and the smashed crucifix lay on the ground, surrounded by bleeding bodies. She could hear the police sirens in the distance, getting louder.

Paul did not move. The bodyguard pulled him up and laid him on the seat, his blood slowly seeping into the velvet upholstery. Free at last, Arianne knelt on the floor. The broken glass cut into her knees, but she did not feel it. She was staring at Paul's face. She knew that mask. For the second time in her life she was facing the dead body of a man she loved, and it was all her fault. She had forced him to come with her. Now she had nothing but her grief and her guilt.

She began to scream. She thought she would never stop.

37

LONDON
September 1988

Pandora flung the file down on her desk. She leaned back in her seat and closed her eyes. Every week her public relations agency sent her copies of press clippings relating either to the business or to herself, although the difference was becoming less and less apparent. 'The magic of Doyle'; 'Doyle bucks the trend'; 'Pandora Doyle and Ted Carson: the dynamic duo'. It went on and on, the copy on the financial pages sometimes as colourful as the gossip columns. At first it had been thrilling, but now she had to fight the temptation to dump the file into the wastepaper basket.

The business had grown beyond anyone's expectations, certainly her own. The licensing arrangements had been a great success, and 'Doyle' shops would soon be found in every major city in Britain. But — regardless of what the press hype efficiently organized by her PR agency said — the economic climate had begun to bite. The consumer boom was being curtailed by the government's efforts to reduce inflation; interest rates had started to climb, and mortgage repayments would soon trim down any disposable income. It had become necessary to run just to stay in the same place, and expansion into America, unlikely as it had seemed a few months ago, could now be the answer. No one was more eager than Ted for the move to take place.

It would mean raising further capital at a time when the dollar was on an upward trend against the pound. If the business in America did not perform as expected, it could jeopardize Pandora's home base as well. She would have to find suitable premises at once. Ted's offer of an American partnership solved both problems at a stroke, and her financial advisers had enthusiastically supported it. She knew she would not be able to delay indefinitely.

Pandora was aware of Ted's ulterior motives. Ever since

their affair began, he had relentlessly tried to intervene in her business, at first with friendly advice, and then through more determined moves. Earlier on, Pandora had told Ted about Arianne's role in setting up her company, and then she found out that he had approached Arianne through his New York bankers to buy her out of 'Doyle'. A major confrontation followed, although it proved unnecessary when Arianne's lawyers notified Ted that Mrs de la Force was not interested in his offer. Nevertheless, the episode made Pandora uncomfortably aware of a side of Ted she had disregarded until then.

The desire to own and to control everything around him was ingrained in his nature. What Ted was like had been clear to Pandora from the beginning, and she accepted that there had been an element of calculation on her side when they had begun their affair. Ted was a visible symbol of her achievement, an enviable scar to heal the wound left by Johnny, but she found herself in a better version of the same trap.

Unlike Johnny, Ted had no apparent trouble in a relationship with a woman who had her own interests. If Pandora had decided to play tennis during her marriage, Johnny would have told her that she was wasting her time because she was no good at it, then he would have stood behind her during her lessons, holding her arm and giving constant instructions until she stopped playing through lack of confidence. Ted was a bigger, more intelligent man. He would have been perfectly happy for Pandora to play tennis whenever she wanted, for as long as she wanted, provided that he owned the court and sat in the umpire's chair. Perhaps it was just a matter of not letting him buy the court.

Otherwise Ted was obviously very fond of her, and she was fond of him. There were no fireworks, but there were no storms either. Pandora found very few fireworks in her life at this point. Her work, which had started in a frenzy of excitement, was less and less a source of personal satisfaction. Her business was a much larger organization now, and she had been forced to delegate most of the jobs she enjoyed in order to concentrate on policy and financial decisions. Her days were now taken up by long meetings on financial matters, stock control, manufacturing and delivery schedules. She was simply supervising others doing what she had originally done herself. Her initial passion had imperceptibly given way to a sort of contentment. Perhaps it was inevitable, and there was no reason why contentment should not also be her aim in her personal life.

Ted's desire to please her was obvious, and tonight was yet another example. Pandora had talked him into sponsoring the forthcoming production of *Das Rheingold* at Covent Garden, and they had been asked to the Royal Box by Lord and Lady Woodfall, to see *L'Italiana in Algeri*. Lord Woodfall was one of the main fund raisers for the Opera, and he obviously knew this particular sponsor: two acts were as far as Ted's patience would go. Unfortunately, the sponsorship was in the name of the property development company, and Vlasos and the dreadful Melissa had also been invited.

Pandora stood up. It was time to go home and change.

The Rolls Royce turned into Floral Street, closely followed by a Bentley. Pandora fixed her eyes on the road ahead to avoid the gaze of the opera-goers on their way to the main entrance on Bow Street, caught by Ted Carson's opulent caravan.

Both cars stopped outside the discreet side entrance and the drivers let their passengers out. Pandora and Ted waited for a moment until Melissa managed to negotiate her voluminous skirts out of the car door, then they led the group into the small foyer where Lord and Lady Woodfall were waiting for them. Lord Woodfall shook hands with the men, introducing them to his wife, and Ted then introduced Pandora and Melissa.

'Aren't you Serena's daughter?' Lady Woodfall asked Pandora.

'Yes, I am. I still remember when Mummy and I went to stay with you, although I must have been very small.'

Lady Woodfall smiled.

'Your mother and I were at school together. Such a

long time ago. She was so beautiful. You look very like her.' Pandora knew she didn't, but either Lady Woodfall's memory was failing or she was adept in small talk. She thanked Lady Woodfall and held on to Lord Woodfall's arm as they began to climb the graceful stair winding its way around the foyer.

'What a handsome man,' Melissa said appreciatively, staring at the silver-framed portrait on the wall showing a distinguished middle-aged man in a light-grey double-breasted suit as they walked past it. A brief silence ensued, broken by Lord Woodfall.

'He's Sir John Tooley, our last Director. We owe him a great deal,' he said, clearly uncertain of how to respond.

Vlasos cast a dagger-like glance at Melissa.

'He's probably not rich enough for you,' he barked.

'I *adore* Rossini,' Lady Woodfall immediately interjected to no one in particular, in a voice loud enough to drown any other conversation, and they all agreed that Rossini was wonderful. A liveried porter opened the double door facing them on the landing, and they entered the antechamber to the Royal Box. A table for six was already laid in the middle of the room and a waiter stood by a small round table in the corner, where a drinks tray and glasses had been set out for them.

Pandora sensed Ted's disappointment at the modest elegance of the room. Melissa's reaction was plain to see. She had obviously expected something out of Imperial Vienna, not a room reminiscent of a small drawing room in a provincial hotel suite. Her eyes were fixed in disgust on the electric fire in the fireplace at one end of the room.

'It's rather . . . charming,' she said finally, with more tact than Pandora had come to expect from her. She walked to the fireplace and admired herself in the mirror above the mantelpiece, quickly retouching her hair.

'What would you like to drink?' asked Lord Woodfall.

'I would *adore* a glass of champagne,' Melissa gushed. Lord Woodfall glanced at the drinks tray. A waiter rushed out, probably on his way to the foyer bar.

'I'm sorry, but we don't seem to have any here. It won't be a moment.'

'You could have given her ginger ale, she wouldn't be able to tell the difference,' Vlasos laughed loudly as Lord Woodfall handed him a whisky.

'I've heard that your garden is glorious,' Pandora said to Lady Woodfall, who gratefully launched into an explanation of her restoration work in the last few years.

Champagne glass in hand, Melissa joined them, and the conversation took off at last, the men on one side of the room discussing business while the women exchanged views first on gardens, and then interior decoration. Lady Woodfall praised Pandora on her remarkable achievement.

'You girls are all doing something worthwhile these days,' she said, 'it's simply wonderful. I'm ashamed to say that the only thing I do is collect porcelain. What do you do, Melissa dear?'

'I collect alimony,' Melissa replied sweetly.

Luckily the first bell rang out.

'I think we ought to take our seats now,' Lord Woodfall said to the company at large. 'We'll have dinner here during the interval.'

'Is there only one interval?' Melissa asked anxiously.

'I'm afraid so, but we will have just one course. Everybody seems to be on a diet these days,' Lady Woodfall smiled. Her hopes of a triumphal stroll through the Crush Bar dashed, Melissa sulkily followed Lady Woodfall and Pandora into the box just as the second bell rang. At last they all sat down, the guests quickly studying their programmes to get some idea of the plot. The lights went down and the overture began. After a while, Pandora saw that Vlasos was losing his hopeless fight to keep his eyes open. She decided to keep a regular check on Ted. At least he was within reach of her elbow.

'Marvellous, just marvellous,' Melissa exclaimed as the waiter served her coffee. The conversation had focused again on the opera.

'Most enjoyable, the singers are very good,' added Ted. Pandora hoped he would not expand on his comment.

Lady Woodfall launched into an explanation of the

merits of Marilyn Horne's voice when the door suddenly opened, bringing her monologue to a halt.

A man in his early thirties walked in. He was wearing a plain cotton suit and no tie, but he did not seem ill at ease among the black-tied company.

'I'm sorry to barge in like this, Uncle Jack, but I saw you in the distance and I thought that I ought to say hello. I hope you still remember me.'

'Andrew! What a surprise!' Lord Woodfall said cheerfully, introducing him to their guests. A waiter brought a chair, and the man sat next to Lady Woodfall.

'Andrew left London a few years ago,' she explained. 'What are you doing these days, dear?'

The newcomer smiled.

'I'm running a bird sanctuary in the Seychelles. Most unprofitable, but very rewarding.' He pulled out a tie from his pocket and showed it to his aunt. 'I was looking more respectable earlier on, but it is very hot where I am sitting.'

'I know. It can get frightfully hot in Covent Garden sometimes. It's such a relief when the curtain opens and there is that wonderful rush of cold air,' Lady Woodfall said sympathetically.

Andrew laughed. 'You have to be in the front stalls to feel it. I'm afraid I can no longer afford seats as good as yours. My seat is so high up you almost need an oxygen mask.'

Ted, sitting next to Lady Woodfall, turned towards the newcomer.

'Why did you choose the Seychelles?' he asked. 'Isn't it a God-forsaken part of the world?'

The bell rang, and Andrew stood up. 'Precisely for that reason,' he replied. 'I used to do something completely different after Cambridge, but I became more and more involved with environmental work, until I realized it was really what I wanted to do. It's too long a story, and I have to climb back up to my seat.' He turned to his aunt. 'I'm here for a while. I'll come and see you at home, if I may,' he said, then kissed her goodbye. He waved absently at the rest of the group, as though he scarcely noticed them, and left.

Obviously amused, Lord Woodfall shook his head.

'My nephew is an unusual chap. He used to work for me at the bank, but then he decided to go away and live in the middle of nowhere.'

'He probably came across Melissa at a party,' Vlasos said from the other end of the table. Eyes glaring, Melissa rushed through the polished mahogany door at one side of the fireplace, and disappeared into the lavatory. She came back a moment later, her lip gloss as shiny as the satisfaction on her face.

'Now I can say I've been to the Queen's loo!' she told Pandora. 'It's very quaint, all panelled and ancient. You ought to see it.' The discreet coat of translucent powder on Lady Woodfall's cheeks was not enough to conceal her sudden blush. She instantly stood up, plunged into a quick explanation of the plot of the final act, and led them all back into the box.

Pandora cast her eyes for the last time over the neatly typed report and accounts covering the last quarter, then signed the short covering note clipped to the front of the document. It was a slightly warmer variation of the 'Please find enclosed . . .' type of letter she signed many times a day. With reluctance, she had given up her attempts to develop a more personal correspondence with Arianne. They were occasionally in touch over the phone, but their conversations after Venice had made it clear that Arianne was wary of talking about anything other than business matters. It was almost as if, having shown too much of herself then, she was now busily rebuilding the impenetrable wall around her.

Pandora regretted it. She owed so much to Arianne, and she hoped that the bond between them would not fade away. She glanced at the letter again, then opened a drawer and took out a small sheet of her personal stationery. 'I hope everything is well. I'd love to hear from you,' she wrote. She attached her message to the top of the report, placed it in her 'Out' tray, and carried on signing the rest of her post.

38

FORMENTOR, MAJORCA
July 1975

It was mid-afternoon, and the hotel was quiet. Most of the guests had retired to their rooms for their after-lunch siesta. There were a few people milling around the lobby, but the bar was empty. The barman was polishing glasses at the far end of the counter, and Charles Murdoch tapped on it to catch his attention.

'A beer, and make sure it's cold,' Charles snapped at him. The barman was surprised by the order. Until then Mr Murdoch had always asked for champagne. He poured Charles an ice-cold 'San Miguel' and went back to his tasks. Experienced barmen know when to leave their customers alone.

Charles was deep in thought. He was down to his last three hundred dollars, and there was no prey in sight. He could get a refund for his return ticket to New York, but he didn't like the idea of giving up his escape route. The idea of selling his gold watch was out of the question.

He now bitterly regretted having annoyed that German woman. He had met her at the casino in Montecarlo, where her diamonds had caught his eye. He did not mind the fact that the diamonds sparkled against lizard-like skin, nor that the woman's waistline had become a long-forgotten memory; he was prepared to service a brick wall if the rewards were right. It had been easy enough to pick her up. They had spent a few days in Montecarlo, which had been ruinous for him since he was paying his own hotel bills, but it had been worth it. The woman had asked him to come with her to her villa in Formentor, giving him a chance to go for the kill.

He had learned early in his career that, in order to make his efforts worthwhile, the last thing to do was to mention money in the early stages of an affair. It put women on their guard. It was far more productive to wait until the right moment came along, when the illusion of

431

a relationship had been created, and then mention some worthy educational project he would undertake, were it not for his limited resources. A year in Florence studying restoration of frescoes seemed to be particularly effective with his clients. Like him, they knew nothing about it, but it probably made them feel good to sponsor his cause. A generous cheque usually followed his plea for help. After showing more than adequate gratitude, he always made it clear that the money was a loan, to be paid back as soon as his circumstances allowed.

If the target proved unresponsive, then he relied on his second line of attack. He travelled with an assortment of jeweller's tools and paste diamonds in various sizes and shapes; he would substitute some of them for the woman's jewellery before parting company. It could be even more lucrative than cultural sponsorship at times, but it could also lead to trouble with the police, and Charles wanted a quiet life. His problem was that his understanding of a quiet life was a very expensive one, and his money never seemed to last for long.

Things had progressed smoothly with the German woman, and by their second night together in Formentor he endeavoured to bring his performance to an even higher standard than usual, in preparation for his request for educational assistance. He had been too successful. Brought to a frenzy of pleasure, the woman began to shriek, waking her chihuahua from his sleep in one corner of the bedroom. Believing that his mistress was being attacked, the dog leaped on them and sunk his teeth into Charles' thigh. Blinded by pain and rage, he had grabbed the rat-like creature and flung it away, but he miscalculated his strength. The dog flew out of the first-floor window, landing in the swimming pool below. Nothing worse happened to the damn animal other than shock and a slight chill, but the woman became hysterical and threw Charles out of the villa on the spot. He had now been in the hotel for nearly two fruitless weeks. The real money was in the villas nearby, and their occupants seemed to keep to themselves.

Eager for anything to take his mind off his problems,

he began to listen to the conversation between one of the waiters and the barman. He understood a little Spanish from his early days in New York, when he had been surrounded by Puerto-Rican neighbours, and managed to pick up a word here and there, enough to guess that it might be useful to join in.

'What are you talking about?' he asked.

'Pedro was just saying that a huge yacht has anchored outside the Cape. Apparently the world's richest widow is on board,' the barman told him.

Charles stood up. It was nearly five o'clock, and he had to change. There was no time to lose. He signed his bill and left the bar.

The sight of Cape Formentor, the sheer white rock faces rising to the sky from the vivid blue waters, is one of the wonders of the Mediterranean. But for Arianne, lying in a deck chair on her yacht a quarter of a mile away, it was just a fuzzy outline.

She was waiting for another day to go by. Since leaving Buenos Aires after Paul's death weeks ago, she had lived in a daze of Scotch and Valium. She was in no state to face Gloria and Nana in Cap d'Ail, and had flown directly to her yacht. When the captain had asked for their destination, she had tried to focus on the nautical chart and pointed at Cyprus, furthest away from where they were. Once they reached the island, she looked at the map again. Majorca was at the other end of the chart now, so that was where she wanted to go next.

She would never come ashore, ever. The shore was a place for pain, and she wanted to spend the rest of her life like this, floating aimlessly between sea and sky. Radio and telex messages were brought to her daily from the bridge. She would crumple them in her hand and throw them into the sea without reading them, watching them sink slowly in the wake of the yacht. Unlike her memories of Paul.

She noticed that the outline of the coast was becoming clearer. Time for another pill. She struggled to get it out of the box and took a sip from the whisky tumbler by her side to wash it down. It was nearly empty, but a steward immediately refilled it. Good man, Arianne thought. It was nice to have good men around her. She lay back in her chair. It would soon be time for something. Lunch, dinner, she wasn't sure, and she didn't care. She felt the wind on her face. She liked it. The wind blew things away.

'Blow, blow, the wind blows,' she told the nice man nearby.

'Yes, madam,' the steward said impassively.

She raised her eyes towards the sky, but the bright light made her dizzy and she closed them. She could hear the wind, only the wind. And then she heard something else, someone shouting. She opened her eyes again and saw the steward rushing to the other side of the deck.

'Help!' It was a man's voice, but she couldn't tell where it came from. The steward threw a lifebelt overboard, and two sailors joined him to pull at the rope. After a moment, she saw a man climb on board. He was wearing only very brief white swimming trunks, and he was coughing up water.

Her sailors helped the man to his feet, holding him until he seemed able to stand on his own. The man looked at Arianne, then staggered across the deck and knelt by her side.

'I'm Charles Murdoch,' he told her. 'I can't tell you how grateful I am. You've saved my life.' He meant it. The boatman he had hired on the beach to take him to the tip of the cape had warned him that the tide would be strong, and his plight had become more real than he had intended. He was an exceptional swimmer, but it had been a close call.

'It's nice to save a man's life. *Very* nice,' Arianne mumbled, taking a long sip from her glass. Charles stared at her. The woman was drunk, but even so she was ravishing. It could be his lucky day after all.

But she wasn't saying anything, she was just staring at him with glazed eyes. Charles decided to stand up to give her a chance to appreciate how tall and handsome he was, then he collapsed into the deck chair next to her. It would be dangerous to give the impression that he had already recovered enough to be sent back to shore.

434

'I'm still a bit weak. I'm sorry if I'm delaying your cruise,' he said apologetically.

Arianne waved her hand dismissively.

'Don't worry, I'm not in a hurry. I've plenty of time. Nothing but time. All the time in the world . . .'

She felt euphoric. Here was a nice man by her side, a man from the sea. He came from the sea, and he would soon go back to the sea. Like a fish. She enjoyed talking to a fish.

'You're a fish!' she suddenly giggled. Charles forced himself to laugh. She liked his laugh. He was a friend.

'Maybe,' he replied. 'But you are a truly lovely lady,' he added.

'Yes, I'm lovely. *Veeery* lovely. So lovely that any man that gets close to me drops dead. Don't drop dead, fish,' she said, helping herself to another pill. Charles caught her hand to stop her. The woman was clearly mad, but he didn't want her to fall asleep just yet.

'Those are no good for you. You should have something to eat,' he said, taking the pill away.

'You care for me, fish. A caring fish, I like that. I have plenty of pills in my cabin, though. Lots of wonderful pills.' Arianne waved her hand towards the portholes a few yards away from them. 'But you're right, we should have something to eat.' She tried to stand up but she stumbled. Charles put his arm around her waist and helped her regain her balance.

'Why do you say that men who get close to you drop dead?' he asked as they made slow progress towards the dining room. He was almost dragging her along. He knew little about her, and he panicked for a moment. She couldn't be Mafia, could she? She didn't sound Italian or American, but it was better to find out more about her before going too far.

'Because they do, fish, they do. The first one . . . the first one had an accident, the second one died of disappointment, and the third one . . . the third one . . .' she began to cry, then almost as suddenly, she started to laugh. 'It's funny to die of disappointment, isn't it? I told him that I couldn't have children, and he died. Right there. Just like that.'

Charles half-listened to her drivel. The woman stank of whisky. She was not going to make it through dinner, and he could not afford for her to fall asleep, as she was likely to do any minute now. It was still light enough for him to be taken to shore as soon as she collapsed and her staff took her to bed. He had seen the motor boat on board. He had to act now. It would make all the difference in the morning.

As they walked past the door leading to her cabin, he pulled her close to him and began to kiss her. She offered no resistance. After a moment, he picked her up in his arms and carried her inside.

The sun poured through the windows of the cabin, and the polished silver frame around the photograph on the bedside table shone in the light. It was the first thing Arianne saw when she opened her eyes. The figures were in sharp focus for the first time in ages. She had probably forgotten to take her pills last night. She stretched her hand towards the drawer when she heard a noise next to her. She turned around and saw a naked man quietly snoring by her side.

She jumped out of bed and realized she was naked as well. She had no idea who he was, nor could she remember anything about last night, other than a vague recollection of talking to someone about fish. But the scene was eloquent enough, and the thought of a stranger touching her made her feel sick. She rushed to the bathroom, turned on the shower full force, and scrubbed herself until her skin burned. She stood under the shower for a long time, the water mixing with her tears.

Arianne came out at last and returned to the cabin. She did not look at the bed; she could not bear the sight. She could not bear the thought of her last weeks either, of what she had become. She had seen the yacht as her cocoon, but it had become her jail. She had to get out of here. She quickly threw on some clothes, picked up her address book, and rushed out of the cabin. She ran to the drawing room and made a couple of ship-to-shore calls. Then she rang the bridge, and asked the captain to come to see her without delay.

'I'm leaving now,' she told him as soon as he entered the room. 'Please have the boat ready to take me to shore immediately. I won't be coming back. I'll stay with some friends at Son Sard until tomorrow, and I've asked for the plane to pick me up at Palma. Take the yacht back to Montecarlo.' She paused for a moment, then turned her face from him.

'I had a ... guest last night. Once I'm gone, wake him up and take him to shore.' She hated herself for having to say the words, for her unnecessary humiliation.

'Yes, Mrs de la Force. Is there anything else?'

'No, that's all.' She noticed that the captain had not needed to ask where the guest was.

'Mummy, look!' Gloria shouted before diving off the edge of the pool. Arianne was soaked by the splash and laughed.

'You're a little pest, and I'm going to catch you!' she yelled. Gloria was delighted at the prospect of the chase, and Arianne was about to dive in after her when she saw the maid approaching.

'There's a gentleman to see you, Madame. His name is Charles Murdoch. He says it is about Mr de la Force.'

The man's name meant nothing to Arianne. She had spent ten days in Paris catching up with business matters before joining Gloria and Nana in the villa at Cap d'Ail a few days ago, and he had probably been sent by the Paris office, although anyone there should know better than to refer to Simon after all these years.

'I'm sorry, darling, I have to go into the house for a minute.' Gloria continued to splash as hard as she could as Arianne put on her beach wrap.

'Show him to the study. I'll be there in a moment,' she told the maid.

The man was already sitting down, but he stood up and held out his hand when she came in. He smiled broadly. There was something proprietorial about his attitude, almost as if he were the host and she were the guest. Other than the fact that he was very handsome, his face meant nothing to her at first, but then she froze. He noticed it.

'Hi! I'm the fish. I'm glad you remember me,' Charles said. 'It's a pity you don't want to shake hands, but I can understand.'

'How did you know where to find me?' Arianne asked frostily.

He smiled again, and she was repelled. Her instinct was to leave the room at once, but she knew that he must be here for a reason.

'I'm a very persistent man. I have my ways.' His eye fell on the drinks tray at the corner. He walked over and poured himself a Campari and soda.

'Would you like anything?'

'I don't drink during the day.'

He raised his eyebrows, and then returned to his seat.

'I suppose you must be wondering why I'm here. It's very simple. I think we ought to take up where we left off. It was a very pleasant night, and it would be as much in your interest as in mine.'

She went to the door and opened it.

'I think it's better if you leave now. I'll call my security staff and they'll see you out.'

Charles sat back and took a long sip of his drink before replying.

'I don't think you would like your servants to hear what I have to say.'

The old fear took over, but Arianne instantly dismissed it. He could not possibly have found out about Ruben's murder, but she was curious now. She closed the door and went across the room to sit behind her desk, as far from him as possible.

'I knew you would be sensible,' he said. He made himself comfortable before continuing.

'I have to confess that I had never come across a woman like you before, and our conversation intrigued me. I found out who you were, and decided it would be useful to do some more research. I went to Madrid, and had a most interesting time reading old newspapers at the Argentine College library in the University. I found out that your

438

husband died of a heart attack on your wedding night. From my experiences with you the other night, I can understand that.'

Arianne was enraged by his coarseness.

'I read the Argentine papers at the time, and there's nothing you can tell me that I don't already know. If that's all you have to say, there is no point in continuing this conversation. I would like you to leave now.'

'What I've got to say won't take very long.' He took another gulp of his drink, then looked at her long and hard. 'Please have a little patience.' She found his politeness even more unbearable than his attempts at intimacy.

'Finding out about your husband's death threw your comment about one of the men close to you dying of disappointment into a very different light. You said it happened when you told him that you were unable to have children. It made sense to me that the only man who could have been so affected by the news was the one who married you.' Arianne hoped her face showed nothing. She couldn't see what he was getting at, but she was becoming anxious.

'I can understand one of the world's richest men being bitterly disappointed by the news,' the man went on. 'According to his obituary, he was not a young man, and he had no children. As his wife, you were his heir. Having seen your yacht, and having read about the size of his business, I can also understand why you didn't want to disappoint him *before* the wedding. It's just my guess, but I would say you only told him after he had married you.'

Arianne was alarmed now. He was wrong about her reasons, but he was clever. 'Get to the point,' she said impatiently.

Charles glanced at his cheap watch. He still regretted the loss of his old one, but it had been a wise decision to sell it to pay for his expenses in Madrid.

'It will take me only a minute to finish. It cost me some money, but I then consulted a Spanish lawyer who is very experienced in Argentine law. It seems that a marriage where one of the parties withholds information relevant to the intentions of the marriage from the other is not

439

valid in Argentina. The creation of a family is considered one of the intentions of marriage there, and your husband married you in that belief, although you knew it wasn't possible. That means your married is void, and your husband's estate should have gone to his sisters, not to you. I imagine that they would be interested in my little discovery, but I would prefer to deal with you direct.'

Arianne's immediate reaction was to stand up and throw him out, but she sensed that he was probably right about the legalities. He wouldn't be stupid enough to start something like this without being certain of his ground, and a medical check-up would prove that she was barren. But there was no evidence that she hadn't told Simon about it before their marriage. There were no witnesses, and it would be her word, her almighty word against Simon's sisters, seconded by this rat, assuming that any lawyer would want to represent them. They had no money, and therefore little prospect of getting their hands on hers.

She relaxed a little. In a moment he would be out on the street, where he belonged. She started to say 'Get out!' but the words never came. She had remembered something else.

There *were* witnesses. Hundreds of them. Her mind raced back to their wedding party, when Simon had told whoever cared to listen that they were going to have a child as soon as possible, boasting about the son she would soon give him. They all knew Simon's overwhelming pride. He would never have boasted about anything that would lead to a loss of face. Her lie would still have to be proven in court, but the evidence was strong enough to tempt a greedy lawyer into taking up the case. The first thing any lawyer would do was check up on her background. If this man had been able to find out what he had merely by reading newspapers and having a consultation with a Madrid lawyer, she could not afford to have detectives in Paris and Rio digging up the rest.

'How much do you want?' She could pay him off.

Charles left his seat and came to Arianne. He sat on her desk and crossed his legs with nonchalance, as if he were

440

at home. Arianne wished she could wipe that awful smile off his face.

'It's not exactly money I need. My price is that we spend the rest of our lives together. From now on I can't afford to lose sight of you. As you said, men who get close to you drop dead. I'm not suggesting for a second that you might be tempted to take a contract out on me after this conversation, but it would be much more unlikely if I publicly become your live-in lover. If I were to die in suspicious circumstances, you would then be the prime suspect. But this is a morbid conversation, and completely unnecessary. Let's say that I like your life-style, and I would love to share it with you. We've got on very well so far.' He saw the flash in her eyes. 'Don't worry, I wouldn't want you to do anything against your wishes. I'll live my life discreetly in that respect, and I'll never embarrass you. But I want your answer now. There's a flight to Buenos Aires tonight; I wouldn't want to miss it.'

His price rocked her. Even at arm's length, she wasn't going to spend the rest of her life with this vermin. She needed time to find a way out.

'I'm amazed at your audacity. I've never heard such rubbish in my life and . . .' He interrupted her.

'We are wasting time. You have an hour to decide . . . I'll be waiting for your call at the bar at the Miramar.' He stood up and walked to the door. 'If I were you, I would think twice before making inquiries,' he said before leaving the room.

Her hand went to the telephone as soon as the door closed behind him, but she paused for a minute, then dropped it back in its cradle. He was right. She couldn't make any inquiries with anyone in Buenos Aires without setting off suspicions, followed by rumours. Once the validity of her marriage was questioned, it would only be a matter of time before the de la Force family decided to try their luck in court.

The option was to hand over Simon's estate to his family now. But even if she were prepared to consider losing everything she owned, she could not afford the consequences. Once she relinquished control of the estate, the lawyer retained by Simon would then release the information about her to the Brazilian police. Arianne would not only lose her money; she would go to jail, and she couldn't face losing Gloria. Simon's letter with its threat of disclosure had originally trapped her for ten years. Those years would soon run out, but now the same threat had been extended indefinitely by the possibility of her past being dug up. She was trapped, and she knew it.

She sat in silence for a long while, until she picked up the phone at last and asked the operator to connect her to the Miramar. The conversation that followed took less than a minute. She was to pay the price for many years.

Nana locked the door to her room, then took a suitcase from under her bed, and began to pack her belongings. Nana could not understand why Arianne had allowed this man Charles to move in with them a year ago. She did not like him, not one bit, and Arianne did not seem to like him either. They were together in public, but they lived totally separate lives at home. Arianne had not loved Simon, but at least Nana could understand why she had married him. This Charles was nothing but a good-looking leech.

He was worse than that. He was the worst thing anyone could be in Nana's eyes. He upset Gloria. Not by his actions, because he hardly took any notice of the child. In fact, he seemed to go out of his way to avoid her, but ever since his appearance Gloria had become impossible, and Arianne had begun to avoid her as well. It was difficult to deal with a child who constantly shouted that she hated her mother and the man she had chosen to live with, but sending Gloria away to boarding school in Switzerland, as Arianne had just done, was cruel. Nana had learned to respect Arianne for her loyalty and her kindness. But now she had chosen to send Gloria away, and the only explanation was that Arianne wanted to make her own life as easy as possible.

Nana knew that Gloria would grow up away from her now. The child was as effectively gone from her as her own daughter was, and Nana's life had become simply a matter of waiting for time to pass. She had told Arianne a moment ago that she wanted to live somewhere else, away from them all. Arianne had refused at first, but she had eventually relented, and had asked Nana where she would like to go.

Her choice had surprised Arianne. She did not want to live in Paris, or even in France. There were too many memories there. Nana chose 'La Encantada', Arianne's holiday home in Punta del Este. The hills and the sea reminded Nana of her childhood home, and she could live there on her own most of the time. Arianne assured her that she would make a point of going to Punta del Este with Gloria during her Christmas school holidays, which coincided with the beginning of the Argentine summer.

She would still be able to see her granddaughter, and she would live on her own, away from this madness. If it weren't for the fact that she blamed her for Gloria's unhappiness, Nana could almost feel sorry for Arianne. But she had chosen her life. She had chosen her husband, and now she had chosen this man. Arianne was a strong woman, and life had put her in a position where she could choose whatever and whoever she wanted. She had made the wrong choice, but it was her privilege.

LONDON
November 1988

Pandora had had a particularly tough day at work. There were distribution problems in the Midlands, the postal strike was a nuisance, and a large shipment of her new chintz collection made in Taiwan had been ruined, either in transit or at a port somewhere. She had been screaming into the phone at some man at the other end of the world when exhausted, and fed-up, she had finally slammed the receiver down. It was seven o'clock: the Friends of the Earth lecture on their work to save the seals in the North Sea, their immune system weakened by industrial pollution and now struck down by a virus, had begun at 6.30. If she hurried, she could still catch the end of it.

Ted was in New York, and his absence made a difference: he was a reassuring, comforting presence. He could also be overwhelming and over-protective, but she could live with that. As she scanned every aspect of their relationship, she was convinced it was a good one, and she should count herself lucky. But, in spite of her reluctance to admit it, she was glad to be on her own when he was away. Maybe I just needed a breathing space, she thought as she parked her car near University College.

By the time she walked into the building, the lecture had just finished, and people were coming out of the lecture hall into the foyer. She was on her way to the exit when someone tapped her on the shoulder. She turned around.

'Hi, remember me? I'm Andrew Macadam. I met you at Covent Garden a few months ago. You were having dinner with my aunt and uncle. I'm sorry, but I can't remember your name.'

Pandora had not really taken any notice of him at the Opera, although she remembered his exuberant interruption of a stilted evening. Many people glowed with vitality and health, but his was not the kind that came from sweaty sessions on Nautilus machines and tanning salons in a City basement, but from the sun and sea. His eyes were the same faded blue as his jeans, his lean frame did not require shoulder padding, and he was very attractive.

'I'm Pandora Doyle. I remember you, but you looked different then.'

He laughed.

'Other than the fact that I was wearing my only suit, I can't think why. Maybe you've begun to see people differently now.'

'Maybe,' she agreed. Perhaps he was right.

'I have to go back to the Seychelles tomorrow morning. Lack of time makes one bolder. You look so great that I would ask you to dinner right now, but it is too soon, we hardly know each other, and you would be forced to pretend that I am a nuisance. Why don't we talk for at least five minutes, and then I'll ask? Tell me why a smartly dressed, beautiful woman comes to dull lectures about seals.'

He had the engaging directness of a child, with none of the arrogance that usually accompanies good looks. His admiration rang true, and Pandora felt flattered.

'I am a sponsor of this project,' she told him.

'Rich, attractive, and with a conscience; you are very unusual.'

'Why are *you* here, and what makes you think I'm rich?' Pandora replied, aware of her defensiveness for no apparent reason. At worst, he was just being candid.

'I used to share a flat long ago with the guy who gave the lecture. Why do I think you are rich? It's the way you stand; you stand like a rich person. When I was in banking, I could work out the exact worth of anyone, give or take a million, by the way they walked. I haven't done it for a long time, so I am out of practice. I haven't seen you move yet, but stationary . . .' He crossed his arms and looked at her in mock concentration. 'I would put you in the five to ten million league. Just how rich are you anyway?'

Pandora felt distinctly uncomfortable, then annoyed. The question was much too personal for a ten-minute acquaintance, and she decided to end the conversation there and then.

'I haven't got the faintest idea, and it's none of your business anyway,' she replied coolly.

'You *are* rich, then, I knew it,' Andrew laughed. 'What a pity, that means you are probably a complicated person. Still, we can have a simple dinner.'

'Why should I have dinner with you? I don't know anything about you.'

'A very good reason to have dinner together. Then I can tell you all about myself. I left London five years ago, but there must still be a good Chinese place around here, discreet lights, music from the mysterious East, decent food, bill under ten pounds. Do you have any suggestions?'

The conversation reminded her of her early days in London, when most people she knew had very little money. The unexpected invitation suddenly appealed to her, adding an innocent touch of spice to an otherwise dreary day. It would be fun to listen to his story, and then she would never see him again.

'Not under ten pounds,' Pandora replied. 'I don't think we could eat anywhere much that cheaply, unless your story is very short. They'll throw us out because they will want the table long before the end. Can you stretch the budget? Otherwise I can pay.'

'Don't be deceived by my walk; I *really* don't have much money. Still, I don't take money from women, even London millionairesses. How about going Dutch?' he asked.

'It's a deal,' said Pandora.

'Where are we going?'

'Well, I don't know any cheap Chinese restaurants any more, but I know a nice Indian one. It's the only Indian restaurant with an Austrian décor, and the food isn't bad. It's called the "Moti Mahal". It's in Chelsea, but I've got my car here. I'm parked in Russell Square.'

'Sounds fine. Let's go,' Andrew said cheerfully.

As they left the building, Pandora thought of Ted. For God's sake, we are only having dinner, she told herself, half-listening to Andrew's comments about the lecture. They reached her car. Her black 911 Porsche was one of the prides of her life, but now it seemed too ostentatious. Andrew got in without comment, and she sensed that the car had just not registered with him. Some people don't react to things because they don't know what they are, others because they just don't care. Long ago, she used to know people like that.

She started driving down Southampton Row. Andrew was too tall for the car and his leg was almost touching the gear shift, his hand resting on his thigh, his long brown fingers slightly spread over the top, and Pandora felt ill at ease, too conscious about his presence for her comfort. She forced herself to speak to break the mood.

'So, where are you now?' she asked, glancing at him out of the corner of her eye.

He smiled.

'I was saving my story for later, but I can start now if you want. We have enough time to make it worthwhile.'

The narrow gap in the seats kept them apart, but he moved slightly and their shoulders touched briefly, no more than a second. The air around Pandora felt suffocatingly close. Luckily she had to concentrate on weaving her way through the traffic around Trafalgar Square.

'I left the bank five years ago. I realized that we were all either trying to get rich quick to be able to do something else after we were burned out, or trying to stab each other in the back to reach the top. I did not want to be at the top, and what I wanted did not require that much money anyway. My dream was cheaper than a farm in Wiltshire and expensive schools for children I don't even have.'

'What was this dream of yours?' Pandora asked. She swerved to avoid an idiotic motorcyclist, and her hand touched his leg as she changed gear. For an instant, all her senses were on the outside edge of that left hand. She stared ahead, holding the wheel tightly, and drove straight on down the Mall, the huge flags on either side waving gently in the night breeze.

'I was always interested in birds as a child. So I packed in my job, sold my flat, bought the whole collection of Penguin Classics, and took myself off to the Seychelles. I own a little hotel on one of the islands, I'm writing a book on tropical birds, and I work on bird conservation with a small team of great people. I don't need something like

447

this,' he said, pointing at Buckingham Palace, 'and I would have probably lost my job by now, anyway. Many of my friends did a year ago, after the "Big Bang" went wrong.' Pandora remembered the Stock Market crash, and briefly wondered about Johnny. He had suspended his alimony payments as soon as her name began to appear in the papers. Possibly that was the reason, but Pandora didn't want to find out.

'But aren't you bored?' She was genuinely curious now.

'Boredom is having nothing to do, or doing something you don't like. I have plenty to keep me busy, and I love it. It doesn't make me much money, but that doesn't mean it's boring. The people around here,' he nodded towards the Eaton Square terraces that they were passing, 'must be bored far more often than I am. They don't have to mend their own roofs.'

'It sounds rather self-indulgent to me. It must be a very pleasant life, but does it give you any sense of achievement?' Andrew looked at her sharply.

'Probably not in the sense you mean, but we've been able to reintroduce the Black Paradise Flycatcher, which was almost extinct when I arrived, and there's a lot more to do. I work fourteen hours a day, but I never use a telephone.' His rebuke chastened Pandora, and she said nothing for a while.

At last they turned off the Kings Road into Smith Street, and miraculously she found a parking space in a cul-de-sac near the restaurant. She was glad to get out of the car, to put some space between them as soon as possible. She started to walk towards the restaurant when she felt Andrew's hand on her arm.

'I'm sorry if I sounded angry,' he said gently. She smiled.

'And I'm sorry for sounding dismissive,' she replied, then moved ahead to avoid his eyes. They walked into the restaurant, but they couldn't get much further than the bar. A crowd of young men in pin-stripe suits and their mini-skirted dates blocked their way, loudly ordering white wine. The manager saw her and came over.

'Miss Doyle, you haven't booked, and there won't be a

table for at least another forty minutes. I am so sorry.' The man wrung his hands.

She almost didn't hear him. Andrew was standing behind her, their bodies pressed together by the crowd, his warmth so near to her skin, his breath on her neck. Aware of nothing else, she did not move immediately, then turned around and made an effort to look at him, in spite of her confusion.

'I live around the corner. We could go home and have a drink, and then come back in forty minutes.'

'Fine,' Andrew said. Nothing else.

They walked towards St Leonard's Terrace without saying anything. As they turned the corner he took her hand, holding it tightly. They reached her gate. Andrew stopped and glanced at the front of the house. The wistaria was bare for winter, and she wished he could have seen it in full bloom. He stared at her house for a moment.

'Not bad,' he told her admiringly.

'Your dream was a tropical island, mine was a house in St Leonard's Terrace.

'Mine is cheaper.'

'Mine is easier to get to from work,' Pandora said, standing outside the door and pretending to search for her keys. Her mind clicked into focus as she stopped talking, and she was suddenly filled with apprehension. She didn't know Andrew at all, and she had been carried away. This had never happened to her before. She forced herself to think of Ted, but it made no difference. Then she felt Andrew's hands on her shoulders, and she raised her eyes.

'I think you should open the door,' he said at last, holding her gaze.

They walked in and faced each other in the dim light coming through the open door. She did not dare to close it, but Andrew pushed it shut and they were in darkness, each of them as aware of the other as if in broad daylight, the space between their bodies almost palpable.

They remained still for a moment, the silence only broken by their breathing. Then his arms were around her, his lips on hers.

*   *   *

The ringing of the phone filled the room, and Pandora woke up. She stretched her arm to pick it up; she had no idea of the time, only that the sun was pouring through the window. She also noticed that Andrew was gone.

She picked up the receiver. She thought it was her morning call, but it was Tessa, her assistant. Her shrill voice was the last thing Pandora wanted to hear.

'Pandora, are you all right? Mr Thomas is already here!'

'I'm sorry, there was a burglar alarm going all night, and I haven't had much sleep. I probably didn't hear the phone earlier. I'll be there in a moment.' She put the phone down, turned to the other side of the bed, and touched the hollow in his pillow. Only then did she see the piece of paper by the bedside. 'Flying back this morning. Address on back. Come on the next plane. We will have all the time in the world.'

She didn't want all the time in the world, she wanted *him*. Everything she was or wanted to be had been shaken by their few hours together, everything she owned a poor substitute for what she had found. It had not been a revelation but the confirmation of a certainty, sensed from the moment they had sat next to each other in her car. She went through the day as if it were happening to somebody else, remembering Andrew and their time together, fighting the temptation to take the next plane to find him.

Yet then there was another day, and then another, all of them filled with things to do, people to see, decisions to be made. And Ted was back.

Pandora's longing grew weaker day by day. At first she was able to force her mind away from thoughts of Andrew for a few moments, then a few hours, until eventually she knew that it was just a wonderful, fading memory. Real life was different, and she had worked too hard to find her place in it. Dreams could be dangerous.

40

PUNTA DEL ESTE
September 1988

It was a cold September morning in spite of the sunshine, and Arianne raised her collar. The men lowered the coffin into the freshly dug grave in the Maldonado Cemetery and she dropped the bouquet of white roses she was carrying into the open trench. She walked away before the priest finished his blessing. She did not want him, or anyone else, to see her tears.

As quietly, as silently as anything else she had done, Nana had walked into the sea one week ago. The body had been found on the island in the middle of the bay three days later. Nana had left no message of farewell, no explanation, but it was not necessary. Arianne had phoned her ten days ago, to tell her about Gloria's wedding and the birth of her baby girl.

Arianne had been reluctant to let Nana know about Gloria's marriage. Gloria and Charles had left Venice the night of the ball, before she had had time to speak to her daughter. She had heard nothing from them afterwards, other than friends' gossip that they had married and were living in Connecticut.

Much as she wanted to make contact with her daughter, Arianne thought it would be better to wait until Gloria's feeling of triumph was tempered by the realization of her mistake. Otherwise any contact between them would be nothing but an exchange of recriminations. She had also been restrained by the hope that Gloria would make the first move, but after months of silence she knew that it would be up to her to establish contact. Arianne had avoided speaking to Nana because she knew that while Nana would say nothing to her, she would blame her for Gloria's appalling marriage.

When she heard through friends of the birth of Gloria's child, her wish to contact her daughter was overwhelming. Perhaps as a rehearsal of what would be the more difficult conversation, she had phoned Nana instead to break the news. Now she realized the depth of her mistake. She should have realized that Nana would see Gloria's marriage to Charles as her own ultimate failure. Gloria had always been the centre of her grandmother's life.

Gloria and her child were now all Arianne had, the only ones left to chase away the ghosts. Ruben, Florinda, Simon, Paul, and now Nana had gone from her. But Nana's death gave Arianne a reason to phone Gloria at last, to share her grief. It was not an excuse, it was an inescapable need. She could not wait to get back to New York, to make contact with her daughter at last, and to see the baby. Nothing else mattered.

'Good afternoon, Miss Gloria,' the butler said courteously, holding the door open for Gloria and the nanny behind her, carrying the baby in her arms. His tone was casually polite, as if he still saw Gloria every day. She looked around, and felt as if she had never been away. She was home.

'Good afternoon, François. Please take Sheila to your sitting room,' she said, introducing the nanny. 'I'm sure she would love a cup of tea.' She deliberately avoided any mention of the fact that she had been away for a long time, and took her baby from the nanny. She carefully rearranged the folds of Mercedes' wrap, then turned towards the drawing room as the others walked away. It was then that she saw Arianne standing at the far end of the gallery, witnessing the scene. At any other time she would have thought that her mother was playing her usual power games, letting Gloria come to her, but now she guessed her mother was as eager as she was for a reconciliation, but equally frightened about their meeting. The two women walked slowly towards each other, until Arianne opened her arms and embraced her daughter and grandchild.

'My darling, I'm so glad to see you at last!' Arianne's arm was around Gloria's shoulders, and there were tears on her face. Arianne gingerly pulled the wrap away from Mercedes' face.

'She is the only one who is entitled to cry here, and look

452

how well she is behaving. She is lovely!' Arianne held out her arms in a silent request for the baby, and Gloria handed her over with a smile. Arianne gently cradled the sleeping child, kissing her cheek and nuzzling her downy head.

'Let's go to my bedroom,' she said. 'Mercedes will be much more comfortable on my bed.' They walked into Arianne's dressing room, where Gloria noticed an enormous box of nappies, another box full of baby lotions and an array of soft toys on a chest of drawers.

'I did some shopping this morning, just in case,' Arianne mumbled, then laughed, hugging Mercedes to her. They walked into the bedroom and Arianne very gently laid the baby down on the silk bedspread, meticulously arranging the matching cushions around Mercedes. The two women stood by the edge of the huge four-poster, watching over the small bundle for a moment, until Arianne squeezed Gloria's hand.

'She seems alright. Let's sit down by the fireplace, we can keep an eye on her from there,' she said, ringing the bell by the bed. After a moment, François appeared with a tea service, laid it on the low table by the fireplace, and left the room. Mother and daughter were suddenly conscious that the easy part was over. Now they had to address each other, and Arianne concentrated on serving tea, grateful for the temporary distraction.

She had rehearsed her speech many times during the last few days. Now the time had come to say it, to put an end to twenty years of silence and white lies, to own up. She would have to explain who she really was, what she had been. That was easy, or easier than the rest at least. Nana, the real Arianne, Gloria as a baby, Charles, her whole past had to be unfolded and exorcised, once and for all. She was facing the hardest task of her entire life. She handed a cup to Gloria and sat next to her on the small sofa. She closed her eyes for a moment, then began to talk, staring fixedly ahead.

'I've never been so happy as I am now. Seeing you has made me realize how much I've missed you. There are so many things I want to tell you, things which concern both you and me, and you are entitled to know. Whatever may come out of it, I want you to know that I've always thought of you as my daughter. You are, and have always been, the most important person in my life. I'll always, always, love you, no matter what. If a lie is a distortion of what we really feel, then I have never really lied to you, but I want to tell you about myself, about Nana, about . . . you.' She felt the tears welling in her eyes and stopped, unable to speak for a moment. She was about to continue when she felt Gloria's hand gripping hers.

'Mummy, please don't go any further. I know what you want to say will be very painful for you, and it really doesn't matter any more. You *are* my mother and I love you, the rest makes no difference. I learned many things during this year we've been apart, about myself as well as you, and Mercedes taught me anything else I needed to know. Now that I have a daughter I can understand you at last. You owed me nothing but love, and you gave me that in the best way you could. I tried to hurt you, but I hurt myself more . . .' Gloria stopped.

'I want you to forgive me,' Arianne murmured after a while.

'And I want you to forgive *me*,' Gloria replied. They remained still, and Arianne felt flooded with a mixture of surprise and joy as they sat side by side, their hands clasped together. Until a moment ago she had thought it was essential to spell out the truth about her life, because she had seen it as an obstacle between Gloria and herself. Now Gloria had shown her it was not necessary. Once acknowledged, love had become a truth in itself, more powerful than mere facts.

'There's something else I want to tell you, something I hadn't realized until now. I'm proud of you. Very proud . . .' Arianne briskly composed herself, stood up and walked to the bed, beckoning at Gloria with a mockingly stern face.

'I hope you have not forgotten about her. Obviously I have to keep very close watch on this child . . .' Gloria walked to her side, and both women looked down on the sleeping baby.

'I'm sure that you will,' she laughed.

*   *   *

454

'How much did she give you?' Charles asked anxiously as Gloria walked into the sitting room. He was long past pretending. Ever since their marriage he had been meeting all the bills, and his funds were nearly exhausted. The rent was crippling. He had counted on Arianne softening up soon and chipping in so that she could visit Gloria during her pregnancy, but the bitch had proved tougher than he thought, and the hospital bills after the birth had been shocking. Shortly afterwards he had had to fire the cook and the live-in maid, and they had to make do with a cleaning woman twice a week. Now that winter was setting in it would be possible to sack the gardener as well, but life could not go on like this indefinitely.

Charles had heard through a friend of Gloria that the last surviving sister of Simon de la Force had died in Argentina. Charles' hold on Arianne had come to an end. He was no longer able to blackmail her, and any attempt by him to ask for money would put her on her guard about keeping Gloria as her sole heir. Everything depended on that.

Gloria looked at Charles.

'Sometimes I think you ought to crawl back into the sewer you came from,' she said slowly. 'Unfortunately for you, I didn't ask my mother for any money.'

'How did it go then?' he asked, trying to soften his tone.

'Fine,' she replied. She did not want to talk to Charles about her mother, any more than she had wanted to talk to her mother about Charles. Gloria now wished she had listened to her a year ago. Her marriage was a shambles. Charles' sole concern was her money, her prospects of money. He still put up a good show, hardly ever mentioning the subject, but the birth of Mercedes had dispelled whatever was left of Gloria's naivety. Charles would have cared more for a prize dog than he did for his baby.

'Mummy has asked us to spend Christmas with her in Punta del Este,' she told him. 'I couldn't possibly say no, and I have accepted on your behalf, but I want you to stay here. I won't be coming back. I will talk to the lawyers tomorrow. I want a divorce.'

Charles was thunderstruck, then furious. The girl was a spoiled brat. It took one visit to her mother for her to want to run back home. More to the point, it upset his plans. He did not want to divorce her until the settlement was worth his while, which would mean at least half of her mother's money. But she had to get it first.

'Gloria, you are talking nonsense. I can understand how distraught you must be after an emotional reunion with your mother, but this is not the time to review our marriage. We have to give each other time. You owe it to our daughter.'

The mention of the child enraged her.

'You don't give a damn about Mercedes! If you're counting on the prospect of a fatter settlement the longer we stay together, then forget it. Mummy told me she plans to set up her whole estate as a trust for Mercedes in Liechtenstein. The trust will look after me for life, at the trustees' discretion. I don't think you will rate very highly in their opinion. The arrangement will be in place by next year. Frankly, it's not worth your while hanging around.'

Charles was barely able to conceal his alarm. His whole scheme hinged on the certainty of Arianne's attachment to Gloria, but it had never crossed his mind that their child would give Arianne a reason to bypass her daughter altogether when settling her estate. It would be easier for him to look into the Queen of England's handbag than to probe into a Liechtenstein trust. He needed time, and he had to keep calm.

'Gloria, I'm truly sorry to hear what you've just said. You have totally misjudged me, but I'm not going to argue with you. Have you discussed the divorce idea with your mother?' He hoped that his voice did not betray his anxiety.

'No, I haven't.' Gloria regretted it now, but she had been restrained by a remnant of pride. She could not bring herself to admit openly to her mother during their first meeting after so many months apart that she had been entirely wrong about her marriage.

Charles struggled to conceal his relief. Everything was

not lost. He lowered his eyes and spoke as if with great difficulty.

'I find your decision extremely painful, but I will not put any obstacles in your way. However, Mercedes is my daughter as well as yours, and I need some time to adjust to the idea that I won't see her so often. Let us have at least one Christmas all together, and I promise you that I will agree to a divorce on whatever grounds you want once we are back in New York. Don't talk to the lawyers yet. It would be impossible to have even the illusion of a happy family occasion if we are already entangled in legal procedures. And I would ask you not to tell your mother about your decision until the New Year, to give us one last chance to work things out. I don't think that's asking too much, do you?'

Gloria hesitated for a moment. It was hard to believe that Mercedes was so important to Charles, but after all she was his daughter. It did not matter a great deal, anyway. It was only two months until Christmas, and his cooperation would make things easier afterwards.

'I agree,' she said finally. 'But I will move to the other side of the house until then.' She left the room without looking back.

Charles sighed with relief. Sleeping on his own was almost a blessing. He needed peace and quiet to make his plans.

Awake in her bed, Arianne mulled over the day time and time again. The joy of seeing Gloria and her baby had been as sweet as she had anticipated, only clouded by Gloria's obvious unhappiness. They had both tried their best to be at ease with each other. Perhaps it would have been easier if Arianne had been able to explain to Gloria the true nature of her former relationship with Charles, but it would have meant dwelling on the subject of her past again. Gloria had given her the chance to leave it behind, for her own sake as well as her mother's.

While holding the child in her arms, she had realized that she wanted Mercedes to be a part of her life from now on. She had ruled out further visits in New York for the time being. It would not be possible to avoid the subject of Charles indefinitely. Though Gloria's marriage would soon come undone, Arianne did not want to be seen as instrumental to Gloria's decision. There had been too much rancour in the past because of what Gloria judged to be Arianne's interference in her life. It would have to be Gloria's own choice to bring her marriage to an end, and Gloria had to see it as nothing but that.

But Arianne wanted to create at least a semblance of normality in their relationship, and she had thought of Christmas in Punta del Este as the best possible option. Charles and Gloria could stay on the yacht, miles away from the house, and Charles could sail or water-ski during the day, while she and Gloria spent time in the house with the baby.

Her eagerness to see Mercedes had momentarily blurred the implications. The three of them thrown together again would be an impossible situation. She had to find other people to stay with them, to defuse the situation by turning it into a social gathering.

Arianne went to her desk and began to scan her address book. There were hundreds of names, but they were all either too close to her past with Charles, or not close enough to justify an invitation for Christmas.

The answer struck Arianne suddenly. Pandora Doyle. Arianne felt close enough to her to share this awkward moment, and Pandora was a monument of discretion. Pandora had mentioned that Ted Carson was her boyfriend when he had approached Arianne to buy her out of Pandora's company; the episode had made Arianne think that he was probably cut from the same cloth as Simon, but that was Pandora's concern, not hers. Pandora and Ted Carson, the perfect solution to her dilemma. They would be ideal guests for the occasion.

The bright sunshine filtered through the window, casting blue, red and amber spots on the grey tiled floor. The stained glass picture of Santa Teresa, a plaster image of the Holy Mother and a small wooden crucifix were the only ornaments in the simple room. Mother Rosario sat on one side of a scrubbed pine table, facing Florinda.

'It has not been easy to find you a job with your record, Florinda,' she said sternly. 'But I have watched you during your years in prison, and I believe that your repentance is sincere. You know that the Mother Superior took an interest in your case. It was only because of that that you were released early. Now we have been able to find you something, and you must not let us down.'

'Thank you, Mother Rosario. I just want to be able to get on with my life,' Florinda said quietly, her eyes cast down in humility.

'You must go to the Hotel Praia dos Morros, in San Corrado, and ask for Maria Galvez. She is in charge of the cleaning staff, and she is expecting you.' The nun gave a piece of paper to Florinda. 'Here's the address. May God be with you, my child.'

Florinda leaned forward and kissed the nun's hand.

'Thanks to you I've learned the ways of Our Lord, Mother Rosario. I hope that one day you'll be proud of me,' she mumbled.

As soon as she was outside, Florinda ran along the cloister towards the street. She wanted out of this damn place fast. It was almost as unbearable as the jail where she had rotted for nearly twenty years. She had been out for almost a month, and she had spent most of it saying prayers with the stupid nuns and cleaning their latrines.

It had been worth it, though. Now she was free at last, free to find Silvia, wherever she was. She had rotted in jail for years because of her sister. If she could find her, she would make her pay. If only she could find her . . .

41

PUNTA DEL ESTE
December 1988

Arianne was enjoying the car trip from 'La Encantada' to
Montevideo Airport, where she would pick up Pandora in
a couple of hours. She could have sent someone else, but
she had been glad to have an excuse to get away from
the house.

At long last she sensed that things were taking a turn
for the better. Charles, Gloria and Mercedes had arrived
from New York that morning, but they were resting on
the yacht after the overnight flight. Pandora had phoned
at the last minute from London to say that Ted Carson was
not coming with her after all. But at least there would be
somebody else to defuse the atmosphere in the house, and
that was all that mattered. Arianne stretched out her legs
and leaned back against the soft leather upholstery. As the
car sped down the road towards Montevideo, she could
catch occasional glimpses of the sea through gaps in the
thick pine forests along the coast.

The death of Ines de la Force a few weeks ago had at
long last cancelled Charles' hold over her. For twelve years
she had waited as Simon's sisters died, one by one. In any
event it would be Arianne's twentieth wedding anniversary
next June. Under Argentine law, the matter would simply
lapse through the passage of time. Charles would be better
off to take whatever he could get from her in a divorce
settlement with Gloria. Three or four million dollars was
as much as she was prepared to pay for the sake of seeing
him off without further trouble to her or to her daughter.
Otherwise, she would just let her lawyers loose on him.

It was now a matter of dealing with the future: hers,
Gloria's and the baby's. Her money was truly hers at
last, and Gloria and Mercedes would become the centre
of her life.

Yes, things were taking a turn for the better. It was a
sunny afternoon, and she felt like singing. For a moment,

she thought of the chauffeur's reaction, but then she began to whistle loudly, amused by the chauffeur's surprised glance in the rearview mirror. She didn't care; she was Mrs de la Force, after all.

The plane gathered speed, ready for take off from Rio de Janeiro airport on the last leg of its journey from London to Montevideo. Pandora looked out of the window, anxious for distraction.

Her eyes fell on a would-be Gothic church on top of a mountain nearby, an incongruous sight against the dramatic outline of Rio's *morros*, the church's spires reminding her of monasteries on the Rhine. But the light, the mountains, the trees, everything was different. It was another world, so unlike the one she knew. Perhaps Pandora's problems would seem different, less urgent, from here.

Her most pressing difficulty was in front of her eyes, the large diamond on her finger. She had turned the stone inward as soon as she left Ted yesterday afternoon, but it felt uncomfortable after a while, and the ring was too valuable to take off and drop into her pocket.

Ted must have sensed something after his return from New York three weeks ago, because he had begun to talk about the need to 'work on their relationship'. They had agreed to meet at his flat yesterday evening, to go to the airport for their overnight flight to Montevideo. Pandora had arrived early. They sat on the sofa facing the fire, making small talk, when he suddenly changed the subject.

'I need to know your decision about expanding into America. I can't hold the shops for you indefinitely,' he had said.

'I've told you I'm worried about taking on such a big financial commitment now,' Pandora replied.

'There's a painless way for you to raise the money.'

'Such as?'

'By becoming Mrs Ted Carson, of course.' Ted pulled the ring out of his pocket and slipped it onto her finger. 'I would have no trouble financing the expansion of my wife's business.'

Pandora stared at the ring, avoiding his eyes.

'I . . . I can't give you an answer now,' she said at last.

'Why?'

'Because I've been married before, and it takes more than a ring. It's not as simple as that.' It wasn't, and it had little to do with her previous marriage. A couple of months ago her answer would have been an unequivocal 'yes', but her meeting with Andrew had shattered her contentment.

'I know. I've been married too, and at least you don't have to pay alimony. That isn't any reason not to try again,' Ted replied.

It might not be for him, but Pandora was full of doubts.

'I have to think about it,' she told him.

Ted stood up.

'If you need to think about it, then the answer is "No".' He was clearly upset.

'If I knew the answer I would give it to you now. The fact that you already know what you want on this particular score doesn't mean that I do. I have to think about it.' Pandora also stood up, and faced him.

'Perhaps it would be better if I go to Arianne's alone. I want to be able to do my own thinking in peace and quiet, otherwise you'll influence my judgement. You can be very persuasive — sometimes more than you think,' she said flirtatiously, trying to sound as lighthearted as she could.

Ted frowned for a moment, then he smiled.

'You're right,' he said. 'Maybe being on your own with Arianne de la Force might help my cause. She didn't do badly marrying a rich man.'

Pandora raised her eyebrows. 'Maybe she didn't, but I don't imagine you're keen on following in her husband's footsteps. Nor would I want you to.'

Ted laughed, then took her in his arms. She felt so safe she almost said 'yes' there and then, but something held her back. Now, seven thousand miles away, she wondered if she had been right to postpone her decision.

The screen at the front of the cabin showed the plane's progress on a map of the region. They had just crossed the border between Brazil and Uruguay. They would reach

Montevideo within an hour. She had a week of peace and sunshine ahead of her to make up her mind.

Along the skirting boards, don't miss the socket plates on the wall, up the door frames, then the furniture. Feather-duster in hand, Florinda went around the hotel room, just one of many she had to do on that floor alone, mentally repeating the instructions from her new boss like a mantra. The woman was a dragon. She toured each of the rooms and ran a white cotton glove over all the flat surfaces. Any evidence of dust was enough to send her into a tantrum. Florinda hated her, but at least she had a small room in the attic, shared with another maid, and the salary was just enough to survive on. Otherwise, she would have had to go back to the slum or, even worse, lodge with the nuns again. She had to stick to this job for a while and avoid being fired if she was to get a reference. Her hatred of her boss was almost a relief, a distraction from her growing, relentless obsession with her sister. It was intolerable to have to live like this, watching her every step, not being able to take anything from the rich cretins staying in the hotel. Money, cameras, jewellery, were sometimes carelessly left around in the rooms, just begging to be stolen, but she couldn't run the risk. In the meantime, her sister was probably having a good time.

But maybe she wasn't. Silvia had always been a weak-ling, only good for lying around and letting Ruben or Florinda look after her. Without either of them, she was probably starving. The thought of her sister dressed in rags, trying to survive in the slums on her own, comforted Florinda, but only briefly. It was also possible that she had found another sucker to keep her. She could be sunning herself on the beach right now, while Florinda was scrubbing floors. She ground her teeth in anger and began to make up the bed, savagely beating the pillows into shape, imagining them to be Silvia.

Emptying the wastepaper basket was the last task on her list and the only one likely to yield some slim reward; a not quite empty scent bottle, or a discarded lipstick. Florinda did not find anything as useful as that this time, but at least

463

there was a copy of Brazilian Vogue, and she decided to have a break. She locked the door, then sat down in the armchair and flicked through the pages.

The sight of rich women flaunting their opulent homes, of beautiful girls wearing clothes she could never afford, made Florinda furious. Whores, they were all whores, undeserving of their good fortune. She was glancing at a feature on paintings and their prices, their obscene prices, when the photograph of a woman caught her eye. The face seemed familiar; at first she thought the woman might be one of her former employers, but after some thought she decided it was somebody else. She had seen that face a long, long time ago. Not with that confident, knowing expression, certainly not dressed like that, but she knew she had seen that woman before.

The revelation hit her like a blow in the chest. It was Silvia. The caption gave her name as Arianne de la Force, but Florinda had no doubt. It was her sister. She walked to the mirror, placed the magazine on the dressing table and took a look at herself, pulling back the loose skin on her face, smoothing away the lines brought on by bitterness and poverty as much as the passage of time. It was the same face. Silvia looked younger, less worn, but so would Florinda if she had clothes and jewels like that.

She began to read, and found out that the 'fabulous Mrs de la Force' was said to have bought a painting for fifty-five million dollars. She was described as enormously rich and shy of publicity. Her South American connections were mentioned, and also the fact that she only left her European or New York homes to spend Christmas at her magnificent house in Punta del Este.

Florinda tore the magazine into shreds in her rage. While she had rotted in jail Silvia had been living like a queen, having everything she wanted and more. Now she knew where to find her. The bitch would pay, at last. She would have to give Florinda money for her silence, lots and lots of money. Then she would kill her. Only that would be adequate compensation for Florinda's years of suffering.

Her wages would be paid tomorrow, the day before Christmas Eve. They were enough to cover the bus fare to Uruguay, and it would take her only three or four days to reach Punta del Este. She would be there just in time.

42

The maid came into the room on tiptoe and quietly drew the curtains.

'You don't have to be so careful, Corazon, I'm already awake,' Pandora said from her bed.

'I haven't brought your breakfast, Miss Doyle, because Mrs de la Force told me to ask you if you would like to join her downstairs.'

'Please tell Mrs de la Force that I'll be delighted to join her as soon as I'm ready. It won't take me long,' Pandora told the maid as she jumped out of bed.

'Mrs de la Force is having breakfast on the terrace,' Corazon announced very formally before leaving the room.

Under the shower, Pandora thought it would be the first time Arianne and she had had breakfast together since her arrival a week ago. Pandora had managed to conceal her annoyance with Arianne when she casually mentioned, on the way from Montevideo airport, that Charles, Gloria and their baby would be spending the holiday with them. The reason for the invitation was suddenly clear to her, but she was in Arianne's debt, and she resigned herself to her role as peace-keeper. Her worry was unfounded. Pandora had been quickly taken up by the local set, who provided an endless stream of invitations to parties, yachts and yet more parties, invariably declined by Arianne, and she found herself spending very little time in the house.

Her hostess had been a model of sociability compared to Charles, though. Pandora had only seen him on her first evening there, supposedly the Christmas celebration dinner, although it was hard for Pandora to enter into the Christmas spirit in this beautiful summer weather. Arianne had been at her sparkling best then, mostly talking to Gloria about people they knew, while Charles concentrated on Pandora. His performance was as polished as she remembered it from Geraldine's party nearly two years ago. Only Gloria had shown any signs of discomfort, her tension underlined by Charles and Arianne's apparent ease. From then on she had seen Charles very rarely, and only from a distance.

Having come to terms with the awkwardness of the situation, Pandora was thoroughly enjoying her stay. The social merry-go-round had postponed any thoughts about her own problems. It had been easy to fool herself into believing that there weren't any in a setting like this. She came out of the bathroom and dressed quickly, then left her room through the French doors leading directly to the terrace.

Sitting under a large white umbrella by the balustrade facing the lagoon, a pool of shadow on the huge stone terrace edged by white geraniums in terracotta urns, Arianne held Mercedes in her arms. Ten yards away, the nanny stood against one of the pillars of the gallery, keeping respectful watch on her charge. A maid appeared, carrying a silver breakfast service.

'Perfect timing,' Arianne said to Pandora with a smile. The maid placed the breakfast tray on the table.

'Would that be all, Señora?' she asked.

'Yes, Alma, thank you.' The maid left, and Pandora sat down.

'Would you mind pouring the coffee?' Arianne asked, clicking her fingers for the baby, who tentatively tried to grab them. 'I can't let go of Mercedes. The nanny is dying to have an excuse to take her away from me. Help yourself to whatever you want.' Arianne managed to balance the child on her lap while she buttered her toast, but in the meantime Mercedes dipped her little fingers into the strawberry jam and then rubbed them all over Arianne's white shirt.

'Naughty girl!' she laughed. The nanny came towards them but Arianne waved her hand, dismissing her. Pandora smiled at the scene.

'You're obviously besotted,' she told Arianne.

'She's the best thing that's happened in my life in a very long time. I've learned a few things recently, mainly to care only about what really matters.'

'How can you tell? It's not always easy.'

Arianne glanced at her.

'You *always* can. We may not want to face it, but it's there to see.' She noticed Pandora's hand.

'You complimented me on my rings the first time we met. Now it's my turn. We haven't really spoken since you've been here, so why don't you tell me all about it now? Then I can go on holding Mercedes and her nanny won't have any excuse to whisk her away from me.'

Pandora fidgeted with her ring for a moment, then looked up.

'Ted has asked me to marry him.'

'And you don't want to.'

Pandora sighed. 'I wish it was as clear-cut as that. I know I would have preferred to carry on as we were. He is forcing me to make a choice, to commit myself, and I'm not sure I want the commitment. It's very difficult to be anything other than Mrs Carson if you marry a man like that. On the other hand, I'm not sure if I want my work to be the most important thing in my life either. It fills most of my time, I enjoy it and I'm very proud of what I've achieved, but I still have to go home at the end of the day.'

'I would say that what you don't know is how to get out of your dilemma,' Arianne said, struggling to release Mercedes' sticky grip on the long gold chain around her neck. 'You probably think it's an offer you can't refuse. Or shouldn't. From my experience, beware of offers you can't refuse. They always turn out to be more expensive than you thought.' She called the nanny.

'Mercedes needs a new nappy,' Arianne said as the nanny took the baby. She wet a napkin in her water glass and rubbed it on a damp mark on her white trousers.

'If *Vogue* could see me now,' she sighed mockingly. Both women laughed, then Arianne suddenly became serious.

'You're both going back tomorrow, and I wanted to talk to you before you left. I'm very grateful for what you've done for me by coming here. I'm sure you understand why I asked you.'

Pandora smiled.

'I think I know what you mean, but I'm the one who

has every reason to be grateful. I must confess that I was surprised to find Gloria and Charles here, but it was pretty clear that you didn't want to talk about it, and perhaps some things are better left unsaid.'

'That's a *very* British reaction,' Arianne laughed.

'I *am* very British. I saw it as a problem in New York, but now I take it as a fact of life. And there's no need for you to apologize, not after what you did for me last year.'

'I just invested some money, and that only because I knew it was a viable business. There was little risk. Now that you have your own money, you must have realized that it is very important in some ways, but it's not everything. You gave me something that night in Venice every bit as important to me as the money was to you.'

Pandora tried to remember their conversation then, but she could find no clue.

'My only recollection is that I didn't make much sense that evening, I was so worried by my own problems. What did I give you?' she asked, genuinely puzzled.

Arianne took a sip of her coffee before replying.

'I'll follow your advice about certain things being better left unsaid. It doesn't matter. I just wanted to let you know I'm grateful, particularly in the circumstances.' Her tone indicated to Pandora that there was something else on her mind.

'If you are talking again about Charles and Gloria, I hope my being here has been helpful,' Pandora said. 'Charles certainly seems to keep himself out of sight. Maybe he's embarrassed, and can't face you.'

Arianne shook her head.

'He's up to something. If only I knew what it was. He's been going for long walks in the park every day, and he's not the walking type. He has been there again since he brought Mercedes over this morning.' She briskly clapped her hands. 'Enough of that subject. Let's talk about tonight. The Cullens have asked us to join them at the New Year's Eve party at La Terraza. Gloria and Charles will be going, but dinner on Christmas Eve was enough for me. You and I can have dinner here alone tonight, and then you should go to the party without me.

My driver will take you there, and he can wait to bring you back.'

'I'll stay here with you if you don't want to go,' Pandora offered.

'Absolutely not,' was Arianne's firm reply. 'I'm tired of parties, but you have to start the year doing something more exciting than keeping me company. You may meet the man of your dreams there, although I have the feeling you already have.'

'What do you mean?' Pandora asked, taken aback.

Arianne smiled enigmatically.

'Don't be so defensive. I was only referring to your ring,' she said.

Charles looked around for the last time. He was sure he was alone, but he had to be cautious.

It hadn't taken him long to locate the generator house during his first walk, discreetly concealed by landscaping at the bottom of a slope. Luck was on his side. A recent storm had brought down a few pines at the edge of the forest on top of the hill, and his only concern now was to ensure, during his daily strolls, that they remained in place. It was most unlikely that the trees would be removed today. Nobody liked hard work between Christmas and New Year, certainly not on New Year's Eve.

Charles had not been fooled by Arianne's flawless performance since they had arrived. He knew she would not show herself in public with him and Gloria, particularly somewhere as conspicuous as the party at La Terraza. It had only been a matter of getting that English girl out of the house tonight, and his suggestion that the Cullens ask her along had taken care of that. Arianne always gave the staff the night off after serving dinner on New Year's Eve. Later she would be alone in the house.

Charles had made sure that there would be nobody else on the yacht as well. That morning he had told the captain that the staff could have the night off. More than pleased, he began the long walk back towards the house.

* * *

A breeze rustled the pines on top of the hill, a hundred yards away from where Charles had been a moment ago. The branches creaked, startling Florinda, and she took cover among the fallen trees. After a while she was reassured that she was alone, and loosened her grip on the handle of the small bag she had brought with her from Rio.

As soon as she had arrived three days ago, after the back-breaking bus journey, she had checked the Punta del Este telephone directory, where she found the listing she was looking for: 'A. de la Force, "La Encantada".' But there was no address. She was eventually told at the post office that 'La Encantada' was twelve miles away, on a hill near Punta Ballena. She had to go back to the Onda bus station and take another bus. The fare took most of what was left of her money, but money would soon be no problem.

Florinda found the house at last, after a tiresome walk uphill. She was awed by its magnificence, but she did not linger to take in the view. Her first concern was to find a hiding place before nightfall. The forest was a long way from the house, and clearly a place nobody went to. She slept outdoors, the chill of the night biting into her.

She stalked the house during the next two nights, scavenging the dustbins for food, and drinking water from the fountain on the terrace. One evening Florinda caught sight of her sister in the window at the top of the tower; her joy at discovering where she slept almost cancelled out the surge of rage Florinda felt at the sight of her. Florinda was also able to confirm that there was only one other woman staying in the huge house, sleeping at the opposite end from the tower. She had to hope that her sister would be alone tonight; she knew from her days as a maid that even the rich gave their staff the night off on New Year's Eve. If her sister went to a party, she would wait for her return. She had waited long enough; a few more hours would make no difference.

She opened her bag and pulled out the gun she had stolen from the manager's office before leaving the hotel. The feel of the polished metal filled her with pleasure. The gun was almost identical to Ruben's.

471

43

Charles glanced at the time once again before going into the galley. It was nearly nine o'clock. From the bottom step he could see Pepa putting the finishing touches to the dinner trays laid on the long stainless steel top.

'I'm sorry to disturb you so late, Pepa. I know you're about to go home, but I've just noticed that I'm missing my American Express card. I may have left it in the pocket of the shirt I gave you to be laundered this afternoon.' Charles flashed his most ingratiating smile. 'Could you find it for me now? I would do it myself if only I knew where to look.' The laundry was on the lower deck, so it would take Pepa a few minutes to get there and back.

'Of course, Señor. I won't be a moment,' Pepa said.

'Don't hurry. I don't want you slipping down the stairs in a rush. I can wait.' As soon as Pepa left, Charles pulled a bottle of Seconal out of his pocket. He had asked for beer with dinner that evening. The beer mug made his dinner tray easy to identify.

Gloria had ordered gazpacho. He quickly sprinkled the contents of two Seconal capsules into the bowls on Gloria's and the nanny's trays, stirring them until he could see no trace of the powder in the soup. By the time Pepa returned, he was inspecting the spice rack on the wall.

'Here's your card,' Pepa told him. Charles slipped it into his pocket.

'I'm so glad you found it,' he said. He had known that she would. He had put it there on purpose. Pepa picked up Gloria's tray and Charles courteously stood aside to let her go first.

The clock struck eleven. Their dinner over, the two women were alone in the dining room, lingering over coffee.

'Do you have a wish for the New Year?' Arianne asked. She noticed Pandora's expression, and smiled.

'Don't worry, I'm not expecting you to disclose your secrets. But it's your first New Year's Eve here, and it is very easy to see shooting stars in the summer sky in this part of the world. Look for one, and make your wish. It will come true.'

Pandora raised her eyes. 'Just like that?' she asked.

Arianne smiled.

'You have to help your wishes come true, but it's better to have some support from above.'

Pandora suddenly felt very lonely.

'I do have a wish,' she said after a while, 'and I'll tell you what it is. I hope I'll see someone again.'

Arianne stood up and picked up the wine bottle from the silver wine cooler.

'Probably not the same someone who makes that ring feel so uncomfortable on your finger,' she said as she refilled Pandora's glass before going back to her own seat. 'There's truth in wine, so why don't you tell me about him?'

'I met him in London not long ago. He lives in the Seychelles, and he went back soon after. It's probably just a fantasy of mine,' Pandora explained rather apologetically.

'You shouldn't dismiss fantasies so lightly. They give us something to achieve. If nothing else, they're the spice of life, after all. Do you love him?'

'I wish I knew,' Pandora sighed. 'It would make everything so much easier. How can you tell if you love someone after only a few hours together?'

Arianne seemed suddenly pensive.

'Time has nothing to do with it,' she replied after a while. 'You don't love someone simply because you spend your life with them. Love is not a habit, but you have to make allowances for the fact that I am a tempestuous South American,' she said jokingly. Then she became serious. 'Don't analyse love, just let it happen,' she murmured.

'Even if it means giving up everything else in your life, and puts in question everything you value or is important to you?'

'Yes, if it *is* what you really want. What we really want

473

is what counts in the end,' Arianne said in a voice that reminded Pandora of their conversation in Venice.

'You're entitled to think I have no right to ask you this, but what you're saying is very important to me, and I'm asking for my sake, not yours. It is more than obvious that you don't love Charles. Now that I know you better, I guess you never did. If, as you say, loving a man is so significant in one's life, why did you ever choose him?'

Arianne left her chair and walked to the French doors. She stared at the clouds gathering over the moon, her back to Pandora.

'Because I couldn't afford not to. We have to make our choices along the way. They make certain things possible, but not everything. What matters is not to discover that what you left behind counted more in the end than what you've got. There are personal prices you can pay, and others you simply can't afford. That's ultimately what I discovered through our conversation in Venice, although it wasn't so clear at the time. You helped me then and that's the reason why I'm so grateful to you, why I decided at the time to help you.'

Pandora wondered what she had said that could have affected Arianne so much, but she was no more able to remember the full conversation than she had been over breakfast.

'I think you ought to go now,' she heard Arianne say. 'You should be there before midnight, and it's a long way from here. La Terraza is past the Casino in San Rafael.'

Pandora stood up. 'Are you sure you don't want me to stay? I don't like to leave you all alone on New Year's Eve.'

Arianne smiled. 'Most certainly not, particularly after all you've told me. The last thing you need is to be left alone with your thoughts, and I'm tired. I just want to go to bed. But we can toast the New Year early,' she said, walking across the huge room towards the sideboard. She took a champagne bottle out of the silver bucket and opened it. The cork shot out, falling at Pandora's feet.

'There's a local superstition that if you are single and

a champagne cork falls on you, you'll get married soon,' Arianne said, pouring the wine into two champagne flutes.

'You aimed the bottle at me, so it doesn't count,' Pandora laughed. Arianne handed her a glass.

'It's an innocent game and you have to cheat sometimes if you are going to get what you deserve,' she said. 'Happy New Year,' she added, raising her glass. The identical emeralds on her fingers sparkled in the candlelight.

'Happy New Year,' answered Pandora. She hoped it would be. 'Do *you* have a New Year's wish?' she asked.

Arianne smiled.

'I think I've already got mine. Gloria told me this afternoon that she'll start divorce proceedings as soon as we are all back in New York.' Arianne's happiness as she spoke was plain to see.

'I'm delighted, for you as well as her,' Pandora said. They sipped their champagne, then Arianne put down her glass.

'Time for you to go. Have a wonderful time, and remember to look for shooting stars.'

They walked across the dark hall, the Moorish tiles gleaming in the light from the waiting car outside, visible through the glass doors.

Arianne waited until the car drove away. She turned towards the stairs to her bedroom, then stopped when she heard a noise outside. Probably the wind knocking over one of the chairs on the terrace, she thought. But she was suddenly uneasy, conscious of being on her own in the huge, dark house.

She remembered Simon's gun, lying in the bottom drawer of her desk. It was silly, but perhaps she should get it.

Charles hummed softly as he drove along the empty coastal road, trying not to think about the knot of tension in his stomach. He saw the lights of a car coming towards him in the distance, so he pulled to the side and ducked his head down until he heard it drive past, then he went on.

The early part of his plan had worked as he had expected, and Gloria and the nanny were both asleep in their cabins, slumped on their beds. He would tell Gloria tomorrow morning that she had been sleeping so soundly he had hated the thought of waking her up for the sake of a party. He might even take a Seconal himself, and let them find *him* asleep in his bed later.

He came to the side road, almost a track, leading to 'La Encantada'. He turned off the car lights and began to drive uphill until he reached the gates. He parked at the side of the road, behind the huge shrubs, and picked up the shoulder bag from the back seat.

He walked until he was in sight of the house. The only lights were in Arianne's bedroom, outlining the louvered shutters, and in the hall downstairs, but the entrance lights were left on during the night at all times.

He turned left, and began to walk towards the forest. After a while he reached the top of the hill, and came to the fallen trees. A sea wind had begun to blow, and the trees creaked around him. Good. It would be one possible explanation in the morning.

He waited for half an hour, then he gently shoved the small, bushy pine along the ground until it began to roll downhill, crashing against the building at the bottom of the slope. Charles followed it, pushing it tight against the ventilation grate in the lower section of the wall, a dense mass of pine needles blocking the outlet for the power generator's exhaust. Choked by its own fumes, the engine soon stalled.

Charles ran towards the house. 'La Encantada' was now in complete darkness. It was one o'clock. He would give Arianne half an hour to fall asleep, then he would make his final move.

The party at La Terraza was in full swing. After the rush of champagne toasts, hugs and kisses one hour ago, the dancing had continued with a vengeance in the main building, in the gardens, and around the floodlit swimming pool. Pandora was one of the few who did not join in.

Charles and Gloria had not appeared, and she was worried. Arianne had said she thought Charles was up to something, and Pandora regretted having left her alone. There was no point in staying any longer now that it was well past midnight. She would ask the driver to take her back to the house right away.

She walked across the lawn, down the stone steps leading to the car park, the wind blowing her hair. In spite of her worries, she could not avoid being struck by the view in front of her, the infinite expanse of sea gleaming in the moonlight, under the stars. She had reached the bottom of the steps when she saw a single shooting star flying brightly across the night sky under the Southern Cross.

By the time she reached the car she had made her wish.

Half past one, time to go. Charles stood up and walked across the silent courtyard. He opened the front door with his key and slipped into the house. He collected a small brass candlestick from one of the hall tables, and paused for a moment at the bottom of the stairs, but he heard no noise. He began to climb.

He reached the door at the top, and waited again. Everything was quiet. Gently, very gently, he opened the door a fraction and peered into the room. In the moonlight filtering through the shutters he could see Arianne asleep on the bed.

He took off his shoes and lifted the heavy spanner out of his bag. He went into the bedroom; the room reeked of Arianne's scent, making him as aware of her presence as if the lights were on. He walked on tiptoe until he almost reached the edge of the bed, holding the spanner high, ready to knock Arianne unconscious. Suddenly he stopped. The only noise he could hear was the beat of his own heart, but he was terrified.

He had to regain his calm, otherwise he might not knock her out at first, and he had to be careful not to crush her skull. It must all look like a terrible accident. Details were crucial, and he had to avoid making mistakes. Perhaps it would be better to set up the scene first. He put the spanner in his pocket and, walking backward step by step, his heart pounding with every creak of the floorboards, he returned to the landing. Arianne did not stir.

He pulled out a screwdriver and a large can of floor

wax from his bag and laid them on the floor. He loosened the screws in the door handle on the bedroom side of the door and put the screwdriver away, then he picked up the can of wax and the candlestick. Back inside the bedroom, he carefully placed an open book by Arianne's side, as if she had been reading, then he put the candlestick on the bedside table. He was moving in slow motion, but he could feel sweat trickling down his forehead. He paused for a moment, waiting for his heart to slow down, then he opened the can of liquid wax and poured the thick contents on the valance and the floor under the bed, the solvent fumes filling the air. Once the can was empty, he slipped it inside his shirt. The scene was set: it would be just a mishap, someone falling asleep while reading by candlelight, not at all uncommon around here during power cuts at night.

Charles was ready at last, but suddenly the room fell into pitch darkness. The wind had gathered the clouds, and there was no moonlight. He needed a little light to aim his blow accurately, otherwise he might break her nose. Even a provincial doctor would notice that. He thought of going back to his bag to get the torch, when Arianne stirred. He didn't dare move; the creaking floorboards might wake her up. Time was running out. He grabbed the spanner, searched in his pocket for his lighter, and lit the candle. Able to see again, he raised his arm and brought the spanner down on Arianne's head.

An explosion deafened him, then he screamed in agony. The bitch had gone to bed with a gun, and the bullet had shattered his kneecap. His hand flung backward in the spasm of pain and swept across the table. The candle fell to the floor, the wick dipping into the pool of wax. Flames immediately leaped around the bed; Charles limped towards the door when the gun went off again, slamming into his back. Suddenly he was short of breath, and his legs gave way. He managed to drag himself across the room, his blood oozing onto the floor. He tried to make it through the half-open door but he couldn't. He collapsed in front of it, his inert weight pushing the door shut.

The flames climbed up the panelled walls so lovingly

waxed over the years. They spread onto the ceiling, and Charles could hear Arianne screaming somewhere behind him. She sounded a million miles away but she must have been next to him, because her feet kicked at him, trying to shift his body while she pulled desperately at the door handle. He thought she screamed again when the handle came loose in her hand, but he could have imagined it. He could just see, but as if he was underwater, like a fish, a fish surrounded by fire and smoke, lots and lots of smoke. Arianne collapsed on top of him; by now his sight was dimming, until all he could see was the section of the wall in front of him, where a painting of a woman was being destroyed by the flames. He knew he had seen that painting before, but where . . .?

The fire turned every surface into a sheet of flames. The portrait on the wall was soon only a pile of ashes, like everything else in the burning room.

'Go faster!' Pandora urged the driver as the car raced through the open gates. The wind suddenly broke the cloud, and at last she saw 'La Encantada' ahead of them, the top of the tower wrapped in flames. The car stopped in the forecourt and Pandora ran inside the house.

For a second, everything looked as she had left it. Then the insidious smell of smoke and the horrifying screams from the tower shattered the illusion of calm. She rushed up the stairs. She did not think about herself; her only thought was for Arianne.

Epilogue

Pandora's memories of that terrible night would never fade. She would eventually learn to keep them at bay, wild animals pinned in a corner, but that morning they were as real as the view, a part of it. The fire had been brought under control, but the smoke was noticeable in the distance, a tracery on the cloudless sky. 'La Encantada', only yesterday another monument to Arianne's power, was now her tomb, as it would have been Pandora's had the firemen not appeared seconds after she lost consciousness.

She was alone on the terrace of the café. She stirred her coffee mindlessly as she gazed at the view. It was so perfect: the bay rimmed by an endless line of pale sand, the pine forest bordering the coastline, the mountains behind fading into a lavender haze, and then the sky, a shimmering pale cobalt blue, reflected in the water, a flawless backdrop for a carefree summer – or so it had seemed to her until a few hours ago. The men were rich, the women good-looking, the world as it should be when the living is easy.

Soon the island in the middle of the bay, a couple of miles from the shore, would be festooned with big white yachts, the scene for long lunches on deck under white awnings, served by white-jacketed waiters, while the Rivas, glistening black against the foam of their wakes, pulled the water-skiers across the bay. Pandora had been part of that life and she had loved it, but now it was over.

As she picked up her coffee cup, the sunshine brought out shards of light from her ring. Until yesterday, her work, Ted, Andrew, had seemed an insoluble conundrum, but she had decided last night at the party to turn down Ted's offer of marriage. Her midnight wish had been that she could be with Andrew again, but that had been before the horror at 'La Encantada'. Now it hardly mattered at all. Arianne was dead. Like a shooting star, she had made Pandora's wishes possible and now she was gone. Perhaps it was only

483

sensible to go back to London and continue with her life as she had left it, to find comfort in certainties.

She noticed a car approaching slowly from the harbour. It was one of Arianne's cars. Charles or Gloria must have sent for her, or maybe the police. She shuddered to think about what would happen next. The statements, the inquest, the trial that would inevitably follow if her suspicions were correct. When she was discharged earlier that morning from the Maldonado Infirmary, she had been told that the police might want to contact her during the day. She couldn't bring herself to return to the house, and told the nurse that she would be at the harbour café, having breakfast. She should really go to the bus terminal a few blocks away, take a bus to Montevideo now and board her flight to London that afternoon before the police could find her.

What could she tell them? She knew that Charles had murdered Arianne, but she could not prove it. Arianne had told her about her suspicions, and she knew his mind better than anyone else. Suddenly, the memory of her friend overshadowed everything else.

The police would want facts, and she tried to remember every detail of the night before. The clue to Arianne's murder could be somewhere in her memory. But there were many facts about Arianne that she did not know. Now she never would.

Charles must have been clever enough to cover his tracks, or else the police would be swarming over the yacht by now. But the yacht was there, a few hundred yards away, and nothing disturbed its peaceful rolling in the morning swell. Gloria would get her mother's money at last. Even if she divorced Charles, as Arianne had hoped she would, he would be entitled to a massive settlement. Life would go on.

Perhaps that was the best one could hope for. Arianne's example had been one of the determining factors behind Pandora's wish to prove herself, and Arianne's money had made her business a reality. Her doubts were based on nothing but a crazy fantasy about a man she hardly knew.

Pandora stared at her diamond, a beacon of security. Was she going to be silly enough to give up a man like Ted? Yet it wasn't Ted she wanted by her side now to comfort her, it was Andrew, but Andrew was so far away ... For all Pandora knew, he would have forgotten her by now. What did she *really* want? She had spent the last two years trying to answer that question, but it didn't matter now. The only thing that really mattered to her was to do whatever she could to help catch Arianne's murderer.

The car was very close now. She could not bring herself to face Charles, and there was no time to call the waiter. She stood up and dropped some money on the table, ready to leave. The car stopped a few yards away from her table and the driver got out.

Pandora looked away. She did not want Charles to see her face, a picture of impotent rage, any more than she wanted to see his own, glowing in triumph. But she was instantly ashamed by her reaction. She owed it to Arianne to face him. She might not be able to prove anything, but she could at least confront him with the truth. She raised her eyes at the approaching figure, then froze in disbelief.

It was Arianne, walking towards her with the same elegant ease, the same smile on her face as when she had walked into her New York drawing room two years ago. Pandora's grief, so overwhelming until a second ago, was instantly cancelled by her joy at seeing Arianne, alive and beautiful, as if nothing at all had happened last night. Pandora ran towards her. There were tears in her eyes as she embraced her friend.

'I thought you were dead!' she cried again and again. Arianne smiled and put her arm around Pandora's shoulders.

'Never believe anything until you actually see it happen,' she told her.

They walked back towards the table, and Arianne began to talk as soon as they sat down.

'I wasn't in the house when the fire broke out. I went out for a while. The firemen were already there when I came back. They told me that you had been taken to

Maldonado Hospital, so I went there immediately. I was told you were asleep, and that you would be discharged in the morning. Then I went to the yacht, to check on Gloria and Mercedes. Everybody was asleep, and I spent the night there. I spoke to the hospital a little while ago, but you had already checked out. They told me where to find you.'

Pandora gripped Arianne's hand.

'But what happened last night? I heard screams from your room!' Even in her confusion, Pandora noticed that Arianne's face showed a mixture of emotions, as though she couldn't quite bring off her usual perfect performance.

'I can't tell you everything in one sentence. Please be patient, and I'll explain.'

'I just want to know who was in the room when I tried to open the door. Then tell me the rest.'

Arianne remained silent for a moment.

'It was . . . it was someone who was close to me in Brazil when I was very young, but then we lost touch. I have even forgotten her last name. I was getting ready for bed when she rang the bell, and I let her in. She was obviously in great distress, and I felt sorry for her. She had come to see me to ask for money. I don't know why, but she needed it there and then. It wasn't much, just a few hundred dollars, but I keep hardly any money in the house. I thought I could cash a cheque in the casino, and I told her to wait for me. I stupidly forgot that the casino would be closed on New Year's Eve. I spoke to the security men but they obviously couldn't help me. Then I went back to the house, and I've already told you the rest. The police assume that Charles was in the house for some reason, and that he found her in my bedroom. He must have thought she was a thief; I don't know what happened, but the police are satisfied that nobody else was involved. The chief of police is a charming man. He's gone out of his way to minimize any inconvenience for me, and he told me there was no need for me to identify the woman's body. Apparently she was burned beyond recognition. They will try to formally identify her through her dental records, but they have so little information on her that it is almost certainly an impossible task . . .' Arianne's hands fluttered in urbane despondency, as if the chief of police's predicament was her own. 'I explained to the police that, other than the fact that her name was Silvia, I remember little or nothing about her, and I have no idea where she was living. My gardener has been kind enough to identify Charles' body in the morgue, to save Gloria and me any distress.'

'Is Charles dead?' Pandora asked, trying to take it all in.

'Yes. It's very sad, but he was apparently shot by this woman. She must have had a gun, although I didn't see it. Perhaps Charles disturbed her while she was trying to steal my jewellery. The police think she set the room on fire to destroy any evidence, but was unable to get out.'

Pandora was momentarily speechless. The whole thing was too preposterous. She was perplexed by Arianne's glossing over Charles' presence in the house. She was sure Arianne was not telling her the true story, but it no longer mattered. Her friend was alive, and that was all she cared about.

'I'm glad I won't have to speak to the police after all. But I'll stay here with you for as long as you need me,' Pandora said eventually.

Arianne wasn't listening. She closed her eyes and her hands gripped the edges of the table, her lips tightly drawn, her mouth turned into a thin, trembling line. After a moment she opened her eyes again, and sighed. She then started to speak again in a quiet but determined voice.

'No, it wasn't like that at all. I'm ashamed that I've tried to deceive you, but old habits die hard. In Venice . . .' she stopped for a moment, then continued. 'Let's not make things unnecessarily complicated. Truth matters, and I owe you the truth.' She took a long sip of water from Pandora's glass, then leaned forward, her eyes focused on the far distance.

'I had a sister. I hadn't seen her, or heard from her, since I left Brazil many years ago. Last night, after you'd gone, I heard a noise. It frightened me, so I decided to look for Simon's old gun, but as soon as I found it I realized I was being absurd. I wouldn't know how to use it in any case, so I went to my bedroom. I was looking at the portrait of Madame Claire when I heard the door open . . .'

'Was the painting in your bedroom?' Pandora interrupted Arianne, in spite of her curiosity to know the rest of the story. The painting had brought about their first encounter, and Arianne had never mentioned that it was now in Punta del Este.

'Yes. As I told you in New York, at first I didn't know where to hang it. But over the last few months I grew more and more fond of that portrait. I came to see the similarity between that woman looking at herself in the mirror and me. We were both busy admiring ourselves until something else, something more urgent, made us look back at reality. She and I had become relevant to the world only because we were worth a lot of money. It sounds silly, but I came to see her as my alter ego, and I decided to bring the painting with me to Punta del Este.' Arianne's mouth curved into a dry little smile. 'But I'm still here and I'm still worth a lot of money, while poor Madame Claire is a pile of ashes.'

'Better than the other way round,' Pandora said. 'Please go on.'

'I suddenly heard the floorboards creak. I turned around, and found myself facing my sister again, a gun in her hand . . .'

'Don't move!' the woman said.

Arianne's first shock of fear was overtaken by the feeling that she had seen her before, this ghastly, demented woman pointing a gun at her, her face splattered with mud, pine needles in her hair. Suddenly she froze.

'I knew you would recognize me,' Florinda said with glee. 'I'm sure you're thrilled to see your long-lost sister. I don't look as good as you do, you bitch, but I haven't changed that much.' The hatred in her voice made Arianne shiver. Even if she tried, she would not have been able to move. She stood still, staring at her sister, a nightmarish reflection of herself.

'I know what you are thinking, little sister: that I look like shit. Unlike you, I never found someone to keep me, and I've spent years rotting in jail, paying for a murder you *committed*. Yes, *I was found guilty on your behalf. But you can put that right at last,'* she seethed.

Arianne felt the same fury as she experienced over twenty years ago, when she had faced Florinda at Ruben's office. As then, her sister was out of control, a gun in her hand. She was enraged by Florinda's allegation that Ruben's death had been her responsibility. That was a lie. As then, Florinda could not see anything other than her own hatred. But it would be pointless to confront her with the truth now.

'What do you want?' Arianne asked quietly. Even in her fear, she registered the implication of what Florinda had said. Ruben's murder, the root of all her troubles, was a closed case at last.

'Money!' Florinda barked. 'Lots of it.'

'How much?' Arianne asked calmly. She had to keep Florinda talking. She was acutely aware of her sister's finger on the trigger.

'I want a hundred thousand dollars now. The rest we can talk about later.'

Arianne sighed. 'Do you think I keep that sort of money around the house? There's my jewellery,' she said, pointing towards the case on her dressing table. 'You can take that.'

Still aiming the gun at her, Florinda walked to the table and pulled the case open. She gasped at its contents.

'I'll take this alright,' Florinda said, her fingers raking through the jewels. She glared at her sister. 'And the money. You must have money in the house; you have one minute to think where you're going to find it.'

'I really don't have much money here. You can look in my purse if you want. I promise you I don't keep any elsewhere in the house, and I can hardly go to the bank now.' Arianne struggled to keep her voice level.

Florinda thought for a moment.

'Maybe you are telling the truth,' she said slowly. She grabbed a handful of jewellery and thrust it uncomfortably close to Arianne's face.

'While you were wearing these, I've been cleaning up the shit of rich bitches like you in Rio and São Paulo, and

I know only too well that people like you don't keep any real money lying around.' She laughed hoarsely. 'You are afraid of being robbed by scum like me.' Her voice became more shrill as she spoke, her rancour taking over.

'It's a pity you don't have the money, but your jewels are enough. We'd better say goodbye.' She aimed the gun at her sister's head and was ready to pull the trigger.

'Wait!' Arianne shouted. Florinda smiled grimly.

'I knew you would think of something. Guns have a way of making people think,' she said.

'I could try to cash a cheque at the casino. They know me there. But it will take me more than an hour to get there and back.'

Florinda raised the gun again.

'Do you think I'm stupid? You're planning to come back with the police! We've wasted enough time already.' She took aim.

'I don't want the police involved in this. Please don't shoot!' Arianne cried.

Florinda thought for a moment, then laughed.

'You're right. You wouldn't like your friends to find out who your sister is. I don't think the police would do you much good. I think you should go to the casino.'

Relieved to have found a way out, Arianne pulled her cheque book and the car keys from her bag, Florinda watching her every move. Arianne could only think about the next minute, when she would be out of this room. She was almost ready to leave when Florinda stopped her.

'Not so fast. We have plenty of time. Don't count on your friend coming back. I have enough bullets for two.'

'What do you want now?' Arianne asked, trying to conceal her despair. Perhaps Florinda's agreement had simply been a cat and mouse game to let her think that she would survive after all, but Arianne was not going to break down in front of her sister, as she used to do. She wasn't going to give her that last satisfaction.

'I told you that I've been a maid for years. Now it's your turn to find out what it's like.' She waved the gun at Arianne, pointing towards the bathroom.

'Run my bath, cow!' she shrieked.

Arianne turned and walked into the bathroom, Florinda behind her. She turned the taps on.

'Don't forget the bubbly stuff, I like that,' Florinda told her. Arianne reached towards a huge bottle of Chanel Bath Foam on the ledge and sprinkled some of it into the water.

'All of it,' said Florinda, prodding at Arianne's ribs with the gun. 'And don't forget to put in something that smells nice as well.' She picked up the largest bottle of Arianne's 'Bal a Versailles' scent, and sniffed it.

'Nicer than this,' she said with a grimace, pouring the scent into the washbasin. Arianne picked up a bottle of Floris Bath Oil and emptied it in the bath, by now filled with a mountain of suds. When the bath was ready, Florinda removed the cord from Arianne's dressing gown and grabbed her arm, pushing her back into the bedroom.

'Now take off those pretty clothes you are wearing,' she ordered.

Arianne hesitated.

'Do what I say!' Florinda screamed. Arianne undressed, fighting her shame. Florinda flung the dressing gown cord at her.

'Tie your feet together. Tightly.' Arianne sat on the floor and did as she was told. Florinda then wrenched her hands behind her back and tied Arianne's wrists with a stocking. Arianne lay on the floor and Florinda prodded her with her foot.

'Now roll towards the door. I want to keep watch on you from the bath.' Arianne followed her instructions, and struggled until she lay across the entrance to the bathroom. Florinda stepped on her as she walked in.

'You make a nice doormat, whore,' she said as she flung her cheap cotton dress on the floor. She lay in the bath for a long time, trying every soap in the large silver dish. At last she got out, luxuriantly rubbing herself dry with Arianne's monogrammed bath sheet. Florinda returned to the bedroom and put on Arianne's clothes, then sat at the dressing table and pinned her hair back, like Arianne's. She stared across at Arianne's face, then made herself up with her cosmetics. Finally satisfied, she picked up her gun again and released Arianne's hands, noticing the emerald rings on her sister's fingers for the first time. She pulled them off, and slipped them onto her own.

'You can untie your own feet, I'm not your maid,' she barked. 'Now put on my dress.'

Even in the overpowering steamy atmosphere, drenched in scent, Arianne could smell her sister's filthy dress as she pulled it over her head. Florinda took her by the arm and led her towards the mirror, then she pulled the pins out of Arianne's hair and messed it up with her fingers.

'There you are! I'm you and you are me. We are not very different after all, are we? In fact we are not different at all.' Arianne looked in the mirror, and was repelled by what she saw, as if the last twenty years of her life had never existed.

Florinda yawned. 'Enough of this game. On your way now, bitch. And don't get ideas about finding a gun somewhere, or coming back with someone to help you. I'll be waiting for you outside, under cover. You come back with the money, on your own, and stand in the middle of the courtyard, with your hands up, where I can see them. You have an hour and a half, no more. Otherwise I'll leave the house, but I'll come back and shoot you later, or that lovely baby I've seen you playing with. So get going . . .'

Arianne ran down the stairs. Florinda watched her from the landing until she heard the car start. Holding the gun, she made herself comfortable on her sister's bed, and prepared for a long wait.

Her gaze was caught by the silver-framed photograph on the bedside table. She picked it up and looked at it for a moment. It had once been hers, and she had treasured it. Like so much else, Silvia had taken it from her. Now she could have it back, but she didn't want it. It meant nothing to her after all these years. She flung it onto the table, the glass shattering into splintered shards.

She lazily stretched out her arms, admiring the emeralds on her hands. They were her rings now. The gleam of the emeralds was as pleasant as the touch of the silk shirt on her skin, and she sighed in contentment. She felt really *good after the hot bath, and she closed her eyes for a moment . . .*

'I suddenly heard the floorboards creak, turned round, and found myself facing my sister, a gun in her hand . . .' Arianne suddenly shifted her eyes away from Pandora, and was quiet for a while.

'There's something else I ought to explain to you,' she said at last. 'Something I've never told anyone else before. There was a man in Rio, a man I loved very much. I may have . . .' Arianne's voice was almost a murmur now. Pandora took one look at her agonized face and interrupted her before she could continue.

'I just want to know what happened last night. Anything else is in your past, and I have no right to know it. It would make no difference to me, anyway,' Pandora said firmly.

Hearing her, Arianne was reminded of Gloria's almost identical words during their reunion in New York. She leaned across the table and held Pandora's hand affectionately in hers.

'I thought I owed you the truth,' she said quietly.

'There are no debts in friendship. Even if you hadn't told me what really happened last night, you would still be my friend. No other woman has ever had so much influence on me, and you're the one entitled to call in debts.' Arianne was nearly crying now, and Pandora stopped.

'Did your sister ask you for money?' she asked once Arianne had calmed down.

'Yes,' Arianne whispered.

'And the rest of the story is just as you told me before?'

'Yes. I have no idea what Charles was doing in the house, but I'd rather not know.'

'I think we both know.' Pandora called the waiter, then faced Arianne again. Their eyes locked for a second, in silent agreement to leave last night behind them now.

'Do you want me to stay and help you sort it all out?' Pandora asked. Arianne shook her head, only her warm smile belying her usual cool composure.

'I'm very touched by your offer, but it's really unnecessary. There's no point in you staying here any longer.

493

The house is a mess, and I have to arrange for builders and decorators to come in before leaving for New York. Gloria, Mercedes and I will be flying back as soon as possible. This is obviously a shock for Gloria, and I want to spend as much time as I can with her from now on.'

Arianne settled the bill.

'Shall we go? Your side of the house was not touched by the fire, and Corazon has packed your bags. I've arranged for your luggage to be taken to the airport; I'll drive you there myself. There's no need for you to delay your departure.' She paused for a moment, a mischievous glint in her eyes. 'Please don't think that I'm in a rush to get rid of you, but I'm sure there are better ways for you to use extra holiday time than by keeping me company.'

They climbed into the car, and drove away. The smoke was still visible as they approached Punta Ballena.

'It's a nuisance, but I hope the house will be clear of the smell by next summer. I want to sell "La Encantada".' It was all Arianne said.

'What about you? What are you going to do now?' Arianne asked. Pandora took a deep breath.

'You told me yesterday that we always know what's right in our hearts. It is true. You also said that one should only be concerned about what truly matters. Suddenly seeing you alive after thinking that you were dead has made me realize there are very few things that are really important. Once I'm back in London, I'll have to decide if I want to continue with the business or not. I might well sell it, but your investment is secure no matter what, I promise you. I'm sure you'll make a good profit,' she told Arianne.

'I'm always good at that at least,' Arianne replied with a smile.

They remained silent until they reached the airport. They parked outside and Pandora walked towards the *Aerolineas Argentinas* counter. Arianne's driver was already there with her luggage.

'How do I get to the Seychelles?' Pandora asked the girl in the pale blue uniform. The girl was used to passengers asking about the next flight to Buenos Aires, not to places she had never heard of. She opened a thick manual and looked through it for a while before replying.

'It's a *very* long journey. You have to fly to Johannesburg first. We have a flight there this afternoon. If you catch the plane to Buenos Aires now, you'll probably make it.' Pandora handed over her credit card, and the girl busied herself at her computer terminal. Pandora left Arianne at the counter and walked to the kiosk nearby, where she bought a small box of chocolates and a brown envelope. She emptied the chocolates into the nearest bin, then wrote an address on the envelope and gave it to Arianne.

'Would you mind sending this back to Ted by registered post from New York?' Pandora asked, dropping her diamond ring into the box. 'I'll phone him from somewhere along the way.'

Arianne took the box and slipped it inside the envelope. She smiled in amusement.

'You seem to be solving your problems,' she said.

'And so do you.' Pandora took her ticket and the boarding card. 'I owe it to myself to find Andrew, and then I'll see what happens. Either I'll find out that he was just a fantasy of mine, or that he is really important to me. I have to give it a chance.'

They walked towards the boarding gate; the plane was fifty yards away. Pandora stopped and faced Arianne.

'What will *you* do?' she asked.

'Oh, I'll always have plenty to do, don't worry. Don't forget I have Gloria and Mercedes now. Can you believe I'm a grandmother!' Arianne replied, joy dancing in her honey-coloured eyes. They laughed until they reached the gate, where they suddenly became silent and stood face to face.

They hugged each other for a long moment, the morning sunshine casting their shadows behind them. Then Pandora turned towards the waiting plane, and began to run. She ran towards her future now, without looking back.

COMPETITION

WIN A TRIP FOR TWO TO
ARGENTINA

All things nice... HarperCollins*Publishers* together with Eldorado Enterprises are offering you the chance to win a fabulous trip for two to Argentina. To include seven nights free accommodation at a first-class Buenos Aires hotel and with an exciting excursion programme – a visit to Iguazu Falls, two tickets for a Tango show, an afternoon's shopping in Florida's – Buenos Aires' exclusive shopping mall – dinner at Argentina's leading steak house, and much, much more... — it will be the trip of a lifetime!

To enter all you have to do is answer the eight simple questions below about Argentina and *Sugar and Spice*, William Gill's spellbinding blockbuster of passion and drama, attach the entry voucher to be found at the front of your copy of *Sugar and Spice*, and send them to the address below. Ten runners-up will each receive £100 worth of Grafton Paperbacks of their choice.

COMPETITION RULES

★ Answer the 8 questions and send them with your entry voucher to the address given below.

★ Only one entry allowed per person. Entries not accepted without an entry voucher to be found at the front of *Sugar and Spice* .

★ Closing date for all entries is 30th June 1992. The first prize will be awarded for the first entry with 8 correct answers drawn from a hat. The judges' decision is final.

★ The winner will be notified by post by 31 July 1992. The trip must be taken between the beginning of September and the end of November 1992.

★ Open to all residents of the UK and Ireland excluding employees of HarperCollins Publishers and Eldorado Enterprises and their families.

---

1. Where did Pandora first encounter Ariane ? _____

2. Which fashion house did Sylvia work for in Paris ? _____

3. At which New York restaurant does Gloria outrage her mother? _____

4. What did Pandora dress up as to attend Ariane's ball in Venice ? _____

5. Where do Andrew Macadam and Pandora first meet ? _____

6. Who died in the fire at La Encantada ? _____

7. What is the capital of Argentina ? _____

8. In what year was Juan Péron first elected President of Argentina ? _____

Send your answers with your entry voucher to:

SUGAR & SPICE **COMPETITION,**

Marketing Dept., HarperCollins Publishers, 77-85 Fulham Palace Road, London W6 8JB